FOUR KICK-BUTT HEROINES.
FOUR BESTSELLING MASTERS OF URBAN FANTASY AND PARANORMAL ROMANCE . . .

PATRICIA BRIGGS . . .

". . . is an inventive, engaging writer, whose talent for combining magic of all kinds—from spells to love—with fantastic characters should certainly win her a huge following, and a place on many bookshelves." —*SF Site*

EILEEN WILKS . . .

". . . takes a chance—and readers are the winners."
—*Midwest Book Review*

KAREN CHANCE . . .

". . . will enthrall you with her world of vampires, mages, and a fair maiden tough enough to kick their butts."
—*USA Today* bestselling author Rebecca York

SUNNY . . .

"Fans of Laurell K. Hamilton will love Sunny."
—*New York Times* bestselling author Lori Foster

ON THE *Prowl*

PATRICIA BRIGGS

EILEEN WILKS

KAREN CHANCE

SUNNY

BERKLEY BOOKS, NEW YORK

THE BERKLEY PUBLISHING GROUP
Published by the Penguin Group
Penguin Group (USA) Inc.
375 Hudson Street, New York, New York 10014, USA
Penguin Group (Canada), 90 Eglinton Avenue East, Suite 700, Toronto, Ontario M4P 2Y3, Canada
(a division of Pearson Penguin Canada Inc.)
Penguin Books Ltd., 80 Strand, London WC2R 0RL, England
Penguin Group Ireland, 25 St. Stephen's Green, Dublin 2, Ireland (a division of Penguin Books Ltd.)
Penguin Group (Australia), 250 Camberwell Road, Camberwell, Victoria 3124, Australia
(a division of Pearson Australia Group Pty. Ltd.)
Penguin Books India Pvt. Ltd., 11 Community Centre, Panchsheel Park, New Delhi—110 017, India
Penguin Group (NZ), 67 Apollo Drive, Rosedale, North Shore 0745, Auckland, New Zealand
(a division of Pearson New Zealand Ltd.)
Penguin Books (South Africa) (Pty.) Ltd., 24 Sturdee Avenue, Rosebank, Johannesburg 2196,
South Africa

Penguin Books Ltd., Registered Offices: 80 Strand, London WC2R 0RL, England

This is a work of fiction. Names, characters, places, and incidents either are the product of the authors' imagination or are used fictitiously, and any resemblance to actual persons, living or dead, business establishments, events, or locales is entirely coincidental. The publisher does not have any control over and does not assume any responsibility for author or third-party websites or their content.

ON THE PROWL

A Berkley Book / published by arrangement with the authors

PRINTING HISTORY
Berkley edition / August 2007

Copyright © 2007 by The Berkley Publishing Group.
"Alpha and Omega" by Patricia Briggs copyright © 2007 by Hurog, Inc.
"Inhuman" by Eileen Wilks copyright © 2007 by Eileen Wilks.
"Buying Trouble" by Karen Chance copyright © 2007 by Karen Chance.
"Mona Lisa Betwining" by Sunny copyright © 2007 by DS Studies Inc.
Cover illustration by Tony Mauro.
Cover design by Rita Frangie.
Interior text design by Kristin del Rosario.

All rights reserved.
No part of this book may be reproduced, scanned, or distributed in any printed or electronic form without permission. Please do not participate in or encourage piracy of copyrighted materials in violation of the authors' rights. Purchase only authorized editions.
For information, address: The Berkley Publishing Group,
a division of Penguin Group (USA) Inc.,
375 Hudson Street, New York, New York 10014.

ISBN: 978-0-425-21659-0

BERKLEY®
Berkley Books are published by The Berkley Publishing Group,
a division of Penguin Group (USA) Inc.,
375 Hudson Street, New York, New York 10014.
BERKLEY® is a registered trademark of Penguin Group (USA) Inc.
The "B" design is a trademark belonging to Penguin Group (USA) Inc.

PRINTED IN THE UNITED STATES OF AMERICA

10 9 8 7 6 5 4 3 2 1

If you purchased this book without a cover, you should be aware that this book is stolen property. It was reported as "unsold and destroyed" to the publisher, and neither the authors nor the publisher has received any payment for this "stripped book."

CONTENTS

Alpha and Omega

PATRICIA BRIGGS

CHAPTER 1

THE wind was chill and the cold froze the ends of her toes. One of these days she was going to break down and buy boots—if only she didn't need to eat.

Anna laughed and buried her nose in her jacket, trudging the last half mile to her home. It was true that being a werewolf gave her greater strength and endurance, even in human form. But the twelve-hour shift she'd just finished at Scorci's was enough to make even *her* bones ache. You'd think that people would have better things to do on Thanksgiving than go eat at an Italian restaurant.

Tim, the restaurant owner (who was Irish, not Italian for all that he made the best gnocchi in Chicago) let her take extra shifts—though he wouldn't let her work more than fifty hours a week. The biggest bonus was the free meal she got each shift. Even so, she was afraid she was going to have to find a second job to cover her expenses: life as a werewolf, she had found, was as expensive financially as it was personally.

She used her keys to get into the entryway. There was

nothing in her mailbox, so she got Kara's mail and newspaper and climbed the stairs to Kara's third-floor apartment. When she opened the door, Kara's Siamese cat, Mouser, took one look at her, spat in disgust, and disappeared behind the couch.

For six months she'd been feeding the cat whenever her neighbor was gone—which was often since Kara worked at a travel agency arranging tours. Mouser still hated her. From his hiding place he swore at her, as only a Siamese could do.

With a sigh, Anna tossed the mail and newspaper on the small table in the dining room and opened a can of cat food, setting it down near the water dish. She sat down at the table and closed her eyes. She was ready to go to her own apartment, one floor up, but she had to wait for the cat to eat. If she just left him there, she'd come back in the morning to a can of untouched food. Hate her he might, but Mouser wouldn't eat unless there was someone with him—even if it was a werewolf he didn't trust.

Usually she turned on the TV and watched whatever happened to be on, but tonight she was too tired to make the effort, so she unfolded the newspaper to see what had happened since the last time she'd picked one up a couple of months ago.

She skimmed through the headline articles on the front page without interest. Still complaining, Mouser emerged and stalked resentfully into the kitchen.

She turned the page so Mouser would know that she was really reading it—and drew in a sharp breath at the picture of a young man. It was a head shot, obviously a school picture, and next to it was a similar shot of a girl of the same age. The headline read: "Blood Found at Crime Scene Belongs to Missing Naperville Teen."

Feeling a little frantic, she read the article's review of the crime for those, like her, who had missed the initial reports.

Two months ago, Alan MacKenzie Frazier had disappeared from a high school dance the same night his date's body had been found on the school grounds. Cause of death was difficult to determine as the dead girl's body had been mauled by animals—there had been a pack of strays troubling the neighborhood for the past few months. Authorities had been uncertain whether the missing boy was a suspect or not. Finding his blood led them to suspect he was another victim.

Anna touched Alan Frazier's smiling face with trembling fingers. She knew. She knew.

She jumped up from the table, ignoring Mouser's unhappy yowl, and ran cold water from the kitchen sink over her wrists, trying to keep nausea at bay. *That poor boy.*

It took another hour for Mouser to finish his food. By that time Anna had the article memorized—and had come to a decision. Truthfully, she'd known as soon as she read the paper, but it had taken her the full hour to work up the courage to act upon it: if she'd learned anything in her three years as a werewolf, it was that you didn't want to do anything that might attract one of the dominant wolves' attention. Calling the Marrok, who ruled all the wolves in North America, would certainly attract his attention.

She didn't have a phone in her apartment, so she borrowed Kara's. She waited for her hands and her breathing to steady, but when that didn't seem to be happening, she dialed the number on the battered piece of paper anyway.

Three rings—and she realized that one o'clock in Chicago would be considerably different in Montana, where the area code indicated she was dialing. Was it a two-hour difference or three? Earlier or later? She hastily hung up the phone.

What was she going to tell him, anyway? That she'd seen the boy, obviously the victim of a werewolf attack, weeks after his disappearance, in a cage in her Alpha's house? That she thought the Alpha had ordered the attack?

All Leo had to do was tell the Marrok that he'd come upon the kid later—that he hadn't sanctioned it. Maybe that was how it happened. Maybe she was projecting from her own experience.

She didn't even know if the Marrok would object to the attack. Maybe werewolves were allowed to attack whomever they pleased. That's what had happened to her.

She turned away from the phone and saw the boy's face looking out at her from the open newspaper. She looked at him a moment more and then dialed the number again—surely the Marrok would at least object to the publicity it had attracted. This time her call was answered on the first ring.

"This is Bran."

He didn't sound threatening.

"My name is Anna," she said, wishing her voice wouldn't quiver. There was a time, she thought a little bitterly, when she hadn't been afraid of her own shadow. Who'd have thought that turning into a werewolf would turn her into a coward? But now she knew the monsters were real.

Angry with herself she might have been, but she couldn't force another word out of her throat. If Leo knew she called the Marrok, she might as well shoot herself with that silver bullet she'd bought a few months ago and save him some trouble.

"You are calling from Chicago, Anna?" It startled her for a moment, but then she realized he must have caller ID on his phone. He didn't sound angry that she'd disturbed him—and that wasn't like any dominant she'd ever met. Maybe he was a secretary or something. That made better sense. The Marrok's personal number wouldn't be something that would be passed around.

The hope that she wasn't actually talking to the Marrok helped steady her. Even Leo was afraid of the Marrok. She didn't bother to answer his question—he already knew the answer. "I called to talk to the Marrok, but maybe you could help me."

There was a pause, then Bran said, a little regretfully, "I am the Marrok, child."

Panic set in again, but before she could excuse herself and hang up, he said soothingly, "It's all right, Anna. You've done nothing wrong. Tell me why you called."

She sucked in a deep breath, conscious that this was her last chance to ignore what she'd seen and protect herself.

Instead she explained about the newspaper article—and that she'd seen the missing boy in Leo's house, in one of the cages he kept for new wolves.

"I see," murmured the wolf at the other end of the phone line.

"I couldn't prove that anything was wrong until I saw the newspaper," she told him.

"Does Leo know you saw the boy?"

"Yes." There were two Alphas in the Chicago area. Briefly she wondered how he'd known which one she was talking about.

"How did he react?"

Anna swallowed hard, trying to forget what had happened afterward. Once Leo's mate had intervened, the Alpha had mostly quit passing her around to the other wolves at his whim, but that night Leo had felt that Justin deserved a reward. She didn't have to tell the Marrok that, surely?

He saved her the humiliation by clarifying his question. "Was he angry that you had seen the boy?"

"No. He was . . . happy with the man who'd brought him in." There had still been blood on Justin's face and he stank with the excitement of the hunt.

Leo had been happy when Justin had first brought Anna to him, too. It had been Justin who had been angry—he hadn't realized she'd be a submissive wolf. Submissive meant that Anna's place was at the very bottom of the pack. Justin had quickly decided he made a mistake when he Changed her. She thought he had, too.

"I see."

For some reason she had the strange feeling that he did.

"Where are you now, Anna?"

"At a friend's house."

"Another werewolf?"

"No." Then realizing he might think she'd told someone about what she was—something that was strictly forbidden—she hurried to explain. "I don't have a phone at my place. My neighbor is gone and I'm taking care of her cat. I used her phone."

"I see," he said. "I want you to stay away from Leo and your pack for right now—it might not be safe for you if someone figures out you called me."

That was an understatement. "All right."

"As it happens," the Marrok said, "I have recently been made aware of problems in Chicago."

The realization that she had risked everything unnecessarily made his next few words pass by her unheard.

"—I would normally have contacted the nearest pack. However, if Leo is murdering people, I don't see how the other Chicago Alpha wouldn't be aware of it. Since Jaimie hasn't contacted me, I have to assume that both Alphas are involved to one degree or another."

"It's not Leo who's making the werewolves," she told him. "It's Justin, his second."

"The Alpha is responsible for the actions of his pack," replied the Marrok coolly. "I've sent out an . . . investigator. As it happens he is flying into Chicago tonight. I'd like you to meet him."

Which was how Anna ended up naked between a couple of parked cars in the middle of the night at O'Hare International Airport. She didn't have a car or money for a taxi, but, as the crow flies, the airport was only about five miles from her apartment. It was after midnight and her wolf form was black as pitch and smallish as far as werewolves were concerned. The chances of someone seeing her and thinking she was anything but a stray dog were slight.

It had gotten colder, and she shivered as she pulled on the T-shirt she'd brought. There hadn't been room in her small pack for her coat once she'd stuffed it with shoes, jeans, and a top—all of which were more necessary.

She hadn't ever actually been to O'Hare before, and it took her a while to find the right terminal. By the time she got there, *he* was already waiting for her.

Only after she'd hung up the phone had she realized that the Marrok had given her no description of his investigator. She'd fretted all the way to the airport about it, but she needn't have. There was no mistaking him. Even in the busy terminal, people stopped to look at him, before furtively looking away.

Native Americans, while fairly rare in Chicago, weren't so unheard of as to cause all the attention he was gathering. None of the humans walking past him would probably have been able to explain exactly why they had to look—but Anna knew. It was something common to very dominant wolves. Leo had it, too—but not to this extent.

He was tall, taller even than Leo, and he wore his black, black hair in a thick braid that swung below his bead-and-leather belt. His jeans were dark and new-looking, a contrast to his battered cowboy boots. He turned his head a little and the lights caught a gleam from the gold studs he wore in his ears. Somehow he didn't look like the kind of man who would pierce his ears.

The features under the youth-taut, teak-colored skin were broad and flat and carried an expression that was oppressive in its very blankness. His black eyes traveled slowly over the bustling crowd, looking for something. They stopped on her for a moment, and the impact made her catch her breath. Then his gaze drifted on.

CHARLES hated flying. He especially hated flying when someone else was piloting. He'd flown himself to Salt Lake, but landing his small jet in Chicago could have alerted his quarry—and he preferred to take Leo by surprise. Besides, after they'd closed Meigs Field, he'd quit flying himself into Chicago. There was too much traffic at O'Hare and Midway.

He hated big cities. There were so many smells that they clogged his nose, so much noise that he caught bits of a hundred different conversations without trying—but could miss entirely the sound of someone sneaking up behind him. Someone had bumped by him on the walkway as he left the plane, and he had to work to keep from bumping back, harder. Flying into O'Hare in the middle of the night had at least avoided the largest crowds, but there were still too many people around for his comfort.

He hated cell phones, too. When he'd turned his on after the plane had landed, a message from his father was waiting. Now instead of going to the car rental desk and then to his hotel, he was going to have to locate some woman and stay with her so that Leo or his other wolves didn't kill her. All he had was a first name—Bran hadn't seen fit to give him a description of her.

He stopped outside the security gates and let his gaze drift where it would, hoping instincts would find the woman. He could smell another werewolf, but the ventilation in the airport defeated his ability to pinpoint the scent. His gaze caught first on a young girl with an Irish-pale complexion, whiskey-colored curly hair, and the defeated look of someone who was beaten on a regular basis. She looked tired, cold, and far too thin. It made him angry to see it, and he was already too angry to be safe, so he forced his gaze away.

There was a woman dressed in a business suit that echoed the warm chocolate of her skin. She didn't look quite like an Anna, but she carried herself in such a way that he could see her defying her Alpha to call the Marrok. She was obviously looking for someone. He almost started forward, but then her face changed as she found the person she was looking for—and it was not him.

He started a second sweep of the airport when a small, hesitant voice from just to his left said, "Sir, have you just come from Montana?"

It was the whiskey-haired girl. She must have approached him while he'd been looking elsewhere—something she wouldn't have been able to do if he weren't standing in the middle of a freaking airport.

At least he didn't have to look for his father's contact anymore. With her this close, not even the artificial air currents could hide that she was a werewolf. But it wasn't his nose alone that told him that she was something far rarer.

At first he thought she was submissive. Most werewolves were more or less dominant. Gentler-natured people weren't usually cussed enough to survive the brutal transformation from human to werewolf. Which meant that submissive werewolves were few and far between.

Then he realized that the sudden change in his anger and the irrational desire to protect her from the crowds streaming past were indications of something else. She wasn't a submissive either, though many might mistake her for that: She was an Omega.

Right then he knew that whatever else he did in Chicago, he was going to kill whoever had given her that bruised look.

UP close he was even more impressive; she could feel his energy licking lightly over her like a snake tasting its prey. Anna kept her gaze fully on the floor, waiting for his answer.

"I am Charles Cornick," he said. "The Marrok's son. You must be Anna."

She nodded.

"Did you drive here or catch a cab?"

"I don't have a car," she said.

He growled something she didn't quite catch. "Can you drive?"

She nodded.

"Good."

SHE drove well, if a little overcautiously—which trait he didn't mind at all, though it didn't stop him from bracing one hand against the dash of the rental. She hadn't said anything when he told her to drive them to her apartment, though he hadn't missed the dismay she felt.

He could have told her that his father had instructed him to keep her alive if he could—and to do that he had to stick close. He didn't want to scare her any more than she already was. He could have told her that he had no intention of bedding her, but he tried not to lie. Not even to himself. So he stayed silent.

As she drove them down the expressway in the rented SUV, his wolf-brother had gone from the killing rage caused by the crowded airplane to a relaxed contentment Charles had never felt before. The two other Omega wolves he'd met in his long lifetime had done something similar to him, but not to this extent.

This must be what it was like to be fully human.

The anger and the hunter's wariness that his wolf always held was only a faint memory, leaving behind only the determination to take this one to mate—Charles had never felt anything like that either.

She was pretty enough, though he'd like to feed her up and soften the stiff wariness in her shoulders. The wolf wanted to bed her and claim her as his own. Being of a more cautious nature than his wolf, he would wait until he knew her a little better before deciding to court her.

"My apartment isn't much," she said in an obvious effort to break the silence. The small rasp in her voice told him that her throat was dry.

She was frightened of him. Being his father's chosen executioner, he was used to being feared, though he'd never enjoyed it.

He leaned against the door to give her a little more space and looked out at the city lights so she'd feel safe stealing a few glances at him if she wanted to. He'd been quiet, hoping she would get used to him, but he thought now that might have been a mistake.

"Don't worry," he told her. "I am not fussy. Whatever your apartment is like, it is doubtless more civilized than the Indian lodge I grew up in."

"An Indian lodge?"

"I'm a little older than I look," he said, smiling a little. "Two hundred years ago, an Indian lodge was pretty fancy housing in Montana." Like most old wolves he didn't like talking about the past, but he found he'd do worse than that to set her at ease.

"I'd forgotten you might be older than you look," she said apologetically. She'd seen the smile, he thought, because the level of her fear dropped appreciably. "There aren't any older wolves in the pack here."

"A few," he disagreed with her as he noted that she said "*the* pack" not "*my* pack." Leo was seventy or eighty, and his wife was a lot older than that—old enough that they should have appreciated the gift of an Omega instead of allowing her to be reduced to this abased child who cringed whenever he looked at her too long. "It can be difficult to tell how old a wolf is. Most of us don't talk about it. It's hard enough adjusting without chatting incessantly about the old days."

She didn't reply, and he looked for something else they could talk about. Conversation wasn't his forte; he left that to his father and his brother, who both had clever tongues.

"What tribe are you from?" she asked before he found a topic. "I don't know a lot about the Montana tribes."

"My mother was Salish," he said. "Of the Flathead tribe."

She snuck a quick look at his perfectly normal forehead. Ah, he thought, relieved, there was a good story he could tell her. "Do you know how the Flatheads got their name?"

She shook her head. Her face was so solemn he was tempted to make something up to tease her. But she didn't know him well enough for that, so he told her the truth.

"Many of the Indian tribes in the Columbia Basin, mostly other Salish peoples, used to flatten the foreheads of their infants—the Flatheads were among the few tribes that did not."

"So why are they the ones called Flatheads?" she asked.

"Because the other tribes weren't trying to alter their foreheads, but to give themselves a peak at the top of their heads. Since the Flatheads did not, the other tribes called us 'flat heads.' It wasn't a compliment."

The scent of her fear faded further as she followed his story.

"We were the ugly, barbarian cousins, you see." He laughed. "Ironically, the white trappers misunderstood the name. We were infamous for a long time for a practice we didn't follow. So the white men, like our cousins, thought we were barbarians."

"You said your mother was Salish," she said. "Is the Marrok Native American?"

He shook his head. "Father is a Welshman. He came over and hunted furs in the days of the fur trappers and stayed because he fell in love with the scent of pine and snow." His father put it just that way. Charles found himself smiling again, a real smile this time and felt her relax further—and his face didn't hurt at all. He'd have to call his brother, Samuel, and tell him that he'd finally learned that his face wouldn't crack if he smiled. All it had taken to teach him was an Omega werewolf.

She turned into an alley and pulled into a small parking lot behind one of the ubiquitous four-story brick apartment buildings that filled the older suburbs of this part of town.

"Which city are we in?" he asked.

"Oak Park," she said. "Home of Frank Lloyd Wright, Edgar Rice Burroughs, and Scorci's."

"Scorci's?"

She nodded her head and hopped out of the car. "The best Italian restaurant in Chicago and my current place of employment."

Ah. That's why she smelled of garlic.

"So your opinion is unbiased?" He slid out of the car with a feeling of relief. His brother made fun of his dislike of cars since even a bad accident was unlikely to kill him. But Charles wasn't worried about dying—it was just that cars went too fast. He couldn't get a feel for the land they passed through. And if he felt like dozing a bit as he traveled, they couldn't follow the trail on their own. He preferred horses.

After he got his suitcase out of the back, Anna locked the car with the key fob. The car honked once, making him jump, and he gave it an irritated look. When he turned back, Anna was staring hard at the ground.

The anger that being in her presence had dissipated surged back full force at the strength of her fear. Someone had really done a number on her.

"Sorry," she whispered. If she'd been in wolf form she'd have been cowering with her tail tucked beneath her.

"For what?" he asked, unable to banish the rage that sent his voice down an octave. "Because I'm jumpy around cars? Not your fault."

He was going to have to be careful this time, he realized as he tried to pull the wolf back under control. Usually when his father sent him out to deal with trouble, he could do it coldly. But with a damaged Omega wolf around, one that he found himself responding to on several different levels, he was going to have to hold tight to his temper.

"Anna," he said, fully in control again. "I am my father's hit man. It is my job as his second. But that doesn't mean that I take pleasure in it. I am not going to hurt you, my word on it."

"Yes, sir," she said, clearly not believing him.

He reminded himself that a man's word didn't count for much in this modern day. It helped his control that he scented as much anger on her as fear—she hadn't been completely broken.

He decided that further attempts to reassure her were likely to do the opposite. She would have to learn to accept that he was a man of his word. In the meantime he would give her something to think about.

"Besides," he told her gently, "my wolf is more interested in courting you than in asserting his dominance."

He walked past her before he smiled at the way her fear and anger had disappeared, replaced by shock . . . and something that might have been the beginning of interest.

She had keys to the outer door of the building and led the way through the entry and up the stairs without looking at him at all. By the second flight her scent had dulled of every emotion besides weariness.

She was visibly dragging as she climbed the stairs to the top floor. Her hand shook as she tried to get her key into the deadbolt of one of the two doors at the top. She needed to eat more. Werewolves shouldn't let themselves get so thin—it could be dangerous to those around them.

HE was an executioner, he said, sent by his father to settle problems among the werewolves. He must be even more dangerous than Leo to have survived doing that job. She could feel how dominant he was, and she knew what dominants were like. She had to stay alert, ready for any aggressive moves he might make—ready to handle the pain and the panic so she didn't run and make him worse.

So why was it that the longer he was around, the safer he made her feel?

He followed her up all four flights of stairs without a word, and she refused to apologize again for her apartment. He'd invited himself, after all. It was his own fault that he'd end up sleeping on a twin-size futon instead of a nice hotel bed. She didn't know what to feed him—hopefully he'd eaten while he traveled. Tomorrow she'd run out and get something; she had the check from Scorci's on her fridge awaiting deposit in the bank.

There had once been a pair of two-bedroom apartments on her floor, but in the seventies someone had reapportioned the fourth floor into a three-bedroom and her studio.

Her home looked shabby and empty, with no more furniture than her futon, a card table, and a pair of folding chairs. Only the polished oak floor gave it any appeal.

She glanced at him as he walked through the doorway behind her, but his face revealed very little he didn't want it to. She couldn't see what he thought, though she imagined his eyes lingered a little on the futon that worked fine for her, but was going to be much too small for him.

"The bathroom's through that door," she told him unnecessarily, as the door stood open and the bathtub was clearly visible.

He nodded, watching her with eyes that were opaque in the dim illumination of her overhead light. "Do you have to work tomorrow?" he asked.

"No. Not until Saturday."

"Good. We can talk in the morning, then." He took his small suitcase with him into the bathroom.

She tried not to listen to the unfamiliar sounds of someone else getting ready for bed as she rummaged in her closet for the old blanket she kept in it, wishing again for a nice cheap carpet instead of the gleaming hardwood floor that was pretty to look at, but cold on bare feet and sure to be hard on her backside when she tried to sleep.

The door opened while she was kneeling on the floor, folding the blanket into a makeshift mattress as far as she could from where he would be sleeping. "You can take the bed," she began as she turned around and found herself at eye level with a large reddish-brown werewolf.

He wagged his tail and smiled at her obvious surprise before brushing past her and curling up on the blanket. He wiggled a bit and then put his head down on his forepaws and closed his eyes, to all appearances dropping off immediately to sleep. She knew better, but he didn't stir as she went into the bathroom herself or when she came out dressed in her warmest pair of sweats.

She wouldn't have been able to sleep with a man in her apartment, but somehow, the wolf was less threatening. *This* wolf was less threatening. She bolted the door, turned out the light, and crawled into bed feeling safer than she had since the night she'd found out that there were monsters in the world.

THE footsteps on the stairs the next morning didn't bother her at first. The family who lived across from her was in and out at all times of the day or night. She pulled the pillow over her head to block the noise out, but then Anna realized the brisk, no-nonsense tread belonged to Kara—and that she had a werewolf in her apartment. She sat bolt upright and looked at Charles.

The wolf was more beautiful in the daylight than he had been at night, his fur really red, she saw, set off by black on his legs and paws. He raised his head when she sat up and got to his feet when she did.

She put a finger to her lips as Kara knocked sharply on the door.

"Anna, you in there, girl? Did you know that someone is parked in your spot again? Do you want me to call the tow truck or do you have a man in there for once?"

Kara wouldn't just go away.

"I'm here, just a minute." She looked around frantically,

but there was nowhere to hide a werewolf. He wouldn't fit in the closet, and if she closed the bathroom door, Kara would want to know why—just as she'd demand to know why Anna suddenly had a dog the size of an Irish wolfhound and not nearly as friendly looking in her living room.

She gave Charles one last frantic look and then hurried over to the door as he trotted off to the bathroom. She heard it click shut behind him as she unbolted the door.

"I'm back," said Kara breezily as she came in, setting a pair of bags down on the table. Her dark-as-night skin looked richer than usual for her week of tropical sun. "I stopped on the way home and bought some breakfast for us. You don't eat enough to keep a mouse alive."

Her gaze caught on the closed bathroom door. "You do have someone here." She smiled, but her eyes were wary. Kara had made no secret of the fact that she didn't like Justin, who Anna had explained away, truthfully enough, as an old boyfriend.

"Mmm." Anna was miserably aware that Kara wouldn't leave until she saw who was in the bathroom. For some reason Kara had taken Anna under her wing the very first day she'd moved in, shortly after she'd been Changed.

Just then, Charles opened the bathroom door and stepped just through the doorway. "Do you have a rubber band, Anna?"

He was fully dressed and human, but Anna knew that was impossible. It had been less than five minutes since he'd gone into the bathroom, and a werewolf took a lot longer than that to change back to human form.

She cast a frantic glance at Kara—but her neighbor was too busy staring at the man in the bathroom doorway to take note of Anna's shock.

Kara's rapt gaze made Anna take a second look as well; she had to admit that Charles, his blue-black hair hanging free to his waist in a thick sheet that made him look strangely naked despite his perfectly respectable flannel shirt and jeans, was worth staring at. He gave Kara a small smile before turning his attention back to Anna.

"I seem to have misplaced my hair band. Do you have another one?"

She gave him a jerky nod and brushed past him into the bathroom. How had he changed so fast? She could hardly ask him how he'd done it with Kara in the room, however.

He smelled good. Even after three years it was disconcerting to notice such things about people. Usually she tried to ignore what her nose told her—but she had to force herself not to stop and take a deep lungful of his rich scent.

"And just who are you?" Anna heard Kara ask suspiciously.

"Charles Cornick." She couldn't tell by the sound of his voice whether he was bothered by Kara's unfriendliness or not. "You are?"

"This is Kara, my downstairs neighbor," Anna told him, handing him a hair band as she slipped by him and back into the main room. "Sorry, I should have introduced you. Kara, meet Charles Cornick who is visiting from Montana. Charles, meet Kara Mosley, my downstairs neighbor. Now shake and be nice."

She'd meant the admonition for Kara, who could be acerbic if she took a dislike to someone—but Charles raised an eyebrow at her before he turned back to Kara and offered a long-fingered hand.

"From Montana?" asked Kara as she took his hand and shook it firmly once.

He nodded and began French-braiding his hair with quick, practiced motions. "My father sent me out here because he'd heard there was a man giving Anna a bad time."

And with that one statement, Anna knew, he won Kara over completely.

"Justin? You're gonna take care of that rat bastard?" She gave Charles an appraising look. "Now you're in good shape, don't get me wrong—but Justin is a bad piece of business. I lived in Cabrini Green until my mama got smart and married her a good man. Those projects, though, they grew a certain sort of predator—the kind that loves violence for its own sake. That Justin, he has dead eyes—sent me back twenty years the first time I saw him. He's hurt people before and liked it. You're not going to frighten him off with just a warning."

The corner of Charles's lip turned up and his eyes warmed, changing his appearance entirely. "Thank you for the heads-up," he told her.

Kara gave him a regal nod. "If I know Anna, there's not an ounce of food to be found in the whole apartment. You need to feed that girl up. There's bagels and cream cheese in those bags on the table—and no, I don't mean to stay. I've got a week's worth of work waiting on me, but I couldn't go without knowing that Anna would eat something."

"I'll see that she does," Charles told her, the small smile still on his face.

Kara reached way up and patted his cheek in a motherly gesture. "Thank you." She gave Anna a quick hug and pulled an envelope out of her pocket and set it on the table next to the bagels. "You take this for watching the cat so I don't have to take him to the kennels with all those dogs he hates and pay them four times this amount. I find it in my cookie jar again, and I'll take him to the kennels just for spite because it will make you feel guilty."

Then she was gone.

Anna waited until the sound of her footsteps reached the next landing, then said, "How did you change so fast?"

"Do you want garlic or blueberry?" Charles asked, opening the bag.

When she didn't answer his question, he put both hands on the table and sighed. "You mean you haven't heard the story of the Marrok and his Indian maiden?" She couldn't read his voice and his face was tilted away from her so she couldn't read that either.

"No," she said.

He gave a short laugh, though she didn't think there was any humor behind it. "My mother was beautiful, and it saved her life. She'd been out gathering herbs and surprised a moose. It ran over her and she was dying from it when my father, attracted by the noise, came upon her. He saved my mother's life by turning her into a werewolf."

He took out the bagels and set them on the table with napkins. He sat down and waved her to the other seat. "Start eating and I'll tell you the rest of the story."

He'd given her the blueberry one. She sat opposite him and took a bite.

He gave a satisfied nod and then continued. "It was one of those love at first sight things on both their parts, apparently. Must have been looks, because neither one of them could speak the other's language at first. All was well until she became pregnant. My mother's father was a person of magic and he helped her when she told him that she needed to stay human until I was born. So every month, when my father and brother hunted under the moon she stayed human. And every moon she grew weaker and weaker. My father argued with her and with her father, worried that she was killing herself."

"Why did she do that?" Anna asked.

Charles frowned at her. "How long have you been a werewolf?"

"Three years last August."

"Werewolf women can't have children," he said. "The change is too hard on the fetus. They miscarry in the third or fourth month."

Anna stared at him. No one had ever told her that.

"Are you all right?"

She didn't know how to answer him. She hadn't exactly been planning on having children—especially as weird as her life had been for the last few years. She just hadn't planned on *not* having children either.

"This should have been explained to you before you chose to Change," he said.

It was her turn to laugh. "No one explained anything. No, it's all right. Please tell me the rest of your story."

He watched her for a long moment, then gave her an oddly solemn nod. "Despite my father's protests, she held out until my birth. Weakened by the magic of fighting the moon's call, she did not survive it. I was born a werewolf, not Changed as all the rest are. It gives me a few extra abilities—like being able to change fast."

"That would be nice," she said with feeling.

"It still hurts," he added.

She played with a piece of bagel. "Are you going to look for the missing boy?"

His mouth tightened. "No. We know where Alan Frazier is."

Something in his voice told her. "He's dead?"

He nodded. "There are some good people looking into his death, they'll find out who is responsible. He was Changed without his consent, the girl who was with him was killed. Then he was sold to be used as a laboratory guinea pig. The person responsible will pay for their crimes."

She started to ask him something more, but the door to her apartment flew open and hit the wall behind it, leaving Justin standing in the open doorway.

She'd been so intent on Charles, she hadn't heard Justin coming up the stairs. She'd forgotten to lock her door after Kara left. Not that it would have done her much good. Justin had a key to her apartment.

She couldn't help her flinch as he strode through the door as if he owned the place. "Payday," he said. "You owe me a check." He looked at Charles. "Time for you to go. The lady and I have some business."

Anna couldn't believe that even Justin would take that tone with Charles. She looked at him to gauge his reaction and saw why Justin had put his foot in it.

Charles was fussing with his plate, his eyes on his hands. All his awesome force of personality was bottled up and stuffed somewhere it didn't show.

"I don't think I'd better go," he murmured, still looking down. "She might need my help."

Justin's lip curled. "Where'd you pick this one up, bitch? Wait until I let Leo know you've found a stray and haven't told him about it." He crossed the room and took a handful of her hair. He used it to force her to her feet and up against the wall, shoving her with a hip in a gesture that was both sexual and violent. He leaned his face into hers. "Just you wait. Maybe he'll decide to let me punish you again. I'd like that."

She remembered the last time he'd been allowed to punish her and couldn't suppress her reaction. He enjoyed her panic and was pressed close enough that she could feel it.

"I don't think that she's the one who is going to be punished," Charles said, his voice still soft. But something in Anna loosened. He wouldn't let Justin hurt her.

She couldn't have said why she knew that—she'd certainly found out that just because a wolf wouldn't hurt her didn't mean he wouldn't stop anyone else from hurting her.

"I didn't tell you to talk," Justin snarled, his head snapping away from her so he could glare at the other man. "I'll deal with you when I'm finished."

The legs of Charles's chair made a rough sound on the floor as he stood. Anna could hear him dust off his hands lightly.

"I think you are finished here," he said in a completely different voice. "Let her go."

She felt the power of those words go through her bones and warm her stomach, which had been chill with fear. Justin liked to hurt her even more than he desired her unwilling body. She'd fought him until she realized that pleased him even more. She'd learned quickly that there was no way for her to win a struggle between them. He was stronger and faster, and the only time she'd broken away from him, the rest of the pack had held her for him.

At Charles's words, though, Justin released her so quickly that she staggered, though that didn't slow her down as she ran as far away from him as she could get, which was the kitchen. She picked up the marble rolling pin that had been her grandmother's and held it warily.

Justin had his back to her, but Charles saw her weapon and, briefly, his eyes smiled at her before he turned his attention to Justin.

"Who the hell are you?" Justin spat, but Anna heard beyond the anger to fear.

"I could return the question," said Charles. "I have a list of all the werewolves in the Chicago packs and your name is not on it. But that is only part of my business here. Go home and tell Leo that Charles Cornick is here to talk with him. I will meet him at his house at seven this evening. He may bring his first six and his mate, but the rest of his pack will stay away."

To Anna's shock, Justin snarled once, but, with no more protest than that, he left.

CHAPTER 2

THE wolf who scared Anna so badly hadn't wanted to leave, but he wasn't dominant enough to do anything about it as long as Charles was watching. Which was why Charles waited a few seconds and then quietly followed him down the stairs.

The next flight down, he found Justin standing in front of a door prepared to knock on it. He was pretty sure it was Kara's door. Somehow it didn't surprise him that Justin would look for another way to punish Anna for his forced retreat. Charles scuffed his boot on the stairs and watched the other wolf stiffen and drop his arm.

"Kara's not home," Charles told him. "And hurting her would not be advisable."

Charles wondered if he should just kill him now . . . but he had a reputation that his father couldn't afford for him to lose. He only killed those who broke the Marrok's rules, and he only did it after their guilt was established.

Anna had told his father that Justin was the wolf who changed Alan MacKenzie Frazier against his will, but since there were so many things wrong in this pack there might have been mitigating circumstances. Anna had been a werewolf for three years and no one had told her that she could not have children. If Anna knew so little, then it was more than possible that this wolf didn't know the rules either.

Whether the wolf was ignorant of his crimes or not, Charles still wanted to kill him. When Justin turned around to face him, Charles let his beast peer out of his eyes and watched the other wolf blanch and start back down the stairs.

"You should find Leo and give him the message," Charles said. This time he let Justin know that he was following him, let him feel, a little, the way it was to be prey for a larger predator.

He was tough, this Justin. He kept turning around to confront Charles—only to meet his eyes and be forced away again. The chase aroused his wolf; and Charles, still angry at the way Justin had manhandled Anna, let the wolf out just a little more than he should have. It was a fight to stop at the outside door and let Justin go free. The wolf had been given a hunt and it was much, much too short.

Brother wolf hadn't liked seeing Anna frightened either. He'd staked his claim and it had taken all of Charles's control not to just kill Justin in Anna's apartment. Only the strong suspicion that she'd go back to being afraid of him had allowed him to stay seated until he was sure he could control himself.

Climbing four flights of stairs should have given him enough time to silence the wolf. It might have, except that Anna was waiting for him, rolling pin in hand, on the landing below her apartment.

He paused halfway up the stairs, and she turned around without a word. He stalked her back to her apartment and into the kitchen area, where she set the rolling pin on its stand—right next to a small pot that held a handful of knives.

"Why the rolling pin and not a knife?" he asked, his voice raspy with the need for action.

She looked at him for the first time since she'd seen his

face on the stairs. "A knife wouldn't even slow him down, but bones take time to heal."

He liked that. Who'd have thought he'd get turned on by a woman with a rolling pin? "All right," he said. "All right."

He turned abruptly and left her standing in front of the counter because if he'd stayed there he would have taken her, seduced her. The apartment wasn't large enough either to pace or to get much distance between them. Her scent, blended with fear and arousal, was dangerous. He needed a distraction.

He pulled one of the chairs around and sat on it, leaning back until it was propped on two legs. He folded his arms behind his head and assumed a deliberately relaxed posture, half-closed his eyes, and said, "I want you to tell me about your Change." He hadn't missed the clues, he thought, watching her flinch a little. There was something wrong with how she'd been Changed. He focused on that.

"Why?" she asked, challenging him—still caught up in the adrenaline rush of Justin's visit, he imagined. She caught herself and turned away, cringing as if she expected him to explode.

He closed his eyes entirely. Another moment and he was going to put all the gentlemanly behavior his father had taught him aside and take her, willing or not. Oh, that would teach her not to be afraid of him, he thought.

"I need to know how Leo's pack is run," he told her patiently, though at the moment he could have cared less. "I'd rather do that through your impressions first, and then I'll ask you questions. It'll give me a better insight into what he's doing and why."

ANNA gave him a wary look, but he hadn't moved. She could still smell the anger in the air, but it might just have been a remnant from when Justin had been there. Charles was aroused, too—and she found herself responding to it though she knew it was a common result of victorious confrontations among males. He was ignoring it, so she could, too.

She took a deep breath, and his scent filled her lungs.

Clearing her throat, she tried to find the beginning of her story. "I was working in a music store in the Loop when I first met Justin. He told me he was a guitarist like me, and he started coming in a couple of times a week, buying strings, music . . . small-ticket stuff. He'd flirt and tease." She gave an exasperated huff for her foolishness. "I thought he was a nice guy. So when he asked me out for lunch, I said sure."

She looked at Charles, but he looked as though he might have fallen asleep. The muscles in his shoulders were relaxed and his breathing was slow and easy.

"We dated a couple of times. He took me to this little restaurant near a park, one of the forest preserves. When we were finished he took me for a walk in the woods. 'To look at the moon,' he told me." Even now, with the night long over, she could hear the tension in her voice. "He asked me to wait a minute, said he'd be right back."

He'd been excited, she remembered, almost frantic with suppressed emotion. He'd patted his pockets, then said he'd left something in his car. She'd been worried that he had gone to get a wedding ring. She'd practiced gentle ways of saying no while she waited. They had very little in common and no chemistry at all. Though he seemed nice enough, she'd been getting the feeling that there was something a little off about him, too, and her instincts told her that she needed to break it off.

"It took longer than a minute, and I was just about to go back to the car myself when I heard something in the bushes." The skin on her face tingled with fear, just as it had that night.

"You didn't know he was a werewolf?" Charles's voice reminded her that she was safe in her apartment.

"No. I thought that werewolves were just stories."

"Tell me about after the attack."

She didn't need to tell him about how Justin had stalked her for an hour, herding her back from the edge of the preserve every time she came close to getting out. He only wanted to know about Leo's pack. Anna hid her sigh of relief.

"I woke up in Leo's house. He was excited at first. His pack only has one other woman. Then they discovered what I am."

"And what are you, Anna?" His voice was like smoke, she thought, soft and weightless.

"Submissive," she said. "The lowest of the low." And then because his eyes were still closed she added, "Useless."

"Is that what they told you?" he asked thoughtfully.

"It's the truth." She ought to be more upset about it—the wolves who didn't despise her treated her with pity. But she didn't want to be dominant and have to fight and hurt people.

He didn't say anything so she continued her story, trying to give him all the details she could remember. He asked some questions:

"Who helped you gain control of the wolf?" (No one, she'd done that on her own—another black mark against her that proved she wasn't dominant, they'd told her.)

"Who gave you the Marrok's phone number?" (Leo's third, Boyd Hamilton.)

"When and why?" (Just before Leo's mate stepped in and stopped him from passing Anna around to whatever male he wanted to reward. Anna tried to avoid the higher-ranking wolves—she had no idea why he'd given her that number and no desire to ask.)

"How many new members have come into the pack since you?" (Three, all male—but two of them couldn't control themselves and had had to be killed.)

"How many members of the pack?" (Twenty-six.)

When she finally wound down to a stop she was almost surprised to find herself sitting on the floor across the room from Charles with her back against the wall. Slowly Charles let his chair drop back to the floor and pinched the bridge of his nose. He sighed heavily and then looked at her directly for the first time since she'd begun speaking.

She sucked in her breath at the bright gold of his eyes. He was very near a change forced by some strong emotion—and despite seeing his eyes, she couldn't read it in his body or his scent—he'd managed to mask it from her.

"There are rules. First is that no person may be Changed against their will. Second is that no person may be Changed until they have been counseled and passed a simple test to demonstrate that they understand what that Change means."

She didn't know what to say, but she finally remembered to drop her eyes away from his intense stare.

"From what you've said, Leo is adding new wolves and missing others—he didn't report that to the Marrok. Last year he came to our annual meeting with his mate and his fourth—that Boyd Hamilton—and told us that his second and third were tied up."

Anna frowned at him. "Boyd's been his third for as long as I have been in the pack and Justin is his second."

"You said that there is only one female in the pack besides you?"

"Yes."

"There should have been four."

"No one has mentioned any others," she told him.

He looked over at the check on her fridge.

"They take your paycheck. How much do they give you back?" His voice was bass-deep with the heat of the change behind it.

"Sixty percent."

"Ah." He closed his eyes again and breathed deeply. She could smell the musk of his anger now, though his shoulders still looked relaxed.

When he didn't say anything more, she said quietly, "Is there anything I can do to help? Do you want me to leave or talk or turn on music?" She didn't have a TV, but she still had her old stereo.

His eyes stayed closed but he smiled, just a twitch of his lips. "My control is usually better than this."

She waited, but it seemed to get worse rather than better.

His eyes snapped open and his cold yellow gaze pinned her against the wall where she sat as he uncoiled and prowled across the room.

Her pulse jumped unsteadily and she bowed her head, curling up to be smaller. She felt rather than saw him crouch in front of her. His hands when they cupped her face were so hot she flinched—and regretted it when he growled.

He dropped to his knees, nuzzling against her neck, then rested his body, now taut as iron, against hers, trapping her between him and the wall. He put his hands on the wall, one to each side of her, and then quit moving. His breath was hot on her neck.

She sat as still as she could, terrified of doing anything that might break his control. But there was something about him that kept her from being truly scared, something that insisted he wouldn't hurt her. That he never would hurt her.

Which was stupid. All the dominants hurt those beneath them. She'd had that beaten into her more than once. Just because she could heal quickly didn't make getting hurt pleasant. But no matter how much she told herself she ought to be frightened of him, a dominant among dominants, a strange man she'd never seen before last night (or, more accurately, very early this morning), she couldn't.

Though he smelled of anger, he also smelled like spring rain, wolf, and man. She closed her eyes and quit fighting, letting the sweet-sharpness of his scent wash away the fear and anger aroused by telling this man about the worst thing that ever happened to her.

As soon as she relaxed he did as well. His rigid muscles loosened and his imprisoning arms slid down the wall to rest lightly on her shoulders.

After a while, he pulled away slowly, but stayed crouched so his head was only slightly higher than hers. He put a gentle thumb under her chin and raised her head until she gazed into his dark eyes. She had the sudden feeling that if she could look into those eyes for the rest of her life, she would be happy. It scared her a lot more than his anger had.

"Are you doing something to me to make me feel like this?" She asked the question before she had time to censor herself.

He didn't ask her how he made her feel. Instead, he tilted his head, a wolflike gesture, but kept eye contact, though there was no challenge in his scent. Instead, she had the impression he was almost as bewildered as she was. "I don't think so. Certainly not on purpose."

He cupped her face in both of his hands. They were large hands, and calloused, and they trembled just a little. He bent down until his chin rested on the top of her head. "I've never felt this way before either."

HE could have stayed there forever, despite the discomfort of kneeling on the hardwood floor. He'd never felt anything like this—certainly not with a woman he'd known less than twenty-four hours. He didn't know how to deal with it, didn't want to deal with it, and—most unlike himself—was willing to put off dealing with it indefinitely as long as he could spend the time with her body against his.

Of course there was something he'd rather do, but if he

wasn't mistaken there was someone else coming up the stairs. Four flights of stairs were, evidently, not enough to keep intruders away. He closed his eyes and let his wolf-brother sort through the scents and identify their newest visitor.

There was a knock at the door.

Anna jerked back out of his hold, sucking in her breath. Part of him was pleased that he'd managed to distract her so much that she hadn't noticed anything until then. Part of him worried at her vulnerability.

Reluctantly, he stood up and put a little distance between them. "Come in, Isabelle."

The door opened and Leo's mate stuck her head in. She took a good look at Anna and grinned mischievously. "Interrupting something interesting?"

He'd always liked Isabelle, though he'd tried hard not to show it. As his father's executioner, he'd long ago learned not to get close to anyone he might someday have to kill—which made his circle of friends very small: his father and his brother for the most part.

Anna stood up and returned Isabelle's smile with a shy one of her own, though he could tell she was still shaken. To his surprise, though, she said, "Yes. There was something very interesting going on. Come in anyway."

Once the invitation had been issued, Isabelle blew in like the March wind, as she usually did, simultaneously shutting the door and holding out a hand to Charles. "Charles, it is so good to see you."

He took her hand and bowed over it, kissing it lightly. It smelled of cinnamon and cloves. He'd forgotten that about her, that she used perfume with an eye toward the sharpness of werewolf senses. Just strong enough to mask herself and so give her some protection from the sharp noses of her fellow wolves. Unless she was extremely agitated, no one could tell how she felt from her scent.

"You look beautiful," he said, as he knew she expected. It was true enough.

"I should be looking a nervous wreck," she said, running the hand Charles had kissed through her airy, feathery cut hair that, combined with her fine features, made her look like a fairy princess. She was shorter than Anna and finer-boned, but Charles had never made the mistake of thinking of her as fragile. "Justin came boiling in with some nonsense about a meeting tonight. He was all but incoherent—why did you enrage the boy like that?—and I told Leo I'd drop by to see what you were doing."

This was why he didn't make friends.

"Leo received my message?" Charles asked.

She nodded. "And looked quite frightened, which is not a good look for him, as I told him." She leaned forward and put a too-familiar hand on his arm. "What has brought you to our territory, Charles?"

He stepped back. He didn't much like to touch or be touched—though he seemed to have largely forgotten that while he was around Anna.

His Anna.

Forcefully he brought his attention back to business. "I have come to meet with Leo tonight."

Isabelle's usually cheerful face hardened, and he waited for her to blow up at him. Isabelle was as famous for her temper as she was for her charisma. She was one of the few people to blow up in the Marrok's face and get away with it—Charles's father liked Isabelle, too.

But she didn't say anything more to him. Instead she turned her head to glance at Anna, whom, he suddenly realized, she'd been pointedly ignoring up to that point. When she returned her gaze to Charles, she began speaking, but not to him.

"What tales have you been carrying, Anna, my dear? Complaining about your place in the pack? Choose a mate, if you don't like it. I've told you that before. Justin would take you, I'm sure." There was no venom in her voice. Maybe if Charles hadn't already met Justin, he'd have missed the way Anna's face paled. Maybe he wouldn't have heard the threat.

Anna didn't say anything.

Isabelle continued to stare at Charles, though she was careful to keep from meeting his eyes. He thought she was studying his reactions, but he knew that his face gave nothing away—he'd been prepared for the way his brother wolf surged up in anger to defend Anna this time.

"Are you sleeping with him?" Isabelle asked. "He's a good lover, isn't he?"

Though Isabelle was mated, she had a wandering eye and Leo let her indulge herself as she pleased, a situation almost unique among werewolves. That didn't mean *she* wasn't jealous; Leo couldn't so much as look at another woman. Charles always felt it was an odd relationship, but it had worked for them for a long time. When she'd made a play for him a few years ago, he'd allowed himself to be caught, knowing that there was nothing serious about her offer. He hadn't been surprised when she'd tried to get him to talk his father into letting Leo expand his territory. She had taken his refusal in good humor, though.

The sex had meant nothing to either of them—but it meant something to Anna. He'd have had to be human to miss the hurt and mistrust in her eyes at Isabelle's thrust.

"Play nicely, Isabelle," he told her, abruptly impatient. He put a little force in his voice as he said, "Go home and tell Leo I'll talk to him tonight."

Her eyes lit with rage and she drew herself up.

"I am not my father," he said softly. "You don't want to try the shrew act with me."

Fear cooled her temper—and his, too, for that matter. Her perfume might have hid her scent, but it didn't hide her eyes or her clenched hands. He didn't enjoy frightening people—not usually.

"Go home, Isabelle. You'll have to swallow your curiosity until then."

He shut the door gently behind her and stared at it for a moment, reluctant to face Anna—though he had no idea why he should feel so guilty for doing something long before he'd ever met her.

"Are you going to kill her?"

He looked at Anna then, unable to tell what she thought about it. "I don't know."

Anna bit her lip. "She has been kind to me."

Kind? As far as he could tell kindness had been pretty far from anything that had happened to Anna since her Change. But the worry in her face had him swallowing his sharp reply.

"There is something odd going on in Leo's pack," was all he said. "I'll find out exactly what it is tonight."

"How?"

"I'll ask them," he told her. "They know better than to think they can lie to me—and refusal to answer my questions, or refusal to meet with me is admitting guilt."

She looked puzzled. "Why couldn't they lie to you?"

He tapped a finger on her nose. "Smelling a lie is pretty easy, unless you are dealing with someone who cannot tell truth from lie, but there are other ways to detect them."

Her stomach growled.

"Enough of this," he said, deciding it was time to feed her up a little. A bagel was not enough. "Get your coat."

He didn't want to take the car into the Loop, where it would be difficult to find parking, because his temper was too uncertain around her. He couldn't talk her into a taxi, which was a new experience for him—not many people refused to listen when he told them what to do. But then, she was an Omega, and not constrained by an instinctive need to obey a more dominant wolf. With an inward sigh, he followed her down a few blocks to the nearest L station.

He'd never been on Chicago's elevated train before, and, if it weren't for a certain stubborn woman, he wouldn't have ridden one this time. Though he admitted, if only to himself, that he rather enjoyed it when a rowdy group of thugs disguised as teenagers decided to give him a bad time.

"Hey, Injun Joe," said a baggy-clothed boy. "You a stranger in town? That's a foxy lady you have there. If she likes her meat brown, there's plenty here to go 'round." He tapped himself on his chest.

There were real gangs in Chicago, raised in the eat-or-be-eaten world of the inner city. But these boys were imitators, probably out of school for the holidays and bored. So they decided to entertain themselves by scaring the adults who couldn't differentiate between amateurs and the real deal. Not that a pack of boys couldn't be dangerous under the wrong circumstances . . .

An old woman sitting next to them shrank back, and the smell of her fear washed away his tolerance.

Charles got to his feet, smiled, and watched their smugness evaporate at his confidence. "She's foxy, all right," he said. "But she belongs to me."

"Hey, man," said the boy just behind the one who had spoken. "No hard feelings, man."

He let his smile widen and watched them shuffle backward. "It's a nice day. I think that you should go sit in those empty seats up there where you see your way more clearly."

They scuttled to the front of the car and, after they had all taken a seat, Charles sat back down next to Anna.

THERE was such satisfaction in his face when he sat down that Anna had to suppress a grin for fear that one of the boys would look back and think she was laughing at one of them.

"That was a prime example of testosterone poisoning," she observed dryly. "Are you going to go after Girl Scouts next?"

Charles's eyes glinted with amusement. "Now they know that they need to pick their prey more cautiously."

Anna seldom traveled to the Loop anymore—everything she needed she could find closer to home. He evidently knew it better than she did, despite being a visitor. He chose the stop they got off on and took her directly to a little Greek place tucked in the shadow of the L train tracks, where they greeted him by name and took him to a private room with only one table.

He let her give her order and then doubled it, adding a few dishes on the side.

While they were waiting for their food, he took a small, worn-looking, leather-bound three-ring notebook from his jacket pocket. He popped the rings and took out a couple of sheets of lined paper and handed them to her with a pen.

"I'd like you to write down the names of the members of your pack. It would help if you list them from the most dominant and go to the least."

She tried. She didn't know everyone's last name and, since everyone outranked her, she hadn't paid strict attention to rank.

She handed the paper and pen back to him with a frown. "I'm forgetting people, and other than the top four or five wolves, I could be mistaken on rank."

He set her pages down on the table and then took out a couple of sheets with writing already on them and compared the two lists, marking them up. Anna took her chair and scooted it around the table until she sat next to him and could see what he was doing.

He took his list and set it before her. "These are the people who should be in your pack. I've checked the names of the ones who don't appear on your list."

She scanned down it, then grabbed the pen back and marked out one of his checks. "He's still here. I just forgot about him. And this one, too."

He took the list back. "All the women are gone. Most of the rest who are missing are older wolves. Not *old.* But there's not a wolf left who is older than Leo. There are a few younger wolves missing as well." He tapped a finger on a couple of names. "These were young. Paul Lebshak, here, would have been only four years a werewolf. George not much older."

"Do you know all the werewolves?"

He smiled. "I know the Alphas. We have yearly meetings with all of them. I know most of the seconds and thirds. One of the things we do at the meetings is update the pack memberships. The Alphas are supposed to keep the Marrok informed when people die, or when new wolves are Changed. If my father had known so many wolves were gone, he would have investigated. Though Leo's lost a third of the pack membership, he's done a fair job of replacing them."

He gave back the list she'd written—a number of names, including hers, were also checked. "These are all new. From what you've told me, I'd guess that they are all forced Changes. The survival rate of random attack victims is very poor. Your Leo has killed a lot of people over the past few years in order to keep the number of his pack where it is. Enough that it should have attracted the attention of the authorities. How many of these people were made wolves after you?"

"None of them. The only new wolf I've seen was that poor boy." She tapped the paper with her pen. "If they didn't leave bodies and spread out the hunt, they could have easily hidden the disappearance of a hundred people in the greater Chicago area over a few years."

He leaned back and closed his eyes, then he shook his

head. "I don't remember dates too well anymore. I haven't met most of the missing wolves, and I don't remember the last time I saw Leo's old second except that it was within the last ten years. So whatever happened was after that."

"Whatever happened to what?"

"To Leo, I'd guess. Something happened that made him kill all the women in his pack except Isabelle and most of his older wolves—the wolves who would have objected when he started attacking innocent people, or quit teaching new wolves the rules and rights that belong to them. I can see why he'd have to kill *them*—but why the women? And why didn't the other Chicago Alpha say anything to my father when it happened?"

"He might not have known. Leo and Jaimie stay away from each other, and our pack is not allowed to go into Jaimie's territory at all. The Loop is neutral territory, but we can't go north of here unless we get special permission."

"Oh? Interesting. Have you heard anything about why they aren't getting along?"

She shrugged. There had been a lot of talk. "Someone told me that Jaimie wouldn't sleep with Isabelle. Someone else said that they had an affair and he broke it off, and she was insulted. Or that he wouldn't break it off and Leo had to step in. Another story is that Jaimie and Leo never got along. I don't know."

She looked at the checks that marked the newer wolves in her pack and suddenly laughed.

"What?"

"It's just stupid." She shook her head.

"Tell me."

Her cheeks flushed with embarrassment. "Fine. You were looking for something that all the newer wolves had in common. I was just thinking that if someone wanted to list the most handsome men in the pack, they would all make the cut."

Both of them were surprised by the flash of territorial jealousy that he didn't bother to hide from her.

It was probably a good time for the waiter to come in with the first course of food.

Anna started to move her chair back to where it had been, but the waiter sat his tray down and took it from her, seating her properly before he got back to setting out the dishes.

"And how have you been, sir?" he said to Charles. "Still haven't given up and moved to civilization?"

"Civilization is vastly overrated," Charles returned as he put the sheets of paper into his notebook and shut the cover. "As long as I can come up once or twice a year and eat here, I am content."

The waiter shook his head with mock sadness. "Mountains are beautiful, but not as beautiful as our skyline. One of these days I'll take you out for a night on the town and you'll never leave again."

"Phillip!" A bird-thin woman stepped into the room. "While you are here chatting with Mr. Cornick, our other guests are going hungry."

The waiter grinned and winked at Anna. He dropped a kiss on the woman's cheek and slipped through the door.

The woman suppressed a smile and shook her head. "That one. Always talking. He needs a good wife to keep him in line. I am too old." She threw up her hands and then followed the waiter.

The next twenty minutes brought a series of waiters and waitresses who all looked as though they were related. They carried food on trays and never said anything about it being odd that two people should eat so much food.

Charles filled his plate, looked at hers, and said, "You should have told me you didn't like lamb."

She looked at her plate. "I do."

He frowned at her, took the serving spoon, and added to the amount on her plate. "You should be eating more. A lot more. The change requires a lot of energy. You have to eat more as a werewolf to maintain your weight."

After that, by mutual consent Anna and Charles confined their conversations to generalities. They talked about Chicago and city living. She took a little of a rice dish and he looked at her until she took a second spoonful. He told her a little about Montana. She found he was very well spoken and the easiest way to stop a conversation cold was to ask him about anything personal. It wasn't that he didn't want to talk about himself, she thought, it was that he didn't find himself very interesting.

The door swung open one last time, and a girl of about fourteen came in with dessert.

"Aren't you supposed to be in school?" Charles asked her.

She sighed. "Vacation. Everyone else gets time off. But me? I get to work in the restaurant. It sucks."

"I see," he said. "Perhaps you should call child welfare and tell them you're being abused?"

She grinned at him. "Wouldn't that get Papa riled up. I'm tempted to do it just to see his face. If I told him it was your suggestion do ya suppose he'd get mad at you instead of me?" She wrinkled her nose. "Probably not."

"Tell your mother that the food was perfect."

She braced the empty tray on her hip and backed out the door. "I'll tell her, but she already told me to tell you that it wasn't. The lamb was a little stringy, but that's all she could get."

"I gather you come here often," Anna said, unenthusiastically picking at a huge piece of baklava. Not that she had anything against baklava—as long as she hadn't eaten a week's worth of food first.

"Too often," he said. *He* was having no trouble eating more, she noticed. "We have some business interests here, so I have to come three or four times a year. The owner of the restaurant is a wolf, one of Jaimie's. I sometimes find it convenient to discuss business here."

"I thought you were your father's hit man," she said with interest. "You have to hunt down people in Chicago three or four times a year?"

He laughed out loud. The sound was rusty, as if he didn't do it very often—though he ought to, it looked good on him. Good enough that she ate the forkful of baklava she'd been playing with and then had to figure out how to swallow it when her stomach was telling her that it didn't need any more food sent its way.

"No, I have other duties as well. I take care of my father's pack's business interests. I am very good at both of my jobs," he said without any hint of modesty.

"I bet you are." He was a person who would be very good at whatever he decided to do. "I'd let you invest my savings. I think I have twenty-two dollars and ninety-seven cents right now."

He frowned at her, all amusement gone.

"It was a joke," she explained.

But he ignored her. "Most Alphas have their members give ten percent of their earnings for the good of the pack, especially when the pack is new. This money is used to ensure there is a safe house, for instance. Once a pack is firmly established, though, the need for money lessens. My father's pack has been established for a long time—there is no need for a tithe because we own the land we live on and there are investments enough for the future. Leo has been here for thirty years: time enough to be well established. I've never heard of a pack demanding forty percent from its members—which leads me to believe that Leo's pack is in financial trouble. He sold that young man you called my father about, and several others like him, to someone who was using them to develop a way to make drugs work on us as well as they work on humans. He had to kill a number of humans in order to get a single survivor werewolf."

She thought about the implications. "Who wanted the drugs?"

"I'll know that when Leo tells me who he sold the boy to."

"So why didn't he sell me?" She wasn't worth much to the pack.

He leaned back in his chair. "If an Alpha sold one of his pack, he'd have a rebellion on his hands. Besides, Leo went to a lot of trouble to get you. There haven't been any pack members killed or gone missing since you became a member."

It wasn't a question, but she answered him anyway. "No."

"I think maybe you are the key to Leo's mystery."

She couldn't help a snort of derision. "Me? Leo needed a new doormat?"

He leaned suddenly forward, knocking his chair over as he swept her off of her own and stood her on her feet. She'd thought she was used to the speed and strength of the wolves, but he stole her breath.

As she stood still and shocked, he prowled around her until he came back around the front and kissed her, a long, dark, deep kiss that left her breathless for another reason entirely.

"Leo found you and decided that he needed you," he told her. "He sent Justin after you, because any of his other wolves would know what you were. Even before your Change, they'd have known. So he sent a half-crazy wolf because any other would have been unable to attack you."

Hurt, she flinched away from him. He made her sound special, but she knew he was lying. He sounded like he was telling the truth, but she was no prize. She was nothing. For three years she had been nothing. He had made her feel special today, but she knew better.

His hands, when they came down on her shoulders, were

hard and impossible to resist. "Let me tell you something about Omega wolves, Anna. *Look* at me."

She blinked back tears, and, unable to resist his command, raised her eyes to glare at him.

"Almost unique," he said and gave her a little shake. "I work with numbers and percentages all the time, Anna. I might not be able to figure the odds exactly, but I'll tell you that the chances that Justin picked you out to Change by sheer chance are almost infinitesimal. No werewolf, acting on instincts alone, would attack an Omega. And Justin strikes me as a wolf who acts on very little else."

"Why not? Why wouldn't he have attacked me? And what is an Omega?"

It was evidently the right question because Charles stilled, his former agitation gone. "You are an Omega, Anna. I bet that when you walk into a room, people come to you. I bet complete strangers tell you things they wouldn't tell their own mothers."

Incredulous, she stared at him. "You saw Justin this morning. Did he look calm to you?"

"I saw Justin," he agreed slowly. "And I think that in any other pack he would have been killed shortly after he was made because his control is not good enough. I don't know why he was not. But I think you allow him to control his wolf—and he hates you for it.

"You should not be ranked last in your pack." His hands slid down her shoulders until he held her hands. Oddly that felt more intimate than his kiss had. "An Omega wolf is like the Indian medicine men, outside of the normal pack rankings. They had to teach you to lower your eyes, didn't they? To submissive wolves, such things are instinctive. You, they had to beat down.

"You bring peace to all those around you, Anna," he said intently, his eyes on hers. "A werewolf, especially a dominant wolf, is always on the edge of violence. After being shut in an aircraft with too many people for hours,

I came into the airport craving bloodshed like a junkie craves his next fix. But when you came up to me, the anger, the hunger left."

He squeezed her hands. "You are a gift, Anna. An Omega wolf in the pack means that more wolves survive the Change from human to wolf because they can find control easier with you there. It means that we lose fewer males to stupid dominance fights because an Omega brings a calmness to all those around him. Or her."

There was a hole in his argument. "But what about earlier, when you almost changed because you were so angry?"

Something happened to his face, an emotion she didn't know him well enough to read, except to know that it was strong.

When he spoke it was with visible effort, as if his throat had tightened. "Most werewolves find someone they love, get married, and spend a long time with their spouse before the wolf accepts her as his mate." He dropped her gaze and turned away, walking across the room and giving her his back.

Without the warmth of his body, she felt cold and alone. Scared.

"Sometimes it doesn't happen that way," he told the wall. "Let it rest there, for now, Anna. You have been through enough without this."

"I am so tired of being ignorant," she spat, suddenly hugely angry. "You've changed all the rules on me—so you can *damned* well tell me what the new rules are." As abruptly as the anger had come, it was gone, leaving her shaky and on the verge of tears.

He turned and his eyes had gone gold, reflecting the dim light of the room until they glowed. "Fine. You should have let it be, but you want truth." His voice rumbled like thunder, though it wasn't very loud. "My brother wolf has taken you for his mate. If you were *nothing* to me, I would have never allowed such abuse as you have suffered since your

Change. But you are mine, and the thought of you hurt, of being able to do nothing about it, is an anger that even an Omega wolf cannot easily soothe."

Well, she thought, stunned. She'd known he was interested in her, but she'd assumed it had been a casual thing. Leo was the only mated wolf she knew. She didn't know any of the rules. What did it mean that he said his wolf had decided she was his mate? Did she have a choice in the matter? Did the way he aroused her without trying, the way he made her feel—as if she'd known him forever and wanted to wake up next to him for the rest of her life, though she'd known him only hours, really—was that his fault?

"If you had let me," he said, "I'd have courted you gently and won your heart." He closed his eyes. "I didn't mean to frighten you."

She should have been frightened. Instead, suddenly, she felt very, very calm, like the eye in a hurricane of emotion.

"I don't like sex," she told him, because it seemed like something he ought to know under the circumstances.

He choked and opened his eyes, their bright color giving way to human dark as she watched.

"I wasn't enthusiastic before the Change," she told him plainly. "And after being passed around like a whore for a year, until Isabelle put a stop to it, I like it even less."

His mouth tightened, but he didn't say anything, so she continued. "And I won't be forced. Never again." She pulled up the sleeves of her shirt to show him the long scars on the underside of her arm, wrist to elbow. She'd made them with a silver knife, and if Isabelle hadn't found her, she'd have killed herself. "This is why Isabelle made Leo stop making me sleep with whatever male pleased him enough. She found me and kept me alive. After that I bought a gun and silver bullets."

He growled softly, but not at her, she was pretty sure.

"I'm not threatening to kill myself. But you need to

know this about me because—if you want to be my mate—I won't be like Leo. I won't let you sleep around with anyone else. I won't be forced either. I've had enough. If that makes me a dog in the manger, so be it. But if I am yours, then you *damned* well are going to be mine."

"A dog in the manger?" He let out a gusty breath of air that might have been a half-laugh. He closed his eyes again and said in a reasonable tone, "If Leo survives tonight, I shall be very surprised. If I survive you, I'll be equally surprised." He looked at her. "And very little surprises me anymore."

He strode across the floor, picking up his chair and setting it where it belonged as he passed it. He stopped just in front of her and touched her raised chin gently, then laughed. Still smiling he tucked a piece of her hair behind her ear. "I promise you will enjoy sex with me," he murmured.

Somehow she managed to keep her spine straight. She wasn't ready to fall into a puddle at his feet quite yet. "Isabelle said you were a good lover."

He laughed again. "You have no need for jealousy. Sex with Isabelle meant no more to me than a good belly scratch and rather less to her, I think. Nothing worth repeating for either of us." There was a whisper of sound outside the room and he took her hand. "Time for us to go."

He paid polite compliments to the meal as he handed over a credit card to a young-looking man who called him "sir" and smelled of werewolf. The owner of the restaurant, Anna supposed.

"So where would you like to go next?" she asked as she stepped out onto the busy sidewalk.

He pulled his jacket on the rest of the way and dodged a woman in high heels who carried a leather briefcase. "Somewhere with fewer people."

"We could go to the zoo," she suggested. "This time of year it's pretty deserted, even with the kids out of school for Thanksgiving."

He turned his head and started to speak when something in a window caught his attention. He grabbed her and threw her on the ground, falling on top of her. There was a loud bang, like a backfiring car, and he jerked once, then lay still on top of her.

Chapter 3

IT had been a long time since he'd been shot, but the sizzling burn of the silver bullet was still familiar. He hadn't been quite fast enough—and the crowd of people made sure that he couldn't go after the car that had taken off as soon as the gun had fired. He hadn't even gotten a good look at the shooter, just an impression.

"Charles?" Beneath him, Anna's eyes were black with shock and she patted his shoulders. "Was someone shooting at us? Are you all right?"

"Yes," he said, though he couldn't really assess the damage until he moved, which he didn't want to much.

"Stay where you are until I can get a look," said a firm voice. "I'm an EMT."

The command in the EMT's voice forced Charles to move—he didn't take orders from anyone except his father. He pushed himself off of Anna and got to his feet, then leaned down and grabbed her hand to pull her up from the frozen sidewalk.

"Damn it, man, you're bleeding. Don't be stupid," snapped the stranger. "Sit down."

Being shot had enraged the wolf in him, and Charles turned to snarl at the EMT, a competent-looking middle-aged man with sandy hair and a graying red moustache.

Then Anna squeezed his hand, which she still held, and said, "Thank you," to the EMT and then to Charles "Let him take a look"—and he was able to hold back the snarl.

He did growl low in his throat, though, when the stranger looked at his wound: never show weakness to a possible enemy. He felt too exposed on the sidewalk, too many people were looking at him—they had acquired quite an audience.

"Ignore him," Anna told the EMT. "He gets grumpy when he's hurt."

George, the werewolf who owned the restaurant, brought out a chair for him to sit on. Someone had called the police; two cars came with flashing lights and sirens that hurt his ears, followed by an ambulance.

The bullet had cut through skin and a fine layer of muscle across the back of his shoulders without doing a lot of damage, he was told. Did he have any enemies? It was Anna who told them that he'd just flown in from Montana, that it must have been just a drive-by shooting, though this wasn't the usual neighborhood for that kind of crime.

If the cop had had a werewolf's nose, he would never have let her lie pass. He was a seasoned cop, however, and her answer made him a little uneasy. But when Charles showed him his Montana driver's license, he relaxed.

Anna's presence allowed Charles to submit to cleaning and bandaging and questioning, but nothing would make him get into an ambulance and be dragged to a hospital, even though silver-bullet wounds healed human-slow. Even now he could feel the hot ache of the silver as it seeped into his muscles.

While he sat beneath the hands of strangers and fought not to loose control, he couldn't get the image of the shooter out of his head. He'd looked in the window and saw the reflection of the gun, then the face of the person who held it, wrapped in a winter scarf and wearing dark glasses. Not enough to identify the gunman, just a glimpse—but he would swear that the man had not been looking at him when his gloved finger pulled the trigger. He'd been looking at Anna.

Which didn't make much sense. Why would someone be trying to kill Anna?

They didn't go to the zoo.

While he used the restaurant bathroom to clean up, George procured a jacket to cover the bandages so Charles wouldn't have to advertise his weakness to everyone who saw him. This time Anna didn't object when he asked her to call a taxi.

His phone rang on the way back to Anna's apartment, but he silenced it without looking at it. It might have been his father, Bran, who had an uncanny knack for knowing when he'd been hurt. But he had no desire to talk with the Marrok while the taxi driver could hear every word. More probably it was Jaimie. George would have called his Alpha as soon as Charles was shot. In either case, they would wait until he was someplace more private.

He made Anna wait in the taxi when they got to her apartment building until he had a chance to take a good look around. No one had followed them from the Loop, but the most likely assailants were Leo's people—and they all knew where Anna lived. He hadn't recognized the shooter, but then he didn't know every werewolf in Chicago.

Anna was patient with him. She didn't argue about waiting but the cabdriver looked at him as though he were crazy.

Her patience helped his control—which was shakier than it had been in a long time. He wondered how he'd be behaving if his Anna hadn't been an Omega whose soothing effect was almost good enough to override the protective rage roused by the attempt on her life. The painful burn of his shoulders, worsening as silver-caused wounds always did for a while, didn't help his temperament, nor did the knowledge that his ability to fight was impaired.

Someone was trying to kill Anna. It didn't make sense, but somewhere during the trip back to Oak Park, he'd accepted that it was so.

Satisfied there was no immediate threat in or around the apartment building, he held out his hand to Anna to help her out of the taxi and then paid the fare, all the while letting his eyes roam, looking for anything out of place. But there was nothing.

Just inside the front door of the lobby, a man who was getting his mail smiled and greeted Anna. They exchanged a sentence or two, but after a good look at Charles's face, she started up the stairs.

Charles had not been able to parse a word she'd said, which was a very bad sign. Grimly he followed her up the stairs, shoulders throbbing with the beat of his heart. He flexed his fingers as she unlocked her door. His joints ached with the need to change, but he held off—only just. If he was this bad in human form, the wolf would be in control if he shifted.

He sat on the futon and watched her open her fridge and then her freezer. Finally she dug in the depths of a cabinet and came out with a large can. She opened it and dumped the unappealing contents into a pot, which she set on the stove.

Then she knelt on the floor in front of him. She touched his face and said, very clearly, "Change," and a number of other things that brushed by his ears like a flight of butterflies.

He closed his eyes against her.

There was some urgent reason he shouldn't change, but he'd forgotten it while he'd been watching her.

"You have five hours before the meeting," she said slowly, her voice making more sense once his eyes were shut. "If you can change to the wolf and back, it will help you heal."

"I have no control," he told her. That was it. That was the reason. "The wound's not that bad—it's the silver. My changing will be too dangerous for you. I can't."

There was a pause and then she said, "If I am your mate, your wolf won't harm me no matter how much control you lack, right?" She sounded more hopeful than certain, and he couldn't think clearly enough to know if she was correct.

DOMINANTS were touchy about taking suggestions from lesser wolves, so she left Charles to make up his own mind while she stirred the beef stew to keep it from burning. Not that burning would make it taste any worse. She'd bought it on sale about six months ago, and had never been hungry enough to eat it. But it had protein, which he needed after being wounded, and it was the only meat in the house.

The wound had looked painful, but not unmanageable to her, and none of the EMTs had seemed overly concerned.

She took the metal ball out of the pocket of her jeans and felt it burn her skin. While the EMTs had been working on his back, Charles had caught her eye and then looked at the small, bloody slug on the sidewalk.

At his silent direction, she'd pocketed it. Now she set it on her counter. Silver was bad. It meant that it really hadn't been a random shooting. She hadn't seen who fired the shot, but she could only assume that it had been one of her pack mates, probably Justin.

Silver injuries wouldn't heal in minutes or hours, and Charles would have to go wounded to Leo's house.

Claws clicked on the hardwood floor and the fox-colored wolf who was Charles walked over and collapsed on the floor, near enough to rest his head on one of her feet. There were bits and pieces of torn cloth caught here and there on his body. A glance at the futon told her he hadn't bothered to strip out of his clothes, and the bandages hadn't survived the change. The cut across his shoulder blades was deep and oozing blood.

He seemed more weary than wild and ravenous, though, so she assumed his fears about how much control he'd have had not been borne out. An out-of-control werewolf, in her experience, would be growling and pacing, not lying quietly at her feet. She put the stew in a bowl and set it in front of him.

He took a bite and then paused after the first mouthful.

"I know," she told him apologetically, "it's not haute cuisine. I could go downstairs and see if Kara has any steaks or roasts I could borrow."

He went back to eating, but she knew from healing her own wounds that he'd be better off with more meat. Kara wouldn't be home, but Anna had a key, and she knew Kara wouldn't mind if she borrowed a roast as long as she replaced it.

Charles seemed to be engrossed in his meal so she started for the door. Before she was halfway there, he'd abandoned the food and stalked at her heels. It hurt him to move—she wasn't quite sure how she knew that, since he neither limped nor slowed visibly.

"You need to stay here," she told him. "I'll be right back."

But when she tried to open the door, he stepped in front of it.

"Charles," she said and then she saw his eyes and swallowed hard. There was nothing of Charles left in the wolf's yellow gaze.

Leaving the apartment wasn't an option.

She walked back to the kitchen and stopped by the food bowl she'd left him. He stayed at the door for a moment before following her. When he had finished eating she sat down on the futon. He jumped up beside her, put his head in her lap, and closed his eyes with a heavy sigh.

He opened one eye and then closed it again. She ran her fingers through his pelt, carefully avoiding the wound.

Were they mated? She thought not. Wouldn't something like that have a more formal ceremony? She hadn't actually told him that she accepted him—no more than he had really asked her.

Still . . . she closed her eyes and let his scent flow through her and her hand closed possessively in a handful of fur. When she opened her eyes, she found herself staring into his clear gold ones.

His phone rang from somewhere underneath her. She reached down to the floor and snagged the remnant of his pants and pulled the phone out and checked the number. She turned it so he could see the display.

"It says *father*," she told him. But evidently the wolf was still in control, because he didn't even look at the phone. "I guess you can call him back when you're back to yourself." She hoped that would be soon. Even with silver poisoning, he ought to be better in a few hours, she hoped.

The phone quit ringing for a moment. Then started again. It rang three times. Stopped. Then rang three more times. Stopped. When it rang again she answered it reluctantly.

"Hello?"

"Is he all right?"

She remembered the werewolf who had brought out a chair for Charles to sit on while the EMTs worked on him. He must have called the Marrok.

"I think so. The wound wasn't so bad, pretty much a deep cut across his shoulder blades, but the bullet was silver and he seems to be having a bad reaction to it."

There was a little pause. "Can I speak to him?"

"He's in wolf form," she told him, "but he is listening to you now." One of his ears was cocked toward the phone.

"Do you need help with Charles? His reaction to silver can be a little extreme."

"No. He's not causing any problems."

"Silver leaves Charles's wolf uncontrolled," crooned the Marrok softly. "But he's giving you no problems? Why would that be?"

She'd never met the Marrok, but she wasn't dumb. That croon was dangerous. Did he think she had something to do with Charles being shot and was now holding him prisoner somewhere? She tried to answer his question, despite the possible embarrassment.

"Um. Charles thinks that his wolf has chosen me as a mate."

"In less than one full day?" It did sound dumb when he said it that way.

"Yes." She couldn't keep the uncertainty out of her voice, though, and it bothered Charles. He rolled to his feet and growled softly.

"Charles also said I was an Omega wolf," she told his father. "That might have something to do with it as well."

Silence lengthened and she began to think that the cell phone might have dropped the connection. Then the Marrok laughed softly. "Oh, his brother is going to tease him unmercifully about this. Why don't you tell me everything that has happened. Start with picking Charles up at the airport please."

HER knuckles were white on the steering wheel, but Charles was in no mood to ease Anna's fears.

He'd tried to leave her behind. He had no desire to have Anna in the middle of the fight that was probable tonight. He didn't want her hurt—and he didn't want her to see him in the role that had been chosen for him so long ago.

"I know where Leo lives," she told him. "If you don't take me with you, I'll just hire a taxi and follow you. You are not going in there alone. You still smell of your wounds—and they'll take that as a sign of weakness."

The truth of her words had almost made him cruel. It had been on the tip of his tongue to ask her what she thought she, an Omega female, could do to help him in a fight—but his brother wolf had frozen his tongue. She had been wounded enough, and the wolf wouldn't allow any more. It was the only time he could ever remember that the wolf put the restraints on his human half rather than the reverse. The words would have been wrong, too. He remembered her holding that marble rolling pin. She might not be aggressive, but she had a limit to how far she could be pushed.

He found himself meekly agreeing to her company, though as they got closer to Leo's house in Naperville, his repentance hadn't been up to making him happy with her presence.

"Leo's house is on fifteen acres," she told him. "Big enough for the pack to hunt on, but we still have to be pretty quiet."

Her voice was tight. He thought she was trying to make conversation with him to keep her anxiety in check. Angry as he was, he couldn't help but come to her aid.

"It's hard to hunt in the big cities," he agreed. Then, to check her reaction because they'd never had a chance to really finish their discussion about what she was to him, he said, "I'll take you for a real hunt in Montana. You'll never want to live near a big city again. We usually hunt deer or elk, but the moose populations are up high enough that we hunt them sometimes, too. Moose are a real challenge."

"I think I'd rather stick to rabbits, if it's all the same to you," she said. "Mostly I just trail behind the hunt." She gave him a little smile. "I think I watched *Bambi* one too many times."

He laughed. Yes, he was going to keep her. She was giving up without a fight. A challenge, perhaps—he thought about her telling him that she wasn't much interested in sex—but not a fight. "Hunting is part of what we are. We aren't cats to prolong the kill, and the animals we hunt need thinning to keep their herds strong and healthy. But if it bothers you, you can follow behind the hunt in Montana, too. You'll still enjoy the run."

She drove up to a keypad on a post in front of a graying cedar gate and pushed in four numbers. After a pause the chain on the top of the gate began to move and the gate slid back along the wall.

He'd been here twice before. The first time had been more than a century ago and the house had been little more than a cabin. There had been fifty acres then and the Alpha had been a little Irish Catholic named Willie O'Shaughnessy who had fit in surprisingly well with his mostly German and Lutheran neighbors. The second time had been in the early twentieth century for Willie's funeral. Willie had been old, nearly as old as the Marrok. There was a madness that came sometimes to those who live too long. When the first signs of it had manifested in him, Willie had quit eating—a display of the willpower that had made him an Alpha. Charles remembered his father's grief at Willie's passing. They—Charles and his brother, Samuel—had been worried for months afterward that their father would decide to follow Willie.

Willie's house and lands had passed on to the next Alpha, a German werewolf who was married to O'Shaughnessy's daughter. Charles couldn't remember what had happened to that one or even his name. There had been several Alphas here after him, though, before Leo took over.

Willie and a handful of fine German stonemasons had built the house with a craftsmanship that would have been prohibitively expensive to replace now. Several of the windows were thickened on the bottom with age. He remembered when those windows had been new.

Charles hated being reminded how old he was.

Anna turned off the engine and started opening her door, but he stopped her.

"Wait a moment." A hint of unease was brushing across the senses bequeathed to him by his gifted mother, and he'd learned to pay attention. He looked at Anna and scowled—she was too vulnerable. If something happened to him, they'd tear her to bits.

"I need you to change," he told her. Something inside him relaxed: that was it. "If something happens to me, I want you to run like hell, get somewhere safe, then call my father and tell him to get you out of here."

She hesitated.

It was not his nature to explain himself. As a dominant wolf in his father's pack, he seldom had to. For her, though, he would make an effort.

"There is something important about you being in wolf form when we go in there." He shrugged. "I've learned to trust my instincts."

"All right."

She took a while. He had time to open his notebook and look at her list. He'd told Justin that Leo could have Isabelle and his first five. According to Anna's list, other than Isabelle, of those six only Boyd was on the list of names his father had given him. If Justin was Leo's second, then there wasn't a wolf other than Leo who was a threat to him.

The ache of his wound gave lie to that thought, so he corrected it. There were none of them who would give him a run for his money in a straightforward fight.

Anna finished her change and sat panting heavily on the driver's side seat. She was beautiful, he thought. Coal black with a dash of white over her nose. She was on the small side for a werewolf, but still much larger than a German shepherd. Her eyes were a pale, pale blue, which was strange because her human eyes were brown.

"Are you ready?" he asked her.

She whined as she got to her feet, her claws making small holes in the leather seat. She shook herself once, as if she'd been wet, then bobbed her head once.

He didn't see anyone watching them from the windows, but there was a small security camera cleverly tucked into a bit of the gingerbread woodwork on the porch. He got out of the SUV, making sure that he didn't show any sign of the pain he was in.

He'd checked in the bathroom of Anna's house and he didn't think the wound would slow him appreciably now that the worst of the silver poisoning had passed. He'd considered acting more hurt than he was—and he might have if he'd been sure that it was Leo who was responsible for all the dead. Acting wounded might lead Leo to attack him—and Charles had no intention of killing Leo until he knew just exactly what had been going on.

He held the SUV door open until Anna hopped out, then closed it and walked with her to the house. He didn't bother knocking on the door; this wasn't a friendly visit.

Inside, the house had changed a lot. Dark paneling had been bleached light and electric lights replaced the old gas chandeliers. Anna walked beside him, but he didn't need her guidance to find the formal parlor because that was the only room with people in it.

Everything else in the house might have changed, but they had left Willie's pride and joy: the huge hand-carved granite fireplace still dominated the parlor. Isabelle, who liked to be the center of attention, was perched on the polished cherry mantel. Leo was positioned squarely in front of her. Justin stood on his left, Boyd on his right. The other three men Charles had allowed him were seated in dainty, Victorian-era chairs. All of them except for Leo himself were dressed in dark, pin-striped suits. Leo wore nothing but a pair of black slacks, revealing that he was tanned and fit.

The effect of their united threat was somewhat mitigated by the pinkish-purple of the upholstery and walls—and by Isabelle, who was dressed in jeans and a half shirt of the same color.

Charles took two steps into the room and stopped. Anna

pressed against his legs, not hard enough to unbalance him, just enough to remind him that she was there.

No one spoke, because it was for him to break the silence first. He took a deep breath into his lungs and held it, waiting for what his senses could tell him. He had gotten more from his mother than his skin and features, more than the ability to change faster than the other werewolves. She had given him the ability to *see*. Not with his eyes, but with his whole spirit.

And there was something sick in Leo's pack; he could feel the wrongness of it.

He looked into Leo's clear, sky-blue eyes and saw nothing that he hadn't seen before. No hint of madness. Not him, then, but someone in his pack.

He looked at the three wolves he had not met—and he saw what Anna had meant about their looks. Leo was not unhandsome in his own Danish Viking sort of way, but he was a warrior and he looked like a warrior. Boyd had a long blade of a nose and the military cut of his hair made his ears appear to stick out even farther than they really did.

All the wolves Charles didn't know looked like the sort of men who modeled tuxedos at a rental shop. Thin and edgy, with no real flesh to mar the lines of a jacket. Despite differences in coloring, there was a certain sameness about them. Isabelle pulled her bare feet onto the mantel with the rest of her and heaved a big sigh.

He ignored her impatience because she wasn't important just now—Leo was.

Charles met the Alpha's eyes and said, "The Marrok has sent me here to ask you why you sold your child into bondage."

Clearly, it wasn't the question Leo had expected. Isabelle had thought it was Anna, and Charles hadn't disabused her of the notion. They would deal with Anna, too, but his father's question was a better starting place because it was unexpected.

"I have no children," said Leo.

Charles shook his head. "All your wolves are your children, Leo, you know that. They are yours to love and feed, to guard and protect, to guide and to teach. You sold a young man named Alan Mackenzie Frazier. To whom and why?"

"He wasn't pack." Leo spread his arms, palms outward. "It is expensive to keep so many wolves happy here in the city. I needed the money. I am happy to give you the name of the buyer, though I believe he was only acting as a middleman."

True. All true. But Leo was being very careful how he worded his reply.

"My father would like the name and the method you used to contact him."

Leo nodded at one of the handsome men, who passed Charles with his eyes on the ground, though he spared an instant to glare at Anna. She flattened her ears at him and growled.

He had been a poor influence on her, Charles thought unrepentantly.

"Is there anything more I can help you with?" Leo asked politely.

They had, all of Leo's wolves, used Isabelle's trick with perfume, but Charles had a keen nose and Leo was . . . sad.

"You haven't updated your pack membership for five or six years," Charles said, wondering at Leo's reaction. He'd been met with defiance, anger, fear, but never with sadness.

"I thought you might catch that. Did you and Anna compare lists? Yes, I had something of a coup attempt I had to put down a little harshly."

Truth, but, again, not all of it. Leo had a lawyer's understanding of how to be careful with the truth and use it to lie by leading a false trail.

"Is that why you killed all the women of your pack? Did they all rebel against you?"

"There weren't so many women, there never are."

Again. There was something he wasn't catching. Leo hadn't been the wolf who had attacked young Frazier—it had been Justin.

Leo's wolf was back. He handed Charles a note with a name and phone number written in purple ink.

Charles tucked the note in his pocket and then nodded. "You are right. There are not enough females—so those we have ought to be protected, not killed. Did you kill them yourself?"

"All the women? No."

"Which of them did you kill?"

Leo didn't answer, and Charles felt his wolf perk up as the hunt commenced.

"You didn't kill any of the women," Charles said. He looked at the model-perfect men and at Justin who was beautiful in an unfinished sort of way.

Leo was protecting someone. Charles looked up at Isabelle, who loved beautiful men. Isabelle, who was older than old Willie O'Shaughnessy had been when he'd begun to go crazy.

He wondered how long Leo had known she was mad.

He looked back at the Alpha. "You should have asked the Marrok for help."

LEO shook his head. "You know what he would have done. He'd have killed her."

Charles would dearly have loved to see what Isabelle was doing, but he couldn't afford to take his eyes off Leo: a cornered wolf was a dangerous wolf.

"And how many have died instead? How many of your pack are lost? The women she killed for jealousy, and their mates you had to kill to protect her? The wolves who rebelled at what the two of you were doing? How many?"

Leo raised his chin. "None for three years."

Rage rose its ugly head. "Yes," Charles agreed, very softly. "Not since you had your little bully boy attack a defenseless woman and Change her without her consent. A woman who you then proceeded to brutalize."

"If I'd protected her, Isabelle would have hated her," Leo explained. "I forced Isabelle to protect her instead. It worked, Charles. Isabelle has been stable for three years."

Until she'd come to Anna's today and realized that Charles was interested in Anna. Isabelle had never liked anyone paying attention to other females when she was around.

He risked a glance and saw that though she hadn't moved from the mantel, Isabelle's legs were back to dangling down so she could hop down quickly if she wanted to. Her eyes had changed and watched with pale impatience for the violence she knew was to come. She licked her lips and rocked her weight from side to side in her eagerness.

Charles felt sick at the waste of it all. He turned his attention back to the Alpha. "No deaths because you have an Omega to keep her calm. And because there are no females to compete with except for Anna, who doesn't want any of your wolves, not after they raped her on your orders."

"It kept Anna alive," Leo insisted. "Kept them both alive." He ducked his head, an appeal for protection. "Tell your father that she is stable. Tell him I'll see she doesn't harm anyone else."

"She tried to kill Anna, today," Charles said gently. "And if she hadn't . . . She is insane, Leo."

He watched the last trace of hope leave Leo's face. The Alpha knew Charles wouldn't let Isabelle live—she was too dangerous, too unpredictable. Leo knew that he was dead, too. He had worked too hard to save his mate.

Leo didn't give any warning before he attacked—but Charles had been ready for him. Leo wasn't the kind of wolf to submit easily to death. There would be no bared throats in this fight.

But they both knew who would win.

* * *

ANNA had been stunned to stillness by what Leo had revealed, but that ended when Leo attacked. She couldn't help the little yip she let out, anymore than she could help her instinctive lunge forward to protect Charles.

A strong pair of workman's hands gripped her by the ruff of her neck and pulled her back despite the scrabbling of her claws on the hardwood floor.

"Here, now," Boyd's rumble hit her ears. "Steady on. This isn't your fight."

His voice, one she was used to obeying, calmed her so she could think. It also helped that Charles avoided Leo's first strike with a minimal movement of his shoulders.

The other wolves had come to their feet and part of her registered Justin's insistent chanting, "Kill him, kill him." She wasn't sure which wolf he wanted to die. He hated Leo for controlling him and for being Isabelle's mate. Maybe he didn't care which one died.

Leo struck three times in rapid succession, missing each time. He'd committed to the last blow, and when it didn't land he had to take an awkward step forward.

Charles took advantage of the stumble and stepped into Leo, and in a graceful movement she couldn't quite follow did something to Leo's shoulder that had the Alpha roaring in rage and pain.

The next few things happened so fast, Anna was never certain in what order they occurred.

There was a rapid double bark of a gun. Boyd's hands loosened their grip on her fur as he swore, and Isabelle gave a frenetic, excited laugh.

It took Anna only a glance to see what had happened. Isabelle was holding a gun, watching the fight, waiting for another clear shot at Charles.

Anna broke free of Boyd's loosened grip and sprinted across the room.

From the mantel, Isabelle looked Anna squarely in her eyes and said sharply, "Stop, Anna."

She was so sure of Anna's obedience, she didn't even wait to make certain Anna listened before turning her attention back to the battling men.

Anna felt the force of Isabelle's command as it rolled by her like a breeze that ruffled her hair. It didn't slow her down at all.

She gathered her hind quarters underneath her and launched. Her teeth closed on Isabelle's arm, and she felt the bone crack with a noise that satisfied the wolf's anger. The force of her leap was such that she pulled Isabelle off the six-foot-high mantel and slammed her into the fireplace as they both tumbled down—Anna's jaws still locked around the arm that had held the gun.

She crouched there, waiting for Isabelle to do something, but the other woman just lay there. Someone came up behind them, and Anna growled a warning.

"Easy," Boyd said, his calm voice touching her as Isabelle's order had not.

His hand rested on her back and she increased her growl, but he didn't pay any attention to her: he was looking at Isabelle.

"Dead," he grunted. "Serves her right for forgetting you aren't just another submissive wolf who has to listen to her. Let go, Anna. You caved her head in on the fireplace. She's gone." But when Anna reluctantly let go, Boyd made sure Isabelle was dead by twisting her head until her neck made a sick-sounding pop. He picked the gun up off the floor.

Staring at Isabelle's broken body, Anna began to shake. She lifted a foot, but she didn't know whether she was going to take a step closer or a step away. A chair hit her in the side and reminded her that there was a fight going on—and Isabelle had shot at Charles twice.

If he was hurt, he showed no sign of it. He was moving as easily as he had in the beginning, and Leo was staggering, one arm limp at his side. Charles swept behind him and hit him in the back of the neck with the edge of his hand and Leo collapsed like a kite when the wind dies.

A soft, moaning howl rose from Boyd, who was still standing beside her, echoed by the other wolves as they mourned their Alpha's passing.

Ignoring them, Charles knelt beside Leo and, with the same motion Boyd had used on Isabelle, he made sure the broken neck was permanent.

He stayed there, on one knee and one foot, like a man proposing. He bowed his head and reached out again, this time to caress the dead man's face.

Justin's move was so fast, Anna didn't have a chance to sing a warning. She hadn't even noticed when he'd changed to his wolf form. He hit Charles like a battering ram and Charles went down beneath him.

But if Anna was frozen, Boyd was not. He shot Justin in the eye a split second before Justin's body hit Charles.

That fast it was over.

Boyd hauled Justin's limp body off Charles and dumped him to one side. Anna didn't remember moving but suddenly she was astraddle Charles and growling at Boyd.

He backed up slowly, his hands raised and empty. The gun was tucked into the belt of his slacks.

As soon as Boyd ceased to feel like a threat, Anna turned her attention to Charles. He was lying facedown on the floor, covered with blood—her nose told her that some of it was Boyd's, but some of it was his, too.

Despite the way he'd been fighting Leo, Isabelle had hit him at least once, she could see the bloody hole in his back. In wolf form she couldn't help him and it would take her too long to change.

She looked over her shoulder at Boyd.

He shrugged. "I can't help him unless I get closer than this."

She stared at him, challenging him with her eyes in a

way she would never have done before today. It didn't seem to bother him. He just waited for her to make up her mind. The wolf didn't want to trust anyone with her mate—but she knew she didn't have a choice.

She hopped all the way over Charles's body, giving Boyd access. But she couldn't help her snarl when he rolled him over to check him for wounds. He found a second bullet hole in Charles's left calf.

Boyd shed his suit jacket and ripped off his dress shirt, scattering buttons all over the floor. He tore the silk shirt into strips and then, as he was bandaging Charles's with rapid experience, he began giving orders. "Holden, call in the rest of the pack—and start with Rashid. Tell him we need him to bring whatever he needs to treat a silver bullet wound—both bullets are out. When you've finished, call the Marrok and tell him what has happened. You can find his number in Isabelle's address book in the kitchen drawer under the phone."

Anna whined. Both of Isabelle's shots had hit.

"He's not going to die," Boyd told her, tying off the last bandage. He glanced around the room and swore. "This place looks like the last scene in *Hamlet*. Gardner, you and Simon start getting this mess cleaned up. Let's get Charles someplace quieter. He's not going to be a happy camper when he wakes, and all this blood isn't going to help." He picked Charles up. When he carried him out of the room, Anna was at his heels.

BACK in human form, Anna lay on the bed beside Charles. Rashid, who was a real doctor as well as a werewolf, had come and gone, replacing Boyd's makeshift bandage with something more sterile-looking. He told Anna that Charles was unconscious due to blood loss.

Boyd had come in afterward and advised her to leave

Charles before he woke up. The room was reinforced to withstand an enraged wolf—Anna was not.

He hadn't argued when she refused. He'd just bolted the door behind him when he left. She waited until he was gone and then changed. There was clothing in the old-fashioned wardrobe, lots of things that were one size fits all. She found a T-shirt and a pair of jeans that didn't fit too badly.

Charles didn't notice when she got on the bed with him. She put her head next to his on the pillow and listened to him breathe.

HE didn't wake quietly. One moment he was limp and the next he'd exploded to his feet. She'd never watched him shift and, although she knew his change was miraculously swift, she hadn't known it was beautiful. It started with his feet, then like a blanket of red fur the change rolled up his body, leaving behind it a malevolent, very angry werewolf dripping blood and bandages.

Bright yellow eyes glanced around the room, taking in the closed door, the bars on the windows, and then her.

She lay very still, letting him absorb his surroundings and see there was no threat. When he looked at her a second time, she sat up and went to work on his bandages.

He growled at her, and she tapped his nose gently. "You've lost enough blood today. The bandages don't advertise your weakness any more than bleeding all over would. At least this way, you aren't going to ruin the carpet."

When she finished, she threaded her fingers through the ruff of fur around his neck and bent her head to his.

"I thought I had lost you."

He stood for her embrace for a minute before wriggling free. He got off the bed and stalked to the door.

"It's bolted," she told him, hopping off the bed and padding after him.

He gave her a patient look.

There was a click and the door was opened by a slender, unremarkable-looking man who appeared to be in his early twenties. He crouched on his heels and stared Charles in the face before glancing up at her.

The force of personality in his eyes hit her like a blow to the stomach, so she wasn't entirely surprised when she recognized his voice.

"Shot three times in one day," the Marrok murmured. "I think Chicago has been harder on you than usual, my son. I'd best take you home, don't you think?"

She didn't know what to say so she didn't say anything. She put her hand on Charles's back and swallowed.

Charles looked at his father.

"Have you asked her?"

Charles growled low in his chest.

The Marrok laughed and stood up. "Nevertheless, I will ask. You are Anna?" It wasn't quite a question.

Her throat was too dry to say anything, so she nodded.

"My son would like you to accompany us to Montana. I assure you that if anything is not to your liking, I'll see to it that you can relocate to wherever suits you better."

Charles growled and Bran raised an eyebrow as he looked at him. "*I* am the Marrok, Charles. If the child wants to go elsewhere, she can."

Anna leaned against Charles's hip. "I think I'd like to see Montana," she said.

Look for the continuation of
Charles and Anna's story in
August 2008 from Ace Books.

Inhuman

EILEEN WILKS

CHAPTER 1

KAI Tallman Michalski stood at her kitchen sink looking out the window. In daytime she would have seen mesquite, tumbleweed, and the pale grasses of winter stretched across land as flat as her frying pan. But it was after eight o'clock at night in late January, and her apartment complex perched at the very edge of town. Beyond the reach of the parking area's lights, across the wide road that ran along the back of the complex, darkness waited.

Lightning stitched from one black-hung pocket of sky to the next. Eight seconds later, thunder rumbled like a giarit's empty belly.

Her own belly tightened.

"Where's your plastic wrap?"

She twitched all over like a nervous horse.

"Chill," Jackie said. "It's just me."

Kai turned away from the window to see her friend standing in a tiny kitchen aglow with color. Ghostly patterns swam through the air, some soft as a soap bubble, some so vibrant they seemed almost solid.

She clenched her fist, digging her fingernails into her palm. Pain was a quick way to focus—handy, too, since it was always available. The colors faded to a transparent overlay, barely visible. "Sorry. I phased out watching the storm rolling in on us. Listen, y'all don't have to clean up."

Jackie rolled her eyes. The transparent sea around her was olive shaded with royal blue. Small, discrete shapes swam in her colors like agitated minnows. "Plastic wrap," she repeated. She jiggled the platter she held, still half-full of broccoli, carrots, and bell pepper.

As usual, the vegetables had gone largely unappreciated. Kai always put them out—she liked them, even if no one else did. "In the bottom drawer by the stove. But there isn't much mess, and the storm—"

"Now, Kai." A chunky blonde zipped through the arch between the kitchen and the living area, her hands full of glasses. The colors swimming around her were as quick and lively as her hands as she plunked glasses in the dishwasher. Ginger was twenty years older than Kai and Jackie, but she didn't move like it. "That storm will bother you a lot more than it does us. You need to learn to accept help gracefully, like Jackie does."

Kai's smile stretched across her face, slow and amused. "Jackie does almost everything gracefully. Then she opens her mouth."

"Hey." Jackie's eyebrows lifted above eyes almost the same warm mocha as her skin. "You think I can't chew on my foot gracefully?"

Ginger patted the taller woman on the arm. "We love you anyway, sweetie. So," she said, ripping off a paper towel and turning on the water to dampen it. "Y'all are going to the rally tomorrow, right?"

"Count me out." Jackie's colors looked upset, the shapes breaking up and re-forming. "If what Kai said about those two people who were killed is true—"

"It is," Kai said quietly, opening the refrigerator to put away three unopened Cokes and two cans of Dr Pepper. "You won't read about it in the paper, but they were both Gifted."

"So we're supposed to band together and march in public, demanding our rights?" Jackie snorted. "Might as well hang a sign around my neck: *Gifted here. Come get me*. Even if the psycho who whacked those two people doesn't come after me, other nulls might. Like my boss. Or the idiots in Reverend Barclay's congregation. Bet they'd be thrilled to know exactly who to hate."

"We've got to do *something*." Ginger was uncharacteristically serious. "We can't let them march us off a cliff without speaking up."

"Not everyone has your nerve," Kai said. "But I suppose I'll go. If you . . ." Her voice trailed off.

Jackie's colors were too jumpy, too dark. She was a deeply reluctant medium who did her best not to contact the dead, but sometimes they pushed their way in. "Hey." She put a hand on Jackie's shoulder. "What's wrong? Is one of the dearly departed giving you a hard time?"

"No. It's nothing. Here." Jackie thrust the wrapped veggies at her.

Deliberate lies were snot green. Something was wrong, but Jackie didn't want to talk about it, so she lied.

Kai didn't call her on it. She accepted the platter and found room for it in the refrigerator. People lied in so many ways, for so many reasons. Most lies weren't malicious. People dodged the truth to spare someone's feelings, to avoid long explanations, to get what they wanted, to fit in, to avoid the consequences of their actions.

Kai knew that good people lied, sometimes for good reasons. She just wished they'd stop. Which, of course, made her quite the hypocrite. She might only lie about one thing, but it was a whopper.

"So how's Nathan?" Ginger asked, whisking herself back into the living room, paper towel in hand.

The question wasn't the non sequitur it seemed. Kai had told everyone who showed up tonight about the two victims being Gifted; she wanted her friends to be wary. She hadn't told them how she knew, but they would assume the information came from Nathan.

As, of course, it had.

"More to the point," Jackie added, "*where's* Nathan? How come he didn't show? He always comes to your parties."

Ginger laughed. "Comes? He's usually here anyway."

"He had to work tonight." Kai looked around. The kitchen was spotless, so she headed for the living area. "Besides, this wasn't my usual sort of get-together. Ginger, there isn't a thing left to clean in here."

"I guess you'd know his schedule." Ginger tossed her a grin as she wiped down the coffee table, a garage-sale find Kai had painted turquoise and coral and black. "Though I can't believe y'all are still paying for two apartments when you spend most of your time in just one."

Jackie's dark, angular face broke out in a smile. "So you and Nathan aren't just friends! I didn't see how you could be. I mean, the guy is seriously hot in a tall, dark, and uncommunicative sort of way, and you're hetero, right? And the two of you look good together, like bookends. You're both so buff and bony."

Ginger hooted. "Jackie's mouth strikes again!"

Jackie grimaced. "I didn't mean—"

"No, of course you didn't." Kai smiled. "But Nathan and I aren't lovers. We spend a lot of time together because we're friends, and because he's teaching me self-defense. He—"

"And you're teaching him computers," Ginger broke in. "And you run together. And eat dinner together half the time."

Kai looked at Jackie. "Ginger likes to think she's matchmaking with these little comments she makes. It's annoying, but I haven't been able to hint her into stopping."

"Hint!" Ginger laughed. "If I ever learn how to say things as bluntly as you do without people wanting to slap me—"

"It's that Buddha smile," Jackie said. "She smiles like that and you can't get mad."

"I think I'm blushing," Kai said.

"Really?" Ginger made a point of pressing her hand to Kai's cheek. "Nope. Not a hint of heat."

Kai looped an arm around Ginger's shoulders and hugged her. "Okay, not blushing, but I feel like I should be. Now, that gully washer is nearly here, so you two need to be on your way. I don't want to worry about you getting home safely."

Ginger returned the hug. "We'll be fine. But you'll do better if we aren't around when it hits, won't you?"

"What?" Jackie frowned, looking from one of them to the other. "I'm missing something here."

"You know Kai's Gift has a hitch in its gallop?"

"Well, yeah, but erratic empathy isn't such a bad deal. Who wants to feel *everything* everyone else feels all the time?"

"So true. Problem is, it goes wonky when there's a storm. Sometimes she gets nothing. Sometimes every feeling for a mile around washes right in on her."

Jackie looked appalled.

"Not to worry." Kai patted Jackie's arm reassuringly. "Someone gave me a recipe for a tea that helps. It's got a little magical boost that helps me shut things down. But I'll sleep after drinking it, and I can't do that until—"

"Until your guests are gone," Jackie finished for her. "Got it." She retrieved her coat from the couch and handed Ginger her jacket. "Come on, Ginger. I can't leave until you do, remember? I rode here with you."

Ginger just grinned. "Would that friend who gave you the tea be Nathan, by any chance?"

"If I'd wanted you to know who it was, I would have used his or her name. Go home, Ginger."

"Because I've wondered if Nathan was Wiccan. That's not a big deal in some parts of the country, but here in the Bible Belt it can be. Especially now. With Nathan being a deputy, it could mean trouble if he were known to be a witch. So I thought that might be his big secret. He'd have to be a solo practitioner, since he's not part of my coven, but—"

"Home." Kai grabbed Ginger's purse from the couch and held it out.

A few minutes later, Kai shut the door behind her friends. She breathed a sigh of relief. She loved Ginger dearly, but her friend's inquisitiveness could be a trial, and Nathan's secrets weren't hers to disclose.

Not that she knew many of his secrets, but she knew the biggie. Part of it, anyway. Nathan wasn't Wiccan or Gifted because those were human labels. And Nathan wasn't human.

Kai wandered around her small apartment, fluffing a pillow, straightening a stack of books, too twitchy to settle. It was barely nine o'clock. She didn't want to sleep, dammit, but with that storm . . . maybe she should listen to the weather forecast. She clicked on the radio.

"The president announced the expansion of the task force initially formed to study the effects of the power winds that shifted the balance of magic five weeks ago. Speaking to a crowded town-hall type meeting in Boston, she said . . ."

Kai snorted. She doubted a task force was going to help. They couldn't remake the world back into its old shape—though a few dozen more dragons to soak up excess magic leaking from nodes all over the world would help. Maybe they'd find a way to conjure or contact some.

Here in Midland, the Turning hadn't caused as many problems as elsewhere. With only one small node in the city, the ambient magic level hadn't risen enough to interfere badly with computers. They hadn't been troubled with things blown in by the power winds, either, like the goblins that hit a little town near Austin, or the hell-rain in Houston.

That had blazed for days in spite of the efforts of firefighters from all over the nation. It might be burning still if the FBI's Magical Crimes Division hadn't sent three covens to extinguish it.

Of course, the hates-magic crowd thought the covens had started the fire in the first place. Never mind that experts said the Turning was caused by a shift in the realms—they blamed witches.

Now that most of the big, showy problems caused by the Turning had been dealt with, people were noticing another change. The population of Gifted had pretty much doubled. Turned out that a lot of people possessed a potential for magic, but so slight it had gone unnoticed until the power winds blew through in December. Existing Gifts had been strengthened. Nascent Gifts had bloomed into the real thing—delighting some, traumatizing some, and feeding the antimagic hysteria that spread like a fungus in others.

People always wanted someone to blame, didn't they? Fear tied knots in reason and shut down compassion, even in basically decent people.

Not everyone was basically decent. Politicians pandering to fear and prejudice had introduced a bill in the Texas House to require all Gifted to register their Gift. They wanted it put on driver's licenses and employment applications, loans, and several types of professional licenses. It made Kai think of the way the Nazis made Jews wear Stars of David on their clothing.

She bent to pick up a crumpled napkin Ginger had missed in her frenzy of cleaning. The truth was, she was afraid, too—not of magic, but of people. Which wasn't like her.

Kai gave a lot of parties, though she wasn't an extrovert in the usual sense. She just liked people. She especially liked bringing together those who'd never ordinarily have a chance to get acquainted, and her job took her into homes all over the city, so she knew people from all walks of life.

She threw good parties, too. Like a chef, she took a little of this, a little of that, and stirred up a delicious gathering. But tonight's party hadn't been her usual get-together. Tonight she'd asked her Gifted friends and a few concerned spouses or partners over to talk about the prejudice that had blown into Texas along with the power winds . . . and to pass on Nathan's warning.

Two people had been killed in the past month, their bodies drained of blood. Reverend Barclay and his ilk blamed some demonic cult, but Nathan said both victims had been Gifted.

"In other news," the NPR announcer was saying, "Republican House Leader Brent Trott renewed his opposition to the Dragon Accords, referring to them as 'deals with the devil.' The Accords, sometimes referred to as Dragon Treaties, were passed last week by strong majorities in both the House and the Senate, and the president is expected to sign them into law tomorrow. In China . . ."

Kai turned the radio off. She didn't need a weather report to know the storm was close. She'd better get her tea brewing.

In the kitchen she got down her teapot, filled it with water purified by more than reverse osmosis, and set it on the burner. Her stomach churned with guilt.

What she'd said outright was true: the tea helped protect her from the effects of the storm. The rest had been half-truth, misdirection, and lies.

The tea hadn't come from Nathan, as she'd allowed Ginger to assume, but from a shaman of her mother's tribe. That misdirection was for Nathan's sake. It was best if even tolerant people like Ginger continued to think him human. Nor did the brew knock her out. It enhanced her focus so she could put herself *in* sleep—a trance state that shut down her Gift along with her conscious mind. That half-truth had been for her own sake, to spare herself explanations she couldn't afford because of her one big lie.

Kai wasn't an empath.

While she waited for the water to boil, she wandered over to the sliding glass doors that opened onto a tiny balcony. Impulsively she yanked open the blinds, but the lighting tricked her out of a view. Instead she saw her own face, ghostly in its reflected state, looking back.

The face she saw was . . . *bony*, she thought, and chuckled. Trust Jackie! It was as good a description as any. Better than plain, which is what she usually thought when she looked in the mirror. Her features didn't rise to the extravagance of real ugliness, but they didn't add up to anything as smooth as prettiness, either. That sharp blade of a nose would have done any Diné warrior proud.

Like her grandfather. She smiled and her ghost smiled back. That beak looked great on that fierce old man. She did have good skin, and she thought her neck was rather elegant. Her hair was okay. It was thick, at least, though straight as poured water, and the color hit a bland halfway point between her mother's shiny black and her father's dusty blond.

The woman in the glass lost her smile. The root-ripping torrent of grief had long since subsided, and memory ran smoothly in its beds, a quietly welcoming stream. Yet she'd never stopped missing them. She'd give almost anything to hear her father's belly laugh one more time, or be back in her mother's kitchen making fry bread.

Her mother had been a pretty, feminine woman. Maybe if she'd taken after her mother more, Nathan would . . .

Oh, stop. She yanked the blinds closed. There were plenty of pretty women in Midland. She'd never known him to bring one of them home. Nor any pretty boys, for that matter. For awhile she'd wondered if his moral code precluded sex outside of marriage, or if he'd taken some kind of vow. A couple months ago she'd been nervy enough to ask.

He'd looked startled, then said, simply, "No."

Nothing more, just that one word. With anyone else, it would have been a rebuke for having pried. With Nathan, it was a mark of trust that he'd answered at all.

She could only suppose that human women didn't ring his chimes. Pity he rang hers so well.

The whistling of the teapot drew her back to the kitchen. She took down the glass jar where she kept the herbal mixture, filled a mesh tea ball, and placed it in a glass mug. The herbs had an odd, not unpleasant aroma dominated by the anise scent of giant hyssop. As soon as she'd poured the hot water she covered the mug with her left hand and began chanting. Heat and moisture dampened her palm as she repeated the chant three times, then thanked the Powers. She covered the mug with a glass saucer and left the tea to finish steeping.

In the bathroom she pulled on her faded flannel pj's, put her clothes in the hamper, washed her face, and brushed her teeth. Her contacts went into their case and the world turned blurry, but she didn't bother with glasses. She retrieved the mug and brought it into her bedroom, where aqua walls and white wicker unknotted some of her tension.

Color mattered. Kai knew that better than most. She could see the way people responded to the colors around them. She'd painted this apartment as soon as she moved in last year—aqua in the bedroom, a warm tan in the living area, sandy tan in the kitchen, with a turquoise stripe wrapping the two areas to unite them.

She tugged down the covers and turned off the bedside lamp, leaving the one on in the kitchen. Childish, foolish . . . she promised herself again to stop with the name-calling, but it did embarrass her. Eleven years after the accident, and she still didn't like the dark.

She cozied into her nest of pillows and drank the tea in three big swallows. And shuddered.

The stuff tasted nastier than it smelled, but it worked fast. Even as she snuggled down flat, warmth opened in her middle like a blossom and began sending out tendrils.

She lay in the darkness breathing quietly, listening to the wind as it kicked up a fuss outside. Warmth continued to spread, reaching places that made her think of Nathan and wishes . . . a wish that hovered in the air, its wistful lavender woven threaded with silver and red. A nice carnal shade of red.

A sensible woman would be glad their relationship hadn't gone in the direction she'd wanted. He was leaving, wasn't he? He'd told her that three months ago. People he worked with were beginning to be suspicious about him. He couldn't stay in Midland much longer.

Surely it would hurt worse when he left if they'd become lovers. As it was, loss already ached inside her like a tooth going bad.

Maybe he wouldn't leave if . . .

Yes, he would. Dammit, she knew that.

Rain tapped its first, uncertain fingertips on the window. Time to finish putting herself out . . . not for her own sake, but for everyone else's. Her Gift might not be empathy, as she claimed, but it was skewed.

Which was just as well, since that was probably why she wasn't crazy. Telepaths usually were.

Kai didn't read minds. She saw thoughts and the emotions connected to those thoughts, and sometimes she changed minds. Literally. If she stayed awake for tonight's storm, there was a good chance that some of her thoughts would split off to tangle themselves up in other people's heads.

This wasn't unusual. The biggest null on the planet left a residue of thoughts and feelings behind, but such a faded wash that only a strong psychometry Gift could read anything from it. Strong emotions caused many people to project, and a few others were natural projectors.

But normal thought-bodies evaporated soon after separating from their origin. Kai's didn't. Her stray thoughts might cause her neighbors no more than a brief confusion or bad dream, but it could be worse. Much worse. And with the way her Gift had strengthened since the Turning, she couldn't take any chances.

Kai no longer needed to speak the entire spell aloud. Long practice plus the focusing property of the tea allowed her to carry only a single word deep inside, where she released it. In a dizzy, immaterial shift she slid into white fog, a place diffuse and warm where thought slowed . . . and slowed . . . and faded away.

CHAPTER 2

IT was the sobbing that woke her.

Kai hung in the blurred state between sleep and waking, eyes closed, hearing the wash of rain drained of its earlier frenzy, the wail of her neighbor's Siamese cat, and the sobbing. Deep sobs, bereft of hope, aching with a terrible loneliness.

And familiar. She'd heard this before, in other dreams. *Oh, sweetheart—there now, you aren't alone, I'm here. I'm . . .*

Her eyes opened. The sound of that terrible sorrow died, but the colors of it lingered for a second in alien shapes of black and silver before dissolving.

Kai sat up, shaken. She'd brought those thoughts back with her. *That* had never happened before. And she never experienced the emotions connected to thoughts.

Was her lie somehow coming true? Was she was turning into an empath as well as a weird-ass telepath?

That fear, put into words, sounded so silly she was able to set it aside. She'd been asleep, after all—normal sleep, not in-sleep; the trance state never lasted more than a couple hours. She'd connected with someone's thoughts, but her dreaming mind must have translated colors and shapes to conjure the experience of grief instead of the sight of it.

Could it have been Nathan's mind she'd touched?

She frowned, not liking the idea. She'd caught such a quick glimpse of those thoughts . . . for some reason they hadn't struck her as human, but she wasn't sure why. Nathan was lonely, though. Deeply so. That was one reason she'd reached out to him when they first met, both of them out running in the early morning.

That, and his incredible thighs. And shoulders. And . . .

And that was enough of that sort of thinking. She shook her head at herself and glanced at the red numerals on her clock, bought because the numbers were big enough for her to read them without contacts or glasses.

Two-ten.

Well, shit. She grimaced and reached for her glasses. No point in trying to go back to sleep. The in-sleep state rested her deeply, and with a couple hours of real sleep on top of it, her tank was topped off. She might as well read for awhile.

Someone pounded on her door.

What the . . . it couldn't be good news, not at this hour. Kai swung out of bed, heart pounding, mentally sorting through various disasters as she hurried to her living area.

The police, arriving with some terrible news? A drunk? A neighbor with an emergency?

Her last guess was right, she saw as she neared the door. Patterns clung to it, coming from the person on the other side—patterns she recognized.

Nathan. And pain. She fumbled with the locks, swung the door open, and let in a rush of cold, wet air.

The man standing in the puddle of yellow light from her porch light didn't move. He was on the lanky side of lean with a long face, black hair, and weathered skin that suggested native or Hispanic blood, though his features were

Anglo. His clothes were dark and dripping. No jacket. He was cradling his left arm with his right, but she didn't see any blood.

"Nathan. Come in. What— No, come in first, then tell me."

"There's a bullet in my shoulder."

"An ambulance. I'll call . . . or do you want me to take you to the hospital? I'll get my coat." Keys. She needed her keys. She turned.

"Eh." One long arm reached out and stopped her. "No hospital. I don't want that. Will you take the bullet out?"

Her mouth gaped. She shut it. "I'm a physical therapist, not a doctor. Certainly not a surgeon."

"I don't need a surgeon. You know how a body is put together."

"I don't know how to—" She heard her voice rising and shut herself up, took a breath, and said more quietly, "I can at least clean it and wrap some gauze around it. Come inside."

"I shouldn't have bothered you." He turned.

This time she grabbed his arm. "*In*, dammit."

He looked down at her hand, then up at her face, and smiled a singularly sweet smile. That was typical. Nathan's smiles were rare, but each arrived as a new discovery, invented on the spot. "Yes, ma'am."

Standing still, Nathan didn't draw the eye. When he moved, men stood straighter and watched, wary. Women just watched. When he moved, Nathan was power.

Power with a bullet in the shoulder. A bullet. God! Kai shut the door, locked it, and stalked around behind him to look at the wound. How dare he get himself shot. How dare someone shoot him. And he wanted her to cut into him! She wanted to punch things. She was furious and irrational and hoped she'd get over it soon, but she wanted to punch things first.

His cotton shirt clung to his back, soaked through. There

was a small, neat hole in the cloth in the neighborhood between his spine and his left scapula. "There's hardly any blood."

"It's usually best not to bleed."

She couldn't help but smile, which made it hard to hold on to her anger. "Bleeding isn't optional for most of us. What about pain? Is that optional, too? Unless you can shut the pain off, it's going to hurt badly if I start digging around in you."

"Shutting pain off is dangerous."

"Can you do it?" she asked, startled.

He didn't answer. He did that sometimes. If she asked a question he didn't want to answer, he said nothing—no evasions, no anger. And no lies. In the eighteen months she'd known him, Nathan had never lied to her.

The last of her temper poofed out like mummy dust. "Nathan, I'm not qualified. You know that. You need a doctor."

He turned to face her. "Being cut will hurt, but I'm already in pain. Removing the bullet will allow me to heal properly. You're worried that you might damage me, but you won't. I'll direct you. If your hand slips and you cut where you shouldn't, I'll heal it. I heal quickly."

He spoke patiently, as if she were making a fuss over a simple favor. Maybe to him that's all this was. "And if I don't remove the bullet?"

"My body will push it out in a few days, but my range of motion will be impaired until then, and my healing delayed."

Not to mention the pain thing. "I guess a doctor would notice the quick healing. You don't want that."

"Yes. He or she would also have to report a gunshot wound."

Her neighbor's cat had quieted. The apartment was silent except for the shushing of the rain outside. Kai's heart thudded hard in her chest and her palms were damp. Was she seriously considering doing what he wanted?

She met his eyes. They were steel gray like a winter sky, and heavily lashed, striking beneath his dark brows. As usual, they gave away nothing. But the slow, indigo shapes of the thoughts weaving around his head and torso kept spiking into ragged scarlet, toothy orange. Pain colors, when they shaped themselves that way.

He'd given her what he considered enough information to make a decision. He wouldn't ask again. "Who shot you?"

"A city cop. I was somewhere I wasn't supposed to be."

"You'll tell me," she said fiercely. "If I do this, you'll tell me why you were shot, what you were doing—all of it."

He nodded.

"All right. I'm insane, but I'll do it."

CHAPTER 3

NATHAN lay on his stomach on Kai's couch, waiting for her to return with whatever medical supplies she thought she needed. He heard her muttering to herself as she rummaged in the medicine cabinet in the bathroom.

He'd already selected the knife—a short, sharp paring knife from her kitchen, part of a set he'd given her last Winterfaire.

Not Winterfaire. Christmas. That's what they called the celebration of the winter solstice here. Even after all these years, in the privacy of his mind he sometimes forgot to name things in the common way.

She'd given him a present, too—a suede shirt the color of sand, soft as a mare's nose. He was glad he hadn't worn it tonight . . . but that was silly thinking. He wanted to keep it for as long as possible, so he seldom wore it. Certainly not for a hunt, even such a limited one as tonight's had been.

Kai had laughed when she opened his gift and said something about the difference between men's presents and women's. She did see him as a man. Sometimes he wanted to ask her why. Was it only his shape that made her think of him that way? Or were his thoughts man-shaped in some ways?

That could be. He'd been here a long time. Perhaps he wasn't as far from human as he sometimes felt.

Feelings spiked in him at the thought. Complicated feelings. Humans dwelled within their complications so consistently, even as they squirmed and disavowed and tried to make the world simple by thinking it so. Nathan had never grown accustomed to human complexities, even—especially—when he experienced them. This wash of huge, contradictory feelings made him want to weep.

Instead he paid attention to the texture of the blanket beneath him, the rhythm of his breath, and the hot pain in his shoulder.

Tonight's shirt was ruined, but it was only cloth, not a gift. She'd helped him remove it. At his suggestion, she'd placed a blanket on the couch to keep it dry, since he hadn't taken off his wet jeans. He'd have been more comfortable without them, but that would have sent a sexual signal.

The blanket would also absorb blood, and there would be some. He could limit bleeding, but he couldn't stop it entirely without prematurely sealing the wound.

The first bright shock of pain from the bullet's entry had long since subsided to a crimson haze, unpleasant but manageable. Controlling pain did not mean setting up some magical shield to deny it, but going into it, accepting it fully. Just as his muscles would accept the knife's message when it sliced into him.

Harder, much harder, was making himself vulnerable to that knife. But Kai would be wielding it, so that was all right.

He lay quietly, waiting, bemused at himself. How odd that he'd come here. It had been instinct, of course. He'd been hurt, in need of help. He'd come to his friend.

His friend. Nathan basked in the wonder of that. He'd known he liked Kai, that he felt good around her, but hadn't realized . . . gods. He'd just found her. A year ago he would have felt nothing but joy at the finding. Now . . .

"Okay, I've got gauze and antibiotic ointment and peroxide," Kai said. Her footsteps, soft as they were on the carpet, were audible to him as she approached. "And I found my tweezers. I sterilized them with the peroxide, but I should probably boil them and the knife."

"Not necessary. I'm not susceptible to bacteria or viruses."

"Oh." She took a deep breath. "I'll still clean the area around the wound. It will make me feel better, and I need to get the dried blood off so I can see what I'm doing."

"All right." He slowed his breathing further, closing his eyes. The couch smelled musty; she gave off the fresh, bright scent of a healthy young woman, plus the subtle mix that said *Kai* to him.

He couldn't go under all the way. Her scent might be enough to keep him from interpreting the knife as an attack, but he wouldn't risk it. Besides, he needed to guide her.

"Where were you that you weren't supposed to be?"

The peroxide was cool and wet. Her touch was firm enough to do the job without being rough. It hurt, but he liked having her touch him. He wished she could do it more often. "At the morgue."

"Are you going to make me pull your story out question by question?"

He smiled at the image of her extracting answers with her tweezers. "I'd prefer to discuss it after the bullet's out."

Another deep breath. "I guess I'm trying to delay."

"Are your hands shaking?"

A pause. "No." She sounded surprised.

"You know how to cause pain when it's needed for healing." They'd talked about that, about how she'd had to learn to allow, even encourage, others to hurt in order to help them reclaim their bodies.

"Yes. Yes, I do. All right. Let's do it."

"You see the entry."

"Yes. It, ah, it's scabbed over and looks about three days old, but I see it."

"Good. The bullet's path was slightly up and to the left, leaving it wedged just beneath the edge of the shoulder blade. I've delayed the internal healing enough that I think you'll be able to see its path. Make a vertical cut, starting about two inches above the entry hole and extending an inch below to give you room to work. There will be some bleeding. I can't prevent that entirely without sealing up around the knife."

The next several minutes went about as he'd expected. Nathan didn't like pain, but it was a familiar enemy. He only tensed once, when her knife skidded across the bullet, sending it deeper.

Otherwise she did well. Kai wasn't trained in this sort of thing, but she understood the basic layout of the body. Her hand remained steady and she followed his directions meticulously. Still, by the time she finished it was a relief to relinquish control and let his body heal. He lay there and panted, exhausted.

She seemed to be doing the same, sitting back on her heels with her eyes closed and her face pale. After a moment she spoke. "It's closing up."

Her voice sounded odd. Spooked, maybe. He couldn't think of what he was supposed to say—agreeing that the wound was, indeed, closing seemed pointless. Perhaps she wanted to know what to expect. "The visible part of the wound heals first, to seal it. Since no vital organs were affected and I'm not in combat, the rest will heal more slowly."

"How slowly?"

"Several hours, probably."

"If you were in combat, it would heal faster?"

"Yes."

"Do you control the healing?"

"No." He reconsidered. That wasn't entirely accurate. "I can, to some extent. I slowed it on the way here, but it's difficult. Tiring."

"Your body prioritizes for you." A thread of humor lightened her voice.

She wasn't too spooked, then. Relieved, he made the effort to sit up. The pain was much less now. "Yes. A good way to put it. May I see the bullet?"

Her eyebrows lifted. "Ghoulish interest, or a souvenir?" She handed him the clump of bloody gauze where she'd dropped the slug.

"I haven't been shot in a long time, and ammunition has changed. It could be useful to know what kind of damage to expect from today's weapons."

"If you're well enough to sit up and examine your bullet, you're well enough to explain why a cop shot you in the back."

"He couldn't shoot me from the front. I was running away." He inspected the smashed lump. Hollow point, as he'd expected. That was standard police-issue and what he used himself. Good stopping power, and less likely to pass through the target and harm a nearby civilian or hostage. Probably a lightweight .38, he decided. Some of the older officers clung to their .38s.

"The officer will be disciplined, I imagine." He lifted his hip so he could slip the slug in his pocket. "He was too hasty in using his weapon. Chief Roberts thinks within narrow channels, but he's correct within his limits."

She huffed out a breath. "That is not an explanation."

He felt a smile start. Kai was angry. If he told her she was pretty when temper brought that flush to her skin, she might pick up the knife again. But she was.

Her Gift was linked to water, and she wore its colors often. The soft flannel she wore tonight was a pale green that made him think of one of the many bright pools in the Summer Lady's land. Her throat rose from the neck of her pajamas, a strong and beautiful pillar the color of warm, wet sand. She would smell so good right there, in the hollow between neck and collarbone.

He took a moment to rein in his body, but the smile lingered inside. "I've been searching for the killer."

"I know that. I don't know why you were at the morgue. Or why you were shot for being there."

"I wanted to see the bodies of the two who were slain. I didn't have permission." The two victims had been killed within city limits, so the city police were handling the investigation. Chief Roberts didn't play well with others, particularly those in the sheriff's office. "I hoped to pick up a . . . a scent. Traces left by the killer."

"Are you a—a werewolf? A lupus, I mean."

"Eh." The question startled him. Kai had always been careful not to pry, not to ask too many direct questions. But she was his friend. He knew her secret; he could give her more of his. "No," he said, then decided that wasn't enough. "This is the only realm with lupi. They're native to it. I'm not."

She nodded solemnly.

His muscles loosened in relief. She didn't fear him, wasn't upset—and she didn't go on to ask the obvious questions, the ones he wasn't sure he could answer. "I said I wanted to find the killer's scent. I meant the physical scent, but I . . . there's more, for me. I pick up other traces, psychic traces, but sensually, as a smell. Like you receive thoughts visually."

"Oh." She cocked her head. "I like that. It makes me feel less of a freak to know your talent works a bit like mine."

"You are not a freak."

She tapped her head. "This knows that." She touched her chest. "This doesn't. Did you get a scent from the bodies?"

He grimaced. "I never reached the bodies. The police have them under guard."

"I guess the morgue usually has someone there. An attendant."

"I allowed for that," he said dryly. He'd been sloppy, but not that sloppy. "I didn't expect officers to be stationed at the bodies." He could have killed or disarmed them, of course, but one action would have been immoral, the other stupid. He shook his head. "I don't understand why they were there. Chief Roberts is narrow, not stupid. He must have some reason to guard the bodies, but I can't come up with one."

"He may be thinking of vampires. A lot of people are right now. The bodies were drained of blood, right? So he might have posted people to watch and make sure they don't—well, rise or something."

Nathan snorted. "If he's trying to find a vampire, he's wasting his time. They don't exist. Not the way they're depicted in fiction."

"But . . . they do exist?"

"Blood-drinkers are real, but not native to this realm. Most of them aren't intelligent, and none of them reproduce by endowing their victims with the ability to rise from the dead."

She grinned. "Or go around seducing young virgins?"

They'd watched *Interview With the Vampire* together last Halloween. Funny show. He'd chuckled at what she claimed were all the wrong places. "Exactly."

"So you think it's a human who killed those people?"

"Unlikely. A deranged or evil human might drink blood, but he or she couldn't suck out the entire ten pints in the average body. Nor is it easy to drain a body completely in other ways, and the victims were apparently exsanguinated in the same places the bodies were found."

"Then it's an animal of some sort. Something that came in on the power wind."

"Probably." He considered his words for a moment. "By 'animal' I don't just mean inhuman. I mean a species incapable of complex communication."

"Communication? You think that's the dividing line

between animal and, uh . . . I guess I can't say human, but I'm not sure how to put it."

"Sentient is the closest word in English."

"Okay, then. I would have thought the level of sentience depended on intelligence, the ability to reason."

"Reason can be defined in different ways, and intelligence is a slippery scale to apply. Is a severely retarded man a beast?"

She grimaced. "You make your point."

"Sophisticated communication which conveys concepts rather than just 'danger' or 'food' is essential because without it, intelligence and moral reasoning don't develop. A potentially intelligent being that is unable to communicate effectively never develops its potential. Take cats, for example."

"Uh . . . cats?"

"Cats are potentially sentient, but only those who live closely with other sentients develop fully because they lack the stimulus of clear communication. Not all cats develop a high level of sentience," he added. "But some do. The ones with good telepathic skills."

"Cats." Her voice and expression were blank. Then a smile spread across her face like the early colors of dawn. She shook her head, rueful, smiling. "I think I'm weirded out. Also wiped," she said, rising. "And so are you. Do you want to stay here for what's left of the night?"

"That would be good." Healing drained him. Delaying the healing drained him more. "Did you see that in my colors?" he asked, suddenly curious. "That I need rest?"

"Not the colors so much as the way they're behaving. Droopy and sluggish."

He nodded. That made sense—his thoughts felt sluggish. "Thank you. For the offer of your couch, and for helping."

"You're welcome. I'll get you a pillow and a cover." A yawn caught her, and she stretched.

Long-buried feelings stirred inside him. He had to be stern with his body in order to quiet it before she noticed. "A sheet would be welcome. I don't need a blanket. Is it all right if I remove my jeans? They're wet."

"Sure." Her smile came a shade too quickly, a tint too bright. "I'll get you that sheet."

He didn't remove his pants yet. He'd do that after she was in bed. Kai couldn't regulate her body the way he did, nor could she hide her response from him. He couldn't hide his response from her, either, for that matter—she'd see it in his colors if he allowed himself to become aroused. So he hadn't. He didn't want to raise expectations. But he allowed himself the rare indulgence of enjoying the way her body moved beneath her loose pajamas as she left the room. Maybe . . .

He wouldn't rush things. But he knew her now for a friend, so . . . maybe.

CHAPTER 4

IT was still dark when Nathan woke to three bars from the *William Tell Overture*. He rolled into a sitting position, reached for his jeans, and pulled his cell phone out of the pocket.

Six-oh-five, he noted. And the call was from dispatch. "Hunter."

The phone had woken Kai, too. She drifted out to stand in the doorway to her bedroom while he listened, acknowledged his instructions, then disconnected. He stepped into his jeans, which were clammy and damp still. She didn't ask any questions, but they hung, suspended, in her eyes.

"There's been another killing," he told her, running a hand over his chin. Bristles. He'd have to shave. "The body appears to have been exsanguinated, like the others. It's about three miles from here, just off County Road 60."

Her eyes widened. "But that—that's our road. Nathan, who was it?"

"I don't have an ID." She'd had friends over last night. Gifted friends. She'd worry that the victim was one of them, and with reason. Last night's party and the proximity of the body might not be coincidence. "All I know is that the victim was male."

"Pete . . . Pete was with Meagan. They wouldn't have gone that way. Neither would Ryan, but Mark—he and Andrew live in Odessa. They might have taken 60. It runs into 1788, which would bring them back to 191, so—but you know all that." She scrubbed both hands over her face as if trying to rub sense in, sleep out. She dropped her hands. "I'm babbling. You know all those roads."

He could see the fear swimming in her eyes, could all but feel the cold breath of it on her neck. Impulsively he reached out, took her arms. She was warm beneath the flannel. He didn't want to let go. "I don't know when the killing took place. The body could have been there awhile. I don't know yet."

She nodded, mute in her fear.

"I'll call. As soon as I'm able and have an ID, I'll call."

"That's right—you'll be investigating, won't you? That's outside city limits."

"Yes." The sheriff's office would handle this one. He'd be able to hunt openly. Eagerness burned in him, a cold fire since he lacked a target. But not, he hoped, for much longer.

Reluctantly he released her. He seldom touched her, as touch made things harder for both of them, but he couldn't regret it this time. He paused at the door. "We don't know that the killer only strikes at night. Be careful."

She shoved her hair back. "You, too."

"I'm not in the kind of danger you are."

"You may not be Gifted, but you . . . whatever you are, you're of the Blood. It might want your blood, too."

He couldn't argue with her logic. "Of the Blood" meant one of the inherently magical races, and he surely fit that description. Whatever was drinking blood seemed to be after the punch of magic some carried in their blood. His would do very well for that. Better, probably, than any other in this world.

He nodded. "Maybe it will. That would simplify things."

A flash of temper lit her eyes. "Of all the stupid, macho bullshit—"

"I'm not being . . . macho." He'd been about to say "vainglorious," but the newer word suited. "It's unlikely the killer could damage me seriously." And it—or he, or she—couldn't kill Nathan. If something powerful enough to do that had crossed, he would have known.

Anger still flew flags in her cheeks. "Define 'seriously.' Oh, never mind." She waved at the door. "You have to go. I know that. But I'm going to ask, Nathan. I thought I wouldn't need to, but I do."

Emotion washed through him, tightening his chest. Words, never his strength, failed him entirely. He nodded at her, acknowledging that she would ask him what he was without having any idea how he would answer. And he left.

Nine minutes later, Nathan started his vehicle. His apartment was directly below Kai's; he'd run down and emptied his bladder, washed quickly, and pulled on a clean uniform. As he pulled out of his parking spot he took his cordless razor from the glove compartment.

For the ten thousandth time he wondered why his queen hadn't arranged things differently. She seldom overlooked a detail, but he could see no advantage to the erratic way his beard and hair grew. Sometimes he went a week without shaving. Sometimes he had to shave three times in one day.

Of course, men had mostly worn beards back when she'd sent him here. Perhaps she'd simply failed to anticipate fashion.

Haircuts were more trouble than shaving, given the need to catch every hair that fell, but less frequent. Kai had cut his hair last time he needed a trim.

Once more feeling sluiced through him, rich as wine and more baffling.

What would he tell her? How much would he be able to say?

Dawn was the vaguest of promises in the sky behind him and the county road taking him west was empty of traffic. Nathan turned on the flashing light but left the siren off. He hated the stupid thing. He kept his speed to a reasonable seventy, wanting to finish shaving before he arrived.

He managed that, barely. The flashing red light on top of a sheriff's department car disturbed the darkness just ahead when he cupped the head of the razor in one hand.

There were very few in this realm who would be able to make use of his hair, particularly such tiny scraps of it. And none, he believed, who knew what he was. But he wasn't one to take chances. With a wisp of intention he crisped the bits of hair caught in the razor.

Seconds later, he pulled up behind the other official car. It was the only vehicle in sight. He reached for his jacket from habit rather than necessity and climbed out.

The patroller had left his headlights on with the car parked at an angle to illuminate what lay in the trampled grass beside the road's shoulder. The air smelled of car exhaust, wet dirt, and humans—and, very faintly, of something else. An alien scent that raised the small hairs on the back of his neck.

He looked around, tested the air. Already that whiff of otherness was fading. Whatever it was, he decided, it was gone now.

The patroller was surprised to see him, but swallowed it. "Sergeant Hunter."

Technically, Nathan handled the day shift personnel, and didn't come on shift for another forty minutes. This pup was on the night shift, so Nathan didn't know him well. He had caught a few comments not intended for his ears, however. Raines, like several others, suspected that Nathan was lupus, just as Kai had. And he didn't approve.

Nathan gave him his name for greeting, then asked, "Who found him?"

"Fellow named Jeffrey Bates. Lives over yonder." The patroller nodded at a small cluster of houses set back from the road about half a mile. "Says he likes to run early, before traffic's a problem. He's in my car."

"How long since Bates found him?"

"Maybe fifteen minutes. He had a cell phone with him. I was over on 1788, so I responded quickly."

"You touch anything?"

"No, sir. Uh . . . I held a mirror in front of the victim's mouth, checking to see if he was breathing. Just to be sure, you know?"

Nathan nodded. He'd suspected those were Raines's footprints next to the body; they were clear, obviously left after the rain had stopped.

Checking for life would have been instinctive for the young patroller, but Nathan knew the look and smell of death. Even without touching the corpse he could estimate how long this one had been dead: no more than six hours, no less than four.

He moved closer without stepping into the muddy, trampled grass directly around the body. Off in the distance he heard the wail of an ambulance. Wouldn't be long before company arrived, and there were things he preferred to do unobserved. He crouched for a closer inspection.

The body lay on its back, one arm flung wide, the other at its side. No noticeable rigor yet, but it had been a cold night. He'd been young . . . well, they all seemed young to Nathan, but this boy had been in his early twenties. African American, though the blood loss left his skin an odd, ashy color. He wore jeans, a T-shirt, and a denim jacket, all of them soaked through from last night's rain. Tony Lama boots, Nathan noted. Pricey and fairly new.

The jeans had been pulled down. His penis, flaccid and

bloodless, hung out of the opening in his shorts. Two visible wounds: one in his neck, another near the groin, over the femoral artery. The wounds were unnaturally neat, with no blood or tearing—a circle of punctures about the size of a human mouth opened wide, but nothing a human mouth could make.

He'd seen something like them once. Another time, another place . . . when? Where?

Memory didn't return an immediate answer, so he focused on what he saw now. No blood—not in the corpse, not around it. Maybe the killer was exceptionally tidy. Or maybe it had killed and drained this boy somewhere else.

Nathan looked at the arms and hands again. No defensive wounds. He checked the ground around the victim another time. "You pass any parked cars on the way here?"

"I—Yeah, I did. Why?"

"How far away?"

"What does it matter?" Raines's sandy mustache didn't hide the thrust of his lower lip, which made him look like a sulky two-year-old.

Nathan's head came up. He didn't say anything. Just looked at the boy.

"Sorry, sir. I . . . uh, there's a Mustang parked a couple miles west of here, near the turnoff."

"Run the plates. It's probably his."

Raines stood as stiff as the corpse would be soon. "Yes, sir. I'll have to go back there. I didn't memorize the plates."

"Do it." Nathan looked back at the body, not minded to explain his reasoning, but added, "The sheriff will be here soon. Be nice if we could give him a possible ID without disturbing the scene, wouldn't it?"

"Yes, sir."

As soon as the other car pulled away, Nathan stretched out a hand and touched the skin near the wound on the neck, confirming his guess about the time of death. He concentrated briefly, then brought his hand back to his nose, sniffed—and froze, his eyes widening in surprise. Not at what he smelled. At what he didn't.

Surprise unlocked memory. Time, place, and cause tumbled out, making his stomach tighten. Now he knew when he'd seen bite marks like that and what had made them. "Well, shit."

CHAPTER 5

SHERIFF Randy Browning reminded Nathan of a mastiff. He had the heavy frame, the droopy eyes, and the temperament. Patient and unflappable, he was a guardian by nature as well as profession. He didn't like magic, didn't trust it, but he was a practical man. He'd use whatever was necessary to protect his people.

Nathan respected that. He respected the man, too—enough to work with him and allow Browning to consider himself in charge. In some things, he was.

"You want to tell me why you expected Shaw's car to be nearby?" Browning asked.

Jimmy Shaw, age twenty-five. He'd had a DUI six years ago, a couple of speeding tickets since, but was otherwise clean. The address on record was on the west side in a decent, working-class neighborhood that was mostly white and Mexican with a sprinkling of darker faces. He'd bought his 2003 Mustang new, and his body was being loaded into the ambulance now.

Kai didn't know Jimmie Shaw. Nathan had checked.

Nathan's relief about that made it easier to be amused by Browning now. The sheriff was hoping Nathan wouldn't tell him anything too weird. "Tire tracks," he said, nodding at the imprints in the shoulder he'd noticed immediately. They were blurred—made after storm muddied the ground, but before the rain ended.

"I know about the damned tire tracks. Someone pulled up, dumped the body, and drove away. What made you think the car was nearby? It would have made more sense for the killer to keep going."

"It probably doesn't know how to drive."

A muscle in Browning's jaw twitched. "It."

"It may look human, but it isn't."

Browning gave Nathan a disgusted look. The man wasn't happy about the new shape reality had taken since the Turning. Nathan didn't blame him. The sheriff had spent a lifetime learning how to preserve order under the old rules. It would take time to learn new ones, and while he and others figured out what worked and what didn't, some of those in their charge would be harmed.

But he was basically a fair man. Lips tight, he checked out the busy scene around them, then jerked his head at the road. "We'll take a little walk."

The sky was dull steel overhead with threads of rose and saffron in the east, where a hard ball of sun worked to warm the day. Nathan fell into step beside the other man.

Once they were out of earshot the sheriff spoke gruffly. "All right. Why do you think the killer isn't human?"

"It doesn't smell human."

"I'm not going to the DA with that. I'm sure as hell not telling Chief Roberts the killer doesn't smell right."

"No," Nathan agreed. He had other reasons for thinking the killer nonhuman, but Browning wouldn't want to hear them. Which was just as well. Nathan didn't intend to offer them.

This hunt was his, not the sheriff's. If he was right about the nature of this killer, sending humans after it would just result in dead humans. "The bite marks will provide physical evidence, though. You must have noticed. They're punctures, the sort made by sharp canines. Human teeth don't puncture the flesh that way."

Browning had his jaw clenched so tight Nathan could almost hear the teeth grinding. "It'll be a goddamn circus when that gets out. A goddamn circus."

"You going to notify MCD?"

"Damned well have to, don't I? When the autopsy report comes in, anyway."

In the wake of the Turning, Congress had passed a law making it mandatory for local jurisdictions to inform the FBI's Magical Crimes Division of suspected supernatural crimes or attacks. Not that MCD had the personnel to follow up on every report; there was a long waiting list for trained supernatural investigators. But so far, the police chief had resisted notifying them at all, claiming he was waiting for solid evidence a supernatural agent was involved.

Idiot. But a lot of humans swung between denial and hysteria these days, and Chief Roberts was highly territorial.

Browning chewed on his own teeth for a few more paces, then heaved a sigh. "Guess we've been lucky till now. We didn't have a lot of the weird-ass nasties come through in December the way some places did."

Nathan nodded agreeably, though the lack of nasties troubling Midland had little to do with luck. He'd hunted twice since the Turning. The first hunt had mostly been to create a climate for negotiation. Unlike their larger cousins, river trolls weren't entirely unreasonable once you got their attention, and this was a poor spot for them. No flowing water.

The other had been a hunt in truth. You don't negotiate with a ghoul.

"You think this whatever-it-is can't drive?" Browning asked. "Most nonhumans do."

"Lupi do, certainly. Brownies don't, but gnomes can . . . or so I've heard," Nathan added with a polite disregard for truth. "But as you said, this creature isn't native to Earth. It came through with the power wind. It wouldn't know how to drive."

"You think it's smart enough to learn?"

Now Nathan frowned. His picture was mixed. "Might be best to think of it as smart, but not in a predictable way."

"Clever enough to fool people into thinking it's human, though. Shaw engaged in sex with it. Her. Him. Whatever."

"Or the preliminaries to sex. Yes."

"So it looks human."

"Or can." This wouldn't be an easy hunt. The burn in his blood approved of that.

"Illusion? Do you . . . crap." Browning stopped moving to scowl at the plain sedan cruising toward them. "Should've known he'd turn up. You'd better go. We've got Shaw's place of employment—the Exxon station at Midkiff and Wadley. Talk to them, see what you can find out."

"The family?"

"That's my job."

The sedan was slowing. Nathan watched the driver, not the car. Slim and dapper, with a round face that looked like he buffed it after shaving, Eldon Knox was the detective in charge of the city's investigation. He was clever, ambitious, and bigoted, and he hated Nathan.

"Knox is my enemy," Nathan agreed. "But not an important enemy. He won't provoke me."

Browning gave him a look. "Yeah, it's that attitude that makes him love you so much. Fun as it is to see the chief's favorite lapdog froth at the mouth when he gets around you, I'll deal with him better if you're gone. Go on. Clear out."

"Yes, sir." He turned to go.

The detective's car stopped and he climbed out. His door thunked closed. "Hunter!"

Nathan ignored him. Browning could handle the man. When he got in his car he was thinking about enemies, prey, and Kai.

His immediate task was to interview Shaw's employer and coworkers. He didn't expect to learn much; at most he might find out if Shaw was known to be Gifted. That was the way of investigations. Most of what you learned wasn't useful.

But his gut had a different priority.

He'd do both, he decided. It wouldn't take long to swing by the apartments, and Kai wouldn't have a client this early. She'd be home.

Minutes later, he parked and ran lightly up the outside stairs. His shoulder barely twinged. He'd tell her that. She'd be glad to hear that her surgery had worked so well.

He knocked. Nothing.

Knocked again. No answer.

Fear was a startling acid. It flushed thought from his system so fast that for a moment he stood stock-still and saw her bloodless body instead of the bland metal of the door.

Only for a moment. Then his mind performed one of its more human tricks and sneered at him. Was he going to imagine her dead every time she wasn't where he'd expected?

His mind was less amenable to order than his body, but he hushed it as best he could. After a second it produced a more useful thought: She might be running.

Of course. Kai ran when she was stressed or upset. It helped her deal with her Gift as well as her emotions, and both had been given a workout last night.

She'd have her phone with her, he thought as he padded back down the stairs. His was in his car. He could call her, find out where she was. Or he could track her.

The decision floated up from his middle without input from his brain. Tuning in to her scents—both the physical and the psychic—was as automatic as adjusting the focus of his eyes. He set off at an easy lope.

CHAPTER 6

SWEAT stung Kai's eyes. She had her contacts in, so she blinked furiously instead of rubbing and wished she'd remembered her sweatband. One corner of her mind contemplated laser surgery for the hundredth time, but most of her remained cradled in the steady, reassuring thud of her feet against the ground.

When she ran, when she focused on the physical, her thoughts stayed close, tight to her body. She scarcely noticed them at all, and the residue of others' thoughts slipped past, unseen. The world turned crisp, its edges purely material and lovely to her.

"Kai."

The voice behind her jarred her out of her near-trance. She lost the rhythm, found it again, and raised a hand to acknowledge Nathan's greeting. Though she kept moving, she couldn't find the smooth, centered place she'd been floating in. Her thoughts rose around her in a mist of worry-gray.

Why was he here? He was on duty. Was this official? He could have called, but he'd come to find her. Had they misidentified the body earlier and it was someone she knew, after all?

Punctuating the gray were pops of yellow: *Nathan. Nathan's here.*

She lacked the wind to sigh. She'd pushed herself hard enough this morning, she supposed. Her thighs were burning. She slowed to a jog.

"What's up?" she asked as Nathan drew alongside her, not the least bit winded. He never was, which had irritated her at first. She was more resigned now. He did sweat, at least. In the summer. If he ran more than a mile or two, that is, and it was really hot. Like a hundred.

"You're out running. A killer wants to drink your blood, and you're out running."

"*My* blood?" Startled, a little frightened, she looked at him. He faced ahead, his features set in an odd frown. But his thoughts—! They weren't muddy—Nathan's colors were always clear—but they were sure jumpy. Indigo twitched into purple, slid back to blue, flashed into green flickering with tips of angry red.

"You'd make a good meal for it. You've a strong Gift."

"But you don't have any reason to think it's after me, personally. Do you?"

The thought-fish around him slowed and flattened. His voice turned wry. "No. I was . . . generalizing."

Overreacting, more like. Which was very interesting. She jogged along in silence for a moment. "I take it the newest victim was Gifted."

"I suspect he was, but a body drained of life and blood doesn't tell me that."

"Does it tell you other things?"

"Almost always. This one . . . didn't." Trouble bubbled beneath the even surface of his voice. She saw it in the dark swirls that lifted from him, then fell again. His breath huffed out in a rare show of frustration. "This wasn't at all what I came here to tell you. I don't know why I . . . no, I do know. It just . . . surprises me."

He was seesawing, saying one thing, then another; and that was not like him. When he fell silent she wanted to stop, grab him, and shake a few more words out. She settled for a civilized prompt. "And that reason would be . . . ?"

His feet hit the ground three more times before he answered. "I was frightened. I went to your door and you weren't there, and I was afraid for you."

She could have sworn her heart slid around in her chest in an unnatural way. "That's natural, I guess. You'd just come from a murder scene."

"I'm not used to it. Sometimes I . . . friends are rare. I don't find one often."

Now he was squeezing the heart he'd just sent sliding. She couldn't think of what to say. The urge to grab him hit again, but this time she wanted to hold him. To just hold on.

He discovered smiles again and offered her one. "Usually I'm the one who has trouble with words. I seem to have stolen yours this time."

"They'll come back." Eventually.

"I didn't know. That you were my friend, that is. Until last night, I didn't realize you had . . . come inside me that far." He paused. "This isn't what I wanted to talk about."

"I'm enjoying the subject."

"Are you?" This smile arrived so quickly and so lightly it was almost a grin. "Am I inside you, too, Kai?"

The flush of heat hit too fast for her mind to have any chance of controlling her tongue. "Don't I wish."

He stopped, and *he* did the grabbing, seizing her shoulders and making her stop, too. "I'm sorry. I should have thought about how that would sound."

Humiliation rolled over her with its very different heat. "*Joke.* That was a joke. You're supposed to grin and say something stupid back."

"Stupid, I might be able to handle, but I'm not good at jokes. I'm not good at sex, either."

She rolled her eyes. "So not believing you here. About jokes, maybe. You don't always get them, or sometimes you think something's funny that I don't get. But sex?" She shook her head and found her own smile. "Come on."

"I can do sex, of course. But it's too . . ." He shook his head, clearly frustrated. "This doesn't fit into words well. I need a connection. Sex without that connection is too lonely."

Her heart was pounding and it had little to do with her run. "Friendship is a connection."

"Yes."

She searched his face, seeing something different there, but unsure what. She tried to speak lightly. "You're giving me ideas, you know. If that isn't what you had in mind—"

"My mind has become strange territory. I don't know what's in it myself, so I can't tell you." He dropped his hands. "But you'll get chilled, stopping like this when you're sweaty. We should keep moving."

"I need to stretch first." Stretching helped with lactic acid buildup in taxed muscles, making them less likely to stiffen. It would also give her a few minutes to locate her brain, which had to be around here someplace.

Kai untied the jacket she'd fastened around her waist, shrugged it on, and moved to the curb so she could stretch her hamstrings. "So why did you track me down?" Automatically she reached for his shoulder to balance herself. This kind of touching they'd done often.

"I need to let you know about the killer."

"What about him?" She dropped her heels off the curb. "Or it."

"It may be a chameleon."

"You're not talking about a cute little lizard that changes color."

"No, this creature changes its form entirely, not just its color. Chameleon is the closest word in English."

"Not the illusion of change? It really changes?"

"Yes. Mass is preserved, as is the essential brain composition and metabolism. They can look like anything, though, and unlike demons, they change quickly if they have a good pattern for the new shape."

"Scary." She switched positions, this time pulling her knee to her chest to stretch her quads.

He was looking at her legs. He never looked at her legs, not that way. "I wanted you to be watching for something that seems human, but isn't. You'll be able to tell from the way its thoughts look, won't you?"

She nodded, a frown pleating her forehead. "You have any reason to think I'm likely to run into this creature?"

"Not exactly."

"You aren't giving me a warm, fuzzy feeling. And what about you?" She started back at an easy jog. "Can it trick you?"

He fell in beside her. "Since its metabolism doesn't change, I'll smell the truth if I'm close enough."

"But you're not lupus."

This smile was amused. "No."

Personal questions amused him now, instead of making him run the other way? "Is that all you came here to tell me? To watch out for something like looks human, but isn't?"

He nodded. "I may have exaggerated the urgency. I think the killer is a chameleon—that fits what I know—but I'm not certain. They're extremely rare, for one thing, and normally they exist only in high-magic realms."

"Is that where you come from? A high-magic realm?"

"Yes."

Another answer, offered as easily as if his true nature wasn't a big, fat secret.

He added, "Not the realm where chameleons are found, though. They're constructs. That's not allowed in . . . my home realm."

"Constructs."

"Made, not born."

"But—but how could that be possible?"

"As I understand it, the mage—no, it would have to be an adept. He or she would start with—"

"Hold on. There really are mages and adepts? I thought that was just myth, like unicorns or . . . never mind." She'd been about to say "or dragons," but they'd turned out to be real.

"Unicorns are real, too. Or mostly real. They don't exactly live in any of the realms, but . . . wait, wait." He held up a hand, forestalling the questions hovering on her tongue. "I'll explain another time, or try to. I don't understand unicorns myself. For now, accept that if this creature is a chameleon, it's extremely dangerous and may be drawn to those with a strong Gift."

They jogged together quietly after that. Kai was comfortable with the lack of speech; the companionship of silence reminded her of her grandfather, who could go days without using more than a handful of words, but was so present he made conversation with a glance or a gesture.

Nathan was present in much the same way. Last night and today, though, he'd dipped often into words, telling her more about himself than he'd ever revealed in one gulp. Yet much of him remained hints and questions, with a few facts swirling around in the mist.

Fact: He lived longer than humans. A lot longer. She'd learned that a few months ago when they were watching the History Channel and he commented on something that happened in the First World War—something he'd experienced. Fact: He healed fast, faster than she'd have believed possible if she hadn't seen it herself last night. Fact: He came from another realm . . . and oh, but she'd done a good job of pretending her mind wasn't blown by that news. There were stories of other realms, sure, but whatever reality lay behind those tales had been lost or obscured in their telling and retelling over the years.

The Turning had proved that reality was far stranger and broader than they'd known. Other realms were real. So were adepts and unicorns and the creatures he called chameleons.

So was Nathan. Whatever he was.

They reached the parking area of their complex and turned in. "I have to go," he said. "I'm on duty."

"Okay." Which made it all the more strange that he'd hunted her up.

His official car was parked two slots down from her little Toyota. They stopped there. He wasn't breathing hard, but neither was she this time. The easy jog had cooled her down.

Nathan didn't get in his car right away, though. He did something shocking. He put his hands on her face, fingers spread, and ran his thumbs over her jaw. His eyes searched hers, their wintry color alive with something she'd never seen there before. "Why did you not need to ask before now?"

"You didn't want anyone to know, and I respected that." *You would have gone away.*

"But you need to know now?"

He was confusing her badly. "I . . . yes." *You're leaving anyway.*

"You felt it, too." He sounded deeply satisfied. "Things changed for us last night."

Okay, time to roll. She swallowed her fear and plunged ahead. "Are you from Faerie?"

"From one of the Faerie realms, yes. There are many."

That sent a jolt of surprise through her, but as distractions went it couldn't compete with the ripples created by his stroking thumbs. "You're a . . . an elf?"

"I am sidhe."

He said that the way Elizabeth the First might have said, "I am queen"—fact and power so entwined that one made no sense without the other. "Uh . . . doesn't 'sidhe' mean elves?"

"Sidhe means . . . there are many kinds, but we usually speak of three. The High Sidhe are true immortals. A few of them, not many, have an interest in ruling, so they do. The middle sidhe, those you call elfin or faerie lords, have more of a taste for power and caste. Low sidhe is a more fluid term, but is generally understood to mean the less powerful elfin folk, as well as fairies and others you wouldn't recognize. But some sidhe are nothing like humans or elves and live outside those hierarchies. I . . . eh, I'm not sure what I am now."

His hands dropped and he looked at one, turning it over as if veins, muscles, and knuckles scribed some obscure message in his flesh. "It has been so long . . . but whatever else I am or am not, I am of the wild sidhe."

Wild sidhe? She shook her head, not understanding.

This smile was old and sad. A parting smile. "A hellhound, Kai. I was born a hellhound."

CHAPTER 7

THEY called Midland the Tall City because of the downtown, where brick-and-steel stalagmites poked at the sky. The office buildings Nathan was headed toward weren't skyscrapers by any means, but in the middle of the flattest, most featureless land on the continent, they did stick out. To Nathan's mind the skyline looked like it was giving heaven the finger.

He kept that observation to himself. Religion turned some folks belligerent.

He was headed back to the sheriff's office, the hum in his blood clearer to him than the hum of his car's engine. His trip to the service station that morning had led to another lead, then another. Eventually he'd learned where Jimmy Shaw had spent his last night on Earth.

He'd been able to pursue those leads because Sheriff Browning had released him from desk duty for the duration of the investigation. That sort of pragmatic flexibility was one reason Nathan had lingered here longer than was probably wise. But only one.

Since his stranding, Nathan had been many things—

mercenary, guard, rag man, monk, tinker, riverboat pilot, and more. So many more. In his last persona he'd been a private investigator, specializing in finding lost children.

He'd found them, of course. It was impossible to shift a hellhound from a trail he'd been set to—even, Nathan had discovered, when he'd been set to the trail by no one but himself. It had taken him a long time to learn how to put himself to the hunt when there was no true prey, but it had been worth the effort. Finding the children had been good. Satisfying. Even when they'd been brutalized, he'd been able to return them to people who loved them.

Sometimes there had been no living child to find, only a body—killed by exposure, by mischance, or by malice. All too often, by malice. When that happened, he'd hunted their killers.

Those had been true hunts.

Humans were peculiar. They were by turns squeamish and appallingly violent. Eventually Nathan had concluded it was their very bloodthirstiness that made them erect so many legal and social barriers against culling the vicious from their midst. They didn't trust themselves to stop with the obviously evil.

So he'd hunted the child killers in secret. Eventually he'd been caught—or as good as, since he'd had to abandon that persona. Eighteen years later, Colorado still had an outstanding warrant for Samuel Jager. The legal system might be ineffective, but it was tenacious.

It had taken time to build a new identity. The current age had much to recommend it—indoor plumbing, cell phones, various advances in medicine. He considered cars and television mixed blessings, and had grown to like computers, though airplanes were an obvious mistake. Humans were inexplicably fond of them, but Nathan had no intention of meeting death while strapped in a giant metal coffin hurtling through the air at the behest of some stranger.

But technology was seriously inconvenient when it came time to reconstruct himself. That was another reason he'd put off leaving Midland—the sheer nuisance of creating a new identity. But again, it was not the whole story.

He liked police work. It was a restful job, at least in Midland. He seldom dealt with real ugliness, and he worked mostly in the open. He liked being part of a team, able to contribute to the common good. If he ached sometimes for a real hunt, if his particular skills were seldom needed, he had a place here. Even those who noticed that he was different didn't always shun him for it.

Kai hadn't.

And there, of course, was the rest of the story. He'd been ready to leave eighteen months ago, needing a true hunt. Needing to return to his purpose. He'd met Kai and decided to stay awhile longer.

His heartbeat picked up. He'd told her. He could scarcely believe he'd done it, yet it felt right. She'd been shocked, yes, but not repelled. He could swear she hadn't been repelled. Even if she no longer wanted to be lovers, she would remain his friend.

But the timing . . . ah, Lord of Luck, why now? After all the aching years, would his exile end when he'd found a reason to stay?

There was little he could do about that. He'd never known the day or hour when his time here would be over. He still didn't, so he set that thought aside and focused on his hunt. But the tangle of hope and fear remained, along with both yearnings—one old, one new. And opposed to each other.

He would, he thought as his car bumped over the train tracks, probably be rewarded for his candor with a host of questions. His lips quirked. Kai obviously had no idea what a hellhound was. Or much notion of what the sidhe were, much less the wild sidhe.

Questions would be all right. He pulled into his slot

in front of the cream-colored building that housed the sheriff's department. Questions would be fine, as long as she remained his friend. He believed . . . hoped . . . she would.

He climbed out and set off on foot for one of Midland's institutions—a watering hole called The Bar. It was only half a mile away, on the other side of the railroad tracks. Jimmy Shaw had spent his last night on Earth there.

This was one of the peculiarities others noticed about him—his penchant for walking whenever possible. Pedestrians were regarded with some suspicion in Midland, but walking was a habit he'd been unwilling to give up. He couldn't see the point in shutting himself up in a vehicle any more often than he had to, doing damage to the earth and the air in order to avoid using his body.

People did just that all the time, though. Most claimed they needed to save time. It was true they had little enough of that—their lives were so soon ended. But Nathan didn't see them treating time as precious otherwise. They'd sit in their cars at a fast-food place for fifteen minutes when it would be quicker to park and go inside.

No, he blamed the modern culture of urgency. Only the most urgent sensations, emotions, and situations were considered important. They called it living life to the fullest. Not surprisingly, many sought numbness in alcohol or the pervasive voyeurism of reality TV, while others tried to live a perpetual peak experience through drugs, sex, or celebrity. Ordinary lives, ordinary living, had little value.

Nathan thought people needed to wash dishes by hand sometimes. Prepare their own meals more often. And take walks.

THE Bar was a flat, fading structure with little to recommend it from the outside. Inside it was dim and smelled of grilled hamburgers and beer. The five-o'clockers hadn't hit yet, so there weren't many customers. It still took the manager several minutes to find time for him.

The woman was over fifty and over six feet, with poufy hair and lips greased to an immaculate shine. "Jackie Montoya," she said, holding out a hand. "I'm night manager. Is there a problem?"

"No, ma'am." She had a good handshake, firm without trying to prove anything, and she didn't hold on too long. "I'm Sergeant Hunter. I've got some questions about one of your customers last night. Jimmie Shaw."

Her glossy lips tightened. "Look, I want to help and all that, but I already told that other officer all I knew."

Nathan let that sink in a beat. "Other officer?"

"The detective. Cox, Fox—something like that. Little guy with a shiny face."

"Eldon Knox."

"That's him. He's already got his witness, so I don't see what more I can do for you."

The flush of anger took a second to dissipate enough for Nathan to speak calmly. "I apologize for the inconvenience, ma'am. I know you're busy, but I do have to ask some questions. Is there someplace quiet we could talk?"

She heaved a sigh, looked around, and grimaced. "Might as well make it my office. Your uniform puts some of my customers off. Come on."

She set a quick pace in spite of the heels that must kill her feet by the end of the night. Nathan followed.

Her office was a tiny, cluttered cubby just past the restrooms. It stank of ashes and cigarette smoke. She shifted a pile of computer printouts off the wooden chair and told him to have a seat. He did.

Immediately she lit a cigarette. "Okay. Like I told the other guy, Jimmy's a regular. He doesn't—didn't—come in every day, like some. Doesn't work downtown, does he?

But he has—had—a taste for the panty hose crowd, if you get what I mean. Women in heels with office jobs. Did pretty well with them, too."

"How did he do last night?"

Her smile was quick and cocky. "Just fine." The smile died. "Or not so fine, maybe, if she's the one who killed him. He left with her about midnight."

"Who?"

"Well, I didn't know her—don't think I've ever seen her in here before. But Ed Bates did. He's a real regular, in here every night, and he knew her, see? That's why that detective took Ed with him, so he could make a statement. Lord, but Ed'll be full of himself." She inhaled hard enough to sink her cheeks in, then blew the smoke out her nose. "If she turns out to be your killer, he's going to be dining out on his story for months."

"Did you learn the name of this woman?"

"I heard Ed telling the detective about her. We all did. She's the one who did his therapy after he totaled his pickup a few months ago." She paused, puffing. "Some kind of weird-ass name. I can't quite call it to mind, but it sounded foreign."

"Kai?" he asked, his hear pounding. "Was the name Kai Michalski?"

"That's her." Satisfied, she mashed out the stub of her cigarette. "That's the name of the bitch who did that poor boy in."

BETWEEN patients, Kai surfed the Internet.

Hellhounds, it turned out, did not have a great rep. Not here, anyway. Maybe in other realms they were considered upright or cuddly or commonplace. Here they showed up in role-playing games as monsters. They were popular in comic books, too, generally as minions of the devil. Of course, those weren't reliable sources—a search on her own name would suggest she was Japanese, Hawaiian, or a character in a violent video game. But they indicated the general outlook.

Her dictionary, consulted on the run, hadn't been much help. It described a hellhound as "a mythical watchdog of hell." Obviously Nathan was no myth, but she couldn't hold it against the dictionary for getting that part wrong. When it was printed, lots of things were considered myth that turned out to be true, like dragons. But they were just as wrong with the "of hell" part.

At least, she hoped they were. Hell. Hellhound. The connection was obvious, but had to be a mistake, a misnaming. Nothing good came from hell.

Hell itself was misnamed, of course, if by that you meant the demon realm, not a final resting place for sinners. Anglos had long since muddied the two, but Diné tradition held that demons came from another world. Nor was it the same realm elves lived in. Kai was sure of that.

Almost sure. It had been years since Grandfather taught her the stories, and few of them involved the far people, the Navajo term for elves.

She liked Wikipedia's entry better. It mentioned the mythical guardian of the gates of hell, too, but it also spoke of spectral hounds who haunted spots in Great Britain. That didn't seem to apply to Nathan, who was hardly spectral. But it went on to say that hellhounds were part of the Wild Hunt.

The Hunt was connected to Faerie, not hell. She was seriously fuzzy on what the connection was, but she knew that much. And Nathan's surname was Hunter.

Clue, Kai.

But she wasn't going to know, dammit. Not until she saw him again and could ask. At the time, she'd barely been able to stammer, "What? You're what?"

Nathan had just looked at her with that sad smile and

said they would talk later, when she'd had a chance to think things over. He had duties he needed to tend to. And he'd gotten in his car and driven off.

What was she supposed to think over? She wasn't even sure what a hellhound was! Some sort of supernatural dog, yes, and she had to admit that was a breath stealer, but he wasn't a dog now.

Or maybe he was a part-time dog. Did he Change when he wanted to, like lupi? Or according to some involuntary, arcane schedule? Full moons, eclipses, leap years, alternate Wednesdays . . .

Part of the sidhe, he'd said. The wild sidhe.

Kai was in her cubby at the clinic looking up "sidhe" on her laptop when Ginger stuck her head in the door. "Good grief, are you still working? It's nearly five. Shake a leg or we'll be late."

Late? Oh, yeah. "The rally. I'd forgotten. I'm not sure—"

"You're going," her friend told her sternly. "Come on."

CHAPTER 8

THE rally was being held downtown in Centennial Plaza. It was a pretty spot for much of the year, with a fountain perched in tiered stone basins and several oaks slowly growing their way toward stature. In the warmer seasons the trees stood ready to flutter their leaves and freckle the ground with shade.

Not today, though. Today the trees were bare, the fountain dry. But everything else was full.

"There's a lot more here than I'd expected." Ginger sounded torn between anxiety and delight. "I expected to see mostly students. And the coven—several of them promised to come. But this . . ."

"You did a good job of getting the word out. There must be a couple hundred people here. Maybe more." All of them talking at the same time, all of them revved—uneasy, angry, excited. To Kai, the air was a colorful din. "The TV people showed up, too."

"Are you doing okay?"

"I'm fine." Aside from the guilt. Had Kai been a true

empath, such a large crowd would have been uncomfortable at best. Kai hated the deceit, hated worrying Ginger for no reason. But not enough to tell her the truth. Ginger would feel sorry for her.

Kai could handle the sting of rejection—and had, plenty of times. She understood why people feared the loss of privacy. But pity labeled her pathetic, and she couldn't tolerate that.

In the eleven years since the accident, Kai had moved seven times. In each new place she'd hoped to find friends. And she had, until she tried trusting them with the truth about herself. Whenever she told someone she saw thoughts, they changed. Most withdrew, fearing judgment or invasion. Those who didn't withdraw physically did so in other ways, watching for signs of insanity . . . because everyone knew telepaths went crazy sooner or later.

Everyone but Nathan. She didn't know how she'd found the courage to tell him, but she knew why. He didn't lie to her, not even a rosy little social lie. How could she keep lying to him? So six months ago she'd told him. He'd nodded, asked a few questions, and said he'd never heard of a telepathic Gift like hers, but it sounded easier to live with than the usual sort. And that was it.

"You sure you're okay?" Ginger put a hand on Kai's shoulder. "I need to make my way to the front. I'm supposed to speak after Charley."

"You didn't tell me you were one of the speakers!" Kai patted her hand. "Go on. I'm going to hang here at the back." She might not have the problems a real empath would, but the excited crowd made her nervous. "You might see if you can calm folks down a bit. They're wired."

Ginger grinned. "Charley will help with that. He can put a class to sleep in under ten minutes."

"Hey, I'll bet his students stay awake. They'd want to see

if he does." Charley, like Ginger, taught at the local community college. He was actually a wonderful speaker, but so laid-back he looked like he might doze off mid-word.

Ginger started threading herself through knots of people. The moment she left, Kai dug her nails into her palms.

She might not feel the emotions swirling around her, but if she weren't careful they'd still suck her in. Kai called it fuguing, the way she could slip away, entranced by the colors and shapes of the minds around her. As a baby she'd apparently been lost in fugue so often that she'd been diagnosed as autistic.

Grandfather had known better. When she was three he'd taken her to another shaman, and together they'd performed a rare ritual that suppressed Kai's Gift. For eleven years she'd been normal—until the day she woke, weeping, from a week-long coma. She'd had no memory of the accident, but from the instant she awoke she'd known her parents were dead.

Therapy had saved her in more ways than one. Therapy and Grandfather. She'd needed the intense physical focus to learn how to mute the Gift that had woken, full-force, while she was in a coma. She'd needed Grandfather to teach her how to go on.

Fugue had never captured her completely, the way she was told it had when she was a baby, but it brought other dangers. When in fugue, she could play with the patterns, change them, intrude her patterns into others. When in fugue, she *wanted* to. She'd see something in the patterns that needed fixing, and—

"Kai. Kai!"

Startled, Kai swung around to see Jackie a few feet away, trouble writ as large on her face as it was in her colors. "What is it?"

"Damned ghosts." She scowled. "I'm supposed to get you out of here. Or Ginger. Or both."

* * *

"AFTERNOON, Doug. This is Sergeant Hunter," Sheriff Browning said. "He has some information you need to listen to."

Midland's chief of police made Nathan think of a whip—quick, taut, and snappish. He even looked the part, being over six feet and under one-sixty. His hair and eyes were dark, his forehead high and getting higher. His mustache might have been laid out with a ruler.

"Randy." Chief Roberts nodded at the sheriff. He had a nod for Nathan, too, but no word of greeting. Nor did he offer either of them a handshake, remaining behind his wide desk, its shine interrupted by very few objects—reading glasses, a file folder, a pen, a phone, a wire basket holding papers. "I imagine you're here to complain that I'm intruding into your territory. I'm behind, so I hope you can make this quick."

"Quick enough." Browning took the seat he hadn't been offered, so Nathan sat, too. "Knox hauled off a possible witness to my case. You want to explain that?"

"If you're talking about the Shaw murder—"

"You know I am."

"There's no evidence he was killed outside city limits, and every reason to think his death is connected to the two Knox is already handling. He found a witness. He brought the man in to make a statement. That's his job. However"—he spared Browning a thin smile—"I'm not trying to keep evidence from you. Here's a copy of that statement." He handed Browning the file folder.

The sheriff took the folder but didn't open it. "Doug, in your rush to make this your collar instead of mine, you've screwed up. I know the gist of this. Knox found a witness who identified the woman Shaw left The Bar with last night."

Though the smile remained thin, the dark eyes were smug. "That's right."

"Kai Michalski."

Nathan's heartbeat didn't speed up this time. He knew Knox had Kai in his sights and assumed the chief was backing him, so he had his body under rigid control. But deep inside, in a part of him that had never been and would never be human, he was howling.

Beings in thirteen realms would have known that howl, in their blood and bones if not their conscious minds. And feared.

"That's right," Roberts said again. "I assume someone in the judge's office tipped you. I wonder who that was?"

Browning continued as if the other man hadn't spoken. "You persuaded Judge Walker to issue a warrant for her arrest based on that witness's testimony. But you screwed up. Aside from the sheer lack of evidence—"

"I've got plenty to link her." Roberts leaned forward now, his eyes glowing with suppressed excitement. "Delia Rodriguez—the first victim—lived just two doors down from one of Michalski's patients. The second victim used to date another of her patients."

"Good God, Doug, this is Midland. Half the people here have some second- or thirdhand connection to one or more of the victims."

"But half the people here aren't witches. She is."

"No," Nathan said, his voice steady. "She isn't. Not that it would be an indictment if she was, but you've got your facts wrong."

Roberts's gaze flickered to Nathan—then darted away. Probably hadn't liked what he saw in Nathan's eyes. "She sure as hell is. Michalski is friends with that witch out at the college. And don't tell me Ginger Hemmings isn't a witch. She's open enough about her perversions."

Nathan kept his voice from descending to a growl. "Wicca is a recognized religion. Ginger is Wiccan. Kai isn't."

Roberts had decided to pretend Nathan didn't exist. He laced his fingers together on top of his desk and spoke to

Browning. "We've learned that they had one of their coven meetings last night. Held it at Michalski's apartment just a few hours before she picked Shaw up at the Bar. That's when they prepared for their black rites, when they drained Shaw of blood."

Browning shook his head. "That's all assumptions based on prejudice."

"Don't you accuse me of prejudice. No one has a better record of hiring and promoting—"

"Prejudice against the magical part of the population! Dammit, Doug, you and I have had our differences, but you've always been a good cop. You're so far off base this time you can't even see the base!"

"It isn't prejudice when it's based on facts. I know they met at Michalski's place last night. I know Shaw was later drained of blood. I know Michalski left The Bar with Shaw shortly before he died."

"No," Nathan said. "You don't."

Roberts still wouldn't look at him. "I've got a witness who ID'ed her and three more who gave a good description."

"Mistaken identity."

"What the hell is your man talking about?" Roberts demanded of Browning.

Nathan had had enough. He didn't change position or offer threat openly—but he used a voice the other man would not be able to ignore. "Kai Tallman Michalski was with me at the time your witness claims to have seen her at The Bar."

Roberts jerked. He narrowed his eyes and for the first time looked directly at Nathan. "You're lying."

He was, actually, but the chief had no way of knowing that. "She was with me the rest of the night, too. You think you can get a conviction with an officer of the law swearing he was with her all night?"

The man's lip lifted in a sneer, but underneath it Nathan saw the fear. Smelled it. "You think a jury's going to care what you say? I don't know what you are, but you aren't human." Relief shaded his voice when he turned back to Browning. "That's going to cost you in the next election, Randy. Keeping this—this man, for want of a better word—on as a sergeant even though you have to know that . . ."

Nathan didn't hear the rest. He was already out the door and closing it softly behind him.

He stopped at the desk where Roberts's secretary sat and forced ease on his voice and body. He gave himself a moment to appreciate the soft floral scent of her perfume so he'd have a reason to smile at her. Humans smiled when they didn't feel it, but that trick was beyond him. "While my boss dukes it out with yours, I thought I'd see if I could catch up with Knox. Maybe if I'm in on the arrest, the sheriff won't take it so hard. Do you know if Knox has served his warrant yet?"

She tapped her pen against the desk, then said, "Guess it won't hurt to tell you. I haven't heard from him, so he probably hasn't."

He thanked her and left, taking the stairs, urgency riding him and instinct guiding him. Thoughts floated on that sea of need and knowing, crisp and useful.

Knox didn't know where Kai was. Chances were he'd go to the clinic, then to her apartment—and she wasn't either place. Nathan scented her as much closer. Downtown. He could get to her first.

He didn't ask himself what he would do when he found her. He had no plan, felt no need for one. He knew enough: Knox and Roberts intended to arrest her, to lock her away. It didn't matter at this moment if conviction was likely. The arrest itself would damage her. Jail would damage her. A trial would damage her.

So he would prevent the arrest. She was his. His. No one was allowed to harm her.

CHAPTER 9

"KEEP talking," Kai said.

"This haunt has been trying to get my attention since last night." Jackie grimaced. "I should have listened, I guess. When I gave up and let him in, he didn't have much to say. Not even his name, which is weird. They're usually eager to give me their names, their stories. He did give me a picture—this place, filled with people like it is now. So here I am."

"He?" Maybe the message was from her father. A twist of longing tugged at her, because she wanted that to be true.

"Definitely he, though that's about all I know about him. 'Get her out of there,' he said."

"Who?"

"I don't know. Dammit, you'd think . . . but it's got to be either you or Ginger. I don't know anyone else here well."

"If something bad is going to happen—"

"See, that's just the thing. People think those on the other side have all this insight into events here, when half the time they don't have a clue. But . . . well, if a message is really specific, there's usually something to it."

Charley stepped up to the mike. His soothing voice drifted out over the crowd as he welcomed them, and the colorful soup began to settle.

"I take it this one's specific?"

"As such things go, yeah." Jackie chewed on her lip. "I'd better tell Ginger, too. Do you know where she is?"

"Up at the front. She's supposed to speak."

"Shit. She won't want to leave."

"I'll go with you."

"No, you won't. You'll leave, then I'll have one less to worry about. Go on." Jackie gave her a little push. "Go."

But once she was turned around, Kai saw what Jackie had come to warn about. Though the colors around the crowd had calmed, a small group of men—maybe twenty—kept to themselves off to one side. Kai didn't like the look of their thoughts or the murky swirl they swam in.

"Jackie," she started, turning around—but her friend was gone, swallowed up in people.

It was Kai's turn for some lip chewing. Earlier she'd seen a couple of police officers over by the Midland Center, the brick building whose wall made one boundary for the plaza. Maybe she should find them, see if she could persuade them there was trouble brewing. Or maybe . . . *no, dammit. Don't even think about it.*

Telling herself not to think about something was hopeless, of course. *Don't think about an elephant* inevitably conjures the image of an elephant. Once it occurred to Kai that she might be able to stop the ugliness before it erupted by calming those thoughts, she couldn't banish the idea by telling herself to drop it.

Okay, then. Consider it logically, pros and cons, she told herself as she began weaving through the packed bodies, heading for the Midland Center.

The pro was that she might be able to prevent violence. The con was—well, there were several. First, ugly thoughts didn't necessarily lead to violence. Second, she had no idea what she might do to any minds she tampered with. That was a good reason, an excellent reason, not to interfere. Third, she didn't even know if she could do it.

"Thou shalt not suffer a witch to live!" someone yelled from the back of the crowd.

Kai turned—and those thoughts were roiling now, seething with colors that made her think of storms and blood. There were more shouts, the volume and venom in them mounting every second.

Someone cried out in startlement or fear, someone else in anger. Kai couldn't see what was happening, but the people near her started moving—most trying to get away from the commotion at the rear, some shoving their way toward the trouble. She heard Charley's amplified voice telling everyone to stay calm, stay calm, but no one was listening.

She heard screams.

And the patterns—! The air was thick with the bleached yellow of fear, rippling with electric green and swirls of dark ocher, darker gray, mud brown. The wrongness of the patterns sucked at her. Kai breathed in raggedly—and let herself go, falling into fugue. She had to try—

Someone bumped her, hard. She fell against another someone, which kept her from hitting the ground, and found herself engulfed in a moving knot of people. An elbow jabbed her ribs. She heard screams, cries, yelling. Panic sent her heartbeat rocketing. She fought to keep her feet.

Suddenly she found herself in a pocket of space left inexplicably open in the shoving crowd. She started to reach again for fugue—then saw the body lying on the ground.

It was Jackie.

Kai threw herself to her knees beside her friend. Terror keened her senses, drowning the immaterial in a flood of physical. She shivered as she reached for the pulse point on Jackie's throat . . . strong. Jackie's heart beat strongly.

Kai shuddered in relief. She ran her hands over Jackie's head, looking . . . there, yes, there. On her temple, a knot. The skin wasn't broken, but something had hit her, knocked her out.

Another shiver hit. The air was freezing all of a sudden. Jackie had on a warm jacket, but was it enough? Maybe—

A woman built like a small rhino lumbered into the open space around Jackie. Kai pushed to her feet, thrusting out a hand and calling out for her to stop. Her voice was lost in the din.

The woman's face crumpled in fear. She pushed right back into the crowd.

Kai blinked. She'd never scared anyone off by waving at her before. What in the . . . oh. The cold. The cleared space. Even nulls sensed ghosts sometimes. Kai imagined spirits ringing her and Jackie, pushing back at everyone. She'd have to tell Jackie her ghostly friends weren't useless after all. Once Jackie was . . . oh, God. She had to be all right. She had to.

A sudden surge of people broke past the ghosts' ability to frighten—a mob with neither intention nor control over where it went, pressed willy-nilly by others behind them. The blood drained from Kai's face. She shoved a man aside. Another, a woman, was pushed almost on top of them, but saw Jackie at the last second and managed to stagger over her body without stepping on her

Too many. There were too many, pressed by too many others. She couldn't—

Then a man in a khaki uniform slipped through the rush of people streaming the other way. Nathan. He bent and scooped Jackie up in his arms. "Get behind me!" he shouted. "Hold my belt."

Kai all but plastered herself against him. She gripped his belt as if her life depended on it, and rode in his wake as he cut sideways through the mob.

They broke out of the crowd near the fountain. Nathan

didn't stop, but stepped up into the first stone tier, drained and dry now for winter. Carefully he laid Jackie down, running his hands over her much as Kai had done, then lifting each eyelid. "Concussed," he said, voice raised enough that she could hear. "What happened?"

"I don't know! It happened so fast—these people, the ones with ugly colors, they started yelling at us. At the Gifted, I mean, but I couldn't see what they did. Something that scared people, because all of a sudden everyone was—it was—" Kai found herself horribly close to tears. "I couldn't stop it. I couldn't."

He gave her a look, then rose and wrapped his arms around her. She started shaking.

He lowered his head so he could speak softly, close to her ear. "Adrenaline. You'll be okay in a minute."

"Jackie—"

"Can't do anything for her here. She needs the hospital. It's emptying out now," he added. "We need to go."

"Go?" She lifted her head to stare at him.

"I'm sorry. I couldn't prevent it. I . . ." He sighed. "A judge has issued a warrant for your arrest."

NATHAN got Kai moving while she was still too stunned and shocked to protest. First he had to make sure her friend received care, though, so he carried the woman to the makeshift stage that had served as a podium. The speakers had made it to safety inside the Midland Center, but the television people remained, avidly filming. The local news anchor hurled questions at him, but she was easy enough to ignore.

Uniformed officers were clearing out the last of the crowd as he and Kai left, some tending the fallen. Sirens sounded. They reached Nathan's official car on Illinois Street just as a car he recognized pulled up halfway down the block. "That's Knox," he said as he shut his door. Kai was already in the car, but he suspected Knox had seen her. "He's got the warrant."

"He's got it? You mean . . . you mean you aren't arresting me?"

Stunned, Nathan forgot to turn on the ignition. How could she think that? "No. Good God, no." He pulled himself together and started the car. "I came to make sure you weren't arrested. The riot delayed me. Good thing it was a small one."

She made a choked sound. After a moment, he realized it was a laugh. He glanced at her, unsure whether this was a time when their humor diverged or if she was hysterical.

She seemed all right, though pale. "The riot delayed you. God. All right. If you aren't arresting me, what are you doing?"

"Keeping Knox from arresting you."

"But . . . Nathan, if they've got a warrant, I can't just hide. I don't want to be arrested, but it's a mistake. It's not like they have any real evidence against me. They can't, so they'll have to let me go. But if I evade arrest I look guilty, which will make it harder to persuade them . . ." Her voice wobbled. "How could they think it was me? This doesn't make sense. Are you sure there isn't a mistake?"

"I'm sure. The sheriff and I discussed the case with Chief Roberts. Roberts is deeply prejudiced against the Gifted. He knows about the meeting you had at your apartment last night, though he's mistaken about its nature—thinks it was a coven meeting. He has a witness who saw you leave The Bar with Jimmie Shaw last night just after midnight."

"The Bar?" She was bewildered. "But I don't go there. I've never been there."

"I told them I was with you at that time. The sheriff believed me. Roberts didn't. He said a jury wouldn't accept my testimony since I'm not human."

"You told them . . . but I was home at midnight, asleep. Asleep alone. You didn't get there until two o'clock."

"Yes," he said, patient. "But they can't know what time I arrived. Do you mind if they believe we're lovers?"

She waved that away. "That's not the problem. You tried to give me an alibi, and you meant well, but that witness—she couldn't have seen me. It's someone else, someone who looks like me."

Someone who looked like her, yes. Or something. "He. The witness is Ed Bates. He was your patient, I understand."

"Soft tissue trauma to the neck and shoulders. We had several sessions . . . but Ed knows me. He must know that wasn't . . . was he drunk? That's it," she said, sounding pleased that something at last made sense. "He must have been drunk."

"Three other witnesses gave descriptions of the woman who left with Shaw. I spoke with one of them. She has a poor memory for names, but a good one for faces. She described you perfectly."

Kai didn't say anything for several moments. He wanted to take her hand, to reassure her with the alchemy of touch. That was what he would have needed at such a time, but he didn't understand human rules for touching, which changed from one culture to the next, from one decade to the next. He wasn't sure when touch was welcome between friends in this era.

If they were lovers . . .

She spoke before he could make up his mind, looking down at the hands she'd pleated together in her lap. "Do you think I did it, then?"

"No." He was glad to be able to reassure her of that much. "You've never killed."

"Hey. The telepath's sitting over here, not behind the steering wheel. You can't know that."

But he could. He did. Nathan struggled to find words for this knowing, but it was woven of so many threads. . . . Some killers possessed a psychic scent, but not all. Not even most. And some humans who had never killed smelled like killers because the potential ran high in them. Those were the ones who wanted to kill, wanted the blood and power and destruction of it. Many killed without having that need—in war or to protect another, because of hunger or fear or a fleeting rage.

And some killed as Nathan did, as part of a hunt, though they hunted nonsentients—deer, rabbits, birds. A very few hunted and killed their fellows, but not as Nathan did. For them, he felt pity. They seemed to have some of the same instincts he possessed, yet they lacked others, those that should have connected them to their fellows, leaving them twisted and terrible. They killed because it was the only connection they understood.

A hellhound did not kill for that reason, but he understood the need for connection, the depth of that need. He'd hunted serial killers because they couldn't be stopped otherwise, but he'd killed them cleanly.

How would Kai feel when she understood that Nathan, too, was a killer? It was a question he didn't want to find in his head, and he tried to shove it out. But it clung like a bramble to the furry underside of his mind. Humans had so many moralities, some of them contradictory.

She would be distressed, he thought. He hated to distress her.

"I know you," he told her at last. "If you had killed for any reason, you would be a . . . a different version of Kai. You would still be my friend, but different than you are now." He slowed the car as thoughts and questions pinged and bounced around inside, making his head noisy.

"Nathan," she said in a surprisingly steady voice, "why are we stopping at a car lot?"

"I'll get a license plate here. The car . . . no, I haven't explained, have I?" His eyebrows twitched into a frown. "I'm making decisions for you. That's wrong. I'm sorry." He unbuckled his seat belt and turned to her. This time he went with his impulse and took her hands in his. "I want to hide you so you aren't arrested while I hunt the real killer, but I need another vehicle. Knox saw me with you. So did the television reporter. Once Knox realizes I didn't bring you in, they'll look for this car."

"But this is crazy! You can't throw away your career, and I don't want to be hidden away!"

He wasn't explaining well. "I don't have a career. I hunt. Working as an officer of the law suits me, but I can do that elsewhere, under another name, if I'm allowed to stay here. Here in this realm, I mean. If you don't want to hide . . ." This was difficult. He swallowed. "I respect your right to make your own choices, but you need to know you aren't safe. The chameleon wore your face, your form when it lured Jimmie Shaw out of the city and killed him. You may be able to help me catch it."

CHAPTER 10

THE house was a simple shingle-sided frame structure south of town, just off Cotton Flat Road. It was empty, had been for years. There was no heat, no electricity, no water, and the only furniture was a lopsided couch that had been a home for several generations of mice. The trash on the cracked linoleum floor announced that two-legged residents had come and gone occasionally, too.

Kai had seen all that earlier, when there was still some light and the place still stank. Nathan had done something to fix the smell before he left. Something that involved speaking in a language she didn't know.

It was taking him a long time to get supplies. That, she knew, was her fault—or at least the result of her decision. He was on foot because she hadn't wanted him to steal a license plate or a car, so they'd ditched his official vehicle to walk the last few miles to get here.

It was full dark now. There was a sliver of moon outside, but the grimy window beside the front door let in none of the meager light. That window might still alert people in the nearest houses to her presence, though, if she used the big police-issue flashlight Nathan had left with her. It was for an emergency, not comfort.

Emergency being, she assumed, something more than the mice she could hear scurrying around. Something bigger, like the blood-drinking creature that had worn her face last night.

Kai shivered. *Nathan warded this place,* she reminded herself. She'd watched him do that before he left, loping silently around the house three times. "I'm no mage to raise wards with a gesture or by singing a little song," he'd said when she asked him about it. "But any of the wild sidhe can wrap a bit of protection around themselves. To do it over a larger area takes a bit more concentration, is all."

The wards were good for hours; they'd keep anything and everything out. But standing in the black, filthy living room with her arms wrapped tightly around her middle, it was easy to wonder how he could be sure. Easy to wonder how she had come to this. How could she have ended up on the run from the police, cold and hungry, alone in the dark and unable to do one damned thing to change any of it?

Stupid question. "Why me" questions always were. She knew that, just as she knew how inevitable those feelings were when life turned topsy-turvy. After the accident she'd been hit by multiple bouts of "why me." Eventually she'd accepted that she wasn't to blame, but neither was she exempt from random tragedy. Shit happens.

If she could just do something! She took two quick steps but stopped, not knowing what she might step on or trip over. She longed for water and a rag to clean a corner of this room, a spot big enough to sit down. And a candle. She'd need light to clean, wouldn't she? Light to hold back the dark that pressed against her skin as if winter itself was running cold fingers over her, trailing shivers and fear.

She should have gone with Nathan. She'd wanted to, but he'd said in his calm pragmatic way that obtaining what they needed would take much longer if she was with him.

Alone, he could move unseen, and quickly. That was undoubtedly true, but she hated being helpless, relying on him to supply her needs.

She hated being alone. If only she could call Grandfather . . . oh, she wanted him. The need for his voice, his presence, washed over her, leaving her shaky inside as well as out.

If, if, if. *"If only" won't get supper on the table,* Grandfather used to tell her. *Can't start from where we wish we were.* That was what he'd said when she lost her parents and he lost his only child. Start from where you are, or you don't start.

Kai consulted her belly and found she'd be starting from cold, hungry, scared . . . and mad. Anger was a relief. Anger made her less of a victim and shut out the whiny voice. What was she doing, handing control of her life over to someone else? Nathan meant well, but—

The door creaked and her stomach flipped back to plain old scared. She spun to face it.

"It's me," Nathan said softly. "Took longer than I expected."

Nathan was a black splotch against the smudged outdoor darkness, surrounded by the slowly moving shapes of his thoughts as they swam through a faint glow of indigo, lilac, and silver.

Those were not upset colors. "I want to talk to you."

"All right." The door creaked closed, shutting out the bit of moonlight. The grease-and-beef smell of fast food entered with him. "Let me fix the window first so we can have some light."

"Light would be good." To her disgust, her voice cracked.

Soft footsteps approached, along with his colors and the food smells. She felt his hand on her cheek. "Action is easy," he said softly. "Waiting is harder. Has it been bad, waiting here?"

"It isn't exactly bringing out the best in me."

"Hold this." Paper rustled as he pressed a paper bag into her hand. "I'll cover the window."

The greasy-fries scent from the contents of the bag hit her smack in the reptile brain. Her stomach growled as his colors moved to the dirty window. The thunk of a hammer twice announced progress in the window covering.

All at once there was light. A ball of it, rosy and welcoming, perched in the air behind Nathan's head as he turned to her.

"Ah . . . that's not a flashlight."

"You'd call it mage light or fairy light." When he crossed to her the light followed like an obedient puppy. It wasn't bright—maybe the equivalent of two or three candles—but was plenty for her to see the blanket draped over his arm. She didn't see the hammer she'd heard him use. "It's a simple trick. You could learn to summon one, if you wished."

"I do wish, but later. Nathan—"

Again he touched her, lightly this time and just on her arm. "You have questions, things you need to say. But we should eat first."

Her stomach seconded the idea. "Is that blanket for us to sit on?"

"Yes." He spread it out. "The drinks are in the car, as well as a few other things. I'll get them."

"What car?" she demanded.

"That was my decision. There's no blame to you for it."

Which meant he'd stolen the car. "Did you steal the supplies, too?"

"No. I prefer not to steal, but that wasn't practical with the car."

She sighed, weary with change, fear, and decisions. Too weary to sort through the wrongs and rights. "I'll help bring things in."

"You can, but I'll have to take down the wards first."

"Do you mean I can't leave until you do that? That I've been trapped in here all this time?"

"Eh." He rubbed his nose, looked at the floor. "Well, yes. I'll fix that later, all right?"

She settled unhappily on the blanket.

When he opened the door, the mage light winked out—no gesture or incantation needed. Every time he returned—first with Cokes, bottled water, and two grocery sacks, then with sleeping bags—the light popped back on, too.

She wanted one.

It was an odd and hasty picnic. With the first bite Kai discovered she was beyond hungry, well into ravenous. She devoured most of the burger and half the fries before speaking again. "I shouldn't have run. I shouldn't be here, hiding. I'd like to help you catch the creature, but—"

"They've released your name to the media."

"What?"

"I heard it on the radio. Knox gave a press conference and spoke of the warrant for your arrest. I suspect your image was on the television news, but I didn't see that."

She put down the uneaten portion of her hamburger, her knotted stomach rejecting the idea of food.

Nathan reached for her hand. "Kai. If you don't hide, you'll be in jail by midnight. I don't know if you'll be safe there, if the chief will take the steps to assure that you are. There's ill-feeling toward all Gifted right now, and—"

"And I'm the wicked witch the house is about to fall on. No one objects when she gets flattened. God!" She shoved to her feet clumsily, knocking over her Coke. His hand shot out, catching the cup before it finished tipping in a motion so quick it blurred.

She stared at his hand. He had long, blunt fingers and a wide palm, with a sprinkling of dark hair at the wrist. Such a human hand, in spite of the speed with which it had just moved. She dragged her gaze back to his face. "Why would it want to look like me?"

Nathan rose much more gracefully than she had. "I

don't know. There's a link, though. It may select its prey ahead of time and take their shape."

Her eyes widened as fear pooled in her belly.

"I won't let it get to you." He closed the distance between them, setting his hands on her shoulders. "If it does come for you, I'll stop it. Kill it, I hope, because we can prove your innocence with its body. If it remains in its natural state, the shape of the mouth and teeth will match the bites on Shaw's body. If it doesn't, its transformed body will still prove that it could have worn your face."

"Posthumous vindication isn't that appealing to me."

He squeezed gently. "Do you think I'd let it harm you? There are beings, creatures, I couldn't be sure of stopping, but this isn't one of them."

"I love your confidence, but you don't know much about chameleons."

"I know mass is conserved when they change form. This one looked enough like you to fool someone who knows you, so its mass is similar to yours. If it comes after you, I can stop it."

She chewed on her lip, trying to think her way past the fear. If she gave herself up to the police, she might be in danger from other prisoners, maybe even the guards. If she hid out, the monster might come after her.

The chameleon was certainly the bigger danger, but here she had Nathan. In jail she wouldn't. And they needed the chameleon to prove she wasn't the killer. "Do you Change? Like a lupus, I mean."

"Eh. No. I've had a human body and brain for more than four hundred years now. I can't go back to my hound body, not on my own."

Four hundred years? She'd known he'd lived much longer than a human, but that . . . that would take some getting used to. "Tell me." She reached for the hand on her shoulder, clasped it. "Tell me how you came to be here. How you came to have that human body and brain."

"My queen sent me, and I needed a human form for the hunt. We knew it would take time for me to track the . . . Kai, are you going to allow me to keep you hidden here?"

"Yes."

Relief stripped him naked. She'd never seen his face so raw with feeling. "May I . . . is it all right to hold you?"

She didn't bother with words. Arms were better, and hers slid around him as naturally as if they were already lovers. His arms answered, wrapping her breath-stealingly tight for a second, then loosening. He ran his hands up and down her back, buried his nose in her hair. "I have *wanted* this," he said fiercely. "For so long, I have wanted . . ." His breath shuddered out.

Silence wrapped itself around them then—a silence of heartbeats and breaths settling into a shared rhythm. Kai closed her eyes so she could absorb the feel of him through muscle, scent, and skin.

Which wasn't touching his, dammit. Though the way their bodies were touching, she knew he wasn't sexually indifferent to her. Not anymore. "I've wanted, too," she said softly. "I still do."

He raised his head. She saw his throat work as he swallowed. "Kai." He said her name the way he smiled—as if he'd just found it, just this moment wrapped his lips around the sound. He ran both hands along her hair. "I can't . . . if I'm to keep you safe, I can't be distracted."

"You're turning me down."

He grimaced. "I'm turning us both down, but it's hard." His eyebrows lifted in brief surprise. "That was a pun, wasn't it?"

Actually, it *wasn't* hard. Not anymore. "Ah . . . did you do something just now? Because you aren't . . . things changed."

"I control my body. I've been controlling it around you from the first day we met. The wanting is still there, but it isn't reinforced physically."

Well. He'd been controlling his desire from the time they met? That struck her as a good news, bad news deal. He'd wanted her all along, but he didn't want to want her . . . because sex was too lonely without a bond, he'd said.

But friendship was a bond, a strong one. That tipped things to the good news side, she decided. "Who's this queen that sent you here?"

"I'll tell you." With a sigh he released her. "Sit with me and I'll tell you whatever you want to know."

CHAPTER 11

WHEN Nathan was sent to Earth to find a renegade mage, a redheaded queen was sitting on England's throne. The Spaniards had just founded the first European settlement in North America at St. Augustine, and William Shakespeare hadn't yet set foot on a London stage. In Italy, a young man named Galileo Galilei was disappointing his father by studying pendulums and other nonsense instead of medicine. And the Purge was just beginning.

For thirty-two years, Nathan had tracked the mage. When he finished his hunt, both Shakespeare and Queen Elizabeth were dead; Jamestown had been established; and the Purge was over, with thousands of Gifted dead at the hands of the Inquisition, their governments, or their own neighbors. And Nathan had been stranded, cut off from all he knew, even from his proper shape.

"Ilké had violated many laws, committed many sins," Nathan said, "but the queens don't intervene in lesser matters. But he crossed one line too many when he practiced death magic."

Kai lay against Nathan's chest, listening to his heartbeat

as well as his voice. His arms were around her; his colors swam with hers. In front of them the mage light burned steadily like a heatless campfire. "Death magic, huh? He must have been a major bad guy."

She heard a smile in his voice. "Hellhounds aren't set on the trail of jaywalkers. You are . . . okay with this? That my purpose was to hunt and kill those who broke the queens' laws?"

"I'm okay with policemen and soldiers. Your role was something like theirs."

He fell silent, toying absently with the ends of her hair in a way she found most distracting. Not that she wanted him to stop. Finally he said, "I haven't killed only at my queen's command. When I was stranded here . . . an able-bodied man can't simply decide to never again use his hands and arms. Common sense and instinct will defeat him. That's how it is for a hound and the hunt. I couldn't simply decide not to hunt, but it was hard, very hard, to learn how to choose my own hunts. The queen never loosed me lightly, so I tried to choose as she might have, but at first I didn't understand human society. Death isn't always a solution. Even when the prey is causing obvious harm, killing can spread ill instead of containing it."

"Have you . . . here in Midland, I mean. Have you hunted here?"

"Not a true hunt. Not to the death, except for the ghoul. I've learned to take satisfaction in lesser hunts, though. I couldn't be a law officer otherwise."

"Ghoul? You mean there was— No, never mind." She set that aside for another time. "I'm having trouble getting my mind around this. I know you, know your colors, the shapes of your thoughts. I've never known anyone with less anger. You aren't a violent man."

"Anger is too big a response for most things. It gets in the way. You haven't seen me on a true hunt. I am violent then, Kai."

He wasn't apologizing. He was stating a fact.

She didn't say anything for several minutes. She wasn't sure how she felt. Nathan killed according to rules she didn't know, but he'd spent years—lifetimes, maybe, by her way of measuring—evolving those rules. He didn't just come from a different culture, but from a different species.

Was she bothered by the violence in him, or did she just think she ought to be? His arms still felt right around her; his heartbeat still soothed her. She didn't understand, no, but maybe—right this moment—she didn't have to. "It took you years to understand how to choose your hunts," she said at last. "It may take me awhile to understand, but I hope it won't be years."

His voice was soft. "You don't regret our bond."

"No. I don't regret it." Though she wished she knew what it meant to him. Kai shifted so she could look at him. "How did this mage—Ilké, you called him. How did Ilké end up here?"

"He knew his crimes had been uncovered to the two queens and fled. Because he was part sidhe and strengthened by death magic, he was able to leave Faerie entirely, hoping my queen would not set me on his trail once he was beyond her territory. Only a hellhound could track him, you see."

"Sometimes you say queen singular, sometimes queens, plural. Which is it?"

"I told you that a few High Sidhe take an interest in governing. The Summer Queen and the Winter Queen are . . . eh, you don't have the right words. Call them the High Lords of the thirteen realms. They don't operate a government, a bureaucracy, such as you're used to, but each queen has her court, her dominion. Each steps in when she sees a need."

"Do they rule together?"

"Not precisely. Their dominions overlap at times. When this happens they discuss the matter and decide which of them will act. For them to act together . . . that hasn't happened in my lifetime."

And how long was that? She decided not to ask. Not yet. "But you speak of 'my queen.' Singular."

"Hellhounds are the Huntsman's to command, and so I was, at first. But the Huntsman is brother to Winter and lover to Summer . . . I saw both queens often, and one day I knew I must go with *zan Al'aran.* With the Winter Queen." A hint of longing underlay the words. "So I became hers, and she became mine. It's hard, being queen. Harder for Winter than Summer, because who doesn't love Summer? She'll have been lonely without me."

Kai felt like squirming. It was pointless to be jealous of an immortal—and no doubt supernally beautiful—elfin queen. But she was. Oh, she was. She tried to take the high road. "I imagine she was upset when the realms shifted and you couldn't return."

"The realms didn't shift then. That happened centuries ago, after the Great War. After that your realm was hard to reach, requiring great power. The magic here wasn't replenished, so by the time I arrived there was little left." He sighed. "The hunt took too long. Over the years my own power lessened because there was less for me to draw on, to absorb. By the time I killed Ilké, I couldn't go home."

"Couldn't your queen have brought you back? If she's so powerful—"

"It doesn't work that way. Hellhounds travel between realms without a gate. It's inborn, that skill, and common to many of the wild sidhe. But to bring someone to you from another realm, you must open a gate. After the Great War, the Old Ones forbade opening gates to Earth."

"Old Ones?"

He nodded. "Strange beings, on the whole. I think they're like unicorns."

"I'm getting seriously dizzy here."

"Unicorns have that effect on me, too."

Kai found herself smiling. Unicorns, Old Ones, elfin queens, renegade mages . . . it all sounded fantastic, even absurd. She accepted that these things were true because Nathan said so, and he didn't lie. But the reality she understood was the warmth of his hand, the chill of the winter air, and the slow, sad song of the wind outside.

Also a steadily glowing mage light. "Did you know you'd be stranded?" she asked quietly. "When your queen set you to track Ilké, did you know you wouldn't be able to return?"

"I knew it was possible, yet I didn't. Not really." His thoughts, usually slow, turned busy—silvery minnows struggling to find a fit as he hunted words. "Hellhounds are sentients, but our brains shape our thoughts, and hellhound brains are not human. What I knew as a hound was different from what I can know as a man. Lesser in some ways, greater in others. I knew I could be trapped here, but that was so apart from my reality that it had no meaning until it happened."

She nodded. "Like unicorns. You tell me they're real and I believe you, but I can't grasp it."

He found one of his smiles, this one holding equal parts sweet and sad. "Yes. The queen told me I could be lost here and I accepted that it was true, but didn't grasp that truth."

"But she sent you. She sent you anyway."

"She's queen." His smile turned gentle, as if Kai had said something mildly foolish. "And she's immortal. A few hundred years isn't long to her. She'd expect me to understand and accept the necessity, and she'd be right. Ilké couldn't be allowed to live. With death magic empowering him and none here able to oppose him, he could have done terrible harm to your world. And those in the thirteen realms needed to know he'd be found and punished."

"How would they know? You didn't find him until years after the Earth was closed to them."

His eyebrows lifted. "The Winter Queen announced

she'd set her hound on his trail. Those of Faerie wouldn't need to be present at the kill to know it happened."

A touch of arrogance there. No, more than a touch. "Are you unstoppable, then?"

"Short of death, yes, and hellhounds are difficult to kill. There are few who can manage it."

"A part-sidhe mage pumped up on death magic wouldn't be one of those few."

His gray eyes warmed with amusement. "As you see, he was not."

"Good point." To her surprise, a yawn overtook her. "Wow. Didn't think I could relax enough to be sleepy, but I am. I don't suppose you've got a toothbrush in one of those sacks?"

"Of course." He stretched out a hand and retrieved one of the grocery bags. "Breakfast is in the other bag—fruit, bread, and peanut butter. I didn't get anything for coffee or tea, I'm afraid."

"I'll tough it out." She dug through the sack he'd handed her. Soap, a washcloth and towel, sunscreen, paper plates and cups, deodorant, tampons—tampons! Her usual brand, too, which she assumed he'd seen in her bathroom at some point. She shook her head, smiling. She didn't need them at the moment, but if she was as punctual as usual, she'd want them in another two days.

How many men would have even thought of tampons?

There was also antibacterial ointment, toothbrushes, toothpaste, contact lens solution, and a roll of toilet paper. She took it out, frowning. "With that water you brought I can brush my teeth over the sink in the kitchen, but I'm not using this bathroom."

"You'll want to go outside. I need to set the wards to let you pass anyway, so we'll do that. But first I need to check the area." He stood.

The wards.

While Nathan scouted around outside, Kai thought about

those mysterious wards. Once he'd determined that the area was safe, he had her stand in the doorway with her hands outstretched while he loped around the house again. That was to somehow mix her energy with his so she could pass through his wards.

When he was done she went out and took care of necessities in the concealing darkness. She came back in and brushed her teeth and washed her face in the kitchen using the bottled water as sparingly as she could—with a tiny bubble of mage light posted to her shoulder. And she thought about Nathan.

To protect her, he'd tossed aside everything. From what she could tell, he hadn't felt an instant of doubt or regret for that decision. She knew the colors of those emotions, the way they muddied thoughts. Nathan's colors remained as clear and true as ever.

The hunt, he'd said, was part of him the way her hands were part of her. She suspected he needed the kill at its end, too, at least sometimes. He'd learned to do without that, but when he spoke of a true hunt, he meant to the death.

He was a killer.

He was the most honest person she'd ever met. He was rare, kind, practical, sometimes too serious, and . . . and innocent. It was an odd word to use for someone hundreds of years old and experienced in ways she couldn't even guess at, but it fit. There was no taint to Nathan.

He'd bought her tampons. Somehow that summed everything up for her.

When Kai finished washing and brushing and went back to the living room, he'd unrolled the sleeping bags. They lay primly side by side in the middle of the room. She paused. "I smell smoke."

"I disposed of the papers and such from supper. Best not to tempt the mice."

She couldn't agree more. Kai walked up to him and put her hand on his chest. His heart beat slow and steady, but his eyebrows lifted in surprise and his colors warmed. He looked at her, waiting.

"You should have put our sleeping bags together."

"I don't expect to sleep. Are you cold? I can warm the air in here, but it will take power I'd rather save for greater need."

She shook her head. "I'm not talking about sleeping, Nathan."

"Kai—"

"You didn't turn me down because you couldn't risk the distraction. Your wards will tell you if anything comes close enough to be a threat. If you have another reason for not making love with me now, tell me what it is."

For a long moment he said nothing, but his thoughts sped up and a rosy hue brightened the purple they swam in. And his heart beat faster. "You're right," he said at last. "I'm afraid. I hadn't realized that."

"Okay." She nodded. "Good. So am I." And she reached for his head and put her hands behind it, went up on tiptoe, and kissed him.

His lips were warm and, for two difficult seconds, completely still. Then he quivered. And exploded.

His arms took over, binding her tightly to him. He wanted his mouth everywhere, not just on hers. He kissed her chin, the crest of her cheek, and licked her ear, then kissed her eyes closed and ran the tip of his tongue along the base of the lashes. Then returned to her mouth. "Beautiful, beautiful," he crooned, his breath soft and warm against her lips. "So beautiful."

It was true. Nathan never lied. Under the glory of his hands coursing her back, her arms, her hips, with his mouth making magic on her skin, she was beautiful. She tried to tell him the same with her mouth and hands—that he was splendid, glorious, and hers. Hers. In this moment, if only for this moment, he was hers.

"A moment," he said, tearing his mouth away to lean his

forehead against hers. His breath came fast. "It's been so long . . . I need a moment, or my control—"

"Nathan." She cupped his face in her two hands. "Will you hurt me? If you turn loose of your bloody control, is there any chance you would hurt me?"

His eyes were so dark, the pupils dilated. So intent. He shook his head once, his eyes never losing their focus on her. "But it's been so long. I don't . . . expectations are different than they used to be. I want to do right by you."

Her breath huffed out. "You don't have to do this right. There is no right way because there is no wrong way, not between us. Do you understand? You can't do this wrong."

"Oh." He blinked. "Oh!" And he laughed, delighted, and the sound of it was young and beautiful. Beautiful. "I see. Of course. You're wise, Kai. *My* Kai." The possessive came out fierce, startling her for an instant—just long enough for him to sweep her into his arms.

He laid her on one of the sleeping bags and crouched over her on hands and knees, tugging off her jacket, then her shirt—a stretchy knit, which was good, because he was not patient with the fabric. And kissing her, kissing whatever part of her his mouth happened to be near as he stripped her.

She was hard put to keep up, but she managed to get his shirt off and his pants unzipped before he yanked her jeans off. And her panties. And her bra. He moved her hands aside and finished stripping himself with the same ruthless efficiency he'd used on her. Her eyes widened briefly as he removed the sheath on his leg—a sheath and a knife she hadn't known was there.

Then he lay down beside her and held her, just held her, pressing skin to skin, touching her hair, her breasts, and whispering to her—English words like "soft" and "beautiful." Words in other languages—French, Spanish, what might be Russian. Words in tongues she'd never heard or heard of.

Her name sounded the same in all of them.

Her hands acquainted themselves with him, too—sandpaper skin on his cheeks, where his beard was growing. Softer skin on his flanks and bottom, coarse hair on thighs tight with muscle. The fascinating flex of muscles in his back and shoulders as he stroked her.

Need pooled in her belly. When his lips closed over her nipple, the liquid tugging turned her as hasty as a kid waking up on Christmas morning. "Now," she said, and, "Oh, yes," as he played with her. "Oh, lovely. Yes. But now, Nathan." She wrapped her hand around him, hard and twitching, and he trembled.

But he wasn't finished. He told her so, and he found more places to touch, turning her on her side, lifting her leg, exploring her until she trembled and clutched him and panted. Before panting turned to cursing—barely before—steady, imperturbable Nathan suddenly shook all over. He flipped her onto her back and centered himself over her and drove home.

With his second stroke, she exploded. On the third, he did, too.

Eons later they lay in the crumpled dark with breaths and legs tangled together, the one still quick, the other limp. Kai found enough wind to say, "I always thought that was an old wives' tale. And I didn't do it myself, either."

"What?" He stroked her hair.

"I've gone blind."

He choked on a laugh. "No, but the mage light . . . you were right, but so was I. Normally keeping it going is automatic, but I was distracted for a few moments there at the end. Extremely distracted."

The light bounced back into being, but muted now, no more than a candle glow hovering over his shoulder. She could see him smiling at her, and that was good. He'd invented a truly lovely smile this time.

But she'd already known he was happy. His colors were so bright. She smiled back, loving him.

"Sleep." He touched her cheek and sat up.

"Wait. Where are you going?"

"Nowhere." He reached for his pants. "But I need to stay alert, and I won't if I lie beside you."

"I'm not . . ." But a yawn caught her, making a lie of what she'd been about to say, so she finished wryly, ". . . not going to argue, I guess. But you'll need to sleep, too."

"I like sleep, but I can do without it, especially on a hunt. One sleepless night is easy enough for me."

There was some shifting necessary so she could zip the sleeping bag up around her. Somehow she hadn't noticed the chill earlier, but she did now. He strapped that sheath with its lethal contents back on his calf and pulled on slacks and shirt, but didn't seem bothered by the cold. Then he settled beside her and took her hand.

The mage light winked out. "Do you mind?" he asked softly. "It's best if I let my eyes accustom themselves to the moonlight."

What moonlight? The air might have turned to ink, it was so black. But she was too exhausted to care, and she had Nathan's hand. Or maybe he had hers, and she pondered that and what difference, if any, it made as sleep drew her down, down, its raven feathers brushing her mind into stillness.

CHAPTER 12

"KAI." Nathan touched her shoulder, frowning. He'd brought the mage light up again, hoping the cessation of dark would calm her. It hadn't. "Kai, it's all right. Wake up."

She stopped making the distressed noises. Her eyes opened. "What . . ."

"You were dreaming, I think." She'd whimpered, turning her head from side to side, then stilled. But her hand clasped his so tightly, and she'd kept making those small, unhappy sounds. "A bad dream."

"It was . . . I've had it before. The crying one." She blinked fuzzily. "So lonely. At first I thought it was you, but this time I knew . . . she just wanted to be held, so I— What? What is it?"

He'd sprung to his feet. The plucking inside him announced the breach of his wards a second before the beast crashed through the window.

Glass smashed, flying everywhere. The chameleon landed on the floor between the window and him—and he stood between it and Kai. It was eight feet long counting the lashing tail, its shaggy fur like mottled smoke. Feline, with an oddly shaped muzzle, tufted ears, and the oversize pads of a mountain or arctic cat. And it needed only a split second to orient itself before launching all eight muscular feet at him.

Kai screamed. He heard that, but his entire being was focused on his prey. He couldn't move and expose Kai to those claws, so he locked himself to the earth and met the attack.

Claws raked his forearm, ripping flesh from bone, spattering blood. He rocked back only an inch as he smashed his other fist inside the gaping mouth, aiming for the roof of it, where bone was thin and could be driven into the brain.

But the beast was fast. It flung itself back, howling—and bunched its hindquarters, readying for another attack.

"No!" Kai cried. "No, don't—don't—stop!"

The beast shook its head. And looked at her.

That second's inattention was all Nathan needed. He had his knife in his hand as he leaped onto the beast's back, seizing the great head so he could draw the blade across its—

"Don't kill her! She can't help it, and she's so lonely, so confused—don't kill her, please. Please."

He froze, panting. His arm shook with the need to *finish.*

But the chameleon wasn't moving, either. It wasn't moving.

"See?" Her voice wobbled, but she came toward them. The idiot woman started toward him and his prey. "She won't hurt me. She won't—won't even save herself, because I told her n-not to hurt you."

The beast's muscles tensed. A fine trembling ran through the great body.

Slowly, slowly, Nathan eased the knife away from its throat, but he held his position otherwise, crouched over the chameleon, his wounded arm strobing pain with each heartbeat. "If you stay back, I won't cut her throat. But stay back."

She stopped. "You're bleeding. Your arm. I need to . . . no, it's stopping already, isn't it? You said you didn't like to bleed in a fight, but . . . Nathan, she couldn't help it. She's so alone, and she was dying."

There were tears on Kai's face, shiny in the small glow of the mage light. Nathan stared at her, stricken. "What have you done?"

"I don't know, exactly. Only I touched her somehow, or she touched me . . . I've dreamt of her before, but tonight was different. I—I reached her. I *feel* her now. She came to me because she couldn't be alone anymore, and I . . . I told her, in my sleep. I said she didn't have to, so she came to me."

Pity twisted through him. He knew what it was to be cut off from all you knew. So alone. . . . "She'll kill again, Kai. As you said, she can't help it. There isn't enough magic to sustain her here."

Kai took another step. "There's more magic in some places, close to the big nodes."

"Not enough." Eventually there might be, but not yet.

Kai was only four feet away now. She held out her hand, and the head Nathan had pinned struggled. "Let her smell me," Kai said. "She won't hurt me. She won't."

Nathan knew that every being had to decide his or her own course. He'd earned that knowledge one painful step at a time when he'd been stranded and had to learn how to make his own choices, all of them. But he felt sick, physically sick, as he slowly released the chameleon's head.

It—she—stretched her head out, sniffed the hand held out to her. And beneath him Nathan felt a vibration start.

She was purring. The beast was purring for Kai.

"Can you send her back?" Kai whispered. "Back where she belongs?"

He couldn't, no. But he knew one who could.

* * *

THE mage light hung, motionless, in the center of the room, a warm orange ball pushing back darkness. Either the moon had set or clouds had moved in, for outside the night was entirely black. Cold, too, and with the window broken, that cold streamed in unhindered.

Kai paced. Nathan, impervious to either cold or nerves, sat on one of the sleeping bags, eating an apple. And in one corner of the room, the killer sought by the entire city slept, her long body curled into the same sort of cozy ball a housecat would use to conserve heat, the tuft on her tail draped over her nose.

She had a name. Kai sensed that, but couldn't find it. What she got from the chameleon weren't exactly thoughts, nothing that clear—sensations, feelings, and only the biggest of those. She knew the animal was hungry and weak, but content for the moment because Kai was nearby. She felt that contentment as a sort of rumbling at the back of her mind, like a sleepy purr.

"How did she get through your wards?" Kai asked without looking at Nathan.

"I'm guessing it was her tie to you. Your energy is in the wards. Somehow she used your key to come in."

Kai reached the wall and turned. "I don't know how to make this sort of decision." She stopped, frowning. "Come to think of it, I don't understand why it *is* my decision. It's your life I'm deciding, too."

Nathan finished chewing as calmly as if they'd been in his apartment, talking over a news report they'd heard on TV. "Part of it was mine to decide," he agreed. "But I've made my choices. I could have chosen not to tell you of the possibility, or I could refuse now to call. But for your sake—and also for hers"—he glanced at the sleeping beast—"I'm willing to do it, if you wish me to."

The Huntsman. Nathan would call the leader of the

Wild Hunt because he could return the chameleon to her own realm. He would do that . . . if Kai asked him to.

"But will the Huntsman do it?" she asked.

"I'm no longer of the Hunt, but if I call, he'll come." Nathan gave a little huff of amusement, his lips quirking. "If nothing else, curiosity would likely bring him. The Huntsman keeps hounds, but he has that much in common with cats—a great, throbbing lump of curiosity."

"No, I mean . . . will he agree to send her back?" Saying it brought a pang deep inside. Kai didn't understand the bond she'd formed with the animal, but sending her away felt hard and sad.

Better than letting her die, though.

"Even his sister doesn't predict the Huntsman. He does what he does, and often won't know himself what that will be until he does it. But he has a fondness for me and a love for all wild things. He might kill your chameleon-cat, but there's a good chance he'll save her instead. Or do something we haven't thought of."

"And . . ." Her throat was so dry she had to swallow to get the question out. "And will you go home with him?"

"Kai." Her name came out startled. He shook his head. "No, of course you don't know. There's been a suddenness to all of this, hasn't there? I could have left two months ago when the Turning arrived, if that were my choice. I could leave now. There's enough magic for it."

Her restless feet brought her to him. She crouched in front of him, her heart pounding. "Why did you stay?"

"For you." He set down the uneaten apple core and took her hand, turning it to study her palm, her fingers. "Of course, for you. Though I didn't understand how deep you'd gone inside me, not until last night. I knew I wanted more time with you. But also for me." He rubbed her palm gently with his thumb. Slowly he looked up, meeting her eyes. "I'm not a hound anymore, not precisely. I've spent too many years in a man's body, with a man's brain. That I could hesitate at all to return to her taught me how much I've changed. But the queen . . ."

The trouble in his voice had her turning her hand in his to clasp it. "Yes?"

"I missed my hound's body, missed it badly, at first. I would miss my hands and my speech even more now. And you." He squeezed her hand. "I would miss you terribly if I had to leave."

"Would the Huntsman make you go back?"

"Well, he can't, which is why I'd call him and not my queen. He could kill me, of course, but—"

"Then, no." Her hand clenched hard on his. "Don't call."

"Wait, wait. I didn't mean he *would* kill me. It's a hunter's way of seeing things, that's all—that he could kill me but can't compel me. He'll come, he'll be curious, he either will or won't do what I ask." He shrugged. "And he'll tell her, tell my queen, about my call at some point, when it occurs to him to do so. But she . . . she'd have known when the realms shifted that I could return. Since I haven't . . ." He shrugged, looking away.

He hurt. She settled herself beside him, careful of his arm. It looked whole beneath the bloody rags of his sleeve, and she knew he healed fast. But she'd seen bone earlier. Surely it wasn't completely healed.

She put her hand on his thigh. "You feel torn in your loyalties."

"If she calls me to her, I'll go," he said quietly. "That hasn't changed, but . . . eh, there's no way to wrap this up in words." He sighed and, oblivious to her worry about his wound, put his arm around her. "It may be I've a choice ahead of me I don't know how to make, but there's no saying when that one will arrive. Calling the Huntsman might hasten it. Or it might not. Your choice is already here, Kai."

I can't let her die. That much was clear, a truth Kai couldn't duck. But she wanted another solution, one that saved the chameleon but didn't draw the attention of Nathan's queen.

One that didn't carry so high a cost, she admitted.

In the corner, the chameleon-cat slept, her mottled coat blending her into the shadows. She'd been beautiful and terrifying in action—built more like a leopard than a lion, only shaggy. She had a lynx's oversize ears and feet, an oddly shaped muzzle, and quiet colors.

Quiet now. During the fight they'd flared in a rage of orange and red, but asleep, her colors softened to a dappled brown, like sun-freckled earth. Her thought-shapes drowsed along in the colors . . . not forming the intricate patterns of human thought, but neither were they beast-simple.

You are so beautiful, she thought. *But what do you want? Who are you?*

The great head lifted, the eyes blinking open. Golden eyes. Even in the shadows, Kai could see they were a brassy gold, like old coins. The thought-shapes stilled, then seemed to struggle. Kai *felt* the struggle as the chameleon tried to answer—felt the creature's need, deep and vital, to be understood. She needed for Kai to know—to know—

"Dell," Kai said, her voice thick with tears. "Her name is Dell, and she trusts me. Call him, Nathan. Call the Huntsman."

CHAPTER 13

THE wind is never gone long in West Texas.

Thirty minutes later, Nathan stood beneath a cloud-hung sky in scrubby dirt that might have once been a yard with that wind tugging at his clothes and hair. Kai was beside him; he doubted she could see at all, for even his vision had trouble picking out details in the darkness.

The chameleon—Dell—had followed, and sat on her haunches on Kai's other side, sniffing the air, unafraid. But she was a night creature, wasn't she? Like him.

His mind was sharp with disbelief. Could his long exile be about to end? *Not yet*, he told himself, which was true, since the Huntsman was unlikely to bring his sister along.

Yet it felt false. Memories crowded him hard, jostling out the nebulous images of what-might-be. He thought of a name, a scent, a face that had once been the dearest in all the worlds to him. The hand that had stroked his head, the voice that had praised him for a good kill.

The Huntsman. After all these years, he would see the Huntsman again . . . but other faces, other scents and names crowded into his head, too. People long dead, those he'd known and liked, some few he'd loved.

And beside him, Kai. Kai.

"Is there anything I should know?" she asked nervously. "I mean, assuming your spell works and he and I understand each other, do I bow, or wait for him to greet me, or shake his hand, or what?"

"Ordinary courtesy will do. The Huntsman has little patience with ceremony. He . . ." Nathan's voice broke. Emotions welled up too strong, too fast, pulling him in too many directions. "He doesn't . . . aieee," he moaned, as the grief of the long-ago sundering rose up as fresh as newly shed blood.

He scarcely noticed when he started weeping, but he felt it clearly when she moved behind him, wrapped her arms around him, and held on. And it was as if at last, at last, someone held him through that first, terrible grief, when he'd nearly gone mad with despair. At last something closed. It could close now, and the raw place inside could begin to heal.

His sobbing died, and he found the stillness inside he'd touched a few times before. Twice, when he stayed with the monks in Tibet. Once when he stood on the edge of suicide and decided not to step off . . . a sensible decision, he'd often thought since, for a hellhound was not easy to kill, and he'd have had the devil of a time making sure of himself.

The cold, arid wind was quickly drying his cheeks. He turned and touched his lips to Kai's forehead. "Love," he said, "is very strange."

And then he faced the night again, and spoke the Huntsman's Name.

KAI heard wind, only wind, yet she saw Nathan's lips move. She knew he'd spoken, but something in her mind refused to hear what he said. But the wind kept rising—blowing harder now, whistling scornfully through her jacket, the cold biting deep.

No. Not just wind. She heard . . . howling.

They came on the darkness, black shapes racing across the black of the sky. Like the darkest of storm clouds they seemed to build, to mount taller rather than draw nearer. Fear, atavistic and complete, numbed her limbs and dried her mouth.

Not Dell's. The chameleon-cat howled back, a wail of fear and defiance. Kai reached for the cat with her hand and her mind, soothing her.

Nathan took her other hand, bent, and whispered, "He likes to make an entrance."

Terror and laughter tangled in her throat, and the choked sound she made was built of both. She held tight to Nathan's hand.

Part of her saw the man come striding down from the sky, his boots as sure on the air as if it were forest floor. Part of her saw him just suddenly *here*—only ten feet away, standing in the ordinary dirt beside a mesquite bush. Him and his hounds. They were black, and many, and varied—some greyhound-lean, some mastiff-strong, all of them tall. And silent. After that howling, they were silent now, and unmoving.

And she hardly noticed them, for she was staring at *him*.

She couldn't have said if he was young or old, tall or short, only that the shape of him was perfectly right. He wore a vest over a hairy chest and rough-sewn trousers tucked into hide boots, with a quiver of arrows slung over his shoulder and a sword at his hip. His skin was brown as a nut, his beard the color of maple leaves after they've faded from flame—still autumn, not winter, but no longer burning. That beard, like his hair, curled madly, with bits of dried grass caught in the tangles.

And his colors—! Rich and warm and earthy, but with

hints of leaf green, the violet of a twilight sky, and arctic white. The thoughts woven through those colors were smooth and somehow complete.

"Nadrellian." His voice was rich as freshly pressed cider, pure as a bell, and it caught on some strong emotion. "Ah, Nadrellian." And he held out his arms.

Nathan took one step, then another, and the Huntsman sprang forward to meet him, and the two men embraced—the Huntsman laughing, then seizing Nathan's face in his two hands and planting a smacking kiss on each cheek. The hounds crowded around them, tails wagging, wanting to greet and be greeted.

After a moment the Huntsman released Nathan, a grin splitting his beard. "Hoy, so this is odd, is it not? To grab you and be grabbed back! What, you won't lick my face now you have hands? Ah, but I've missed you, boy."

Kai heard him. In her mind, she heard and understood him. But her ears heard different sounds, not what her mind reported. She shook her head as if she could shake free of the disconnect that way.

Nathan's laugh rang clear. He rested one hand on the head of a hound who stood hip-high to him. Another hound butted him in the leg, wanting attention. He glanced down fondly. "Ardadamar, where are your manners? And you, sir, claiming you missed me. You've scarcely thought of me."

"No, but I did . . . well." He scratched his ear. "Several times, yes, I did. Is my grief less for being inconstant, eh? I missed you. But why did you call me? You don't need me to come home."

"I've a favor to ask." As the Huntsman's face darkened he added, "And stories for payment. Four hundred years' worth."

"Stories. Well." He fingered his beard, then his gaze shifted. He saw Kai and the beast at her side. He nodded. "Ah. So you called me for this, but it's no favor. How could you think so? Queens' law, boy, and you were wise not to take this hunt on yourself." He reached into thin air—and withdrew a bow.

"What? No," Nathan said. "I'm asking you to return the chameleon to her home."

"Oh, the chameleon. Poor girl. No, she can't be sundered again. The hounds can deal with her, or you can. Better you," he decided. "You'll make it easy on her. But I'll take the binder, don't worry."

"Binder?" Nathan said. His voice came out strangled. He glanced at Kai, emotions skittering across his face and spiking in his colors so fast she couldn't track them—but they ended in horror.

He leaped—made one great, impossible leap, and he landed in front of her. He spun to face the Huntsman, a noise rising from his throat he couldn't have made, deep and inhuman, a growl rising straight from nightmare.

The chameleon sprang to her feet, answering his growl with hers.

Kai thought she might wet her pants. "Nathan?"

The Huntsman stilled and said in a voice too much like Nathan's growl, "You defy me?"

"Mine." Nathan crouched lower, hands out—a fighting posture. "She's Kai, and she's mine."

The Huntsman tilted his head, his eyes narrowing. "Or you are hers. She's a binder, boy. She's caught you."

"She's not. Not a true binder, though I . . . she thinks she's a telepath. I don't know what she is, but she's Kai. I can't let you kill her."

"You can't stop me." All the humor—the fey, Robin Goodfellow pleasantry—fell away, and Kai was looking at death. Beautiful, implacable death was coming for Nathan and for her. The hounds—so friendly a moment ago—spread wide, hackles lifting, heads lowering.

Nathan called out a name.

Kai heard icicles and silence, and silently the air split open in front of them. A woman, all in white, stepped out of that slit in reality. It closed up neatly behind her. She took a single step forward—and Nathan abandoned Kai to reach for his queen, and he held her as she held him, both of them speaking in a liquid roll of syllables that made no echoes of meaning in Kai's head.

Kai stood, stricken and staring. This wasn't the Queen of Winter. She *was* winter.

Her skin was white. Not Caucasian, but truly white—like snow or alabaster or opals, for there was a sheen to it, as if colors played beneath the surface. Her hair was blacker than the hellhounds' midnight fur and spiraled in shiny curls to her waist. Her long, oval face angled in ways no human face would, and her tilted eyes were silver just kissed by blue. Tears spangled those eyes, glistening like melting snow in the lashes and on the white cheeks, as she and Nathan embraced.

She had no colors.

Kai blinked. She focused harder, but still saw none of the colors every living creature possessed. No shapes, intricate or otherwise. No thoughts. No emotions. Nothing. "She's not there," Kai said stupidly.

The queen turned her head, her arm still around Nathan, to look directly at Kai. "Binder." Her voice wasn't bells or flutes or anything Kai had expected. No, it was husky and warm, the welcoming warmth of a fireplace on a winter's night. She spoke English now. Clear, unaccented English. "Did you think I would leave my thoughts dangling free for you to seize?"

"My queen." Nathan inhaled on a shudder and stepped back from her, closer to Kai. "She is not a binder."

Those tilted eyes swung toward him, and the queen spoke gently. "I see what you cannot."

"Yes. But it may be I see what *you* cannot, also."

Her eyebrows lifted. "Nadrellian." She cupped his face in both hands. Her fingers were long and thin and indescribably graceful. "My Nadrellian."

A shudder passed through him. He stared into her eyes, and for several moments neither of them spoke. Finally he said, "I cannot step aside. She is mine."

Kai didn't know if it was courage or ego or simple stupidity pushing her, but she couldn't keep still any longer. "*She* has a name and a voice, and I was raised to think it's rude to discuss people as if they weren't present when they are. Especially if you're talking about killing them."

The queen laughed. "So we are," she said agreeably. And a knife winged through the air, heading straight for Kai.

Nathan's hand slapped out, knocking it aside.

The queen glanced over her shoulder at the Huntsman. *"Iss'athl,"* she said—two precisely inflected syllables that echoed in Kai's mind as something like "lively and clever idiot." "Control yourself."

"She lacks respect."

"She's human." The queen moved around Nathan to study Kai, her gaze traveling up and down. "Mostly human."

Mostly?

The queen stretched out a hand to one side. The chameleon, who had been oddly still until that moment, inched forward to sniff those white fingers, then lick them. "I will discuss your fate with you, then, Kai Tallman Michalski. How did you bring Dell to you?"

"I . . ." Kai licked dry lips. Now that she had the chance to speak, it was hard to do so. Those eyes . . . "I didn't, exactly. I was sleeping, and she asked . . . I don't know how to say it because there weren't words, nothing like words. But she was so alone, and she hurt. I said yes, and just— I fit her in, or she came in."

"She asked?"

"I told you," Nathan said. "Kai is not a binder. She sees thoughts, but doesn't—"

"Hush," the queen said absently. She tipped her head to one side. In that moment, curious and alert, she looked about twenty. "I would examine you. For that, I need your permission. You do not have a wide spectrum of choices, since if you refuse I must let my brother kill you. But still, you have this choice. I will not undertake such an invasion without your consent."

Kai's head buzzed with questions, a dizzying mass of questions. She couldn't speak them. Somehow the words wouldn't form, not while she stood beneath the gaze of this ancient power. "May I talk to Nathan?"

"Nai-thann." She made the syllables longer, more weighted, and turned her head to smile at him. "It was a good choice, that name. Are you Naithann now?"

"As much as I know what I am, yes."

"Very well." The queen nodded and stepped back. "You may speak with Naithann."

CHAPTER 14

NATHAN turned and gripped her arms. "Kai. I didn't know—I never guessed . . . let me hold you. Let me hold you a moment." But he didn't wait for permission, just wrapped himself around her. Gradually his ragged breathing eased.

So did hers. "Okay," she said into his shoulder. She dragged in one more long, uncertain breath and lifted her head to look at him. "Okay. What is a binder, and why does everyone think I am one?"

"They see your energy, your Gift. I don't have that vision, so I can't say what they are seeing, but . . . the chameleon, Kai. You tied her to you. She asked. You didn't force her, but you . . . it didn't occur to me because you're so whole, but this is a thing a binder does."

She swallowed. He thought she was a binder, too. He just didn't want to. "So what is a binder?"

"A rare type of telepath who tampers with others' thoughts, binds their will. They are terribly dangerous, because so few can guard against them. Queens' law calls for . . . it is death to be a binder."

Kai had heard of blood running cold. She'd never experienced it until that moment, and didn't like it at all. When in fugue she *could* tamper with thoughts. She even wanted to, because some patterns were so sad and wrong . . .

"No, Kai," he said firmly, as if he were the telepath, not her. "Binders are warped. They are moral infants who understand only their own needs, their own wants. You aren't like that."

"I'm not like a regular telepath, either." Not that there was much regular about telepathy, but—oh, God. These people wanted to *kill* her—not for anything she'd done, but for what she might do.

She had to think. Kai squeezed her eyes closed and tried. "This examination she wants to give me . . . it's not a true-false quiz."

"No. It can be—almost surely will be—painful. She has entry to me because of our bond, but to find the truth of you she'll have to force her way in. If . . ." He ran his hands down her arms to take her hands. "If she finds what I know is true, Kai—that you don't tamper with others' will—she might not kill you."

Kai licked her lips. "I was hoping for something more certain, like she *won't* kill me."

"She won't," the Huntsman said matter-of-factly. "I will." He squatted beside Dell, scratching behind her ears. The big cat purred for him. "Nadrellian—no, it's Nathan now. I need to remember that. Did you know Dell was a mage's familiar?" He snorted. "Illegal in several realms, to take a chameleon for a familiar, but not a violation of Queens' law. But that's why Dell needed the connection, the communication, so much. Why she knew how to find it, too. When the power winds blew, her master . . . who seems to have been an idiot," he added, giving Dell's chin a good rub, "wasn't he, girl? He was killed, and she was blown here."

"The power wind blew in Dell's realm, too?" Kai asked, startled.

His eyebrows jumped in astonishment. "Everywhere, girl. The realms all shifted, so the winds blew everywhere." His voice softened in what sounded like sympathy. "I kill much cleaner than Winter does, you know."

If he meant that for comfort, he failed. She looked up at Nathan. "You said few beings can kill a hellhound. I'm guessing we've got at least two here who could manage it."

Reluctantly he nodded.

"All right, then." She straightened. "You are not to throw your life away— No, listen to me." She gripped his shoulders. "I always knew I had you for only a time. Maybe that time will turn out to be the rest of my life." The joke fell flat. Her fingers tightened. "I don't want you dead, you hear me?"

"I hear." This smile was so sad it brought tears to her eyes. "But love doesn't give you the right to be making my decisions."

Love. This was the second time he'd spoken the word, and neither moment had been ripe for declarations. But . . . "I do love you. I think you know that, but just in case . . . I love you." She blinked quickly. Dammit, she would not cry. She didn't have time for it. "My choices seem to lie between death now and a chance that maybe none of us will die. So yes," she said, turning to the queen who waited with the stillness of ice. "Yes, you have my consent."

The queen glided up to her. "Hold her, Nathan."

"I don't need to be restrained."

"It's for your comfort, child. And his." In those silver eyes Kai saw a sadness eerily like she'd seen in Nathan's a moment ago. "I offered you a choice, but Winter's choices are always hard."

Nathan moved behind her and wrapped his arms around her. The queen placed her hands on Kai's face, one on each side, and Kai had a moment to think how normal they felt—dry and a little cooler than human, but they were just hands.

Then a scream of white sliced her open.

KAI came back to herself slowly, her head splitting, her mind wholly befuddled. Beneath her aching head, softness . . . ah, her mother's lap, and her mother was humming an old lullaby, one she hadn't heard in so long. . . .

No. Not her mother. Kai's eyes opened.

She lay on the ground with her head pillowed on warm fur that rose and fell in a slow, sleeping rhythm. Dell. It was the Queen of Winter who was humming the wordless tune Sitsi Tallman Michalski used to croon to her daughter when Kai was ill or troubled by night fears.

A tune she'd stolen straight from Kai's mind. Kai started to jerk up—and fell back, groaning. Dell gave a protesting grunt.

"Shh. Give yourself a moment. The pain will fade soon." One of those deceptively normal hands reached out to stroke her temple, and the pain receded. "I would like to meet your grandfather. Perhaps Coyote will introduce us."

"I don't think . . ." But maybe Grandfather did know Coyote. How could she say? He didn't talk about his spirit guides. Maybe he had daily conversations with the trickster god. "I don't think he has a high opinion of Coyote," she said, amending her original thought. "Maybe you should ask Changing Woman or First Man."

Perfect eyebrows arched up. "You are indeed feeling better if you can argue with me."

Kai sat up, moving slowly this time. Her head pounded, but it was no more than an ordinary headache now, and already her memory of what had happened was fading. The examination had taken her to every significant event in her life connected with her Gift . . . at once. Every memory, even those she could have sworn she didn't possess. She'd been a baby when her Gift was suppressed. How could she have any memory of that? But she'd gone there, and to so many others, all of them laid open to an overwhelming and intimate presence.

Nathan sat cross-legged nearby, his face cleaned of expression, unreadable. Behind him approaching dawn banded the sky in shades of gray, with the widest band the same steel as his eyes.

Dawn. Dawn was near, lifting the blackness. She'd been . . . away . . . longer than she'd realized. She searched Nathan's eyes for the answer she needed.

He invented smiles again. This one arrived as fresh as the dawn behind him—a smile holding hints of tomorrow and tomorrow and tomorrow.

Her eyes stung. "She isn't going to kill me."

"No, and nor is the Huntsman. But you may not like the solution she's found."

The Huntsman. Kai looked around, but he was nowhere in sight.

"My brother's a restless sort," the queen said, rising fluidly to her feet. "He's off to other hunts, or possibly to sleep. Dell remains yours," she added, looking down at Kai. "That was her choice. But you can't remain here."

Kai scrambled to her feet. "What do you mean?"

"I've decided on a testing. You have three quests to perform, Kai Tallman Michalski." The rich voice deepened, seeming to echo in the still air. "Three quests that will take you far from this realm, where none can defend against you. You will be allowed to prove yourself and find the true nature of your Gift. Do not suppress it any longer, or it will take you over."

"I don't—"

"The fugue, child. What you call fugue. You must learn to use your Gift fully." Solemnity dropped from her as suddenly as it had arrived. She made a little huff of sound, exasperated. "Human-sidhe mixes produce the oddest results sometimes."

"I'm not sidhe!"

"Only a little, true, but that little has had quite an effect. Nathan was correct when he said you weren't a binder, but neither are you precisely *not* a binder. Your Gift is unlike any I've seen." She turned to Nathan and held out her hands, smiling.

He rose and took them. "It is very strange to get what I've needed for so long, and what I wanted even more, and find I was wrong about the one."

"And right about the other." There followed more of those liquid syllables that had no meaning for Kai.

Nathan chuckled. "Fare thee well, my queen."

"And thee, my hound." She dropped his hands, turned, and a slit opened in the air before her. But she paused to glance over her shoulder, a spark of glee in those silvery eyes. This time she looked about ten, and full of mischief. "Do not worry about your grandfather, Kai. I will explain to him. Nor will the police chief trouble you again."

"But what—"

She was gone.

NATHAN felt the queen leave as clearly as he saw it. Yet she wasn't fully absent, not as she had been for all the long years of separation. She had come when he called—come the second he called her, leaving her court, the press of duty and love and need and laughter there. She had come.

As he would go to her if she called. That had always been true. But now he knew that she, too, would come to him.

Yesterday he hadn't known he needed that. Today he did.

"Did you think," she'd said, *"I'd gone through all the grief of setting you free—and put you through it, too—only so I could force you back into shapes of body and*

mind no longer yours? You are still my hound, as I am your queen. But now you are your own, as well."

Today many things were clear to him. He'd been foolish. He could see that now—how foolish he'd been in thinking the queen hadn't known from the moment she sent him here that by the time he could return, he would no longer need to.

He went to Kai and slid an arm around her waist. "Are you . . ." "Okay" wasn't the right word. What was? She'd be struggling—her life nearly lost, then saved, and now overturned. "Unbearably confused," he finished, "or simply overwhelmed?"

"Yes! Yes and yes." She laughed, or choked—the sound held both. "I'm to leave? To leave Earth?"

"Yes." He pressed his face into her hair and breathed her in. "I'm sorry. Probably not forever, but the leaving is hard. At least we'll have a little time to gather supplies first."

"We?"

"Kai." He smoothed her hair back from her face. "Of course. You and I and that great cat of yours will go together, since she couldn't stand to be parted from you, either."

"I thought . . . you love the queen so much. You've missed her and your home so much. And she clearly loves you."

"I do, and she does, but I've loved many over the years, and in many different ways. She isn't mine, Kai. Not as you are." Words. He would have hated losing speech, but words didn't come easily. How to put this feeling, this certainty, into something as limited as words?

He looked at her beautiful face, so uncertain, and finally found the question in her heart. "Eh. You want to know . . . but of course I love you. I am yours as much as you are mine. That's what I wasn't saying, isn't it?"

She laughed and kissed him and hugged him hard. "Yes. Yes, it is. You are such a *man.*"

That was the word for him, he realized, happy. He wasn't fully human, nor truly hound. He was sidhe—wild sidhe—and he was a man.

Kai and Nathan's story will be continued in Eileen Wilks's next lupi book . . .

Night Season

Buying Trouble

KAREN CHANCE

CHAPTER 1

I saw him across the crowded room. He was standing behind a couple of werewolves and a large troll. One of the Weres was knocking snow off his boots while the other attempted to hand his overcoat to the troll, who was serving as greeter. Since in troll terms that involved stomping on potential troublemakers before they got in the door, then throwing them out on their asses, he wasn't getting very far. The Weres finally figured that out and walked away grumbling.

The other new arrival kept his floor-length cloak on. Of course, he probably had more than one reason for that. The hood was up, so I couldn't see his face, but from underneath the cape spilled a faint nimbus of gold. There aren't too many creatures who cast light shadows, and of those, only one would have any reason to be visiting Brooklyn's seediest occult auction house.

He wasn't here to shop. He was here for me.

I whirled and started for the door to the employees-only area, but a large body in a too-small tux blocked my way. "Claire."

"Matt." I tried to move around him, but he managed to

entirely fill the doorway. If he ever stopped those compulsive gym visits, he'd have to start edging in sideways.

"Where do you think you're going?" The soprano voice out of the gorilla-size chest was always a surprise.

"To the bathroom. My contacts are killing me."

Matt fished my glasses off the top of my head and settled them on my nose. "Suffering builds character."

"I have enough character, thanks." I glanced back over my shoulder. "Matt, please! I need to—"

"Start earning your paycheck, I agree." His small brown eyes flickered here and there nervously as if he knew trouble was about to break out, but wasn't sure of the direction. Considering what was up for sale tonight, he was probably right. "I'd feel better having you closer than the back rooms. We got a lot of volatile stuff here."

I wondered if he meant the customers or the merchandise. Either way, I couldn't appeal to a higher power. Despite the overuse of steroids and the bad crew cut, Matt wasn't a bouncer in a dive on the wrong side of town. He was old man Gerald's darling only son and, since his dad was away on a buying trip, my boss.

"Anything goes nuts and my ass is grass. Dad'll have me cleaning the stockroom for the next decade, and who's gonna pay you under the table then?"

I had a good comeback about just how little he paid me, but it died on my lips. The sight of the gray cloak weaving its way across the room occupied all my attention. There was nothing menacing about it, unless you knew what was underneath.

Except for the fact that it was coming straight at me.

I let Matt maneuver me to the front of the main salon, since his bulk insured that we'd move faster through the crush of bodies than I could have alone. We stopped in front of a semicircle of marble plinths that held the evening's wares. None of tonight's items had been available for preview, which explained the pre-auction crowd. Some were of dubious origin and I don't think Gerald had wanted anyone to examine them too closely before the sale. But others were simply too dangerous to have on display without a major safety precaution. Unfortunately for my plans to cut and run, that happened to be me.

Matt positioned me at center stage, up a short flight of steps from the throng of customers. There had been quite a few people on the platform, despite the attempts of the two trolls stationed at each end to keep it clear. The trolls didn't look happy. They were under orders not to break anyone in two or crack any heads open, which kind of limited their persuasive abilities. But, as usual, my appearance cleared the place faster than a gas leak.

"That's better." Matt surveyed the empty platform with satisfaction.

"You could put up the wards," I pointed out desperately. The plinths were usually surrounded by magical shields, only they don't work so well with me around.

"I don't trust the wards, especially not tonight," Matt said irritably. "What's the matter with you?" His tiny eyes scanned the salon, but there were too many people—and assorted other things—in the way for him to notice my particular problem. And I wasn't planning to tell him. He only paid me a fraction of what I was worth, but a fraction is better than nothing. And until I sorted out some personal issues, this was the only income I had. Freaking Matt out would be extremely bad for my dwindling bank account. And maybe I was wrong. Maybe a Lord of the Light Fey was suddenly interested in acquiring a moldy old talisman of dubious provenance, for which he'd be expected to pay a premium price.

Yeah, right.

"Nothing."

"Okay, then." Matt did one more scan of the room. "I need to keep an eye on the Weres. You think you can manage to stand here and stay out of trouble?"

"Well . . . I can stand here." I didn't have much choice considering that the Fey was between me and the exits.

Matt rolled his eyes and moved off to crowd the two werewolves. I thought that was less than smart. It was another week until the full moon, but they were already vibrating with repressed energy and spoiling for a fight. But it was his call, and I had my own problems: while I'd been distracted, the Fey had disappeared.

I thought for a second that I spotted him trying to meld with the shadows in a corner, but a second glance told me that it was only one of the banshees that the house used as security alarms. I scanned the room again, but it was no use. The Fey was simply gone, and I didn't intend to wait around for him to show up. For once, Matt was going to have to make do without me.

I turned on my heel and pelted down the back stairs of the platform, intending to try for the fire exit, but something was in my way. I crashed into a broad, hard chest, and would have gone sprawling if someone hadn't caught my shoulder. My glasses fell to the tip of my nose and a hand pushed them back up. A very attractive hand, I noticed as sight returned, strong and sun-bronzed. It was attached to an equally beautiful arm, all slender muscles under a silken sleeve, and led to a very handsome face. A face with a slight smile curving its sensual lips and an amused glint in eyes the color of a glacier's heart—a pure, crystalline blue.

Oh, crap.

He stood at the bottom of the stairs, but I still had to look up to meet those eyes. That wouldn't have been true for many men—I'm almost six feet tall—and the step I was balancing on added another few inches. But then, he wasn't a man.

The Fey looked me over as he set me back on my feet. Despite my best efforts, his nearness made me shiver and a broader smile broke over his face. I adjusted a strap on my dress and tried not to let my panic show. Gerald & Company requires formal dress for important sales as a way of letting potential buyers know in advance not to expect any bargains, and I'd thought I looked pretty good. My usually frizzy red mane had been tamed by almost an hour with a curling iron and my moss green gown, while not exactly couture, had once been expensive. Now I was wishing I'd blackened my front teeth or, better yet, called in sick.

"Do you know," he told me, a thread of delight running through his voice, "I'm beginning to think this evening might not be as dull as I'd imagined."

I told myself to pull back, to get some maneuvering room, but my body wasn't listening. There was no slowly building passion, no steadily mounting desire as might have been true with a handsome man. Instead, the attraction was instantaneous and so overwhelming that it left me light-headed. I simply wanted him, so much that I had to fight not to throw myself back into his arms.

Of all the things I hate about the Fey, number one is the way they make my body react. I first encountered them when I was sixteen. Father had invited a delegation to visit the family estate, and I was expected to help entertain. Instead, I dropped things all through dinner, unable to keep my mind on what I was doing with my body suddenly going haywire. Their leader had been especially unnerving, with ancient silver eyes and hair as bright as water in sunlight. I'd been fascinated by the way it cascaded over his shoulders, a platinum waterfall that carved tiny prisms from the light whenever he moved. But my admiration had faded fast when he turned to Father and, without altering the polite, bland expression he'd worn all evening, asked if perhaps I was ill, to be so clumsy. Father had laughed off the insult, but I'd been mortified.

Of course, if I'd known why they were there, I'd have shown up for dinner cross-eyed and twitching.

The Fey slid one hand around my waist, drawing me

against a body that felt like sun-warmed steel. He used his free hand to produce the evening's catalogue from under the cloak and flipped it open. He perused a page, then looked down at me again. "You aren't listed."

"What?"

"It's not surprising, considering the treaty," he continued. "When are we to have the pleasure of bidding on you?"

I could feel my cheeks flush, something that, with my complexion, was probably all too obvious. I closed my eyes and with a sudden movement, wrenched away. I smoothed my rumpled gown with slightly shaking hands and glared at him. "Bite me."

I caught a gleam in those odd eyes. "Right here?"

Of all the things I hate about the Fey, number two would definitely be their sense of humor.

Suddenly, anger started to override fear. I wasn't sixteen anymore, and Gerald & Company employed plenty of guards. Not that they'd bothered to furnish me with one—ordinarily, no magical creature wanted to get close enough to give me trouble—but there were more than enough posted around the room to deal with even a Fey. And considering how well the Dark and Light Fey got along, I thought the trolls might even thank me for the excuse.

I looked around for security, but they'd been distracted by the trouble Matt was having. I hadn't seen what started it, but one of the Weres had attacked the leader of the security team and seemed to be trying to gnaw through its knobby forearm. The troll looked at him in understandable bemusement—their skin is approximately the thickness of rawhide—then snapped his arm, throwing the Were across the room. He hit the far wall with an audible thump before slowly sliding to the floor, leaving a big red mark on the gold-embossed wallpaper.

One of the trolls who usually flanked the stage had moved to assist with the fight, and the other was too preoccupied to notice me. I dodged behind the old couple he was watching through narrow, beady eyes. They'd braved my presence to check out one of the items for sale—a small, gray rune stone sitting in solitary splendor on a black velvet cushion. It was the only thing on the plinth, so I assumed it had to be important, but the description in the catalogue had been unusually vague, just a photo and a date in the tenth century.

"I still say it's a fake," the woman sniffed.

"But what if it isn't?" The man looked at it longingly. "One of the Runes of Langgarn—"

The woman gave what could only be called a snort. "Gerald is bad enough, but I don't trust that son of his at all. I'm telling you, it's not real." She caught sight of me and the usual expression of distaste passed over her features before she could mask it. She nudged her companion. "Let's go."

He ignored her. He was staring at the rune almost as if hypnotized, and before I could stop him, he put out a hand as if to actually touch it. The banshee went off like a hundred police sirens, screeching an alarm that cut through every other sound like a knife. Red lights bathed the stage, and the man quickly found himself dangling from the hand of a very large troll.

"No touching!" the troll bellowed, giving him a little shake. It sent the man's head snapping back and forth hard enough to cause whiplash, but he never took his eyes off the stone. Not, that is, until the troll threw him over his shoulder and carted him off somewhere. The woman had already fled, leaving the platform clear again, except for me and the Fey.

It quickly became obvious that I was on my own. Except for me, Matt and the trolls, the only employees on duty that night were a cadre of vampires. They were on loan from Antonio, their master, a Philadelphia mob boss who was one of the business's shady backers. They were a cynical, vicious bunch who seemed to resent having to work for Gerald even more than I did. One was watching me now, a short, ugly brute with a smirk on his lopsided features. The only other time I'd seen him smile was when he "accidentally" smashed a troll into a brick wall with a five-ton forklift. I didn't bother to ask for his help.

Before I could come up with an alternative, a surprisingly calloused hand engulfed mine. The earlier shock of the Fey's touch was back, all the more powerful against my bare skin. The feeling was nothing like the electric tingle of being near a mage. The static surge when my power meets that of a strong magic user often hurts, especially if the mage in question is deliberately trying to test me. I didn't feel a challenge here, but he was definitely doing something.

Outwardly, it probably looked like he was merely standing there, holding my hand. But I could feel his power all around me, questing, searching, trying to discover my secrets. My anger returned big-time. He wanted to know my secret? I'd be happy to show him.

It felt very weird to deliberately call up my power. Normally, I spend my time tamping it down, trying not to drain every mage I meet. Even my work at Gerald's rarely requires an actual application of strength. Normally, the slight damping field I naturally exude is enough to calm down whatever trinket their scouts have dug up. But now I focused on the Fey's bright blue aura and pulled.

Nothing happened.

I tried again. Zilch. I stared at him in disbelief. I once had a mage tell me that I had no visible aura, just a black hole that radiated outward, trying to suck his magic away. He'd been drunk and none too happy with me at the time, so I'd never known if it was true, but magical creatures certainly acted like it. And that was when I wasn't trying.

"Interesting," the Fey murmured after a moment, drawing me closer. What felt like a metaphysical hand stroked down the length of my body, causing me to shudder. "I've never encountered anyone quite like you."

I could second that emotion. The Fey I'd met before hadn't been as susceptible to my abilities as mages, because their magic works differently from the human variety. But they had definitely felt something. So why didn't he?

"Let me go," I told him, suppressing another shiver. My body was trying to melt against him even as my brain was torn between panic and outrage. I don't think I sounded too convincing.

"Tell me what you are and I will. I like to know what I'm bidding on."

"I'm not part of the auction!"

I noticed that Matt had rounded up the Weres. The unconscious one had been tucked under a troll's huge arm, while the other was dangling from the creature's free hand by his collar. The Were's face was alarmingly red and his eyes were bulging, but they were a hardy breed. He'd get thrown out before he actually choked to death. Probably.

Matt gave me a thumbs-up signal from beside the door, and pointed at his watch. I nodded. It was almost showtime. "If you'll excuse me," I said stiffly, "I have a job to do."

"A job?" The Fey sounded like he didn't understand the term.

"Yes, a job. You know, work? For which I am paid?" After a pause, he released me and stepped back. The room was more than adequately heated, but I suddenly felt cold. I hit the button to start the night's events with a little more force than absolutely necessary.

The lights dimmed even further out on the floor, causing an upsurge in conversation, while those over the plinths glowed brighter. The Fey moved aside as the huge, dragon's-head podium rose out of the floor and into place. It was supposedly the real deal, killed, stuffed and mounted by Gerald's father—or so he claimed. Its fake glass eyes surveyed the room with their usual malevolence, its snout curled into an expression of disdain.

It didn't look like something that had been killed in the

heat of battle to me. More likely, Gerald senior had caught it napping and lopped the head off before it was fully awake, assuming it wasn't a clever fake. Gerald's sold some genuinely valuable pieces, but *caveat emptor* was definitely the house motto. The general feeling was that anyone dumb enough to buy the magical equivalent of snake oil deserved what he got.

The Fey came around the side of the huge head. "You're part of the auction staff?" He sounded surprised. I suppose that was fair—Gerald wasn't in the habit of hiring people who couldn't take care of themselves, and I guess I looked fairly harmless.

Looks can be deceiving.

I waited until a crescendo of canned music and the automated voice-over announcing the imminent start of bidding ended. Then I pointed at the nearest plinth. "Do you know what that is?"

He surveyed the small, quivering box on top of the marble stand for a beat. "No."

"It's a djinn. A very old, very pissed off one. Gerald recently acquired it from the estate of the mage who trapped it. Only the spell he put on the container is deteriorating now that he's dead, and if it goes altogether before they can unload it, he's likely to take out half the block."

The box gave a leap as if it had heard me, and almost managed to jump off its plinth. I gingerly sat it back where it belonged, and it quieted down. For the moment.

"How does your presence prevent that?" the Fey asked, sounding bemused.

I stopped looking for the gavel, which Matt had mislaid somewhere as usual, to stare at him in surprise. "You don't know?"

"Why would I ask if I did?"

"I'm a projective null," I told him slowly. What possible reason could he have for faking ignorance? If he was here for me, he certainly knew what he was getting. And if he wasn't, why would he have come?

"You can block magic?" His expression suddenly became a lot more intense.

"For a certain radius. I'm here to make sure nothing blows up in a customer's face." I smiled at him sweetly. "At least, not before they can pay."

"How much of a radius?" His voice had lost its teasing tone, and was now all business.

I glared at him. I knew it. For all their magical strength, the Fey had never produced a null, a fact that seemed to rankle. They'd been looking for a way to add that particular gift to their magical arsenal for some time, but with so few nulls to choose from, and most of them too weak to do more than disrupt a ward now and then, their hunt had been frustrating. Until they found me.

Father's dinner guests had offered him a deal that he could have refused; instead, he jumped on it like a starving dog does a bone. It must have seemed perfect: a chance to get rid of an unwanted burden—and a constant reminder of his wife's preference for red hair—and get paid handsomely to boot. Too bad for him that I was tipped off.

Great-Uncle Pip had always had a soft spot for the one person who didn't treat him like an idiot child. By the time the deal was finalized, he'd insured that I was nowhere to be found. And no one hides better than a null. The usual tracking spells are useless on us; we simply don't register, not even as a norm—and I can walk through most wards as if they aren't even there. The Fey did not take my disappearance well. The nobles who had intended to escort me into slavery in Faerie instead took back Father's head.

I pushed the memories away and pointed to a spot off the side of the stage. It was where the auction assistants usually stood to bring out new items for bidding. Since everything for sale tonight was already in place, no one was likely to be coming or going. "You can stand over there. We can talk after the sale." Assuming he could grab me before I managed to slip away in the mass exodus.

Matt lumbered up beside us. He was sweating despite the temperature, and his collar appeared to be eating into his thick neck. "Bidders aren't allowed on stage, sir," he told the Fey with fake bonhomie. "Perhaps you would like to take a place in front?"

"What I would like—" the Fey began, but I cut him off with a curse. For the second time that night, someone came through the main doors I really didn't want to see. In fact, I'd have preferred a whole room full of Fey to the sight of that narrow, smirking face.

CHAPTER 2

"WHAT'S wrong?" Matt's head whipped around. He scanned the plinths with anxious eyes, but I wasn't looking at them.

I gripped his arm. "It's Seb!" I pointed to where a tall, elegant figure in a dove gray suit had just entered, surrounded by no fewer than eight bodyguards.

"What?" Matt's eyes practically crossed, trying to take in the whole room at once.

I smacked his arm. "Sebastian! My cousin!"

I turned to run, but Matt's big paw descended on the back of my neck. "You can't leave. We're about to start."

"Didn't you hear me?" I asked furiously. "He isn't here to say hello!" Matt's hand didn't budge. "If I'm dead, I can't keep anything from going haywire," I pointed out.

"He's not here to kill you." Matt suddenly looked much calmer. A minute before, he'd been heading for a stroke; now his flushed face wore an expression of smug satisfaction that sent my own blood pressure skyrocketing.

"And you know this how?"

Matt shrugged. "I'm surprised you didn't notice. There's only twelve plinths, Claire."

It took a second to register, then the words hit home. Despite selling fakes whenever he could get his hands on one, Gerald was a superstitious old coot. He knew better than anyone that some of his merchandise was the real deal, and a witch had told him that selling them in lots of thirteen would be an added safety precaution. I hadn't noticed the omission tonight, but I should have. I'd been so worried about the sudden appearance of the Fey that I'd forgotten—they weren't the main reason I was in hiding.

"You're planning to sell me?" My voice went up an octave and Matt winced.

"I didn't have a choice," he said defensively. "Sebastian's boys tracked you down a couple days ago. I could have handed you over then, but I figured you might do better in an auction. So I told your cousin to show up tonight if he wanted you. Looks like he does."

Seb was staring at me, a little smile curving his thin lips. Match point, he mouthed.

Like hell.

"Matt! What do you think Seb will do with me if he wins?"

"He said something about the family business being tied up so one heir gets it all, and the rest are out of luck."

"And did he happen to mention what they do with the losers?" I almost screamed.

"I guess he forgot that part." It was pretty clear that Matt didn't give a damn. His own inheritance rested on keeping his father happy and showing a profit. What happened after the sale wasn't his problem, a fact he demonstrated by chaining me to the podium.

"I'll kill you," I promised as the manacle snapped shut around my wrist.

Matt laughed. "You're a null, Claire. You couldn't do a

spell to save your life! Now settle down and don't make a fuss."

"You have no idea what kind of a fuss I'm about to make."

Matt didn't bother to reply. He started the bidding on the first item, keeping me for last. Practical. I'd be there to keep the peace until the other items were carried away by successful bidders. Then it would be my turn, unless I could figure a way out of this before then.

I looked around, trying to crush down my rising panic. For a minute, I thought the Fey had gone, then I spotted him propping up the wall just offstage. No help there. Matt must have called him in to give Seb some competition, and run the price up.

After a fierce bidding war, the djinn was sold to a tiny old woman swathed in black silk and pearls the size of cherries. She placidly stowed him in her huge purse, showing no sign of worry about her acquisition. Either she was barking mad, or she was a powerful witch. Considering that she kept well away from me, I was betting on the latter.

Matt started the bidding on the next lot, a nail supposedly taken from the True Cross and said to give the possessor a leg up in battle. As it had been brought back from the Holy Land by a knight of the Second Crusade—which had been a miserable failure by any standards—I was a little dubious. It seemed the rest of the room agreed, because bidding was sluggish and the reserve wasn't met.

Matt quickly passed on to item number three, not wanting to lose momentum. I barely heard him describing the history behind the small fragment of parchment because Seb had moved to the bottom of the steps, his bodyguards having pushed a path through the crowd for him. He usually maintains the air of pompous gravity he thinks is appropriate for the head of one of America's foremost magical houses, but tonight his expression was gleeful.

"How old are you again, Claire?" he asked, taking out a

calculator. "I ask because I have an offer from a couple of Harvesters. And age does make a difference, you know."

I glowered at him, but refused to be baited. Harvesting was what nulls of any strength spend their lives fearing, and I wouldn't give him the satisfaction of seeing me lose it. But inwardly, I wasn't doing so good.

Around the year 900, a mage figured out how to siphon away our energy, and thereby our lives, to make bombs capable of bringing all magic in an area to a standstill. How far and how long the effect extends depends on the strength of the null being sacrificed—the younger and more powerful they are, the more energy they have to give. After the process was discovered, it became fashionable to hunt us, especially in the vampire community, although some mages did it, too. Null harvesting, as it's politely called, was outlawed shortly after the practice began, but the law had less to do with stopping the hunts than the meager quality of the nulls remaining by the Renaissance. Harvesters ran themselves out of business by being too good at their job, not that there weren't a few enterprising types still trying.

"Twenty-two, isn't it?" Seb's nimble fingers ran some calculations with the ease of a trained bean counter, which is what he'd been before father's late, unlamented demise.

"Rot in hell."

"It's too bad we didn't find you earlier. Late teens are optimal for top offers, but I'm sure we'll find someone to take you."

He wandered off as Matt gave up trying to convince anyone that the parchment contained part of one of Merlin's lost spells. The bidding started on item number four, a genuine, if somewhat tattered, grimoire from ancient Egypt. Matt was trying to sell the idea that the papyrus scroll had been part of the library of Alexandria, rescued by a daring priest before the Romans burnt it to the ground. He wasn't doing that great. He lacked his dad's genuine appreciation for the merchandise he handled and it showed.

All Matt cared about was making a buck, and his fake smiles and gushing descriptions were putting people off. But in this case, there was a flurry of bidding nonetheless. Anything from Egypt always went over well.

I was waiting for lot number six, a small birdcage covered by a white cloth. It was pretty much my only shot, now that the old lady had gone off with the djinn. Occasional scratches could be heard from inside, but nothing more distinct. That wasn't surprising since I'd personally seen a handler, with a heavy scarf wrapped around his head, fitting the small creature within with a specially made muzzle. They weren't worried about its bite; in this case, the bark really was far worse.

The cage was sitting on the stand closest to me and the chain on my manacle stretched far enough to reach it. What I couldn't figure out was how to get the latch open and the muzzle off before being pounced on by the trolls. The two guards were back in place at either side of the stage, and although they don't move very fast, they weren't more than six yards away. I'd never make it.

I'd barely had the thought when the front door burst open in a swirl of snow. The Weres were back, and they'd brought friends. In fact, it looked like their whole pack had decided to teach Matt a few much-needed manners. As soon as the trolls moved to intercept, I lunged for the cage.

My fingers had just brushed it when Matt caught me around the waist from behind. "Don't even think about it!" he roared over the sound of the Weres and trolls crashing into each other.

The cage wobbled slightly, then settled back into place with a final sounding thump. Matt started dragging me backward toward the podium. There was nothing I could do—my power only works on magical creatures and Matt, like his old man, was garden-variety human. He had no magic to steal.

As I started kicking him in his oversize calves, more to

take out my frustration than in any hope of escape, the Fey appeared behind the plinth. I stared at him, and he dropped me a wink. I was still trying to absorb that when he flipped open the cage door, allowing the tiny brown bird inside to flutter out. Then a late-arriving troll crashed into him and they both went over the back of the stage.

Instead of flying away, the bird started flitting in circles around my head. Matt saw it and squeaked something rude before releasing me and snatching up a net from inside the podium. He took a swipe at the bird, but it dodged with an arrogant flip of its tiny wings. He tried again, but it moved at the last second in an almost calculated gesture. Unable to redirect his bulk in time, Matt went barreling down the steps to crash into a group of Sebastian's men, scattering them like bowling pins. I smashed my palm down on the release button on the podium, springing the manacle open, and slid my wrist free, but several of Seb's remaining thugs were there before I could so much as take a step.

"Leaving early, Claire? And you the main attraction." Sebastian mounted the steps slowly, his dignity back in place despite the pandemonium. I suppose he thought he was safe, surrounded by the rapidly re-forming posse, but for once his optimism was misplaced.

A nearby Were snatched up one of the gold, satin-striped chairs usually provided for bidders that had been shoved to the side tonight to accommodate the throng. He threw it at the head of a troll who was rhythmically smashing one of his pack member's faces into the side of the steps. He missed his target, but he didn't miss Seb.

One of my guards moved to help his felled boss and the other only had me by one arm. He didn't look too bright, but he made up for it in muscle. His suit bulged even more alarmingly than Matt's, to the point that I expected to see him burst out of it like the Hulk at any moment. He was a norm, brought along as cannon fodder in case of an emergency, to buy time for the mages in the group to hustle the boss out of danger. He obviously didn't view me as a threat, which in his case was pretty accurate. At least until the little bird fluttered down onto the dragon's nose and looked at me inquiringly.

It wasn't easy getting the muzzle off one-handed, but I managed it. "You're lazy and stupid, and nobody thinks you're tough," the gamelan told my guard. "And you look ridiculous in that suit."

The guard collapsed to his knees, holding his ears and shrieking. Gamelans don't merely speak the truth, they rip away all the happy little lies we tell ourselves to mask it, forcing us to acknowledge it deep in our very souls. They make us face the raw facts about our lives, and most of the time, they're not pretty.

Seb had gotten back to his feet, but he took one look at the feathered menace and stumbled back a step. It seemed he'd read the catalogue. Unfortunately for him, he was trapped by his own guards, who had formed a line to hold off the mad brawl the salon had become. "You have no talent for business, and three of your relatives are planning to kill you," the bird informed him, raising its high, thin voice to be heard over the noise. "Oh, and one of them is sleeping with your mistress."

Seb screamed and started clawing at his guards, desperate to get away before he heard any more. But the bird had lost interest in him. I eyed it with apprehension as it sized me up out of one bright black eye. "Your father never loved you, and he wasn't even your real father," it finally informed me.

I looked at it incredulously. "That was your best shot?" I'd figured that much out by the time I was six.

It gave an odd sort of bob with its whole body. "It's no fun when they already know their life sucks," it said to no one in particular, and flew off.

I looked around for an avenue of escape, but everything was chaos. The Weres appeared to be losing the battle, mainly because the customers, annoyed that the auction had been interrupted, had joined the trolls. Or, at least, most of them had. A few had decided to take advantage of the pandemonium to make off with some free merchandise. I saw a vampire, who had been the witch's chief competition for the djinn, make a dive for her. She glanced at him in annoyance and, with a word I couldn't hear, sent him flying across the room into a glass display case. The case broke, scattering shards everywhere and causing him to roar in rage. He didn't roar for long.

The case had held a group of charms and all the magic swirling around activated them. Individually, they wouldn't have been much of a problem for a vampire, but he obviously didn't know how to handle several dozen at once. His body was caught in wild tendrils of magic that wrapped around him like brightly colored ribbons, each with a different function. I couldn't see everything through the sparks and swirls, but a lot of the charms must have been baldness cures, because he ended up enmeshed in a cloud of long black strands that sprang from his own head. He tried to break free, ripping out handfuls of hair by the roots, but it grew back almost immediately. The witch doubled over in laughter.

I didn't wait to see what happened when he got loose, but punched the button to send the podium back underneath the stage. I insinuated myself into the small open area in the back, where the auctioneer's legs usually went, to ride it down. The service ramp used for unloading trucks with big items was adjacent to the lower level. If I was lucky, I could get out that way and circle around to my car while everyone was preoccupied with the fight.

It was a slow mechanism, but no one seemed to be paying me any attention. The only person nearby was the old mage who had seemed so enthralled by the rune. He had somehow fought his way back to the stage, and in the midst of the bedlam, had eyes only for the stone. He grabbed it, ignoring the banshee who immediately started up again, but he didn't take off with it as I'd expected. He started chanting something instead, holding the stone in front of him with a look of rapture on his face.

He was far too concentrated on whatever he was doing to see the Fey come up behind him. He tackled the mage around the ankles and the man hit the floor with a thud. The rune went flying, landing right in front of me. The Fey saw and his eyes widened. He leapt for it, shouting something, but I couldn't hear him. There was a flash, a weightless feeling, and the next thing I knew, I was sagging against a cold stone wall, struggling to lift my head.

My muscles ached and my tongue felt thick in my mouth. I tried to move and tottered, dizziness eating at the edges of my vision. What the hell?

A strong hand clapped over my mouth and I was abruptly pressed against the wall by a tall, muscular form. I couldn't see a damn thing—someone must have left the lights off downstairs—but the way my body reacted told me who it was. I started to protest, but a flash of light illuminated the area at the same moment, and I forgot what I'd been about to say.

The dragon's head stood in front of me, but behind it wasn't the familiar mess of Gerald's stockrooms. Instead, I saw a black sky, with menacing gray-green clouds that rumbled almost continually. Deadly silver streaks provided the only light, giving intermittent glimpses of a cobblestone street and a cluster of two-story wooden buildings.

Just as abruptly as I'd been slammed against the wall, I was dragged behind the podium. "Stay down," was hissed in my ear. I looked up as lightning flashed again to see the Fey from the auction house crouched beside me, looking grim.

"Where are we?" I demanded in an equally low tone.

"Faerie."

I took a minute to process that. "And exactly how did we get here?"

"The rune. The mage activated it and opened a portal just as I reached you."

Almost like it was adding an exclamation point to his sentence, something hit the front of the podium, causing the heavy wood backing to shudder. The Fey was looking at something over my shoulder and I followed his gaze. The street had been clear only seconds before, but now it was filled with about a dozen Fey, all staring in shock at the huge dragon's head. I realized that it was sticking out of an alley, so the lack of a body wasn't apparent. And in the poor light, it probably looked real.

Several of the Fey yelled in a language I didn't know, and something slammed into the cobblestones beside my hand. I jerked back without seeing what it was, but the next lightning flash showed that they had bows in their hands and several more were drawing back to shoot. "Tell them we're friends before they kill us!" I said in a furious whisper.

"I would, except for one problem."

"What?"

"We're not friends."

"But, you're all Fey," I protested. I hadn't been able to make out a lot about our attackers, but I'd seen that much. Their bright silver hair lit up the night like beacons whenever the lightning flared.

"Yes, well, that's one way of looking at it," he muttered, beginning to root through the jumbled mess inside the podium. He was right behind the dragon's face, and arrows rattled against its surface continually, but none got through. Maybe Gerald's old man had been telling the truth about it after all. "Are there any weapons here?"

"Why? Can't you talk to them or something?"

A brief, strobelike flash reflected an exasperated pair of eyes under strands of tangled blond hair. "They're Svarestri," he informed me, like that meant anything. I just looked at him. "I'm not," he added unhelpfully.

I gave up trying to understand and he went back to pawing through the hollow head. "If the rune got us here, can't it get us back?" I asked, after a moment.

His head whipped around. "You have it?"

"No, don't you?"

"No. I couldn't get my hands on it in time. It must have remained on the other side." He held up something he'd discovered in Matt's trash heap. "I don't know human magic well. What is this?"

"An inhaler," I said, going by feel. "Matt has asthma."

"And that would be?"

"Completely unhelpful." I glanced back at the gaping black tunnel behind us. "What about retreat?" I'm not a fan of dark alleys, but it beat staying where we were.

"They've already sent some of their number to flank us," he informed me. I have no idea how he knew—maybe his eyes could see better than mine. Since I'd lost my glasses in the shuffle, that was a good bet. I pushed him out of the way and started my own search inside the podium.

I waded through a nasty pile of used tissues, a half dozen crumpled soft drink cans, piles of broken display containers, several scratched acrylic stands and a pair of old sneakers. No wonder Matt could never find the damn gavel! I had to go mostly on feel, as the lightning flashes were more confusing than helpful, and the dark interior of the podium was no brighter than the alley. But as far as I could tell the most lethal thing inside the dragon's head was the smell of Matt's tennis shoes.

"Nothing."

"You're sure?" It wasn't at all reassuring that the Fey sounded almost as desperate as I felt.

"Just how much do these guys hate you?" It looked like talking our way out of this was the only chance we had.

"Bad enough to kill me if they can—and anyone with me."

This just kept getting better and better. A quick look out at the street told me that the trend was continuing. Not getting any response from the dragon must have made the Fey suspicious. Either that, or they thought they'd killed it. Either way, they were slowly moving closer, arrows nocked and ready. Shit.

I didn't have time to worry about it for long, because someone grabbed me from behind. While I'd been concentrating on the street in front of us, a Fey had snuck up on us through the alley. Several of them, I realized, as two more jumped my companion. I didn't think—there wasn't time. I just focused on my attacker's aura and gave a jerk. And since I hadn't been able to affect the Fey at Gerald's, I put a lot more effort behind it than usual.

The Fey holding me screamed, a high-pitched, almost musical note, and collapsed. I landed in a heap on very hard stones, but hardly noticed. I was too busy trying to figure out what to do with the avalanche of power that had flooded into me from the fallen Fey. It was a crushing weight, strong enough to cause tiny sparks in the air, as if a swarm of lightning bugs had descended on me. I'd never known anything like it and I didn't know what to do with it, but keeping it wasn't an option.

I panicked and sent the whole thing into the pavement, where my hands rested. Instead of grounding it as I'd planned, the surge of power moved under the cobblestones, churning them up like a giant earthworm moving through dirt. A giant, electric earthworm headed straight for our attackers.

The Fey scattered, but the building across the street had nowhere to go. A second later, the power hit it dead-on. It shook violently before erupting in a burst of wood, glass and pretty painted shutters, one of which hurtled across the street and almost decapitated me. I didn't have time to freak out, because my companion had hauled me to my feet and we were sprinting down the street, away from the raining cloud of rubble. I heard yells behind us, but nobody followed. I didn't blame them.

CHAPTER 3

I quickly discovered that high heels and cobblestones are a bad mix, and that bare feet aren't much better. The street had obviously been laid by a sadist, because some stones stuck up almost an inch above the others. I was limping before we'd gone two blocks, and had stubbed my toe half a dozen times.

Then the storm broke, with slanting sheets of rain hitting down so hard as to almost blow us off our feet. We took cover under a building with a second story that protruded out past the first, but it didn't help much. In less than a minute, I was soaked, the chiffon dress clinging to me like Saran Wrap.

"Stay here!" the Fey yelled to be heard over the sound of the storm

"What? No!" Before I could grab him, he was gone, the gray cloak blending perfectly into the darkened street. I stood staring out at the rain, thinking murderous thoughts and wondering what the hell I was supposed to do now. With no one to back up my story about how I got here, I wasn't likely to be believed, even assuming I could keep from getting shot long enough to get a hearing. But I didn't dare go anywhere; without my glasses, everything was a big, dark blur until I was right on top of it—including any guards who might be lurking around.

Before anger and fear could edge over into full-scale panic, the Fey was back. "I've found us a bolt-hole. We should be safe there until the storm blows over." He took off his cloak and wrapped me up like a mummy. "It's not far. Try to keep your eyes down. Dark emerald is not a common color among the Svarestri."

I had no idea what he was talking about, and at the moment I didn't care. I nodded.

"And, er, keep in mind that I didn't have a lot of choice about accommodations."

"Fine, let's just get out of here." Anything had to be better than standing exposed on a street corner, waiting to be attacked again.

The Fey led me through a warren of narrow lanes that were fast turning into little rivers, then made a sudden turn into a dark doorway. The room beyond, although lit only by a few lanterns and a crackling fire, seemed bright after the street. I had a brief impression of raucous laughter, trestle tables filled with people, and the smells of wine and roasted meat. Then a large woman in an apron bustled over to us.

She and the Fey started a conversation while I kept my eyes down, trying to melt into the cloak as much as possible. I hoped I looked calm outwardly, but inside I was panicking. How did I know he wasn't bargaining for his own life by turning me in? I hadn't expected us to walk into one of the houses of the people who had just tried to kill us!

It didn't help that I couldn't follow a word of the conversation, but finally, I heard the chink of coins as the Fey paid the woman for something. Then we were following her across the room and into another one, where the lights were even lower and the activities of some of the people made my eyebrows rise. By the time we reached a flight of wooden stairs, I had seen enough to realize why the Fey had found it necessary to apologize. Several sets of hands tugged at the cloak as I passed, but he whipped it away from them almost before I'd noticed. A question was shouted after us, but I didn't understand it and the Fey didn't respond, so I just kept going.

We found ourselves in a small room with a bed, a window closed against the weather, and a washbasin on a stand. The woman said something, then left, clicking the door shut behind her. I couldn't stand it anymore and collapsed onto the bed in a fit of half-hysterical giggles.

"I didn't know you guys had brothels," I wheezed, after a moment.

The Fey had placed the basin on the floor and was balancing over it, taking off one of his boots. What looked like half a gallon of dirty water flowed out of it. "We don't."

"Then what was going on back there?"

"We could go back and take a look, but we might get more offers to join in." He tossed the basin's contents out the window, letting in a chilly gust of wind and rain before snapping it shut again.

"I thought the Fey had, uh, problems in that area."

"What area?"

"Conception and, um . . ." He looked up from emptying the other boot, amusement filling his eyes, and I trailed off.

"Not for lack of trying," he assured me. He unwrapped a sodden piece of cloth attached to his leg that I realized after a moment was a knife sheath. "This isn't a brothel," he added. "It's a rendezvous point. Our people often marry for fertility instead of attraction, but that tends to pall quickly. Sex isn't as enjoyable if it's being done only to conceive."

I just nodded, getting a clear look at him for the first time. The Light Fey are as legendary for their beauty as the

Dark are for their gruesomeness, but it's a haughty perfection, sharp as pain. There is no softness about it, no sense that underneath the glacial exterior is anything less frozen. They have the awesomeness of primal forces, like an avalanche or a volcanic eruption. And they use their beauty like a weapon, just as effectively as their swords or enchantments.

Which is why it was a surprise to see one looking like a drowned rat.

Beads of moisture clung to his high arched brows and dark lashes and his hair lay plastered to his skull. His soggy blue tunic and leggings outlined a nice body, but for once I was too amused to care. He also didn't seem to be glowing anymore. He could have passed for a very tall, very wet human, except for the pair of gracefully curved ears that stuck up from the dripping mass on his head.

I grinned, and he arched an eyebrow. "You should see yourself," he told me. I was actually glad I couldn't.

"Gerald's is supposed to be neutral territory," I said, trying to figure out what about his face was bugging me. "How did you get a knife past the wards?"

"Mysterious Fey trickery. That and the fact that I didn't take in anything big. Which means that this," he held up the small item he'd wrestled from the sodden sheath, "is our only weapon."

"How do you know I'm not carrying one?"

He smiled, those blue eyes running over me. "That would be a good trick."

I looked down to find that the rain had made the damned evening dress all but transparent, and I hadn't been able to wear much underneath because of its almost nonexistent back. I closed the front of the cloak, and he made a slight moue of disappointment. "I talk too much," he commented.

"Too little." I finally figured out what was odd about him. His jawline was stronger than those of the other Fey

I'd seen, but it was mainly his expressions that were off. He had some.

He leaned against the wall and looked at me quizzically. "Name a subject."

"You could start with why you were trying to buy me." Everyone knew the Fey used to kidnap witches to help with their population problem, but it had been illegal for centuries. I disapproved of slaving in principle, and even more when I was the target.

"We've suspected Gerald of stretching a point on any number of sales through the years," I was told, "but have never been able to catch him doing anything illegal. When I saw you there, I realized you could serve as the witness we needed." He looked at me reproachfully. "You would never have been a slave. The Blarestri don't do that sort of thing." He paused. "Well, not anymore."

"The Blar what?"

"Blarestri." He looked surprised that I didn't automatically know what that meant. "That is my . . . clan, I suppose you would call it."

"And I take it from our reception that we didn't land in your clan's territory?"

He grimaced. "No. We're somewhere in the Svarestri lands, but I'm not certain of the exact location. I'll try to find out tomorrow."

"And the Svarestri are what? Another clan?"

"There are three leading clans of what you call the Light Fey," he said slowly, as if he thought he was being teased. He moved to join me on the bed, ending up a little too close for comfort, but I couldn't very well object as there were no chairs in the room. I suppose the people who came there didn't do a lot of chatting. "Mine is one, the Svarestri are another. We, er, don't get along."

I'd figured that much out on my own. "Why do they hate you?"

"Too many reasons to list. But I'm sure they would be

very interested to know how I was able to get into one of their towns—with a large stuffed dragon's head no less—without being seen." He picked up one of my bruised feet, regarding it with a frown. "You won't be doing any more running for some time. We're going to need a horse."

I refused to be distracted by his touch. "I still don't understand how we got here. I thought all portals into Faerie were well guarded."

"The official ones are," he agreed, beginning absent-mindedly to stroke the length of my arch. I knew I should pull my foot away, but it felt incredibly good. "But, according to legend, the rune can transport its user from any point on Earth to any point in Faerie. Unlike someone using the official portals, which have set targets, with the rune the user has only to think of a destination and there he is."

The Fey's expression told me that there was more going on here than I understood. When he spoke about the rune, he looked almost euphoric. "So?"

"So whoever has the rune could place spies behind enemy lines, put assassins into an enemy leader's bedchamber, or even send an entire army into the heart of their rival's territory—all with no warning being given!"

"You're planning to invade?" I asked nervously.

"Not unless the Svarestri force our hand." His eyes narrowed to sapphire slits. "They once ruled all of Faerie, and have ambitions to do so again. The rune would serve as a significant deterrent."

I put two and two together. "That's why you were at Gerald's."

"One of our human contacts saw the listing and brought it to our attention. We thought it—what is the phrase?—a long shot, but worth investigating."

"Maybe the Svarestri thought the same, and the mage was their contact."

"Unlikely. They despise humans, even magical ones. And they know little about your world, which they frequent only rarely. If he was working for anyone, it would be the Alorestri. Of all our people, they have the most contact with humans."

"Alorestri?" All these Fey names were starting to get confusing, and the slow strokes he was making along my arch weren't helping.

"The Green Fey, as they are commonly known, because their livery is green and white," he explained. "The Svarestri, meaning the Black Fey, wear black and silver in battle. My people are commonly called the Blarestri, because our colors are blue and gold. Our real names, of course, are never used."

That, at least, I understood. Names carried power, and I'd heard rumors that the Fey never told anyone theirs for fear it would strengthen any spells used against them. But something was bugging me. "Then you were thinking about the Svarestri at the auction?"

"No. I assure you, I think about them as little as possible."

"I wasn't thinking about them, either," I told him quietly.

He just looked at me for a second, then his eyes widened. "It was the mage who opened the portal; his thoughts must have determined where we were sent."

I finished the thought for him. "And if he was working for the Alorestri, why was he thinking about the Svarestri when he activated the rune?"

He clenched his jaw. "I must get it back! We would use it as a deterrent, but I do not trust the Svarestri to do the same!"

"How do we get back, if the rune is on the other side of the portal?" Despite Sebastian's interest, I thought my chances would be better back home. Seb would prefer to take me alive, so he could sell me to his damned Harvesters. The Fey didn't seem to have that handicap. And I definitely didn't want to get stuck in the middle of one of their wars.

"That will depend on where we are. The Alorestri try to

maintain good relations with everyone. Their lands run alongside the border with the Dark Fey and they need troops from all of us if they are to hold it. If we can make it into their lands, I should be able to persuade them to let us use one of their portals."

"And if we aren't near the border?"

"Let's hope we are."

I nodded and tried to focus on something other than the interest in his eyes. He was clearly examining my face and seemed to like what he saw. I could only assume he had peculiar tastes, since my hair was frizzing into a big red ball as it dried, and my dress was torn and muddy. But he wasn't looking away even as he saw me recognize his interest for what it was. A particularly charming smile lit up not only his features, but also his eyes.

"I keep thinking of you as 'that beautiful redhead who landed me in so much trouble,' but it's a bit of a mouthful. What should I call you?"

I blinked in surprise, both at the unfairness of the accusation, and at the compliment. I also had no idea what to say. Normally, when dealing with humans the Fey use a false name or a title. Anything personal is reserved for those they hold a lot more intimate. I wasn't sure I wanted to be on that kind of footing with him, but he could hardly call me "hey you" for what might be a long trip. And I didn't feel like making something up and then trying to remember to answer to it.

"I'm Claire," I finally said, throwing caution to the wind.

He nodded thoughtfully. "And if I may ask, what does that mean?"

I shrugged. "I don't know. I never looked it up."

He arched a brow. "You bear a name," he said slowly, "and do not know what it means?"

"A lot of people do."

"Not in Faerie."

"So what's yours?"

"That is a very personal question among the Fey. It is better to ask what people call one. It's considered more polite, as it doesn't directly ask for a personal name."

"Okay, what do people call you?"

"Geisli when I was a child—it means sunbeam," he explained, "or sometimes Haddi, because they said I had too much hair. Asmundir is often used at court, because it is indicative of my function as protector of the people. Alarr means general, but I have never yet led an army in battle so it's somewhat misleading. I believe Father gave it to me to impress the Svarestri. And sometimes I'm referred to as Huitserkir, because my armor is white and gold—"

"What do you like to be called?" I asked, desperate to get away from the warm press of his fingers. The touch was light, but a lot more disturbing than it should have been. And he was right—he talked too much.

He looked puzzled. "Others give us our names."

"Then you don't care?"

"I didn't say that." He thought about it for a ridiculously long time. "Some of my shield brothers gifted me with the name Heidar," he finally said. "It means 'bright lord.' They say my hair is easy to see in battle."

"Okay. Heidar it is, then." I felt like I'd won some sort of major victory, just getting his name. Now maybe he'd let me go.

"I am glad to be known to you, Claire," he said, sounding formal all of a sudden. Then strong arms circled me and a warm mouth closed over mine.

Or maybe not.

The kiss started out tender and brain-meltingly sweet, but didn't stay that way. That was mainly my fault. My hands came up, one grabbing Heidar's shoulder, the other curling around the back of his neck, threading its way through his hair and pulling him close. My tongue darted desperately against his as I thoughtlessly drove the kiss deep. He responded after a moment's startled hesitation, clasping me gently, while running a hand down my bare back to cup one of my hips. His hands on my body felt shockingly, achingly good, and he tasted sweet—of spices and some indefinable sunny flavor. I couldn't get enough of the taste, the scent, the feel of him—it was like I was drunk on it.

When we broke apart for air, I found my tongue tracing the vein throbbing in his neck. I had somehow ended up on his lap, my thighs straddling his, and I could feel him firming against me. Someone made a soft exclamation of need and the sound broke through a little of my haze. I stared at him, wide-eyed and suddenly frightened. I felt vulnerable—I needed this too much and it worried what little part of my mind was still capable of thought.

He noticed my expression and frowned. "What is it?"

"I don't know," I whispered, from a throat half closed with panic. "I think something's wrong with me."

"You were injured?" Two large hands began running over me, looking for wounds I suppose, but I almost screamed from the sensation. I was oversensitized, raw with need to the point of pain wherever he touched me. It felt like my body was something apart from me, a hungry, predatory creature that was no longer completely under control. I was scaring myself, and I didn't know how to stop.

I scrambled away from him to the far side of the room, near the window. "Don't touch me!"

"I'm sorry." He looked perplexed, and I really couldn't blame him. "I thought—"

"Oh, shit!"

"Claire, I'm trying to apologize, if you'll give me a—"

"Svarestri!" I hissed, my problematic libido temporarily forgotten. "Outside."

He was beside me in an instant. A whole cadre of the silver-haired guards were filing through the main door of the tavern. Maybe it was coincidence, but I didn't think so. They didn't have the carefree, laughing manner of people on their way to a good time; they looked like they meant business.

"The roof," Heidar said, throwing open the window as soon as the last guard disappeared from view.

"What about it?" I demanded, hoping he didn't mean what I thought. But he was already outside, balancing on the rain-slick windowsill and looking up. The next second, he disappeared into the dark, just as someone knocked on the door.

I jumped and stared at it, then quickly scrambled out onto the sill. I couldn't see anything but heavy clouds overhead and, where they parted, a dark sky dusted with stars. And rain, a lot of it. It clouded my vision whenever I tried to catch any movement on the roof. "Heidar," I called nervously, as someone started throwing their weight against the door. I stood on the ledge, clinging to the wet planks on the side of the building, trying to figure out if being inside or outside scared me more. Then the decision was made for me when two arms reached down and plucked me off my feet.

For a moment, I dangled above the street, which suddenly looked a lot further down than two stories. A guard came back outside, pulling his collar up against the rain, and caught sight of me suspended there. We just stared at each other for an instant, before he let out a yell and grabbed for his weapon. Luckily, it was under his rain cape and before he could get it free, I was on a flat-topped roof running as fast as my sore feet could carry me.

The rooftops were very close together, almost touching in places, and the storm made us virtually invisible. At least, I assumed it did since I couldn't see a damned thing. I stumbled after Heidar, trying not to slip off a roof or into one of the gaps between buildings. He wasn't doing much better himself, with his boots back in the brothel and the rainwater making the rooftops dangerous, but at least no one was shooting at us.

I'd no sooner had the thought than I felt something whiz

by my ear. Heidar spun us behind a tall chimney, whispered, "Don't move," and disappeared. After a second, I saw him silhouetted in a lightning flash as he jumped to another rooftop and took off. Several dark forms, one with a lit lantern in hand, ran after him, leaving me shivering and alone in the night.

I stayed in the shadow of the chimney, hoping Heidar was planning to backtrack and hadn't just decided that I was an unnecessary burden. I hated feeling this helpless, hated Faerie and, most of all, hated rain. I had started to dry out back in the warm little room, but the downpour had me soaked to the skin once again despite the cloak. Its sodden folds were heavy and clung to my limbs clammily. Then a gutter collapsed on the taller building next door, sending a cold stream to douse me. I sighed. I had reached the point where I literally couldn't get any wetter.

A warm hand suddenly gripped mine, and I turned toward it gratefully. "Let's get out of here."

The hand tightened, and a lantern was shoved in my face. It almost blinded me, but I got a glimpse of opaque, silver eyes, and that was enough. I didn't scream—I was too surprised. I reached for his power, but this one must have been older or stronger than the other Fey, because he fought me. We just stood there for several seconds, teetering on the edge of the building, wrestling metaphysically. It hurts when they resist, and by the time I found a way inside his shields, I was gasping in pain.

He didn't scream like the last one when I pulled on his power, but collapsed heavily against me, his weight almost knocking me off the building. I saw the glint of a blade in the lantern light and realized what he was trying to do: if he couldn't take me out one way, he'd use another. I gathered everything I had and pushed, no direction in mind, no thought, just a desire to get him away. The most I'd hoped for was that it would throw him out of arm's reach. Instead, he went flying off the roof as if shot from a cannon, far out across the city. For some reason, the lantern in his hand didn't go out, making him look weirdly like a comet streaking across the dark sky.

I stood there, staring incredulously after him, as yells came from rooftops on all sides. Heidar ran up the next moment, sounding breathless. His lips, looking strangely bloodless in the moonlight, were parted in shock. "What have you been doing?"

"Surviving! Where the hell were you?"

"Stealing a horse."

I stopped, mid-rant. "Good answer."

Little points of light from the guard's lanterns were starting to converge on our position. "Well, they know where we are now," Heidar said grimly. "Run!"

We ran.

CHAPTER 4

AFTER half a dozen buildings, we dropped to the ground via an outdoor staircase Heidar had discovered. We spent long, tense minutes slipping through dark alleys, watching lanterns flicker in and out of the shadows above us. The Fey seemed to think we were still on the rooftops, at least for now.

Heidar had stuffed the horse behind a cart piled high with barrels. It blocked the only exit to a small alley, creating a makeshift pen. He moved the cart slightly to the side to let the horse out, while I stared at it dubiously. My feet were killing me, but a fact was a fact. "I don't ride, you know."

"What do you mean, you don't ride?"

"I mean, I don't ride. As in, never been on a horse in my life." The very large animal snorted loudly. It didn't seem to appreciate getting rained on any more than I did, or maybe it was me it didn't like. It rolled its eyes and whinnied unhappily every time I came near.

Heidar was looking at me like I'd told him I didn't know how to walk. "Everyone can ride."

"Can you drive a car?"

"No."

I shrugged. "Different worlds."

He grasped me around the waist and tossed me onto the horse's back. "Yes, but we're stuck in this one, at least for now. Hold on." He vaulted up in front of me and I clutched the soggy fabric of his tunic in a death grip. Then we were off.

The horse didn't come equipped with a saddle, and its back was wet and slippery. It took most of my concentration not to slide off one side or the other as we went pelting down a maze of tiny streets, splashing through puddles and constantly changing direction. The sound of hooves striking cobblestones echoed off the surrounding buildings, seeming to come back at us from every direction at once. I could hear shouts and see wildly swinging lanterns, both above us and flickering in and out of dark alleyways. As the minutes passed, more and more of them were on our level. The Fey had figured out that we were no longer on the rooftops, but couldn't quite catch up to Heidar's crazy horsemanship.

Those above us kept shouting to the ones in the street, giving them directions, I suppose, about which way we were headed. One somehow reached a wooden structure that formed a bridge over the street just before we did. When we passed underneath, he pushed a large barrel down almost on top of our heads. It missed, splintering into pieces on the cobblestones right beside us, but the gush of water it threw out hit me like a fist. The force of it knocked me sprawling, but Heidar somehow caught me before I hit the ground, grabbing the waistband of my soggy gown just before I slammed face-first into the hard road.

The wet chiffon stretched across my chest, leaving what felt like welts behind, but amazingly, it didn't rip. Heidar managed to control the rearing horse, which had been reigned in too abruptly for its liking, and maneuvered it back under the bridge for cover. He pulled me up in front of him as the guard overhead started shooting at us.

"Are you all right?" he asked, sounding almost as breathless as I was. I nodded in response, not having enough air left in my lungs to speak. "We have to risk it," he said simply.

I pushed wet hair out of my eyes and saw what he meant. The guard on the bridge had a bad angle, and none of his arrows were connecting, but his shouts had been answered from several points behind us. Half a dozen lanterns swung into the street as I watched, some of the fuzzy shapes running flat out for us, others dropping to their knees to nock arrows. Staying where we were definitely wasn't an option.

I spit out a mouthful of dirty water and nodded. Heidar got a better grip on me, maneuvered the horse to one side of the street, then dug his heels into the animal's flanks. We shot out from under the bridge, racing down the covered arcade to one side of the road. The arcade's roof kept the guard's arrows from hitting us, but enough baskets, covered carts and barrels blocked the way to serve as an obstacle course. I almost got beheaded by an empty clothesline, but Heidar pushed my face down into the horse's mane just in time. And, less than a block later, we left the town behind, bursting out into what looked like endless acres of pastureland.

I foolishly thought we were home free, but although the Fey didn't follow us, the storm certainly did. It actually seemed to be getting worse as we left town. The trees whipped wildly back and forth on either side of the road, and the horse began bucking every time a flash lit the sky. Heidar finally had to get down to lead it into the face of the driving wind, slowing our pace to a crawl.

After what felt like a couple of miles, we stopped in front of a black shape that rose suddenly out of the dark. "It's a barn," Heidar yelled. I thought that was a very optimistic assessment, but any shelter sounded good at the moment. He broke open the door and I dragged my sodden self inside. It was very cramped, made even more so by the horse that was trying to push in after me.

"Leave the animal outside!" I yelled.

Heidar stubbornly led it the rest of the way in, then closed the door behind us. "It would tell anyone who passes where we are."

I didn't think too many people were likely to be passing on a night like this, but said nothing. With the door shut, it was pitch-black, without even the brief lightning bursts to give a clue where anything was. I stood motionless, not wanting to bash my head, while he searched around and somehow made a fire.

The small, flickering flames highlighted the fact that we were definitely not in a barn. It would be a stretch to call it a toolshed, although that seemed to be its main purpose. A pile of gardening equipment was stacked near one wall, which was all of ten feet away. On the other was a drying rack for herbs, a small table, a chair and a bucket. That was it.

The storm was right overhead; sounding like a great battle was taking place outside. It made the structure creak and groan alarmingly, but it had to be sturdier than it looked, because it didn't spring a leak. I stopped contemplating the high-beamed ceiling when the horse nuzzled against me, trying to make up for almost tossing me in a puddle earlier. I wrinkled my nose at it, both because of the smell and the fact that it had grabbed the best position by the fire. I sat down at the table and resigned myself to a long night.

My thoughts were interrupted by a gigantic sneeze. "That doesn't sound good," Heidar commented. "Get out of those wet things and sit by the fire before you become ill."

"How am I supposed to 'sit by the fire' with that animal's backside in the way?"

The Fey sighed and pushed the horse into a corner of the little shed. It neighed in protest, but went. "Now, come to the heat and stop sulking," he told me.

I was about to make a sharp comment when an expression of pain crossed his face. It probably had something to do with the wicked-looking arrow point sticking out below his collarbone. It looked like the guard had been a better shot than I thought.

Old instincts took over. "Let me look at that." Heidar shied away, but I pursued him until his back hit the wall. "Don't be a baby. I'm not going to hurt you." I couldn't believe I was having to say that to someone who had a foot in height and about seventy pounds on me.

"What are you planning to do?"

"To help you, you stupid elf! I'm a nurse." I pulled on his good arm until he settled down at the tiny table.

"We are not called elves," he informed me. I used his knife to cut the tunic fabric away from the problem area, baring a long pale back to view. The dampness had kept the blood from drying around the wound, and the fabric came away easier than I'd expected for soaked cloth. It was the only good thing about the situation, though. "That is a human term. It's considered pejorative in Faerie."

"I'll keep that in mind. I'd hate to offend any Svarestri I meet." He smiled slightly, but the next minute his face drained of color when I snapped off the arrow point in a sudden movement. "Sorry."

He nodded, sweat blooming on his forehead. I tried to pull the shaft out of his back, to get the worst over with, but it wouldn't budge. It took me a minute to realize why. I stared at the ugly wound in disbelief. In the dim lantern-light, it looked black against his pale flesh, but it was about to look a whole lot worse. "This isn't good."

"I know. Do it quick."

"That's what I'm trying to tell you—I can't. I don't understand it, but . . . you've already started to heal. Around the arrow."

"Of course." He said it like every wound closes in less than an hour. "Pull it out before it gets any worse!"

I swallowed. This was not going to be fun. "You, uh, might want to hold onto something," I told him. Then I grasped hold of the feathered end of the shaft and gave a heave.

Heidar made a muffled grunt, and bit his bottom lip white, but overall he took it better than I did. To my relief, the arrow tore free easily, with minimal ripping. The blood that followed the shaft was also less than I'd thought it would be. So why did I suddenly have to sit down on the floor?

"You're a nurse?" He took the bloody shaft from my hand, sounding surprised. I suppose I wasn't acting much like a seasoned professional. Of course, I'd usually worked in the office side of the family business, and paperwork, however messed up, doesn't bleed.

"I'm a Lachesis," I said, blinking away a sudden rush of dizziness. He looked blank. "My family. It's House Lachesis," I clarified. Still blank. That was so bizarre that I actually forgot to be sick. "That means nothing to you?"

"The Disposer. In your mythology, she was one of the three Moirae, the Fates. She measured the spread of human life and determined its length." He looked slightly amused. "I hope you are not politely trying to tell me that my time is up."

"No." My vision cleared slightly. "The rumor is that an ancestor fled Venice after being involved in a poisoning affair that got a little too public. She settled in France, but that was the 1660s and a big poison scare was going on there, too. So she didn't think it smart to use her real name. Considering her profession, I guess Lachesis sort of made sense."

"I'm in the hands of an expert poisoner?" Heidar's smile began to fade around the edges.

"We've been known for centuries as the people to see if you're serious about magical healing."

"Or the reverse?"

He was more perceptive than a lot of our clients. I'd

helped to draw up the contracts for curse removal, until I had an attack of conscience on seeing how many of them were for the same people, over and over again. Our cures would work, but in the process place another curse on the sufferer. Not for nothing was Lachesis known as miracle workers in the healing arts: half the curses we removed were our own.

"I'm retired," I said briefly, getting up to finish the job. "And I'm not likely to poison my only guide in this crazy place."

His tunic tore the rest of the way off with a little help from the knife, leaving me staring at a surprisingly well-muscled torso. All the Fey I'd previously encountered had looked like those tonight—tall, but with a slender, almost willowy build. It probably explained why they moved like gazelles, with a quick, springy grace and perfect balance. This one didn't move like that, and now I understood why. His arms, shoulders and chest were well-defined, and the hard muscles coiled beneath that smooth skin gave him more weight to carry.

He said something, but I didn't hear it. Streams of rain-water had found their way inside the V-neck of his tunic and run down his chest, gathering in the dark hollow of his navel. Water droplets still gleamed here and there, and a damp strand of hair had curled in a sinuous curve across his chest.

Brilliant lapis eyes, their color darkened by the low light, met mine. I realized that my hand had been stroking his arm idly, over a sprinkling of sun freckles near his shoulder. More ran over his nose and across his cheekbones. They were light, almost unnoticeable, but I'd never seen a Fey with freckles before.

"I'll get something for the wound," I told him, tossing the remains of the tunic over the side of the table and moving as far away as I could get in the little room.

"I usually heal well enough on my own," he offered, but

I ignored him. I needed something to do, and just because he healed fast didn't mean he couldn't get an infection.

I found lavender and pretty yellow calendula flowers on the drying rack, along with some other stuff I didn't recognize. The idea of having new, completely unknown herbs to experiment on was almost enough to distract me from the task at hand. The family had traded with the Fey for ingredients—I'd seen the records of payments made in the office—but I'd never been allowed to handle any of the materials myself. They went to the boys in the lab along with all the other esoteric goodies. I promised myself to do some serious gathering before I went home. Assuming I ever did.

I needed a clean cloth and something to use to make tea. The cloth was nowhere to be found, but the bucket was metal and didn't have any holes, so I figured it would do for a makeshift teapot. I pushed open the door and got slapped in the face by more rain. It was still pouring down, enough to quickly fill the bucket partway, but also to turn the area around the door into a muddy mess.

I gratefully turned back to the dryer part of the shed, only to stop dead. The Fey was getting undressed. He'd already spread the cape on the floor on the far side of the table and hung the shredded tunic on a nail I'd overlooked. Now his hand dropped to the lacings of his leggings. The dark blue fabric hugged his body tightly and only came away slowly, baring first creamy buttocks, then silky thighs and finally well-muscled calves to view. He sat back on the chair, his body on careless display, before noticing me.

"What's wrong?" He was regarding me quizzically, his head tilted slightly to the side. In the soft glow from the fire, his hair took on the sheen of antique gold, like ancient treasure. I swallowed, fighting the urge to touch those shining strands.

"Nothing."

I sat my bucket with the herbs inside over the fire and

settled down on its far side—practically the only free space left. That put me next to the now steaming horse, but it beat the hell out of the alternative. I'd heard that the Fey had fewer problems with modesty than humans, but could really have done without a demonstration. I occupied myself trying to find something neutral to look at without turning my back on him completely.

I concentrated on the fire, watching the bits of wood and ash thrown up by the flames, but my eyes kept trying to wander to the well-muscled leg and part of one strong thigh visible just beyond it. They were highlighted with minute golden strands that tantalizingly caught the light. Beads of moisture were starting to dry all over his skin, leaving it warm and rosy. I felt a little dizzy.

"What did you put in there?" he asked, peering into the pot.

I swallowed. "Lavender for an antiseptic and calendula to stem blood flow and reduce scarring. It isn't optimal, but it's the best I can do with the stuff at hand." He nodded, but looked at the pot dubiously. I probably shouldn't have mentioned the poison thing.

"I answered your questions; I would appreciate you answering one of mine," he said after a pause. "Who was the mage you called Sebastian? What did he want with you?"

I watched steam start to rise from the pot and wondered how to reply to that. Summing up my past in a few words was a challenge. I decided on the *Reader's Digest* version.

"My father decided to sell me to the Light Fey. Only a great-uncle found out about it before the deal went through and helped me escape. When Father couldn't produce me as promised, the Fey decided he'd welshed on the deal, so . . ."

"I can guess."

"Sebastian has been looking for me ever since. And tonight he caught up with me. The family blames me for what happened to Father."

"And your cousin wants revenge."

"Something like that." Actually, the whole family had had a vote, and they'd preferred Seb's bribes to my assurances. Normally, the memory was enough to bring me to angry tears, but at the moment, I seemed unable to get worked up about it. Maybe because I was already worked up about something else.

I couldn't seem to stop staring at Heidar's hair. The top layer had started to dry and, unusual for the Fey, it had a slight ripple to it. The underside was still damp and golden tendrils curled intriguingly against his neck. I suddenly had an almost overwhelming urge to run my hands through that heavy mane, to slide them over that beautiful chest, to kiss him until he cried out and couldn't breathe . . . he was giving me that puzzled look again.

"Can you describe these Fey?"

I blinked. "What?"

"The ones who tried to buy you."

"Oh. They, uh, they looked like you. Well, sort of." I forced my mind onto the question. "More like the guards back in the village, actually. Same silver hair, same malicious expressions."

Heidar seemed surprised. "The Svarestri don't buy humans. The Alorestri have always been the biggest participants in the slave trade. They lose more warriors holding the border than we do, and need a higher birthrate to compensate. The Svarestri consider humans . . . unacceptable . . . as mates."

"Well, they were trying to buy me."

Heidar suddenly looked grim. "The Svarestri do not buy humans," he repeated. "If they were trying to buy you, the only explanation I can think of . . ."

"What?" I was starting to get worried.

"There is a good chance they were trying to insure that your power was not transmitted to a rival clan's bloodline."

"So?" Slavery was slavery as far as I could see. What difference did the motivation make?

"In their minds, the best way to make sure you did not marry an enemy would not be to marry you themselves." Heidar looked at me gently. "It would be to kill you."

I swallowed. "So, if I'm caught . . ."

Heidar leaned forward, his face intense. "If we're captured, don't tell them your name. Make something up, tell them I bought you from the Alorestri for a mistress, or that I caught you after you ran away from your master. Tell them anything, but not that you're a null."

"There's a good chance they already know." The attacks in the village hadn't exactly been subtle.

"In this village, yes. But possibly not in the next or in the one after that. I'll do what I can to get us to the border, but if we are captured—"

"I'll remember." Not that it would probably matter. So far, it looked like the Svarestri welcomed guests by shooting them full of holes. No matter who they were.

I stirred the tea, decided it was as good as it was going to get, and took it off the fire. The tunic was still wet, but I tore off long strips and held them close to the flames. I felt the Fey's eyes on me, but I didn't meet them. I was going to have to touch him to dress the wound—there was no alternative since he couldn't reach that high on his back by himself—and I wanted as little stimulus as possible before that.

When the cloth was dry, I gathered everything up and approached him nervously. The tunic strips were soaked in the tea, then wrapped around his shoulder and tied off. It wasn't the prettiest job of dressing a wound I've ever seen, but at least it was done. And with luck, that amazing metabolism would do the rest.

"There. Good as new."

I started to step back, but he caught my hand. "Thank you."

It was a light touch, but it instantly brought all the feelings I'd been trying to suppress roaring back. I stiffened and drew in a ragged breath, my skin suddenly fever hot. His grip tightened, concern coming into those clear blue eyes, and that made everything infinitely worse. It wasn't normal for me to feel this much this quickly, not for anyone. Yet I stood there, swaying slightly, almost able to taste the intoxicating flavor of his skin. I knew something was wrong, that there was more going on here than just attraction, but my need had become almost a tangible thing and I just didn't care.

CHAPTER 5

I closed my eyes, trying to shut down my reaction, and a vision of fair features and waist-length silver hair floated in front of me. He'd been the youngest of the delegation to Father, or so I'd thought. The seemingly teenaged face probably hid hundreds of years of experience, but I hadn't known enough about the Fey at the time to realize it. I could still recall every one of his mocking words when I'd tenuously responded to the heat in his eyes. I really didn't want to see that expression on Heidar's face.

"I'm sorry." I tried to move away, but strong fingers laced with mine.

"For what?"

"I know how you Fey think of us, of humans." I tugged backward, but Heidar held on.

"And how is that?"

I opened my eyes to glare at him. "We're disgusting to you," I said, echoing that long-ago, contemptuous voice. "Nauseating, untouchable."

Heidar's free hand deliberately skimmed down my side.

The play of light and shadow over the muscles in his arm was mesmerizing. "Who told you that?"

"One of the group who tried to buy me."

"Svarestri." The way he said it, the name sounded almost obscene. The glow of the fire bathed his face in flickering vermilion shadows, making him look dangerous. My body liked that; lately, it seemed to like everthing.

"I suppose. He said—"

"Forget what he said." Heidar pulled me onto his lap, those large hands encircling my waist as warm lips ghosted against my hair. "I've heard it all before. They despise anyone of thin blood, as they call it. It's caused them to miss out on wonders before this."

"I'm not a wonder."

A warm finger traced the line of my cheek. "Could have fooled me."

I leaned in to kiss him but he pulled back. "What's wrong?" I demanded. He'd just finished telling me how he didn't think like the Svarestri, and now he didn't want to touch me?

"Claire, have you ever been with one of us?"

I suddenly found it impossible to focus on what those perfect lips were saying—I was too busy thinking of things I would like to have them do. I dragged him into a desperate kiss, hands sliding everywhere, finally running my fingers through that beautiful hair. For a moment, he was right there with me, his passion matching my own, then he was grasping my shoulders, holding us apart.

"Claire, listen to me!" He was talking, saying my name, but he may as well have been speaking whatever language the Fey used, because I couldn't understand him. I felt horribly tangled up inside, and the pressure that had been building in my chest since I first caught sight of him threatened to smother me. I thought I was going to choke, to die; not from lack of air but from lack of him, something I seemed to need almost as badly. Heidar remained where he was, conflict clear on his face as he searched mine. Then, finally, he gave a rueful smile. "I should never have said I like to live dangerously," he commented. I had no idea what he was talking about, but then he was kissing me and it didn't seem to matter.

Warm, agile fingertips brushed all of the sensitive spots along my ribs as his hands smoothed up my body, caressing my skin through the thin silk of my dress. A tongue ran hot and rough along my throat, reducing me to a delirious, aching, raw nerve. I shivered as he brushed aside the straps of my gown, and when his lips found a nipple the explosion of sensation caused me to jerk violently. He lost his balance and we tumbled off the chair, but I kept contact, riding him to the floor.

I started out on top, trapping his body beneath me, leaning forward to suck hard at his lips and tongue, claiming him with a passion that was almost rage. It should have scared me, to feel anything that strong, but I couldn't think and didn't care. For awhile, I almost forgot where I was, even who I was, as a dark tide swept me to a place beyond thought, where worry and apprehension melted into liquid pulsing need.

The hunger I felt was matched in Heidar's kiss, hot and bruising and violently satisfying. He met me with the same level of passion I gave, one hand sliding to my waist, pressing me against him, the other behind my neck to hold me in place while hard lips crushed mine. His tongue in my mouth was possessive and demanding, matching my almost anguished desire. Burning, bruising kisses continued, tongues dueling, thighs intertwined, until I was breathless.

Somehow I ended up on my back, a strong, warm body pressing me down, being kissed with a desire that still matched my own, but was suddenly more tender. His hands glided down my sides, sliding the gown the rest of the way off my body. An alarm was blaring somewhere in my mind, but he had paused to kiss my throat and I couldn't concentrate with his breath on my skin.

His tongue found the edge of a nipple and he traced it lightly, delicately, the strokes barely there, yet sparking down every nerve. He pulled the tight little nub he'd created into his mouth and caught it between his teeth, sharp enough to make me gasp. It was almost a bite, almost pain, but stopped just short. He flicked it with his tongue, swept around the areola, and captured it again. Then he drew that tender flesh completely into his mouth and began to suck.

I felt like I was drowning. There was just too much stimulus—the pull of his lips on my body, the sounds he made deep in his throat, the decadent feeling of his hair falling over my bare skin. The contrast of those silken strands with the hardness suddenly pressing against me made my breath catch. I wanted to wrap all that softness around me while that firmness thrust into me. I wanted to see those intent eyes grow unfocused with pleasure. I wanted to make him scream.

His hands caressed down my sides, while his mouth explored me. I shivered as that tongue swept lower, teasing around my navel and then at the fragile silk barrier that was all that remained of my clothes. Then he paused, looking up at me along the length of my body. "There is something I need to be certain you understand."

His voice poured over me, the words indistinct and meaningless. My brain didn't seem to be working and my eyes kept closing in pleasure. And why bother with words? The raw sensuality in his voice and the glazed eyes behind his lashes spoke a lot clearer. I pulled him up to me, and when he was close enough, I kissed him long and slow. My thumb stroked his lower lip as we broke apart, while my other hand slid through soft curls to warm satin, loving the deep shudder that racked him as I stroked.

"You've convinced me," he gasped. I arched up, relishing the heaviness, and the sheer, wonderful solidity of him. I lost myself for a moment in the rushing bliss of skin on skin. I realized that my hands were digging into the hard muscles of Heidar's back as I tried to meld our bodies even closer, but he didn't seem to mind. He pulled down my remaining scrap of clothing, then he was burying himself in me, his rich-blue eyes closed in bliss.

The feeling was so perfect that I almost passed out, and when he began to move, pleasure blossomed in nerve endings I hadn't even known I had. I wrapped my legs around him, holding him with my entire body as we found a rhythm. The sensations that followed were mindless, exquisite joy. My nerves all seemed to melt and run together, my veins pulsing with heat, and for a moment, it was absolutely glorious.

And then the pain began.

Without warning, the seductive warmth of his touch changed to blazing heat. A scorching tide rolled up my body, sizzling along every nerve, an electric pulse that had nothing to do with pleasure. White-hot fire erupted behind my eyes, and I stiffened, shocked by pain as sudden and intense as the pleasure had been. Blistering, incandescent waves of agony flooded my mind until I knew nothing else, saw it as an almost living thing, possessing me, consuming me. My blood felt like fire in my veins, searing the living tissue around it into dying, charred cinders. I tried to scream, but couldn't.

Every nerve was flame, every breath agony, but worst of all, another presence was suddenly inside my mind, alien and familiar all at once. It was as if someone, or something, long imprisoned had been set free. And it was angry.

I stared at Heidar, but he had rolled off me to crouch a few feet away, looking wary. He said something, but I couldn't hear him over the rushing in my ears; it sounded like the violent windstorm outside was suddenly in my head. I reached out to him, and when I caught sight of my arm, I was finally able to scream.

It wasn't my arm anymore. In place of my pale, freckled skin was a thick crust of blue-gray scales glittering dully in the firelight, and over the top of that, a grayish membrane was unfurling, translucent except for a network of fine azure veins. It took my frozen brain a few seconds to realize that it was a wing, and that it was protruding from my shoulder.

I simply lay there, not able to process what I was seeing. "What's happening?" I finally managed to whisper, and my voice sounded all wrong, lower and gravelly, like I had a mouth full of rocks. I realized a moment later that the rocks were teeth, big ones, that were starting to grow from my suddenly elongated jaw. I yelped, and it took the form of a tortured scream of burning air that hit the Fey, lifting him off his feet and tossing him completely through one wall of the shed.

Rain blew in, dousing the fire and wetting my face, but suddenly I could see everything perfectly. The horse bucked and whinnied, its eyes showing white all around. I tried to yell at it to shut up, to let me think, but instead of words, a cloud of pure fire erupted all around me. It turned half of the shed into a burgeoning hell of midnight flame and ruby luminescence, and baked the poor creature alive.

A bitter taste flooded my mouth, as I scrambled to my feet. But I kept it closed, staring at the smoking remains in disbelief. Blood was pounding in my ears, my heart was beating far too quickly and I was fast reaching a whole new level of horror. I raised my eyes to meet Heidar's shining blue ones. He was peering over the remains of the wall, his tousled hair sticking out wildly in every direction.

"Well, that didn't go so badly," he said, his voice unsteady.

I stared at him, wanting to tell him to run, to get as far away as possible from whatever was happening to me. But

I didn't dare open my mouth, and he slowly climbed into the room, past charred bricks and falling timbers.

He picked up the bucket carefully, letting me see every move as he made it as if I was a wild animal he didn't want to spook. He held the reflective surface in front of me, at eye level. For a moment, all I could see was the reflection of the flames, then I realized what else I was looking at.

My vision was surprisingly clear, but my mind was uncomprehending. The reflection showed me a short gray snout studded with gleaming teeth. Above it rose eyes with evil-looking, slitted pupils, but of a ridiculous pale lavender color. My eyes filled with tears, and so did those staring at me from the side of the bucket. The horrible realization hit home, and I batted the thing away with a hand that had sprouted inch-long talons.

The bucket ricocheted off the wall and landed back at Heidar's feet. He bent to pick it up, and a hiss, low and menacing, issued from between my tightly clenched teeth. Once was enough. I didn't need to see it again.

He let it go, but straightened with a frown on his face. "I think I would like some answers," he announced.

He would like some answers?

He moved forward and I tried to shuffle back, but something stopped me. I looked behind me to see huge, scale-covered haunches and a fat tail, wedged in between the remaining shed walls. Grayish-black wings, like a bat's if they were blown up about a hundred times in size, moved with me, and the sound of them scraping over the scales made me shudder.

"Claire." I whipped around at Heidar's voice and found him within a few feet of me. Had he somehow missed the charred body of the horse? It was slowly crumbling to dust under the driving pressure of the rain, but was still recognizable. Did he want to join it? "This is . . . a little unexpected," he said, putting out a hand to take hold of my clawed paw. He patted it gently. "But we'll get through it."

Get through it? I stared at him, completely at a loss. He was crazier than I was.

"I know it's likely difficult to concentrate right now," he said, then stopped. His face contorted, and he began making a low, strangled sound. After a minute, I realized that he was trying not to laugh. He finally swallowed it back down. "But you need to, ah, try to visualize your old form."

I glared at him, and my newly acquired tail began whipping back and forth. It hit the side of the shed with a crack, knocking most of it out and sending the door spinning away into the night. Without that support, the rest of the building gave way and, with a groan of splintering wood, caved in around us.

Several large roof beams hit the top of my head and bounced off. They hurt, but not badly, which probably explained why Heidar had burrowed beneath my front paws, using my new, huge belly as shelter. I roared in confusion, pain and sheer disbelief, and set a nearby tree on fire. Beyond it, I saw lights flicker on in what my improved vision told me was a farmhouse. Oh, shit.

The farmer must have been having a sleepover, because within seconds, four or five well-armed figures were running toward us, yelling something that didn't sound friendly. Heidar looked up at me, his eyes serious for once. "You have to fly us out of here."

Even if I'd been able to talk, I would probably have been speechless. After a minute, he nodded, swallowing hard. "Okay, plan B." He started pushing at me, and actually succeeded in making me waddle a few steps back. "The tree line," he panted, "run for it!"

I barely heard him. I'd just caught sight of my toes, which were peeking out from under the giant swell of my belly, their two-inch-long talons ripping up the ground as I moved. For some reason, that small detail suddenly overwhelmed me. I'd been treated like a monster all my life, but I'd never looked the part before, and it filled me with shame, deep and bitter and smothering, to the point that it was a struggle just to breathe.

My head started to pound, a vivid, furious pain behind the temples. I raised a hand to my face, but only succeeded in jabbing myself in the snout with a claw. I felt around more carefully after that, and discovered an arrow that had lodged itself between two of my scales that didn't overlap perfectly. I could feel sticky blood leaking down the side of what had once been my face, and it brought me back to my surroundings.

Two Fey were lying on the ground nearby, their long silver hair bright against the black soil. Heidar was battling another, and seemed to be holding his own, as the remainder were content to hide behind the smoldering remains of the shed, lobbing arrows at me. Heidar looked up after knocking out his opponent, a fierce triumph on his features. But in this form, my height was greater than his and I could see the village guards hotfooting it toward us down the road. There had to be fifty of them, and judging by the amount of weapons they carried, they hadn't come to let bygones be bygones. Heidar saw them a second later, after they rounded the bend leading up to the house, and his face lost its happy glow.

They showed none of the caution they'd used before, but ran right at us. "They're thinking of the podium in the alley. They don't think you're real!" Heidar whispered. "Let them get a little closer, then take them out."

I blinked at him in slow horror. He couldn't be serious. He'd seen the horse—did he actually expect me to do that to *people*? I opened my mouth to tell him off, but instead of words, the air erupted in another cloud of gold and ruby fire. Several arrows incinerated mid-air, and a nearby tree exploded in a hail of burning bark and wet leaves. I snapped my mouth shut, horrified, but none of the Fey had been close enough to get charred. They dove for cover in ditches beside the road, sinking beneath the flood that had almost filled them until only the tops of their heads showed.

"Fight or run," Heidar told me urgently. "There are no other choices!" I stood there, looking back and forth from him to the Fey. "This isn't New York," he said, his hands gripping me hard enough that I could feel it even through the scales. "Understand me, Claire. They will kill us if they can."

Almost as if to underscore his point, we were suddenly inundated with a whole swarm of arrows. It seemed wet ones could still fly. Too bad I couldn't. I might have wings, but I didn't know how to use them. I wasn't even sure which muscles to flex to unfurl them, but I had to try.

I managed to get one wing off my back, mostly by luck, but as soon as I tried to raise it, arrows rained down on me from two directions at once. The archers behind the shed had decided to combine their force with those in the ditches, and every single one of them was aiming for me. Pain tore at me as several projectiles ripped through the thin membrane of the wing. It didn't bleed much, but it also didn't look like it was going to fly full of holes.

Most of the other arrows were bouncing harmlessly off my scales, but a few here and there were finding chinks in my armor. Black blood spattered onto Heidar's face from a wound in my shoulder. He wiped it off with his hand and stared at it, his face furious. I wondered in a detached sort of way how long it would take before the blood loss killed me.

Then things managed to get even worse. An inhuman screech echoed across the forest like thunder. For a moment, I thought that's what it was, but all the Fey suddenly stopped firing and looked up. I did the same, but although the rain had finally slowed, I couldn't see anything but angry dark clouds with a sliver of moon behind them.

Then, out of a cloud bank burst a sight from a fairy tale, with glowing, torchlit eyes, leathery wings and scales that glittered like diamonds in the starlight. It swooped down over us and the next second, the road, the shed and the nearby trees erupted in a rush of sound and strange, crimson flame. The Fey scattered, some on fire, for the shelter of the forest. I stayed put with Heidar crouched beneath me, relieved to find that my scales didn't burn.

The person who seemed to be in charge of the guards regrouped them after a few moments, but before they could do more than release a few arrows, there was an ear-shattering boom and a flash of painfully bright light, and a fireball barreled right for them. It was beautiful, red and orange, with little tongues of green flame lapping at the edges. But the Fey didn't seem to appreciate the sight. There was a lot of screaming and running and what little cohesion they'd had broke apart. Then the dragon landed and went on a rampage, devouring the closest guards in a few gulps before beginning to pursue the ones that darted in and out and up the trees in a vain attempt to escape. A few got away, haring back down the road, running past the burning hole in the ground where the fireball had struck. But most remained, either seared alive or serving as dragon-food.

"Claire, listen to me," Heidar said in a furious whisper. "The Dark Fey have a very low birth rate—even worse than ours. Most of them can't interbreed with humans and that, plus losses against the Alorestri, have seriously reduced their numbers."

I looked at him blankly. Why the hell was he telling me this *now*? I could smell the burning flesh on the wind, and hear the sounds of carnage from within the trees. I felt sick.

"He probably won't kill you," Heidar continued, "as long as you show the proper respect. When he emerges, don't challenge him. Just stay perfectly still as he looks you over, wings folded, head down."

I vaguely wondered what else he thought I was going to do. My head was killing me from the arrow still sticking out of it, and my wings were useless. Not to mention that this body I'd somehow acquired looked nothing like the dragon's streamlined, lithe form. I doubted if those little wings could lift my bulk even if I figured out how they worked.

The scene wavered in front of me as the dragon emerged from the woods. He stepped on the body of a fallen Fey, grinding it into the mud. Then he just stood there, looking at me for a long moment. Despite the horrific things I'd seen him do, I couldn't help but be awed. He was a terrible, but strangely beautiful, sight. His golden scales had a reflective quality that mine lacked. Flames from the burning trees reflected off them, painting him dark orange and red in places. His wings, which he didn't seem to have any trouble controlling, were huge, black things that made mine look almost vestigial. As I watched, they folded neatly over his back.

He moved closer, not the clumsy waddle I'd been doing, but with almost snakelike fluidity. His large golden eyes looked me over, taking his time. His long snout nudged Heidar, who I was proud to see didn't go screaming after the other Fey, although he looked like he was thinking about it. Then the snout brushed against my tattered wing and a whimper slipped out between my lips. It was half pain, half knowledge that I was no more match for him than I had been for the guards. His talons were fully six inches long, and glittered like daggers at the end of his paws.

He paused, and reared back at my small cry. He said something, actually spoke, but it was in a language I didn't know. It had a liquid undercurrent that washed over me almost like a caress. Then his form wavered like it was melting. But there was no residue on the ground, nothing to show he'd been there except a tall man with dark red hair and a tender expression.

"You have your mother's eyes," he told me, right before I passed out.

CHAPTER 6

I woke up on a bed in a large room. It was mostly dark, except for the flickering shapes a few low-burning candles sent dancing along the walls. But the fact that everything was slightly out of focus told me that something very good had happened while I was out. A glance at the human-looking arm draped over my stomach confirmed it. I was back.

Somebody groaned nearby and I sat up. A very battered-looking Heidar was lying on a nearby chaise, while an old woman in a white apron finished winding a bandage around his waist. "Stop whining, elf," she told him, "your ribs will be sore for a day or two, but you'll live." She didn't sound happy about it, and the squeeze she gave his shoulder as she pulled down his nightshirt was on the wounded side. He drew in air with a hiss, but didn't retaliate. At the moment, I wasn't sure he could.

"What happened to you?" I asked.

The woman spun around. "Ah, you're awake." She bustled over, beaming.

"You fell on me," Heidar said accusingly.

I blinked at him. He was basically one large bruise, which, thanks to his accelerated healing abilities, had left him with bright orange and lavender splotches all over his body.

"Sorry."

"Don't you apologize to him! From what I hear, you saved his worthless elf hide." The older woman lifted my arm for a look. I got a look at her, too, and realized that I'd been a little hasty. Whatever she was, woman didn't seem to quite fit.

The head was all right, complete with kind blue eyes, wispy white hair pulled back into a neat chignon and a pair of reading glasses perched on the end of her nose. But the body under the apron didn't move like a human's, and the hand she reached out to me with was more like a claw. I looked down and saw three-toed bird feet peeking out from under the flounce on her skirt. I swallowed, and said nothing. Who was I to talk?

I glanced over at Heidar, who had managed to prop himself up on some pillows. "I thought 'elf' was pejorative."

He scowled. "It is."

"You'll be fine," she said kindly, patting my cheek. "Get some rest and don't let that one make you upset." She said the last glaring at Heidar, then turned and made a hopping sort of exit. A black feather blew out from beneath her skirts and floated slowly to the floor.

"Harpy," Heidar said, before I could ask. He moved around, trying to find some comfortable position, but finally gave up. "I think we need to talk." I looked at him warily. I wasn't sure I was ready to talk about what had happened yet. I wasn't sure I ever would be. "If I am stuck in enemy territory with someone, I would like to at least know who—or what—she is," he was saying. "You could start by explaining what you did to those guards."

"Which guards?" I had a vision of exploding trees and burning silver hair.

"The ones in the village, shortly after we arrived. I meant to ask you about it before but I . . . was distracted."

I relaxed slightly. Anything that didn't involve scales claws or fathers, I could handle. "I told you. I'm a projective null."

"Nulls block magic. That was not blocking it!"

"It's never happened that way before." I struggled for words that would make sense. "Usually, it just . . . goes somewhere inside me, like I absorb it somehow, and then it's gone. I've never been able to . . . redirect it . . . before."

He didn't look like he believed me. "You used it as a weapon."

I started to shrug, but stopped because it hurt. My whole right side felt sore, like I'd swum a marathon using only one arm. "It was considered one, a long time ago. Nulls used to serve as bodyguards to anybody worried about a magical assault. They brought down the wards guarding their enemies' lands, and some of the strongest stopped entire battles just by walking onto the field. But that was before the Harvesters almost wiped us out."

"To make null bombs."

"Yeah. In the eyes of most of the supernatural community, I'm not a person, I'm a weapon. And the sooner they drain me into one of their bombs the better."

"But your family protected you," Heidar said, more softly. He seemed to realize he'd hit a nerve.

"If you call trying to sell me to the Fey protection."

"I assumed they did so to keep you away from the Harvesters. If you were part of a powerful Fey family—"

I laughed, but it sounded bitter. "My welfare was not foremost in Father's mind."

I sat up and found that I could move with no trouble except for a little stiffness. Someone had put me in a white nightgown liberally trimmed with lace—not my style—but I didn't feel like complaining. I sat on the edge of the bed and looked at poor, beat-up Heidar. Normally, I didn't like talking about my family history, but under the circumstances, I thought it might be relevant.

"My father was always too ambitious for his own good, especially in politics," I said, grimacing a little at the understatement. "When he discovered that Jonas Marsden, the mage who headed up the Great Council, was retiring, he decided he would have the top spot himself or die trying." It ended up the latter, but the prize glittered so brightly that it had blinded him to the risks.

The Council is the ruling body of the Silver Circle, which controls the actions of the entire western hemisphere's magical community. Whoever leads it wields more power than the U.S. president, the Secretary General of the U.N. and a few prime ministers thrown in for good measure—with the added bonus of fewer checks on his behavior. In return for me, the Fey promised to help Father's campaign with a little timely blackmail. It seemed that his chief opponent would have also sold his firstborn for power, if he hadn't already done so for a seat on the Council. I think the Fey found it amusing that one candidate would tarnish another's name by committing the same sin himself—it fit their sense of irony.

"Sebastian convinced Father that only the Fey could insure his victory. And he only had one thing they wanted."

"You."

"Seb thought it would get me out of the way," I explained, "and clear the road for him to inherit the business. But I doubt he had to talk very hard. I'm almost six feet tall. I tower over the rest of the family like, as Father was fond of saying, the stork forgot to leave the baby and instead took up residence itself. Even worse, I'm a redheaded, green-eyed stork in a family of mostly short, brown-eyed brunets." It was a fact constantly brought up by my relatives—assuming they were my relatives.

"And your mother?"

"Also short, although she was blonde."

"No, I mean, did she ever mention anything about having an . . . unusual encounter?"

"She died shortly after I was born—by falling down a flight of stairs she'd climbed safely a hundred times before. So I don't know much about her. All the family ever said was that she craved hot sauce the whole time she was carrying me." A little tidbit that seemed truly ironic now. "But no one ever mentioned a liaison with anyone tall, dark, and scaly."

Heidar laughed. He looked immediately contrite, but I shrugged. "It's all right. Obviously, it happened."

He raised a brow, then winced as if it had hurt. "You aren't happy to find out about your second nature."

I stared at him. "Happy?"

He sighed and got up, moving stiffly over to the bed. "That's what I thought."

"What part of turning into a monster is supposed to be good news?" I asked, incredulously.

"You aren't a monster, Claire," he told me patiently. "You're simply one of the Two-Natured. There's quite a few of us around, what with all the inbreeding with humans that has taken place over the years. I'm half Light Fey, half human myself."

"Big deal!" I jumped up and a frown creased his forehead as he watched me stride back and forth beside the bed. "In your case, that means you get a great body and wonderful bone structure! The worst you have to put up with is glowing a little sometimes!"

His face brightened. "I have a great body?"

I whirled on him, furious. "And what do I have? That fat, scaly, horrible . . . thing . . . with wings!" I broke off because I was close to tears and I didn't want to cry. I just wanted this not to be real. "I killed that horse, and I don't even eat meat!" I collapsed into a heap, crying anyway, remembering how terrified that poor creature had looked right before I barbecued him. He should have been scared—I certainly was.

I felt strong arms go around me, but I refused to look up. I didn't want to see revulsion in Heidar's eyes. I wondered if, somehow, the Fey that had come to Father's had known. Had they seen something in me that gave it away, some small sign I hadn't known to look for? The young one who had called me disgusting—had he seen what I truly was when the layers were pulled away?

A violent shudder shook me and I realized that I was crying, really sobbing, like a small child. I was a mess of conflicting emotions, with fear being uppermost, and no matter how much I cried, it didn't seem to help. Heidar held me for a while, letting me get it out, but when I didn't stop he lifted my chin. I don't know what I looked like—probably nothing very appealing as my skin goes all blotchy when I cry—but he didn't seem to notice. His usually bright blue eyes were virtually black with some emotion, but there was no revulsion that I could see.

He took one of my hands in his. I stared at it, remembering that he'd used the same gesture on my dragon-form. The scales hadn't seemed to bother him. Suddenly, those sensual lips curved into a smile. "I thought you made a really cute dragon, myself."

I stared at him.

"You had these big pansy-colored eyes, and a little shock of purple fuzz, right here." He tickled my chin.

"You're crazy," I told him. At that moment, I really believed it.

"No, I've simply had a lot longer to learn to deal with being Two-Natured than you have." His face turned serious. "And it's not so bad. Yes, there are . . . challenges . . . but there are advantages, as well. Both of you gain some of the other's abilities, making you far stronger in either form than you would have been otherwise." He thought for a minute. "Which might explain why you're such a strong null. Your dragon twin lends you extra power."

"I'm a monster," I whispered, wondering how he'd somehow missed that.

"No, you're half Fey, like me."

"I'm not like you!" I yelled into his too composed face. What was he, retarded? "Dragons are . . . are . . . *things*, not people!"

"Now you sound like the Svarestri," Heidar said disapprovingly. "There really are no Light and Dark Fey, Claire. It's something we tell ourselves, but our blood is pretty much the same, when you come right down to it. The Svarestri used to rule Faerie, and they took their fall hard. They've never gotten over it, never learned to accept being on a par with the rest of us. So they refuse to believe that they are."

He settled back against the side of the bed, taking me with him. "They say the rest of the Light Elves have thin blood because we've married so many humans over the centuries. They say the Dark Fey are monsters, ancient experiments gone wrong that the gods never bothered to destroy. Only they are pure, only they are fit to rule. But it's all a bunch of nonsense."

"Is it?" I remembered what I'd looked like, felt like, in that other skin, and shuddered.

Heidar suddenly stood up, lifting me in his arms, and carried me over to a large bay window. I hadn't noticed it because it was draped in dark red velvet that, in the shadows, became almost invisible against the deep gray stone of the walls. He sat me on the bench in front of it and drew back the drapes. Early morning sunlight flooded over the balcony, giving the mellow wood of the floor a cheerful golden glow. "Look out there, and tell me you see monsters," he said softly.

Outside, a glorious sunrise was breaking over a wide patchwork of green fields. A river cut a meandering path across the scene, like a ribbon of fire as the sun hit it. Orange and cherry colored clouds framed the rising sun, bathing the dark castle walls below the window in a soft pink blush. We were high, I realized, maybe twenty stories above the ground, because the castle was built over a ravine. But I didn't have to look down to see what Heidar was talking about.

A golden face noticed me and flew over to hover just outside the glass. Huge wings beat the air in powerful strokes, holding him in place as we stared at each other. Sunlight glinted off his scales, making him look like he was wearing tight-fitting, golden armor, and behind him, four more dragons hovered close, trying to catch a view. One was green, one a fiery red and two more a softer gray-blue. Like I had been.

"They're very excited," Heidar whispered against my hair. "A child is a great joy among us, and none of them even knew you existed until last night. Your mother didn't live long enough to tell her lover, or perhaps she was afraid he would want to take you away from her if he knew."

I found myself completely unable to tear my eyes away from the scene outside the window. They looked so . . . free. Something about the way they rode the air—with a command, a presence, an ownership of it—tore at my heart. My dragon form had been fat and clumsy, with small wings that would never have allowed me to fly even if I'd known how. "I'll never do that," I said softly.

Heidar laughed, his blue eyes reflecting the color of the sky. "Your twin self is a newborn, Claire! How many babies know how to walk? Give it time."

"A baby?"

"It's why your father was able to find you," Heidar said, hugging me against him. The compulsion I'd felt to touch him seemed to have gone, but the pleasure remained. I was glad that something, at least, had stayed the same.

"When one of the Two-Natured reaches puberty, they

usually come into their second self. If not, it tends to happen the first time they have intercourse with another Fey. The power unleashed is always considerable, and some families can feel it when a new child manifests. Your father was here, in the Dark Fey lands, when he felt your second nature being born. He left immediately to look for you."

"Good thing." The giant face didn't smile, I wasn't sure it could, but one great eye dropped me a wink. Then he flew away a short distance so the others could get a look. "Who are they?"

"An aunt, two cousins, and your half-brother."

"I have a brother?" It was too much to take in. The closest thing to a sibling I'd ever had was Seb. And for some reason, I'd never really counted him.

"That would be the red one. He was, er, a little perturbed with me, as you can see."

"What?" I turned to see Heidar rubbing the side of his jaw ruefully.

"He packs quite a punch."

"I thought you said I fell on you?"

"You did. Your brother just . . . helped connect the dots, so to speak."

I turned back to see a bright, fire-engine-red snout pressed against the glass. The eyes that met mine were a shocking, vivid green. He reared back when he saw my hand find Heidar's, and those magnificent eyes narrowed to slits. He looked like he was contemplating having Fey for dinner.

"Why is he upset with you?"

Heidar looked sheepish. "For good reason. I knew you were Two-Natured as soon as I met you, but I didn't realize until much later that you had never birthed your second self. And even when I did, I assumed—foolishly—that you were half Light Fey. Our twin's birth tends to be somewhat . . . less dramatic . . . so I wasn't too concerned. Even so, I shouldn't have risked it. As your brother pointed out, I nearly got both of us killed."

"It wasn't your fault." If he could be honest, so could I. "I practically threw myself at you."

"Of course you did." He said it so matter-of-factly, that it took a minute to register.

I withdrew my hand. "What?"

"It was the first time you'd been around another member of Faerie since coming of age—other than those Svarestri sticks in the mud. Of course you were drawn to me. Your twin needed me to manifest." He grinned. "Not to mention that my family has a reputation for being irresistible."

"So you're saying what? It was just hormones?"

"In your case, I don't know. But it was not my first time with another Fey. I could have controlled myself better. I should have." He flushed slightly. "It's simply been a very long time since anyone looked at me the way you did—anyone Fey," he added after a moment.

"I thought you said you were irresistible."

"I'm also half-human. Fey women who are full-bloods want full-blooded children, for the prestige and also because many estates cannot be passed to half-bloods. Those who are already partly human also want a full-blood so as not to weaken the line further." He gave me a slight, lopsided smile. "When it comes to anything permanent, I suppose I am resistible after all."

"It sounds like Fey women are as stupid as the Svarestri," I said, climbing into his lap. If it hurt him, he didn't let it show.

"You could do better," he told me seriously. His eyes had turned the purest dark sapphire, and were brimming with an expression I couldn't quite define. "I'll never inherit, Claire. My father is the Blarestri king, but the throne can only pass to someone with a majority of Fey blood. So our children could never hope to—"

"Aren't you getting a little ahead of things?" I snuggled into his lap and bent my head to his delicate, pointed ear.

Slowly, deliberately, I caressed its outline with my tongue. Within seconds, he was almost vibrating with need, and my own body was starting to feel the onset of another all-consuming tide of pleasure. God, I loved Fey men! "We haven't made a baby yet," I whispered.

Heidar's eyes widened as I began to move against him. "I don't believe that will be a problem."

I waved at the gamboling dragons outside, who were now obviously showing off for my benefit. It would have been a scene to take my breath away, under other circumstances. At the moment, it was just making me dizzy.

"Later," I said when I could trust my voice. "We need to talk about how we're going to get that damned rune back."

Heidar reached up to draw the curtains, and rolled me beneath him, all in one motion. "Much later."

CHAPTER 7

A week later, we were stuck in traffic hell going over the Brooklyn Bridge. We'd reentered Earth through a portal in Manhattan, necessitating a little trip to get back to the auction house. Only, it was rush hour, and we weren't getting anywhere. That would have been nerve-wracking enough on its own, but with a Light Fey and a dragon in the car, it was enough to make anyone testy.

The dragon was Tanet, my newly discovered brother. He'd refused to allow me to go back "into the world of men" without him. He seemed to view New York as a place filled with both wonders and horrors too great to describe, and believed that my willingness to travel there showed great fortitude.

At the moment, I kind of agreed with him. Damn it, we hadn't moved in five minutes! There simply had to be a wreck up ahead somewhere.

"I think we could get there faster by walking," Heidar grumbled, echoing my thoughts. Tanet didn't say anything, being occupied with his lunch. Despite the fact that he was in human form—a gangly, red-haired teenager—his meal consisted of a squirming sack of live rats. I was very carefully not looking at him in the mirror. He had offered me a terrified-looking specimen shortly after we got under way and my dragon twin had immediately started mewling hungrily. Apparently, it hadn't thought much of the salad I'd had for lunch. I'd tamped it down and smiled a refusal at him. My inner beast could damn well learn to eat tofu and like it.

While I glared at the unmoving line of traffic, a woman in the next lane caught sight of Heidar. She stared in open-mouthed astonishment until she rammed her car into the SUV in front of her. I realized that he wasn't wearing his usual all-encompassing cloak, maybe because it was about ninety degrees outside. The Fey timeline doesn't move at the same speed as the human, a fact I'd realized when we arrived back from a week in Faerie to discover that New York had progressed from a cold spring to a scorching summer.

Whether the rune could have lain undiscovered at Gerald's for so long was problematic. But it hadn't been listed for sale again, and no Svarestri army had suddenly appeared in anyone else's lands. So we were hopeful, assuming we could ever make it back to Gerald's in the first place.

"Can you do anything about that?" I demanded, as the woman, heedless of the angry cries of the other drivers, got out of her car and ran over to peer in the passenger window. Wonderful.

Heidar blinked at me as she began hammering on the glass. "Such as?"

"You could try to stop glowing!"

"You know I can't do anything about that."

"Then tell her to go back to her car and forget about us!" I scanned the area for police, but mercifully didn't see any. We had enough weapons in the car to outfit a small army, none of which were registered with the NYPD. I hoped Heidar could manage a strong enough suggestion to overcome her interest; if not, we were in trouble because I certainly couldn't. No magic means no magic, and that includes the mind control variety.

He rolled down his window, but that only made things worse. The driver of the SUV and a motorcycle messenger boy soon joined the woman, worshipping at the new shrine of Heidar. "Do something!" I hissed frantically.

"I'm Alma," the woman breathed, drinking him in with her eyes. "I work for Manhattan Models, and I have to tell you, my boss would offer you a contract before you finished walking through the door! Let me give you my card—"

"I'm Steve," the SUV guy said, thrusting a hand in the window and trying to muscle Alma out of the way. "I'm a freelance photographer, and buddy, could you and I make a mint! We gotta talk—"

He was cut off by a precisely aimed elbow to the ribs. Yeah, Alma was a native. "Back off, I saw him first!"

"It's a free country, lady," Steve gasped, and grabbed for the window ledge. That resulted in a tug of war that landed them in a scuffling fight outside our car. The motorcycle messenger quietly took their place. He didn't say anything, even to introduce himself, just stood there staring at Heidar with a look of wonder.

"I'm open to suggestions," Heidar informed me dryly.

"Do a glamour!" I whispered, having just sighted a red-and-blue light weaving its way toward us. It was pretty far back, but the cop was on a motorcycle, meaning he would be here soon even if the line didn't move. Come on, I thought desperately, how long had we been sitting here? I hit the horn. "Let's move, people!"

"Your power makes working any magic much more difficult," Heidar reminded me. "We don't know what we'll find at the auction house. I cannot afford the drain of a prolonged glamourie."

Tanet caught my eye in the mirror and grinned, his teeth as red as his hair. He rolled his eyes at Heidar and shook his head. Tanet could understand a little English, but so far he spoke about the same number of words of my language as I did of his—roughly five. But he got his point across.

"We aren't going to find anything if we're in jail!" I said. The delivery van in front of me lurched forward a few yards, and I followed on its bumper. Heidar's congregation jogged after us, their vehicles abandoned in their wake.

Alma, looking ruffled and with a tear in her blouse, reached us first. She shoved a card in Heidar's face. "My business number is on the front, but wait—let me give you my home number, too." She started searching frantically in her purse for a pen. "Call me anytime, I mean that!" I noticed her wedding ring and wondered how much her husband would appreciate getting a midnight message from a male client, but the thought didn't appear to faze Alma. Or maybe it simply hadn't occurred to her. She looked pretty bemused.

"The human authorities are the least of our worries," Heidar intoned darkly.

"Fine. Explain that to the cop who's two cars back," I told him, wondering if it was time to cut and run. I really could walk faster than traffic was moving.

Alma's hand brushed Heidar's as she scribbled down her number, and that slight touch seemed to seriously up the amplitude on her fascination. She started trying to crawl through the window, but Steve jerked her away. A couple of matronly ladies in a nearby Volvo began craning their necks to see what all the commotion was about and I got a sudden vision of us besieged by love-struck grandmas.

"Damn it, Heidar, help me!"

"What seems to be the trouble here?" One of New York's finest had pulled up beside us and was attempting to see inside the car. Tanet had just torn off another rat's head in the backseat and was crunching it contentedly. I let my head fall forward onto the steering wheel.

"We require assistance," Heidar told the policeman.

"Yes, sir! And what can I do to help?" I looked up to find the policeman staring at Heidar with the same look of slavish devotion everyone else seemed to be wearing.

"The vehicles do not move," Heidar explained, gesturing at the long line ahead of us.

"I'll see what can be done about your problem, sir!" The cop strode away like a man on a mission and remounted his motorcycle. I watched in complete bewilderment as he turned on his siren and started clearing a path through the crowd, ignoring the fact that Heidar continued to hold court with a growing number of admirers in the middle of the bridge.

"Do the damn glamourie," I whispered, as the two old ladies in the Volvo began blowing him kisses.

I'd barely finished speaking when the florist van ahead of us suddenly burst its seams, engulfed by large climbing vines that broke through the back doors and grew upward from the undercarriage. As if that wasn't enough, a flood of hothouse blooms exploded out of the back, slapping us with a rain of rose petals that made the car's automatic wipers switch on.

I turned them off, and shot Heidar a look.

"You have two magical natures now," he reminded me. "Your power is subsequently greater."

"So?"

"I, er, overcompensated."

We'd discovered that Heidar's dual nature was the reason my power hadn't originally had much effect on him. The human part of him had blocked it from reaching his Fey magic, but now that my Fey half was out and about, he was having some of the same problems that everyone else did. It was only one of a number of issues in our new relationship, most of which involved families who cordially loathed each other. I was still hoping for a fairy-tale ending, but was starting to suspect we'd have to work for it.

We inched around the destroyed van with the help of

our new police escort, who also insured that we reached the auction house in record time. He sat on his motorcycle, scratching his head and looking around uncertainly. He was probably wondering what we were doing at a dilapidated warehouse on the Brooklyn waterfront without so much as a nearby deli to explain its allure. I stayed in the car until Heidar worked his magic on the man's mind and he left happy. Then Tanet and I piled out onto the asphalt.

It was high noon, chosen because the trolls and vamps would be asleep. That didn't mean there wouldn't be security, of course, but after several years on the payroll, I knew Gerald's as well as anyone. Which probably explained why my palms were sweating.

"He uses booby traps in daytime," I told the rest of the team. "Bad ones."

Heidar translated for Tanet, who nodded before transforming into his alter ego and bounding over the chain-link fence. A few flaps of his powerful wings took him up to the second story, and a heave and a wiggle forced his considerable bulk through a window. Unfortunately, he didn't bother to open it first.

So much for the element of surprise.

"What's he doing?" I asked.

Heidar gave me a sardonic look while breaking open the lock on the front gate. "Why do you think your father sent him with us?"

I preceded him through the fence and up a cracked concrete sidewalk. "To help?"

"He wants the rune, Claire. I saw it on his face when you were telling him about how we met. Your brother is here to get it for him."

I sighed. It didn't surprise me. The week I'd spent with my new relatives had been both very strange and eerily familiar. Strange because the family seemed genuinely happy to have me around, a sensation I'd never had growing up. Familiar because, despite the otherworldly surroundings, the plotting and scheming had been exactly the same as I'd heard every day as a child. This time it was Fey politics instead of human, but it gave me an identical queasy feeling in the pit of my stomach. Politics had led Father to try to sell me to the Fey, made the family declare me a murderer, and caused the Svarestri to try to kill me on sight. I hated politics.

"What would happen if the Dark Fey got the rune?" I asked, after Heidar kicked in the front door. The sound of splintering wood made me wince, but it made no sense to try to sneak around when we could hear the crashes a 1,200-pound dragon made as it tore through the place.

"I don't know. The Dark King would persuade your father to give it up sooner or later, in exchange for more lands, a higher title. . . ." He shrugged. "Whatever it took. What he would do with it afterward . . . I don't know," he repeated. He didn't look happy about the prospect.

Unlike Tanet, we headed directly to the lower levels, but all we encountered on the way down was peeling paint and dusty stairs. I didn't see any vamps, but that didn't mean much. If any were powerful enough to be awake, they'd be waiting for us below, well out of the sun.

At the bottom, the light switch didn't work, which meant that the loading area would have been completely dark except that Heidar was glowing like some otherworldly lantern. I'd asked him why he glowed in the human world and not in the Fey, but the answer was really long and complicated, and I'd fallen asleep in the middle of it. So it remained a mystery. But for once, I was grateful for it.

We made our way across the room easily, unimpeded by the usual jumble of pallets, boxes, and packing material that tended to be strewn around. I finally managed to find the button to operate the loading door, but as with the light switch, it didn't work. Heidar manually forced the thing up its tracks, letting in enough sunlight to illuminate the whole room. Not that there was much to see.

I'd never seen the place so clean. The only signs that anyone had ever run a business here were a stenciled logo on the wall for a 1950s-era beer company and a broken pallet. It looked like Gerald's was out of business.

Heidar walked over to where the podium had rested when not in use and managed to pull down the platform. There was nothing on top. The bolts that had once held the giant dragon's head sat empty and, like everything else around us, were covered in dust.

Heidar looked around, his face getting unhappier by the minute. "I don't like this, Claire. It feels too much like a—"

"Trap?"

Heidar spun around at the voice, but I just stiffened. I didn't need to look to know who'd spoken. Heidar tensed, remembering Seb's face from the last time we'd all been here together, but I knew there was nothing he could do. The posse was already fanning out around the room, half of them mages, half well-armed humans.

"I can't drain them all," I told him as Seb walked over. The mages would have trouble getting magic to work with me in the room, but then, they didn't really need it. The guns most of them were holding would work just fine.

"I know."

Seb stopped in front of us, a cautious few yards away. His suit was a light, summer-weight khaki that did nothing for his sallow complexion. It looked hot, or maybe he was more nervous than he was letting on.

I realized that I hadn't heard anything from upstairs in a while, and wondered where Tanet was. If he'd encountered Seb's people, we would certainly have heard the commotion. At least I hoped so. I eyed the mages, but since I didn't know more than a couple of them, I had no way to tell if their power had recently taken a drain. Like enough to kill a young dragon.

Seb's eyes were on Heidar with a speculative gleam. "Claire always did attract unusual friends." He glanced at me. "That roommate of yours came to see me shortly after you disappeared. She seemed to think I might be involved." He smiled. "Of course, I was able to claim quite honestly that I'd had nothing to do with it!"

"Not for lack of trying."

He shrugged. "You gave me little choice. Had you gone to Faerie years ago as planned, we would never have quarreled." He looked back at Heidar. "She can be stubborn."

I was about to demand if Seb thought "quarrel" really covered our relationship, when Heidar spoke. "I've noticed." I turned to look at him, but he didn't even glance at me. His eyes were on Seb, and he was smiling. "Do you have it?"

Sebastian nodded. "I thought one of you would be by eventually." He pulled a hand out of his pocket, something clutched in his fist. "I had this place warded, so I'd know when you showed up."

"Matthew told you I tried to persuade him to sell it ahead of the auction."

"And that he refused. A good businessman always holds out for the best price."

Heidar smiled gently. "And what is your price?"

"What do you think?" Seb shot a glance in my direction and opened his hand. My vision seemed to narrow to the point where all I could see was the small gray rune stone sitting in his sweaty palm. All I could hear was Heidar's voice, telling me how important it was, how whoever had it could make a bid to rule all Faerie. Politics, I thought numbly. Had that been what all this was about? Getting me to trust him enough to come back here with him, so he could make his deal?

"Let me see if I understand," Heidar was saying. "I give you Claire, and I walk out of here with the rune—just like that?"

"I've no wish to make an enemy of the Fey," Seb told him, probably truthfully. "The family would like to do more business in Faerie, not less. This could be the start of a lucrative arrangement between us." He glanced at me again. "I could demand more for the stone, but I'd prefer to make a goodwill gesture. Give me Claire, and we'll part friends."

Heidar looked upward suddenly, for no reason I could see. "You know," he said slowly, "I really don't think we will."

I'm still not entirely sure the order of what happened next. At almost the same time, Tanet dropped out of the sky into the middle of the circle of mages, Heidar stabbed Seb in the neck and the rune went flying. It hit the deck near Tanet's huge front paw, but he didn't notice. He was too busy eating one mage, while using another as a club with which to beat several more. The humans started firing at him, but the bullets had no more effect on dragon scales than the Fey arrows had done. I didn't wait for them to remember about me, but flung myself at the stone. I got my fingertips on it, but with too much force, flipping it across the concrete.

It landed almost on top of a mage's foot. He had been working with several others to try to get a net spell going, but at sight of the stone he stopped chanting and grabbed it, a look of disbelief spreading over his features. It looked like Seb hadn't bothered to tell anyone what he was planning to give away.

I reached for the man's magic and pulled with everything I had. I forgot that we weren't in Faerie anymore, forgot that that much force wasn't necessary against a human. He screamed and dropped to his knees, then collapsed and rolled down the loading ramp, the rune still clutched in his fist. I started for him, but hadn't made even a single step when a wave of magic slammed into me like a tidal wave, a raging torrent of it that threatened to bury me under its sheer volume.

I went down, gasping, unable to breathe, as it gushed inside, falling into that part of me that holds my null abilities. I lay there, waiting for it to stop, trying to swallow it as I always had, but there was too much. It kept coming until I thought I would die of it, until the world became nothing but wave after wave of sparkling power that I couldn't eat and couldn't control.

Someone grabbed my hand, but I couldn't see them, couldn't hear, couldn't breathe. I was being shaken, but I barely felt it. "Claire!" Finally, a voice, tinny and weak, cut through the glittering haze. "Claire! Can you hear me?"

I felt myself being drawn into warm arms, and knew without words whose they were. After a few more minutes, the haze lifted, and I could see again. All around us, light danced on the sides of the warehouse, ripples of it making endless kaleidoscopic patterns on the formerly blank walls. It looked like the reflection of water, only about twenty times as bright. I scrunched up my eyes, almost blinded, and behind me, someone started to laugh.

"I looked up your name," Heidar gasped out. "I was going to gift you with a new one, but I don't think I will now."

"What?" I turned to try to see him better, and the kaleidoscope shifted with me, splashing new, wildly shifting patterns everywhere. Tanet slunk over, still in dragon form, and put a paw over his eyes in protest. I finally realized that, for whatever crazy reason, the source of the light was me.

"It means 'shining one,'" Heidar said, tears of laughter rolling down his cheeks. "Who's glowing now?"

Conclusion

WE finally figured it out. It seems that, when I tried to steal the mage's power, I accidentally also took the rune's. It was July 3, so I managed to get rid of it that evening by putting on an early fireworks display as far out in the woods as we could get. I almost died of heatstroke before then, muffled in ten layers of clothing, which still didn't do much to hide the searchlight the rune had turned me into. I'll never be able to complain about Heidar glowing again.

Nonetheless, I was glad to have the rune gone. No matter who had finally ended up with it, it would have been nothing but trouble. Heidar plans to tell his dad that it was a fake, which is what most Fey seem to have believed from the start. I don't know what Tanet will say. He left shortly after our little adventure, having had his opinion of the dangers of the human world strongly reinforced. I don't think I'll be getting a brotherly visit anytime soon.

Heidar and I talked it over and decided to stay in the human world for awhile. My motivation is pretty simple: from what I understand, my twin is far more likely to manifest in

Faerie than here. And although Heidar keeps telling me that I will come to love my other half, I'd just as soon avoid another journey of self-discovery right now. At least until she loses some of her baby fat.

Heidar's reasons for staying are less straightforward. He says he doesn't want me back in Faerie until he can take some precautions against the Svarestri. They don't know as much about the human world as other Fey, so he thinks we'll have an advantage, should any show up here. But I think he's really trying to work up the nerve to tell his father that he's going to have a daughter-in-law who occasionally goes scaly.

I'm still eating tofu, even though my twin is heartily sick of it. At least that's what I've been blaming all these new cravings on. I haven't resorted to grocery shopping at the pet store yet, but steak is starting to sound really good. Rare steak, with pickles.

And maybe some hot sauce.

Mona Lisa Betwining

SUNNY

CHAPTER 1

THE moon was full and round in the sky, a perfect circle of illumination. It called to us, rose some restlessness within us. Sap rising is what they called it in trees. In humans, they called it spring fever. In the Monère—the children of the moon—it was simply the time for Basking, a time to call down the moon's rays and bathe yourself in the renewing light. Only Queens could call it down and share it with others. That was what I happened to be, a Monère Queen, albeit not the usual kind. Not only Monère blood flowed within my veins, although that predominated, three-quarters of it. The last remaining quarter, however, was human blood. I was what they called a Mixed Blood, the first one ever to be a Queen.

So much had changed in such a short while. Not long ago, I had been alone in a sea of humans, an ER nurse on the lonely island of Manhattan, crowded with people, only not mine. Now here I was in Louisiana, ruler of this territory, ruler of these people—more than four hundred Full Blood Monère constituents. Surrounded by my people. And yet still alone.

Moonlight silvered the room, large and empty. Gryphon's room, my Warrior Lord. The first man I had loved, the first lover I had lost. He was dead now, although not completely gone. He'd had enough psychic power to make the transition to demon dead. But he existed now in another realm, far from my immediate reach.

His scent still lingered along the pillow, on the clothes that hung yet in his closet. But it was faint, so faint now. Almost completely lost in the month I'd been gone when I had lost myself in my other shape, my tiger form, roaming the forest to escape my grief. Had I been purely human, I would not have smelled that last barely there musky fragrance that had been my love. It made me grateful then, in a sad way, for my far acuter Monère senses. But soon, acuter senses notwithstanding, that last whiff of him would be completely gone. He'd been beautiful, like a dark angel, a wicked cherub fallen from the sky, tumbled to earth. White, luminous skin, hair dark as midnight, eyes blue as a summer sky. Would his face soon blur in my memory's eye? Would that fade from me also with time, lost along with the hope of a living remembrance of him?

My hand spread across my stomach, my empty womb. I'd just finished my monthly flow, my red blood spilling down the toilet along with my hopes and dreams of a child from him. But it had been a faint hope, at best. The Monère are not a fertile people, and children are few and far among us.

"Milady."

I whirled to face the man standing in the doorway. Whereas Gryphon had been dark, this man was light, with hair as bright as sunshine, his eyes jade green instead of blue, his shoulders broader, his body more heavily muscled than Gryphon's lean, graceful physique. Whereas Gryphon had been beautiful, this man's features were too masculine, too bold for delicate beauty. He was handsome, strikingly so.

Like a Greek god of old. And he was more than just a pretty face. He was my new master of arms.

"Dontaine."

"Milady. It is almost time for Basking."

"Yes, I know. I feel the moon's call. Is it almost midnight?"

He nodded, his eyes falling to where my hand unconsciously rested low over my belly.

Face flushing, I dropped my hand away, embarrassed to be caught drifting like a ghost in my lover's empty room, mourning my empty womb.

I moved toward the door but he did not step away, allow me to pass. I stopped a mere foot away and looked askance at him. He seemed to be struggling for words. "Did you wish to say something to me, Dontaine?"

"Milady, I know you do not desire my touch, nor particularly my gift." He stopped abruptly, laughed harshly. "Speak truth . . . you abhor my gift." His gift was the rare ability to arrest his change halfway between man and wolf, his other shape. They called it a Half Form. I'd called it monstrous.

"Dontaine, what I said . . ." I spread my hands open helplessly. "It was said in the heat of emotions—"

"And after my touch made you lose control," he said deliberately, like one intentionally prodding a sore spot. His power affected me oddly when he was in his Half Form. If I touched him when he was in his half-shifted shape, it called forth my own beast—something that used to terrify me because my beast took me over completely then, but not any more. He'd been careful not to physically touch me since that first accidental triggering of my beast.

I reached out my hand, laid it over his forearm. To prove to both of us that, *See, it won't hurt us*. Only it backfired. I'd forgotten that his power, his normal power, affected me differently, too. It was like shocking little jolts of electricity danced upon my skin for a moment. Pleasurable in an odd kind of way, but with a hint of sharper, edgier pain if it continued longer. Dontaine didn't exactly flinch at the contact and the reaction, but his jaw tightened, and his face became granite hard. Gently, he stepped back, pulled away from my touch, stopping that odd dancing sensation across our skin. "I know you said that you would never sleep with me. Ever."

I flinched, hearing my words repeated back to me, verbatim. Words that had clearly been seared into his memory. And it hadn't even really been his fault. At the time, Gryphon, my lover, had been trying to throw me into Dontaine's bed so that I might acquire his rare Half Form ability. Another oddity of mine. When Monère men mated with a Queen, they usually gained some of her power, and if lucky, some of her gifts. It worked that way with me, too, but went the other way as well. I tended to gain some of the men's power and gifts, as well. I was like a sexual vampire sucking up gifts instead of blood.

"Forgive me," Dontaine said, seeing the expression on my face. "I did not wish to bring up painful memories for you, though I obviously did so in my clumsy attempt at explanation. What I am trying to say is that I come from a line that has proven fertile. Not just my sister and I. My mother Margaret had two brothers, and her father had a sibling as well. If you desire a child . . ." He stopped speaking and looked at me, his eyes pained by my rejection in the past, yet generous enough to offer this when he'd seen my need.

"Dontaine—"

"Please, before you rebuff me yet again, let me explain that what you feel will only grow stronger with time."

My eyes widened upon hearing this. "What do you mean?"

"Your yearning for a child. It comes to all Monère women of child-bearing age. An inbred instinct, a need that will grow even stronger with each passing year."

"Oh. I'd thought it simply part of my grief for Gryphon, not an in-built species propagation thing. Though I shouldn't be so surprised by it." Lots of other in-built goodies to ensure that our people spread wide and proliferated. It had worked, up to a point.

"I can give you a child," he said.

I looked at him, this extraordinarily proud and handsome man, humbling himself to offer me this tempting gift. But I could not take it. And he saw that answer on my face even before I spoke.

"Thank you," I said, my voice soft, husky. "It is a most generous offer, but—"

"But you still have another lover, Lord Amber."

"And Halcyon," I whispered.

"Ah, the Demon Prince, too." He was quiet for a moment, obviously searching his memory for when Halcyon and I could have come together. "When you helped him return to his realm," he finally said.

Actually, it had been right after we'd rescued him from Queen Louisa, the former ruler of this land. She'd been a little pissed at having to give up her territory to me. But I didn't bother to correct Dontaine's assumption. No need to get into the details of when and how it had happened. Just that it had.

"I understand, my Queen." He smiled ruefully. "You are young, the need for a child is not yet that strong, and your bed is not as empty as I thought." The light smile he'd forced upon his face dropped away. "But my offer will stand open to you . . ."

Indefinitely. For as long as I must wait, were the words he did not say. And that scared me. That offer, that yearning for me. I didn't want it or desire it. Too many men had been willing to wait for me—first Amber, then my Demon Prince—and still I did not know why. Why they desired me, a woman common in looks, less than average in build, and of mixed mongrel blood. Life was too short to have to wait for such a tenuous possibility, even among the long-lived Monère, whose lives could stretch three centuries long. But just because you could live that long, didn't mean you did. Look at Gryphon.

"Don't wait for me," I told Dontaine, looking up into that handsome patrician face. "You can have any woman you want. Go to them. Be with them instead."

His eyes lowered and he bowed and stepped back, face impassive, body held stiffly with sudden tension. As if I'd struck him a literal blow. "As my Queen commands," he said, his voice as blank as his face, both carefully wiped clean of all expression.

He turned to leave, and I had a horrible feeling that something was amiss. I almost let him leave. But my instincts were crying out that something was wrong, that his reaction was too strong just to be from my rebuff alone.

"Dontaine, wait please," I said, reluctantly prolonging the agony for both of us. "You said 'As my Queen commands.' You meant that as a formality, right?"

"I am not certain what you are asking, milady."

I struggled for the proper words. "You used that as a polite phrase, like the English would say, 'Long live the king.' Not as an actual command, right?"

"You mean," Dontaine said carefully, "that it wasn't? A command, that is?" He looked up, his green eyes lovely and unsure, an odd look to see in that usual arrogant face.

"Good God, no! Did you think it was?"

"Yes," he said to my shock.

"Oh," I said faintly. "Well, good thing I stopped you then. What . . . uh, exactly did you think I was telling you to do?"

"To go sleep with our unmarried women. Impregnate them."

Some of it was starting to make horrible sense to me. "Because you told me that you come from a fertile line."

He nodded.

"And you thought I'd use that information to increase our population." And the wealth of my territory. It wasn't just monetary income that counted as prosperity here. It was also in the number of women, usually far outnumbered by males. And in the rare female offspring, of which his line had proven capable of generating.

"You thought I was putting you out to stud," I said with shocked dismay, and had a sudden horrible thought. "Is that what your old Queen, Mona Louisa, did to you?"

"No. She wanted me for herself, even though no child came from our union." He smiled grimly. "Then it became a forked prong for her. She dared not put me out to stud then, as you called it, though it would have profited her to do so. If I proved fertile with other women, it would only prove her barrenness. But with you . . . you do not desire me in your bed. It would have made sense to use me elsewhere."

"Like putting out a stallion, or using a prize bull to service all the available female stock." I shook my head at the thought. "It's not as easy as that, surely. Handsome though you are, some women would have affections, desires elsewhere. Not every woman would have wanted or accepted you."

"It would not have mattered," he said simply. "If I had been ordered to service them, none of us would have had any choice in the matter."

"That's barbaric," I said, aghast.

"In the human value system you were raised up in, perhaps. But our women are brought up expecting no say in their choice of mates."

"You're kidding," I said. "Who decides then, their fathers?"

"No, our Queens. Access to a woman is usually granted as a reward to our Queen's most loyal men or for special feats of service, though some men are given bedding privileges if they come from a fertile line."

"God," I whispered. "And I thought it was just the men who had it bad here." Warriors who grew too powerful were usually killed by their Queens. "That's horrible," I said, "to have no say in whom you marry."

"I made no mention of marriage, milady. Very few are granted that privilege. Most unions decided by the Queen are temporary, lasting only several full moons. Only couples paired for breeding purposes are usually granted several seasons together to try and bear a child. Or, if one came from a proven richly fertile line, such as I, he would be designated to a group of women to lie with during that time, not just one."

I was appalled. "Is . . . is that what everyone is expecting me to do, to tell which men to go to which woman's bed?"

"Yes."

"Jesus Christ."

His eyes fixed upon me intently. "Do you not mean to follow that tradition?"

"Hell, no."

"Then what will you do?"

"Let them choose among themselves whom they would like to"—I flapped my hand—"sleep with, marry, whatever. As long as both parties desire it," I tacked on hastily. Best to make things crystal clear among these archaic people. "No raping allowed."

"A very liberal concept, milady," Dontaine murmured, his face and eyes inscrutable so that I did not know if he approved of the idea or not. But it didn't really matter if he did. That was what I was going to do.

"Please let everyone know this. That it is my wish for them to seek out their own lovers, spouses, their own happiness. God, I'd hate to be responsible for that."

"Freedom of choice, and happiness." He murmured it like it was something foreign to him. "A very human idea."

I gave a short laugh. "Well, no surprise there. I'm partly

human." And I was clinging to my human ways quite fiercely.

"That applies to you, too," I said more quietly. "That's what I meant before. Go find a woman you like and be with her. But only if you wish to. It's the same thing I told my guards before we came here." And their surprise then should have given me a clue. I was still learning the ropes of being a Queen, of being Monère. And still finding some of those ropes hard and rough to grasp.

"As my Queen commands." He bowed and stepped back, allowing me to finally pass through the door. In the hallway, I unfurled my senses a little, and listened and heard nothing in the house, only a humming of slow heartbeats in the distance, out in the forest.

"They're all waiting for us," I said with surprise as I quickly wound my way down the spiral staircase, my long black skirt billowing up around me so that I no doubt looked like a balloon about to take off. Or a bloated black widow spider that had just sucked all the blood out of the poor male she'd mated with, I thought darkly. Black was what Queens were expected to wear, and for tonight, I humored them by wearing a long black formal gown and leaving my dark hair flowing loose down past my shoulders, though jeans, sneakers, and ponytail were more my usual style.

"Careful, milady. No need for haste, we are not late." Mild humor laced Dontaine's voice. "And even if we were, the ceremony cannot start without you."

True enough, but still I walked quickly out into the night, Dontaine beside me, a tall guarding shadow. The wind blew cool and soothing across my restless skin, and the night welcomed us with dark embrace, folding us into its silent shadows as we stepped into the forest. The swish of my sweeping hem across the plants and foliage of the forest ground were the only sounds that marked our passage. Aha, I thought dryly, another reason why they wanted their women in long skirts, so they would be easier to keep track of . . . or chase down. A shiver prickled my skin at the phantom image of unwilling women fleeing, being pursued by warriors awarded rights to their bodies by their Queen.

Sometimes I wondered what I was doing here among these primitive people, in this strange, feudal society. I shivered as I felt the collective power of the gathering ahead of us thrum across my skin like a heavy blanket of awareness. So many of them.

Then I stepped into the clearing and saw him. One of the reasons why I was still here. My other Warrior Lord. A man, tall and majestic like a giant oak tree, powerful in body, rugged in face, blunt of features. As beautiful to me as my Gryphon had been. His sea blue eyes met mine and all others faded away. Oh, how I had missed him. His big body, his big heart, the love and devotion he bore me glimpsed naked in his eyes. Only in those huge arms did I feel safe, loved, protected. "Amber," I whispered.

"Mona Lisa." The low rumble of his voice came to me like a dark rough caress, stirring my body, speeding my heart.

A discreet jolting electric touch on my hand, there then suddenly gone, drew me back to my surroundings and the sea of waiting faces all turned to me. Oh yeah, Basking first. I swallowed, threw Dontaine a thankful glance for his reminding touch, and made my way to where my heart wanted me to go—toward Amber. He was surrounded by faces I did not know. A handful of them were young men from my Louisiana territory who had taken positions with Amber after it became clear they would not have any chance at my bed. Fresh virgin lads, too young to have acquired any threatening power, were usually favored by Queens for indulgent bed sport, picked up and tasted like new candy. *She's different,* was the rumor that had spread about me. *She likes older men.*

I smiled, thinking that the rumor was not without some

merit. All my lovers had indeed been older, Halcyon more than six hundred years old. When the Queen avenue had been nixed, most of the young available men had eagerly elected to serve and train under a powerful Warrior Lord, a rare opportunity. All the previous guards in the western Missouri territory, more than twenty of them, had been slaughtered. Not by me, though I had taken a few lives. Or even by Blaec, Halcyon's father, though he had been the tool in sending them on to the final darkness. But by their Queen, who had ordered them to rush us and try to kill us, a suicide mission against the High Lord of Hell, whose very touch was death. So many wasted lives just to give Mona Louisa a chance to escape.

In the center of the clearing, to the left of Amber, were my own personal guards. Men who had sworn their service to me earlier, before this prosperous territory had even been awarded me; men who had risked their lives to protect mine. Aquila, a man not much taller than my own five foot eight, with brown waved hair. Neat and proper, with a crisp Vandyke beard, you'd never guess him to be a former outlaw rogue—one of those who had kidnapped me, in fact. Tomas, with soft brown eyes, wheat-colored hair, and a voice that spoke with the honeyed flow of the deep South. Both men were older, powerful warriors, one gone rogue, the other just about to before I had saved him from that fate.

Beside them stood a woman, massive of girth and height, towering a couple of inches taller than both my guards. Rosemary, my cook, my unofficial chatelaine who ran the monstrous mansion we now lived in, Belle Vista—a house that had its own name, can you imagine? She'd left her coveted position at High Court to follow me to whatever territory I might be assigned to because of her two children, Tersa and Jamie, Mixed Bloods like me. They were not here tonight. Neither was the other Mixed Blood among us, my brother, Thaddeus. And the most deadly, the most unwanted among my guards, Chami, my chameleon, my assassin, was also not present. He'd stayed behind to stand guard over Rosemary's two children and Thaddeus.

I stopped and took my place before them, Dontaine standing beside me with the rest of my guards. Ringing out behind them in a thick spreading throng was the rest of my people—so many faces and names I did not know. I blocked them out for now, blocked everybody out, and lifted my face up to the night, to our light, our source of power and life—the moon, full and beautiful in her round glory. It called to me, that distant planet, tugged at something within me, and I opened myself to her, loosened that something within me in welcome, in acceptance. *Yes, I am your child. Bestow your blessings on me, and I will anoint the others in your stead as your vessel, Mother Moon.*

A warm, thrumming power unfurled within me, was pulled from me outward, upward, like an invisible arrow reaching for the sky, reaching for the moon, and finding it. Like a soft sigh breathed down from the heavens, light began to shower down, glorious rays that illuminated the night and bathed me in its glow. Little butterflies of light darted within me, filling me anew with energy, with power. Filled me tight, so tightly within, until I overflowed and burst outward, spilling the light onto the others, spreading it to them in a glowing, flowing wave that undulated over them, then entered them, too, bowing their backs. Renewing them, filling them with life and energy and power. Sending us all aglow, incandescent creatures of the night. Children of the moon.

Basking. This was what made me Queen. This was what ran our society. A society that centered around its Queens because only they could call down the lunar rays each full moon, to renew us and to extend our lives. Without Basking, we aged as humans did. We died sooner.

The glow faded, dissipated, disappeared within us. My

duty was done, and the people slowly dispersed into the night. "Don't go," I said, turning to Amber.

"No," he answered, his voice a soft, reassuring rumble in the night.

"The rest of your people?"

"*Your* people," he corrected me gently. "They will return back to Missouri."

"How?" I asked with a small smile. "Flying, crawling, loping?"

He returned the smile with one of his own, a slow curving of lips that stoked warmth within me. "By car. We parked in the woods by the eastern border, half a mile away."

"Stay with me tonight," I said softly.

His blue eyes deepened, darkened. "Yes." He glanced behind me to Dontaine and the rest of my men, and told them, "We'll be at the west cottage tonight. Keep everyone away."

"Yes, my lord," Dontaine replied.

I left, conscious only of the power and presence of the man at my side as he drew me deeper into the woods, darkness folding like a comforting shroud around us. The night breathed with life—the rustling of leaves blown by the wind, the hooting of an owl, the chirping of crickets in song, the swoop of wings, the splash of water in the distant bayou. So alive. Every sensation so sharp, every sound so clear. It felt as if I were coming back to life, emerging from deep hibernation. A painfully long one, away from my love. More than two long weeks since he had left me, though he had done so at my bidding.

Rule for me. Be safe for me. And return to me whenever you can. And he had.

"You haven't touched me," I whispered as we walked, so close, a hairbreadth away from each other, but without that final contact.

He turned his head, looked at me then, and my breath

caught. His eyes burned that rich yellow-gold, the color of his beast. What he had been named for—Amber. The color of his eyes whenever he was moved with passion or power. Or both.

"If I touch you now, I will not stop." His voice was deep and dark and so rich in timbre that it vibrated the air. "And the cottage is yet a mile away."

"I don't want to wait," I said huskily, feeling my own eyes dilating, expanding, so that everything came to me even more sharply, clearer.

"You must," he said, and I blinked at the hard command, the quiet arrogance in those words. He was changing, my Amber. Becoming more confident, more . . . dominant.

I almost purred. "Must I?"

He slanted a look at me, eyes narrowed, a tiny smile lifting his lips. "Yes," he said deliberately, "you must."

Oooh. He wanted to play. Or rather, he wanted to dominate.

I licked my lips and his eyes followed the gesture, darkening. My clothes were suddenly too constricting, my skin too sensitive, my breasts too full, my nipples too peaked. I unzipped the dress and stepped out of it, leaving the discarded, hateful dress on the leaf-strewn ground, and kicked off my shoes. Cool air teased over my skin, wisped through the blush-colored lace of my bra, the triangle of my panties.

Now it was Amber's turn to catch his breath, to run his hot eyes over the unclothed paleness of my skin. For his nostrils to expand and inhale in the rich ready scent of my softening body. My turn to tease him by running a hand down my neck, between my breasts, and trail tantalizingly lower. "Are you sure?" I asked in a slow, languid drawl.

He growled. And I laughed.

In a blink, my laziness slipped away. "Catch me if you can," I challenged. With my eyes aglow, I leaped away.

And large predator that he was, dominant male that he was becoming, he gave chase.

I made him work for it, truly fight to get what he wanted—me. I ran like the hounds of hell were behind, chasing me. I ran like the wind. A blur of soundless speed that whipped the air with my passage. So fast that had a human seen us, he would not have seen anything, only sensed the stirring of movement through the rippling air currents left in our wake. And he was right behind me, as fast as I, his form bigger, stronger, even more powerful. He caught the heel of my foot, tumbled me to the ground. I rolled, went with the momentum, kicked out of his grasp, and bounded away again, my trailing laughter teasing him like a ghost.

I darted among the trees, under overhanging branches, deliberately using my greatest advantage, my smaller size, to my benefit. I glimpsed him to the left of me, running parallel, cutting his own course through the forest rather than follow my height-challenging one, and flashed him a glimpse of my white teeth before veering sharply to the right, leaping over a bushy shrub, then cutting right yet again. He put on a burst of speed and intercepted me. His large arms wrapped around me and brought me down, his big body like a safe cocoon around me as we rolled and rolled until we had safely stopped.

"I've caught you," he said in a gritty rumble, his voice rough, his yellow-gold eyes gleaming. "Now yield."

"No," I said. Grinning, I bucked him off me, leaped to my feet, and sprang away. But he was on me again, magically fast. He caught one of my wrists, mid-leap, and swung me against a thick tree trunk, my back pressing against smooth bark. He captured my other wrist, pinned them both above me. Heaving, straining with effort, I slowly pushed my hands away from the tree, lifting them away from the bark against his resistance . . . one inch . . . then two. Amber's eyes widened, expressing both our surprise. "You are getting stronger," he murmured, just before his head swooped down and he captured my lips.

I melted at the first taste of him, his dark sweet flavor like roasted chestnuts, and he pinned my arms once again above me. When he drew back, both our breaths were coming faster, mingling together in the cool air in frosty puffs. Taking advantage of my pliancy, he shifted his grip so that both my slender wrists were anchored firmly in just one broad hand. His other hand he placed like a victorious raider on my pale skin, sweeping it with low rumbling pleasure across the wings of my collarbones, up the lifted vulnerable undersides of my arm. Back down.

"Not fair," I gasped, that deliberate stroke up and then down tingling my skin. "You distracted me with that kiss."

"All's fair in love and war. Is that not one of your human sayings?" he asked, his breath puffing warmly against my ear as he hunched his big body over my smaller one, pinning my legs down with his great weight. I was surrounded by him, weakened by my desire for him, and not really wanting to escape. Captured, at his mercy. But with that brutally harsh face above me, hard with male excitement and purpose, he didn't look like he had any mercy. He looked so grim, male, implacable. Almost unrecognizable, like a stranger. And his power vibrated strongly against me with more than just his Monère self; the animal part of him thrummed so strongly there at the surface, so clearly that I could feel it, sense it. As if it was ready to burst out in a wash of fur and fluids with but the lightest touch, the slightest willing. He was clearly channeling the greater strength and hunger of his beast.

It shivered a feeling of apprehension in me. A feeling almost of fear as I looked up into that hard, hard face, with those inhuman alien eyes gleaming down with hungry harsh intent upon me.

I stilled, licked my lips, a nervous gesture this time. Swallowed. "You . . . uh, you're not going to eat me, are you?"

"Not yet," he growled. "My hunger for you is too great for such restraint this first time."

"Amber," I said almost desperately as his head dipped down, as I felt the brush of his lips and the alarming edge of his teeth stroke over the base of my neck where my pulse bounded suddenly like a desperate thing. As he lingered over it, fear and desire pumped my heart equally. A delicious combination, that edge of danger. But only if I knew there truly wasn't any.

"Amber," I said more sharply. He lifted his head, his nostrils flaring, his eyes dilating as he breathed in my fear-tanged arousal. "I mean as a meal. You don't see me as food, do you?"

He shook his head as if coming out of a daze. His eyes still looked cold, inhuman, but his voice, his voice was the Amber I knew and loved, warm with reassurance . . . and a bit of amusement. "No, love. I want to fuck you. Not eat you."

"Oh good." The tension left my body, leaving an almost painful, sagging relief in its wake.

His body shook. His breath hitched against my skin as he bent his head once more to my neck. "Amber." Alarm kicked in once more. Had I hurt his feelings?

His head remained lowered.

"Amber, you're not . . . crying, are you?"

"No," he choked, his breath huffing against me.

"Look at me."

He did. Mirth danced in his eyes, not tears.

"Beast," I said succinctly.

"Don't worry," he choked out, "not too much of one."

His body shook with the laughter he was trying to suppress. "Don't be mad, my love." But his words were ruined by the shaking merriment of his heaving body, and he suddenly lost the battle. A shout of laughter burst out. Then another, and another, until he was fairly howling with it, shaking against me not with lust but with hilarity.

Oh, the bastard! He was laughing at me!

My eyes narrowed in a look that would have alarmed him had he seen it. But he was too busy snorting away like a pig to see it.

Without a whiff of compunction, I brought my knee up, taking advantage of his inattention. Only his quick reflexes saved him. He twisted to the side and my knee struck his muscled thigh instead of his groin. But his grip on my wrists loosened with the maneuver and my hands were suddenly free.

"You can take your twisted humor and sleep with that," I snarled, shoving him off me with enough force to tumble him backward onto the ground, and took off.

The laughter stopped abruptly as he came after me, a dark and silent force. I ran this time with determination, with angry cunning. But still he caught me again, his hands catching my wrist. I turned, slashed at him, my nails leaving bloody red furrows down his forearm, and with a twist, was free once more. I ran south toward the house, toward Belle Vista and the rest of my men.

"No," Amber said harshly behind me as he realized my intent. "You are mine tonight."

"In your dreams," I muttered, darting left then right, evading his sudden snatch for me. I put on a burst of speed, but he was even faster.

He tackled me from behind, still gentle in bringing me down, but more determined. I cursed, twisted, and writhed, but in the blink of an eye he had me pinned against a tree again. This time, though, he lifted me so that my feet no longer touched the ground. Standing his full height, he leaned into me, my lower legs immobilized against the trunk by his.

His breath came faster from his effort, and humor was

wiped clean from his face, I saw with some satisfaction. Harsh determination replaced it.

"Yield to me," he demanded.

"Not if your life depended on it," I snarled and tried to bite him. He levered his upper torso away from me, an odd smile on his lips.

"But it does," he said, his rough deep voice gentling. "My life does depend upon it. Upon you."

I shut my eyes but could not shut out his words, the caress of his voice. Anger still stirred within me but with less steam, cooled by his tender words.

"I live for you. I dream of you. I count the days until I can return to you. Do not deny me now, my lady, my Queen, my love. Mona Lisa." He breathed my name like a benediction, a vow. "Be mine again," he whispered, and the last of my anger melted away with his humble plea.

I looked into his bold, craggy face. So harsh, so dear. And suddenly realized I did not want to see this big man humbled, begging, as his former Queen had made him do. She had made him grovel in the dirt.

"Yield yourself to me, please," he whispered against my lips.

I smiled, and that smile drew him back a little, wary. "Make me," I said, my eyes gleaming challenge at him.

The white of his teeth flashed like pearls shining in darkness. He grinned like a pirate. "It shall be my pleasure to."

With a quick maneuver, he shifted both my wrists until they were held secure in just one powerful broad hand of his. An almost gentle tug and my bra snapped apart. A big calloused hand smoothed down low over my belly, then moved down even lower. His eyes had swirled back to blue, as tumultuous as the deep dark sea, and no less dangerous. Perhaps more so in its potent allure. *Come into my depths,* they beckoned, and how I yearned to do just that. Those sea blue eyes darkened as rough fingers whispered over delicate lace, the last barrier that covered me, as they passed over my sultry waiting heat. With a sharp rending tear that stopped my breath and wet me even more with its controlled violence, the lace covered me no longer. That marauding hand paused briefly in its gentle pillage, savoring me, cupping me lightly, then moving on down to my thighs, drawn tightly together.

"Open to me," he murmured, rubbing that calloused palm between my legs as if he could open them with the light stroking tease of his hand. Almost. Tempting. But not enough.

"Like I said . . ." My eyes grew sultry, the lids heavy like my waiting pulsing body. "Make me." And with a smile, I clenched my thighs even tighter together, capturing his hand between them in a firm squeeze.

His breath caught, his hand stilled. Then moved again. Less teasing, less tentative, more bold and commanding. A more purposeful search and find now, coming to rest just above my knees. His eyes holding mine, he slid his fingers in the tight barrier I had created and wrapped them around my right knee. With calm deliberation, he began to pry my legs apart. He growled, a warning rumble as I resisted him. I made him work for it. Made him earn it, sweat for it, only yielding that which he could take by brute overpowering force. When he had opened my legs enough, his knees slid between them, forcing them even farther apart, and he rested his weight full upon me. His thickness was wedged right against me, long, tight, and hard in the opening he had fought for. Almost home. Only problem, his pants were still on.

"You forgot to undress yourself," I said, my lips curving up in laughing feline delight as I saw the realization of his dilemma reach his rueful eyes.

"Will you make me work for it all over again if I step back and undress?" he asked.

I smirked. "You betcha."

He smiled in return, then moved so fast that I did not see

it. Just heard the ripping tear as his lower body left me for one brief splinter of time. And then he surged back, and up, and into my body with one forceful plunge, pushing a startled cry from my throat as my inner muscles convulsed around his thick invading length.

He stilled, halfway in me, his great body shuddering. "Am I hurting you?"

"No," I gasped. "Oh, God." I wriggled, strained against him, but my hands were captured, held firmly by him, my body forced open by his, pinned by his body in the most primitive and effective way of all.

He filled my soft emptiness with his hard fullness. Crammingly so. He was a big man, everywhere. And his sudden invasion stretched me almost unbearably, caught me between the prongs of acute pain and acute pleasure, blurring the line between them.

"I *am* hurting you," he muttered and started to pull back, out of me.

I whimpered, cried out, "No!" and wrapped my legs around him, holding him to me.

"Are you sure?" he asked me fiercely, his cheekbones slashed red, his face as rock hard as how he felt within me.

"Yes."

His eyes narrowed, his nostrils flared. "All right. Then take me. Take all of me." His free hand anchoring my hip, he heaved himself into me, pushing in his long thick length until he was buried in me so deep I thought he'd come out the other side.

I opened my mouth to scream. With pain, with pleasure. I wasn't exactly sure which. And he covered my mouth with his own. Swallowed my cry. Pushed his thick tongue into my mouth so that I was filled with him there too, held suspended by him, chained by his hands, his male hardness buried deep in my soft feminine sheath.

He took me as I had asked him to, challenged him to.

He pulled back out of me—both my inner sheath and

my oral sheath—then pushed with slow, insistent deliberation back within me, stretching me, filling me abundantly simultaneously above and below. I mewed, sucked on his tongue, and echoed the action by tightening around him below, within.

His stomach muscles ridged so hard they felt like stone slabs against me, and he made a desperate sound against my lips as he ground himself even deeper inside me. Pulled out. Then another slow, deliberate, stretching push back into my tightness that had us both groaning, trembling. With the third stroke, it was as if the magical threshold of my body had suddenly been reached. It finally eased its almost unbearable tightness, loosened, became more receptive. And like a leash suddenly let go, Amber began a fast, almost furious rhythm, pistoning, pouring himself into me, his tongue stabbing me above as he stabbed me, pounded me, below. And I welcomed him, clung to him, wrapped my tongue and lips and body around him, and asked him for more with arcing body, sucking cheeks, hungry cries. As hungry to hold him, absorb him, become one with him, as he was to pour himself into me.

Our passion, our pleasure, lowered the barriers of our flesh. Called forth the lunar lightness that dwelt within us, so that our glow illuminated our skin and filled the night with building incandescence, growing brighter and brighter as I wound tighter and tighter. Until I finally crested and burst. And it was like the world trembled with my release. His climax followed a heartbeat after mine. Light streamed from us in almost bursting luminosity. Then faded gently away until darkness once more cloaked the night.

CHAPTER 2

I dreamed of flying, of floating in the air above, and the sweet scent of dead flesh below me, and woke up gasping, alone in my bed. Amber had left before dawn, gone back to his men, his people, safe and unaware of where I would travel that day. To High Court, the ruling seat of our people on this continent, set high and remote in the northern reaches of Minnesota, bordering Canada. They'd summoned me for questioning on Mona Louisa's death, the former Queen who'd ruled my Louisiana territory. The bitch who'd ripped Gryphon's heart out, literally, from his chest, killing him and a part of me. I'd killed her in return, although it was not truly I who killed her finally, though I'd done my best to. It had been Blaec, the High Lord of Hell.

The Council had waited for me. They'd had to, while I roamed the forest in my tiger form, in my separate tiger mind, until the day my human thoughts and feelings had finally filtered into my other self, and I could know and control that animal part of me, and realize that time had indeed eased my grief until it had become bearable.

A Queen had been killed—so had a Warrior Lord, but that was of secondary concern, I learned to my fury—and questions needed to be answered. I was going now to answer them. Up to a point.

The plane landed and we disembarked, Dontaine, Tomas, and I. I'd left all the others behind, those who needed protecting, the youngest among us—Jamie, Tersa, my brother, Thaddeus . . . him, especially, I did not want there—and the others to protect them . . . my ex-outlaw rogue, Aquila, and Chami, my deadly assassin. Left behind deliberately, also, was what remained of my heart—Amber, a powerful Warrior Lord, but even more vulnerable than the children. Queens feared him. Feared his bigness, his power, and the legacy his infamous father had left behind—Sandoor, who had raped his Queen and then faked both their deaths. Sandoor, who had inconveniently returned to life and heaped even greater infamy upon himself when he had been discovered to have kept that Queen captive for over a decade, a Queen whom he'd had service his needs and that of his band of rogues. He was truly dead and gone now, killed by my hand. But his son was still paying for the father's sins. Amber would be looked upon with suspicion forever by other Queens, watched carefully by the High Court to see that he, too, did not turn rogue. Turn upon his Queen.

"Two men are not adequate enough to protect you," Dontaine repeated now, as he had many times before during the flight.

My answer remained unchanged as we disembarked and walked to a waiting gray van. "You and Tomas are enough. And I can protect myself."

"We should have brought Chami and Aquila, milady," Tomas said, speaking up for the first time. His southern twang softened his consonants, stretched out his vowels. Brown of hair, plain of face, as loyal and true as the sword he had sworn into my service, he was one of my trusted guards, an older warrior grown too powerful who had been cast out by his Queen and taken in by me. I smiled bittersweetly. Even plain and simple Tomas knew enough not to suggest Amber, the most powerful among us. And the most defenseless against the suspicions he would have faced at High Court.

"I needed them to watch after the others, see them safe," I said to Tomas.

"With all respect, milady," Tomas said in his soft drawl, "but your safety is the most crucial factor to ensure theirs."

"I will be fine, Tomas. I will be spending most of my time answering questions in the Council Hall. Having you two along is already luxury enough."

"A necessity, not a luxury, my Queen. And barely adequate," Dontaine muttered unhappily as we climbed into the van. "And my presence was only because they wished to question me as well."

True enough. He was one of the newest guards to my service, and the one I was least comfortable with. He'd challenged Amber for right to my bed, and I had agreed to take him into it when I saw that Amber was losing. Amber had ended up winning, unexpectedly. That knowledge and awareness of what might have been, that we could just as easily have been lovers by now, still sat heavily between us in all our dealings.

We traveled the next several miles from the airfield to the compound proper in silence. Then the woods fell abruptly away and we entered High Court, a pocket of civilization carved out among the otherwise untouched, pristine forests that surrounded it. A scattering of small buildings flanked and circled out from a tall, stately, three-storied manor house. Across from it, matching it in height and grandeur, was a domed stone building, the Council Hall where our ruling heads of state, so to speak, the High Council members, gathered.

An impeccably dressed little man, his black hair lined with silver, stood at the foot of the steps leading to the manor house, three footmen arrayed in attendance behind him. He opened the door of the van and assisted me out with a courtly bow.

"Thank you, Mathias," I said, greeting the steward of the Great House, as his small army of footmen fanned out and gathered up our bags and trunks.

"Welcome back, Queen Mona Lisa," Mathias said in formal greeting.

"I'd rather not have returned so quickly," I muttered in reply, and caught the flicker of a smile on the proper steward's face before he smoothed it away.

"It is always a pleasure to have you with us," he returned. Polite words, but he sounded as if he meant them. "The Council will see Warrior Dontaine first, as soon as you have settled into your quarters, and then you, milady, afterward. I've given you the south wing upstairs, the same as last time."

I nodded, grateful for his thoughtfulness, and followed our bags up the stairs and down the right hallway to a large, luxurious suite with two smaller bedrooms adjoining it. With murmured directions from Dontaine, our individual pieces of luggage were sorted out and set in the proper rooms, and the footmen discreetly filed out. With just the three of us, we each had a room to ourselves.

"If you will stay here until I return, my Queen," Dontaine said, his face grim. And though politely couched as a request, it was a clear order. I lifted my brows but had no desire or plans to wander elsewhere, so I simply said, "Sure."

After he left, I showered and changed into a fresh black gown. I had brought all three—all that I owned—with me. No jeans and T-shirts here.

I dried and brushed out my hair, leaving it loose in a dark spilling cloud down my back, and with Tomas glued to my side, ventured downstairs for something to eat, knowing they'd be awhile with Dontaine.

He returned an hour later, as we were finishing our meal.

"That wasn't long," I said, gesturing for him to sit down. Dontaine did so reluctantly.

"There wasn't really much to tell. Nor was it the important part." Meaning, he'd had no actual part in killing the Queen, what the Council was most interested in knowing about. "They will see you now."

I gestured a young footman over, although calling him young might have been inaccurate—all Monère under two hundred and fifty years of age looked young—and told him to bring out the plate of food I'd asked them to prepare for Dontaine. "They can wait five minutes. And"—I smiled—"you can talk fast while you eat. What did they ask you? And even more important, what did you tell them?"

Between gulps of red meat—they liked their meat raw—Dontaine spilled out the details of his testimony. Even with the talking, it didn't even take five minutes to wolf down the entire bloody steak. Part of it was he didn't want to keep the Council waiting long; the other part was that his appetite was back now that his part of it was over, and relatively painlessly so, by his accounting.

Downing the last gulp, he wiped his mouth with the napkin and stood. "If we may go now, milady."

I walked out into the night with my men flanking me, feeling like a prisoner heading for my execution, although that wasn't true. Or at least I hoped not. My greatest danger lay not with the Council, really, but with the secrets I held—and that I had to take great care not to reveal.

A multitude of guards, dressed in various colors according to the Queens they served, crowded the wide corridors of the Council Hall, some sitting, some standing, others milling around, chatting, all waiting. None of each court numbered less than six guards. The two sentries standing watch before the large double doors leading to the inner chamber dipped their head in greeting to me. "It is a private hearing, milady. Your guards must wait outside," one of the sentries said.

I'd kind of gotten that idea already. "Of course."

I walked alone into the high-domed chamber, the heavy doors closing silently behind me. A dozen of the Council seats were occupied, all women but for one man, Warrior Lord Thorane, the Council speaker. Other Queens were there—I felt their distinct irritating buzz against my skin—and over them, I felt the weightier presence of the Queen Mother. But it was a new odd sensation, the awareness of a presence that I should not have been aware of, that caused me to stumble, almost fall. Before I even saw the darker skin, I knew the demon was there. Because I felt him. And I should not have.

Demon dead are children of the moon who have died, but had enough psychic power to make the transition to that other realm. Their hearts did not beat, they did not breathe. Perfect predators, making no noise. Nothing to betray their presence. We barely felt them or sensed them, their presence no longer that sharp rush of attraction as with a Monère male or the comforting recognition with a Full Blood female or the buzzing abrasion with another Queen. We had only a muted awareness of their presence, so that we sensed them only when it was too late, when they were too close to us. Almost upon us.

When I lifted my eyes to the chair on the raised platform to my far right, I knew that the person sitting there would be a flash of warm golden color among the sea of white Monère skin and have nails that were long, sharp, and pointed. All that was true, I found, as my eyes settled upon that suddenly vibrant presence. Not a pull, not a repulsion, but an almost thrilling awareness; like a burn that did not hurt, just tingle a bit. But with this demon, not only its skin was golden. And it was not a he. It was a she. Her hair waved long and thick about the delicate heart of her face, a striking metallic gold color against the duskier hue of her skin. She was incredibly beautiful and incredibly tiny. Not little, per se. Oh no, not that, with her voluptuous bosom straining the burgundy silk of her shirt, and the generous swell of her hips stretching the tight leather of her black pants. The only thing little about her was her height and her wasp-thin waist.

Lucinda, Prince Halcyon's sister. And her presence was a shock to me because I had been expecting to see her brother, my lover, Halcyon. Or his father, the High Lord of Hell.

"Lucinda," I whispered, and fell weakly to my knees, swaying suddenly not only with awareness but with another growing discomfort within me—something sharp, something painful, something like sharp talons ripping me apart inside, trying to be born, trying to get out. I gasped, clutching my belly. With my next breath, I screamed.

Raised voices sounded outside in the hall, and the double doors burst open, spilling in the sentries, and behind them, a sea of guards. Dontaine and Tomas were suddenly there, beside me.

"What is it, milady? What's wrong?" Dontaine demanded, pulling my hands away so he could see if I was injured. With the first touch of him, the little shocking electric jolts that came from contact with him, the pain eased and I gasped, almost cried in relief, sagging against him.

The room was a messy swell of noise and feeling, a collective sudden milling of presences that felt too powerful, too much to all be contained in the same room. Questions and demands were shouted. Then Warrior Lord Thorane was above me, looking down, his older face creased with worry. "Mona Lisa. What's wrong, milady?"

"I don't know," I said, as bewildered as he. "Something inside me just suddenly started to hurt."

That awareness flared over me again, even surrounded as I was with the presence of powerful men and the electric sensation of Dontaine's touch. It pulled me, called to me. I turned my head and, in the sea of encircling faces standing about me, unerringly locked upon that one darker face. I found her not because of her distinguishing color, but because I knew exactly where she stood. And the scratching and clawing inside me, that horrible ripping pain, started again. Shit. I doubled over and another scream was torn from my throat.

"What's wrong, what's wrong?" Tomas shouted, his strong hands trying to pull my hands away as Dontaine held me, huddled upon myself, writhing in his lap.

"Get me away," I whispered, so softly, almost no sound because I had no breath. If I had enough breath, I would have screamed again. But he heard me. They both did. Dontaine lifted me up in his arms and with Tomas's help pushed through the gathered crowd and made his way outside.

"Where?" Dontaine asked, his voice and body hard, while I was soft. Soft with relief against him as the pain lessened with each step he took away.

"The forest," I whispered, my voice hoarse from my screams or from my breathlessness. I wasn't sure.

He plunged into the thick woods. Wrapped in his electric touch, the night cool upon my skin and the soft rays of moonshine falling gently upon me, I felt immediately calmer, the restlessness within me stilling. Dontaine walked in silence, in quiet, and I lay in his arms in blessed painlessness as he took me deeper into the woods until we no longer sensed anything, heard anything, and the chaos of High Court was far away.

"Is this far enough?" Tomas asked.

At my nod, they stopped. "Can you stand?" Dontaine asked.

"Yes," I said, even though I wasn't entirely sure if I could. But my legs held me as Dontaine gently stood me on my feet.

"I never knew how wonderful it was simply not to hurt," I murmured in the quiet of night. The wind blew, rustling leaves in a gentle shuffle, an airy shimmer of sound, moonlight dappling our skin as it shone down through the thick forest of trees.

"What happened back there, milady?" Tomas demanded, his voice clipped and harder sounding, his usual soft drawl absent.

"I don't know."

"Do you not?" came a voice, soft and sultry. I felt her first before I saw her. Felt that tingling vibrant awareness, that sensing of demon dead.

She stepped out as if from the very shadows, a part of it, startling my men because they hadn't sensed her, spinning them around.

She stood far enough away so that I felt her but was not writhing yet in pain. Because I understood now that it was her presence that had caused it, triggering something to life within me, something that wanted to come out, even if it had to claw its way out of me.

"Do you sense me, young Mixed Blood Queen?" she asked, her beautiful face still and unsmiling, looking unreal, like a golden statue come to life.

"Yes," I answered in a quiet voice. "I sense you. How can that be? What have you done to me?"

She smiled then, a human expression that warmed her still perfection, brought it to life. Then she laughed, that touchable laugh, the one that stroked you like a living, tactile thing. We all shivered, my men and I.

"I? I have done nothing," Lucinda said. And though her voice was slow and languid like honeyed syrup, her eyes were hard and observant. "It is from what you have done to yourself."

I frowned. "Because I have been with Halcyon?"

She shook her head, causing her long metallic tresses to dance and shimmer about her face like a flow of hammered gold come suddenly to life.

"No. You could have taken him into your body a thousand times and it would never have caused you to sense him a fraction more. It is that other thing you have taken into your body—Mona Louisa."

My body chilled as her meaning became clear to me. And her words had been deliberate. She had called Mona Louisa a thing. And she had been. A Monère who had drunk demon blood and become a little of both, breaking the demon dead's greatest taboo . . . the tasting of their blood. And for good reason. Because drinking that blood had made Mona Louisa strong, demon dead strong. Blaec, the High Lord of Hell, had killed her and slaughtered her entire retinue of guards to keep that demon secret. He'd let me live because he knew I would keep his secret in return for his keeping mine.

What was my secret? Mona Louisa had been strong enough to kill Gryphon, my first love, by literally ripping the heart out from his chest. She'd killed him, and I'd wanted to kill her in turn, but I had not been strong enough to do so. She'd fought me and was beating me. And in my anger, my despair, my desperation, I'd turned to the source of us all, our Mother Moon, and begged her vengeance, begged her for help.

Then I had done something I hadn't known was possible to do. I'd pulled the moonlight out from within Mona Louisa. When we Queens Basked, we pulled down the moon's rays, and they entered us, resided within us. I'd turned that power that all Queens had and used it upon another Queen: pulled the light out of her and into me. Sucked her power, her essence, her energy into me, drained her dry until she had been nothing but a wrinkled bag of shriveled skin holding together dried bones. Weak, helpless, but still living. I'd beheaded her, but she hadn't died because she had become more than Monère; she'd become part demon, and demons did not die even when beheaded. I could have chopped her into little pieces and she still would have existed. It had taken Blaec's touch to kill her. Make her finally cease to be. Only she hadn't, it seemed. Ceased to entirely be.

My mouth dried and my heart stuttered. And deep, deep within me, it was as if someone laughed. Screeched with glee. I fell to the ground, feeling weak, feeling horribly frightened. Feeling something move within me like the stretching of wings.

"The High Lord should have killed you," Lucinda said in a voice gone quiet, causing a reaction quite opposite from that tranquil sound. Tomas grabbed my hand, staying beside me. But Dontaine moved forward, toward Lucinda. His sword sang free as he pulled it from its sheath. "Leave us, demon," he demanded.

She smiled, standing there calm and serene, a head shorter than Dontaine but not at all frightened. "And if I don't, white knight, will you try and make me?" she purred.

He didn't answer her, just came at her, sword drawn.

"No," I said, but my voice came out weak and thready instead of the harsh command I had intended. Beside me, moonlight from Tomas' sword reflected into my eyes. He'd drawn his weapon too, quietly, less flashy. Just there suddenly in his hand.

"You've drawn your blades. I shall have to draw mine," Lucinda said, the sultry flow of her voice flavored with two things you usually did not hear when a man advanced upon you with a naked sword shining sharp and bright in his hand . . . amusement and eagerness. And it was the latter that scared me most.

A shimmer of power, a darker, more subtler force, and the sharp fingernails of her left hand extended, grew four inches long. Thick, wide, and curving. Became deadly claws like five sharp knives suddenly growing from her hand. "It's not always length that matters most," she said, luscious lips curving, eyes laughing, like a sex kitten about to seriously play.

She sprang. Only you couldn't see her move. She was just suddenly no longer there but behind Dontaine, like a wind blown past him. Something he felt but could not see, she moved so fast. Beside me, Tomas sucked in a shocked breath. Nothing stirred for a moment, then a blonde lock of Dontaine's hair, sliced free, floated lightly down to the ground like a dying leaf parted from a tree.

Lucinda laughed at what she saw on Dontaine's face as he swung about to face her. "Still want to play?" she asked, her dark brown eyes sparkling like hot chocolate, eager to melt, eager to burn.

Dontaine growled. Literally growled, a deep warning animal rumble that sounded odd coming from a human throat. Then he moved, with Monère quickness, a fast blur. But still motion you see. He struck at her but she was no longer there, like a ghost suddenly vanishing to reappear yards away, closer to me, closer to Tomas.

Tomas gave no warning, like the sword he had drawn. He simply rushed to attack her, to fend off the threat he perceived to me. Both my men rushed her from opposite sides, coming together in a blur of motion. And Lucinda stood there, a calm little demon, until they were almost upon her, a fierce light in her eyes, a little smile curling her lips. And then she moved. They all moved. With sound and motion and grunts and thuds as they fought fiercely. As Dontaine went tumbling head over heels, tossed away like a stick playfully thrown for a dog to fetch. As Tomas slammed hard to the ground, Lucinda kneeling on his chest, looking too tiny to have done what she had done—overpower two strong warriors.

Looking like a kitten who had the claws of a monstrous tiger, the sharp points of her left hand were buried like nails through Tomas's wrist, pinning his hand and the sword he still held to the ground in a brutal, effective manner. But his other hand was free and had drawn a hidden dagger.

"Not fair odds." Lucinda tsk-tsked. "Too little men to challenge me. But then I never claimed to be fair." She drew back to strike, to move.

"Don't!" My voice rang out in a hoarse croak. And Tomas's dagger froze in its striking drive, not because of my command, but because Lucinda's tiny hand gripped his. "Don't . . . hurt," I gasped.

"Don't hurt whom? Him or me?" Lucinda asked, both menace and amusement in her voice.

"Both," I whispered. "Both." I tried to stand, to move toward them, but that other thing within me fluttered, stirred in protest. *No,* it screamed. *Not closer. Away. Away from the danger, not to it!* I fought to stand and lost the battle, unable to. But you didn't need to stand to move. I started crawling toward them, on hands and knees, my whole body trembling, shaking, resisting, as I dragged myself closer.

"Halcyon's sister. No, Dontaine," I rasped as I sensed movement behind her. I blinked the sheen of pain-driven tears from my eyes—odd that fear dried your mouth, but pain moistened your eyes—and as my vision cleared, I saw Dontaine frozen like a literal statue behind the dainty golden demon, his sword angled for a downward thrust into her back, held unnaturally poised on the brink of that violence. And I knew it was not from obedience to my command—I would have been too late—but from the invisible power of her will. Her psychic powers were what held him immobile, a frozen prisoner in the tendrils of her invisible force. She didn't need physical touch to stop him. It was not just their physical strength that made demons greatly feared.

She stood, pulled her claws casually from the ground, from Tomas's pierced wrist as his face writhed with silent agony. With a thought, she held him immobile, too. A shimmer of that dark shadowy power, and that hideous claw shrank back down to just pointy nails. She licked each bloody tip, slowly sucking each digit clean, savoring it; her cheeks hollowed with each sucking pull, her lips pursing around her fingers like a puckered kiss, making the motions dangerously sensual. The flash of ivory fangs I glimpsed made her just plain dangerous. She swayed her way to me slowly, seductively, like death come to play.

She crouched down before me, looked into my eyes, those sharp nails freshly cleaned of Tomas's blood inches from my face. Curiosity was in those dark, dangerous eyes. "Halcyon's sister," she said, repeating my words. "What an odd creature you are to wish me no harm just because I am your lover's sister."

The tremors shaking my body were becoming wilder, stronger, with her near presence. It was as if my very skin tried to crawl off me, away from her. The skin on my back, shoulders, and arms rippled, moved, as if it had a will of its own. As if something beneath it was moving, struggling to come out, like a vulture's wings—Mona Louisa's other form. My skin burned as it stretched and I gasped at the pain, at the fight I had within myself just to stay planted there, not scramble away from her as every instinct in me was screaming to do.

"Me," I wheezed, fighting to take the breath back into my lungs that the pain had forced out of me. "Just me. Let my men go." I deserved to die, for so many reasons, not just one. They didn't.

"You would not still be living, breathing, had my brother not claimed you as his mate," Lucinda said, and her voice was no longer sensual. Just hard, as if all pretence had been stripped away. "My kind hunted and killed things like you long ago." Her eyes, dark like bittersweet chocolate, the one feature so like her brother, looked down at me with none of the affection, the warmth, usually in his. And I realized then how cold those eyes could be without emotion. "But he did, and my father spared you when he should have destroyed you after what you had done and become. I shall abide by his choice. For now." She stood and smiled, and it was not a friendly gesture. "I can always kill you later," she said like a soft promise, and walked away.

Like a breeze blowing cobwebs away, the invisible bonds holding my men vanished and they were free. They rushed to my side, crouched protectively in front of me. But she was truly gone, back into the night, a child of darkness. Demon dead. And suddenly all I could smell was blood. The rich heady scent of it, its pounding, throbbing call. I could almost taste it like sweet wine rolling down my tongue. My eyes, my body, my entire being was drawn to the man who stood to my left, slightly before me, the flexing of his hand gripping the sword, pushing the blood out of his wounded wrist, two gaping holes where Lucinda's claws had pierced through like Crucifixion nails. Fat drops of red blood fell to the ground like precious wine spilt wastefully, and an ache started in my body, in my soul, for that dripping blood. An ache that throbbed and grew with each spilling, hypnotic drop . . . *plunck . . . plunck . . . plunck . . .* A thirst that seemed enormous, unquenchable. I wanted to lap that blood up, take it into me like air, as if I would perish and die if I didn't have it. And it was not the hunger of my tiger beast for raw meat. I just wanted to drink down his blood, a horrified part of me realized.

A burning sensation filled my mouth, my gums, my teeth, as if that part of me wished to morph, to change, also. Into what? Dear God, into what? What was I becoming?

Tomas. I forced his name into my mind, tried to see him as a person, and not something I could drink to quench that burning, aching thirst. Wounded, bleeding Tomas. He protected me from a threat in front, already gone, when the real threat now lay behind him, so close, a hand grasp away. My fingers spasmed where they lay planted on the ground as I desperately fought the need to reach out and grab that bleeding wrist, touch my fingers to that blood, squeeze it tighter to wring out even more of that redness. The need punched me hard in the gut, drew a small sound of distress from my throat.

At the sound, my men turned back to look at me, saw me doubled over. "Mona Lisa," Tomas cried, reaching for me. "What's wrong?"

"No. Don't touch me!" I choked, throwing myself back away from him, my eyes fixed on the jagged holes of his pierced wrist, on the torn flesh that cried red tears of sorrow at being wasted so, untasted, unsavored. It drew me, beckoned me like a siren's call. *Taste me. Taste life.*

I shook my head violently, dragging myself farther away from his dripping temptation, frightened that if I tasted his blood, I would have fangs in truth; it was a burning promise a thin skin away from a violent, erupting birth. I pulled myself back until I came up against something solid, something warm, something electric as my skin met it. I turned my head to see Dontaine crouched down behind me, hands set carefully on his spread knees. "Tell me what's wrong," he said in a gentle soothing voice, the kind of voice that one used to talk a jumper down from the roof.

I looked at him with wide wild eyes. "His blood." My voice cracked on the words, on the intensity of my hunger.

"Tomas, leave," Dontaine commanded.

Tomas's honey brown eyes flashed with ire, with rebellion. "I will not leave her like this," he said with a fire I had not seen in him before.

I whimpered as he took a step closer, my eyes fixed on that dripping, red blood.

"Look to where her eyes gaze, Tomas. Your blood is calling her beast's hunger up, and she is trying to fight it. The only way you can help her is to leave."

It was a hunger, all right, but not that of my beast's. That animal hunger was at least something I could understand, relate to. This . . . this was an undead hunger, thirsting for life itself. Heavenly Father, how had Lucinda been able to walk away so calmly from him after she had pierced his skin? How had she not slaughtered us all? Drank us all down?

"Is he right? Do you wish me to leave?" Tomas asked, and I had to force myself to concentrate on his words, to understand them.

"Yes. Please go," I said in a careful trembling voice,

forcing the words out when a larger part of me wanted to scream for him to stay. *Stay and feed me!*

Head bowed, he turned and left us, and that hungry, thirsty part of me howled inside as I saw my food walking away, punished me by driving that sharp longing deeply and fiercely into my body like a dagger thrust. I put my face into the ground and screamed, my fingers digging into the cool damp earth, anchoring me there so I did not run after him, chase him down, and sink my teeth into him.

Little electric jolts ran through me as Dontaine touched my shoulder, trying to distract me, I think, bring me back to myself. But it only served to draw my attention to another food source. Here, too, was blood.

Slowly I turned and looked at him, at his hand, smooth and white, skin so soft-looking, so easy to pierce, to tear open to get to that rich flowing blood beneath. That call of life.

"Your eyes," he whispered. "Dear Goddess, they're blue like Mona Louisa's." And I felt his fear jolt through me with thrilling pleasure, almost as sweet a sensation as blood smeared upon my lips would have been. Crap.

"Don't . . . don't be afraid," I said, my voice strained as my own fear—fear of myself—flooded over me

"Mona Lisa, what's happening?" he asked like a child begging a grown-up to tell him there was no bogeyman in the closet. That he was only imagining it. But he wasn't. And the bogeyman wasn't something hiding in the closet. It was me.

"Touch me, Dontaine," I whispered. "Hold me. Make it go away."

Carefully, he sat me up and held me from behind, so he would not see my disquieting eyes. And perhaps, so my teeth would not be near his throat, a wise move. But though he pressed his chest again my back, wrapped his arms around me, encircling me with his electric presence, it did not chase that terrible blood thirst from me. I was aware, so aware of that slow, beating heart that pounded against me like an ancient primitive drumming. Calling: *Here. Here I am. Come get me.*

And how I yearned to do so. So much that I shuddered.

"It's not working, Dontaine," I said, trembling against him, my voice tight. God, how it was not working. I pushed to free myself from his hold, from that terrible drumming heartbeat pressed against me, but he would not let me go. His arms tightened and that strength inherent in a Full Blood warrior kept me chained, kept me captive for a moment, as long as I did not fight him.

"What are you doing?" I demanded.

"Please, my Queen, I feel your panic... Don't run." I felt him tremble against me. Felt his heart quicken under the flooding surge of adrenaline. "My fear. Your fear. It triggers my beast. If you run . . ."

His words gave me an idea. Made me think of that other thing that dwelled within me—so many things inside me now.

My own beast.

I tried to call it forth, tried to unleash my tiger self to drive out that other thing—and it was a thing, not truly a person—possessing me with its hungers and desires. *Come out, kitty cat. Come out and play.*

Always before it roared out of me. Rushed out the moment I unleashed it. But not this time. There was the faintest stirring, the brush of fur inside me. Then it subsided, once more quiescent within me, unable to come out and save me.

"Dontaine." My hands squeezed the arms holding me, kept them pressed down against me. "Call out my beast."

His arms spasmed around me for a second. "You're asking me to change into my Half Form, and I cannot do that. I will have to leave you then. I will not be able to change back until I have hunted. You will be unprotected."

"Dontaine . . ." Against my volition, my head lowered. My hands wrapped like shackles around his strong, pulsing forearms. And with but a thought, gently, easily, I broke his hold on me and lifted his pulsing wrists up to my mouth. I kept my lips closed, fighting myself, but could not stop myself from whispering those closed lips over that white fragile skin, so thin, where just beneath the surface pounded sweet flowing blood. I smelled it. Literally smelled it like the most alluring perfume. And my mouth, my gums, burned again like something set aflame, and my teeth ached to change, lengthen, become dagger-sharp fangs.

With an effort that made tears spring to my eyes, I lifted my head back up, out of immediate biting reach. But only that one thing I could do. His wrists were still held like willing sacrifices before me.

"Please," I whispered. "Call my beast, I cannot do it, or I fear . . ." My voice dropped to a mere breath of sound. ". . . I fear I may drink you dry."

He heard me, and his body stiffened. First with puzzlement, then with fear. "I thought this was your beast's hunger."

"No." And my voice was careful, so careful. As if one loud sound would be enough to break my restraint. For fangs to break through my gums. For me to sink them into that beating pulse there before me like a waiting present. "Not my beast. Something else."

And there was not much for it to be, that something else. Only two things liked blood. Our animal beast. And demon dead. I could almost feel him reaching this new conclusion. And realize that he wasn't holding me, so much as I was holding him now. Realize that it was not my animal self coming to the fore, giving me that greater strength. Nope, something else already there.

"Please, Dontaine. Call my beast." I said it so calmly when I wanted to scream it, especially when his heart started pounding in fright, in terrifying realization that something worse, much worse, was going on.

"Blessed Night," he whispered. Then he gave me what I asked for. The energy in his arms, only his arms, changed, like a distinct line drawn up to his elbows and stopping there. A hot wash of energy poured out from him, powerful waves coming out as if pushed by a tide from the arms that I held. Beneath my touch I felt his skin shimmer and change under the cloth covering it. Felt his bones shift, elongate, tendons and muscles popping into new positions. His hands, the only things visible, stretched, became wider, the fingers rougher, coarser, the skin thicker, less human and more Other. A sheen of fur flowed over the skin as power spilled down his hands. They spasmed once, then huge hooking claws popped from his fingertips like energy let loose to take form and substance and shape. That hot wash of energy flowed up my hands where I touched him, and into me, tingling and heating my palms, then spilling it up through the rest of my body until I was pulsing, vibrating from head to toe.

That Other in me could not stand beneath that warm flooding power. It was pushed aside, and my animal self rose. My tiger stretched and roared, then snarled, caught, unable to come out, unable to fully rise to the surface. That small lingering presence of that demon-tinged Other interfered with it, so that while my beast presence dominated, it could not totally push out the other entity. Both were caught in incompleteness, one coming, the other going, neither able to reach their destination.

His hands—his claws—pulled from me and I let them go, and turned to look up at Dontaine. He was still in human form, his face still etched with that strong masculine beauty. Only his forearms, his hands, had changed, looking unreal against the normal rest of him. "You didn't change completely."

"Neither did you. Your eyes, though, they are that of your beast's . . . and not of her. Are you better?"

Better? I laughed, and it was a harsh, crying sound. A sound that made Dontaine flinch. "Yes, I'm better. Anything was better than that . . . but I can't completely change.

She won't let my beast come completely out, Dontaine." The urges and needs of my beast, however, were there, though the form was not. The animal hunger, the need to hunt, to bring down prey, to feel the hot spill of blood and quivering meat sliding down my throat . . . it beat within me. Only I was still in human form, like Dontaine, but not because I willed it. Oh, no. My will was being roadblocked by that she-bitch I had sucked into me.

I was caught in a limbo of in between, feeling the needs of my animal self, unable to fulfill it in my human form. And before me stood something that could sate my hunger, something that still looked like prey. I pushed away from him, gasping, falling onto my back, crawling away from him, hysterical giggles choking my throat. I didn't want to drink him anymore. Now I wanted to eat him.

"Don't . . . don't . . ." he warned, and as I watched, his eyes turned from emerald green to autumn-leaf brown. The eyes of his beast, his wolf.

"I'm sorry," I said, knowing I was triggering his own hunting instincts, "but I . . . I can't stay here." I turned, scrambled to my feet, and ran. Fleeing from my fear, my hunger. But, unfortunately, I couldn't flee from myself.

I ran blindly, desperately. Without that natural liquid grace that had always been a part of me, that came from my Monère blood. Now, for the first time in my life, I stumbled, tripped, almost fell. I ran with human clumsiness, as if that limbo I was caught in shut down other parts of myself, my gifts of strength and grace that I had taken for granted, always there like the air I breathed. Only it wasn't there now. I ran and knew even in my panicked confusion that I could not hunt like this. I could not capture, much less bring down even a rabbit in this condition, and without sating that bloodlust, I could not free myself of this state. I lurched up against a tree, felt the hard uneven bark dig into my palms. I pressed into it with my gripping fingertips, and rested my cheek against its cool rough surface, breathing hard.

A sound, an instinct, brought my head up and I found myself looking into the eyes of a gray timber wolf less than three meters away. Its eyes were feral, wild, hungry. Seeing *me* as food. For one wild moment I thought it was Dontaine, changed fully into his wolf self. But another sound, a low threatening rumble, swung my gaze to my right. Dontaine stood a stone's throw away, still in his human form—mostly, at least. Only his arms and hands were that of his animal self.

He stood tall, beautiful, and silent, and was somehow frighteningly wild and feral. Even more dangerous than the natural wolf that hunted me. His eyes locked with that of his wolf brother, and a shuddering roll of electric energy rolled off him like silent echoing thunder. He growled, a deep, vicious warning. A totally animal sound coming from a human throat, and the pure menace it contained alarmed something primal in me. Was even scarier than looking up and finding myself face-to-face with a hungry timber wolf.

The wolf turned and slipped away, ceding his prey to a more powerful predator. I turned back to look once more at Dontaine, at those reflective autumn-brown eyes, not because I wanted to, but because I was afraid not to. He came slowly forward, toward me, his body strong, fluid, deadly, a graceful killer with monstrous claws that could rip you apart with the added power of his beast upon him. I tensed to leap away, to flee, even though I knew I could not hope to outrun him.

"Don't, please," he said, voice raw and deep, as if growling like that had hurt his vocal cords. "Don't run . . . If you do . . ." He took a harsh, deep breath. "I cannot leave you unprotected, and you cannot hunt. Please, my Queen." He stopped several yards away and dropped to his knees, begging me with those animal-brown eyes. "Please."

And I knew suddenly what he asked of me. What he would not put words to. There was only one other way to rid us both of our bloodlust: To channel it into sex. There was no other choice, really. Had Dontaine not followed me, in my almost human state, stripped of my Monère strength and quickness, the timber wolf would have killed me. Only now did I shudder at coming so close to death.

Adrenaline surged like a flooding tide of life within me, and my eyes fixed upon the man kneeling blonde and beautiful before me, asking me to save him, save us both. If I ran from Dontaine now and triggered his beast's hunting instincts fully, instincts that he was vulnerable to only because I had asked it of him, he might end up killing me himself. I'd left him in a terrible dilemma. It was up to me now to get us out of the mess I had gotten us into.

With trembling hands, I reached back, unzipped my gown, and let it fall from me onto the ground. My underwear followed and when I stepped free and naked toward him, I saw his eyes fill with almost overwhelming relief. No heat yet, just plain and painful relief. I came to him, trusting him not to rip my throat out while I still must look like prey to him. Trusting that though I felt not one iota of sexual attraction for him at the moment, not when a part of me was still screaming for me to run away . . . I knew, *knew,* that the innate chemistry between Monère male and Queen would flare to life with close enough proximity. And it did when I was a hand's reach away from him. My *aphidy*—that innate chemistry, that power that all Queens possessed—sprang out with a force that made me gasp and sway toward him, almost fall upon him. I didn't. Fall upon him, that is. Not physically, at least. But that part of me invisible, not seen but felt . . . oh yes, felt . . . that hit him with the force of a flying arrow aimed true, burying itself deep in its target, in a perfect bull's-eye.

Dontaine quivered, his body tensing with a different kind of tension now, his eyes brilliant, almost glowing. I inhaled the musky fragrance of his arousal, and of mine. And welcomed the forceful attraction that sprang up between us, embraced its overwhelming intensity willingly, gave myself over to it fully.

"You're wearing too many clothes," I said, surprised at the seductive huskiness thickening my voice.

"My hands," he said and my eyes fell to his hands—his claws, actually—which he kept lowered at his sides. Monstrous, deadly, and supremely ugly, especially in comparison to the rest of his perfect masculine self. Hands that bothered me hugely. I had no choice but to put aside that discomfort. It could be worse. Oh yes, it could have been much worse.

"Let me," I said, and knelt before him.

My hands whispered down his shirt, freeing the buttons, pulling first one sleeve off, then the other, unable to hide a tremor when my hands brushed over fur. Unable to appreciate the loveliness of his naked chest because of what also had been revealed. Fur covered him up to his elbows. Great hooking claws, looking like curved black exclamation marks, the ends sharp and pointy. It broke the mood of my lustful, blissful state, and I forced my appalled gaze away from it. *Don't look at them,* I told myself, closing my eyes, inhaling the musky scent of his arousal, concentrating on that lovely pull between us instead, a pull that seemed to originate deep within me, from my very womb. A womb that felt empty, aching. Clenching in its need to be filled.

I felt him pull back from me. Felt a shimmer of electric power dance in the air between us, and my eyes flew open. The furry forearms and those monstrous claws shimmered, faded slowly, then were gone. And the beautiful perfection of ivory-white skin, unblemished, and long, sensitive, strong fingers—the hands of a pianist, of an artist—were in their place. I'd never noticed before how beautiful, how well made his hands were. He leaned back, eyes closed, clearly exhausted from the effort of changing back, perspiration dewing his chest, dampening his face.

"You didn't need to do that," I murmured.

His eyes opened, and that reflective animal-brown color gleamed back at me once more. But the expression in those eyes was pure male. "I didn't know if I could change back so soon. But I wanted to touch you," he said, and tired or not, he reached for me, and I fell into his arms, into his saving embrace, and lost myself to the bliss of his touch.

The smooth muscles of his chest flattened my breasts, tingled and sharpened my nipples at the brush of skin with skin. The feel of his lips was soft as he brushed them against mine, like a painter making his first delicate stroke on clean canvas.

"Mona Lisa," he murmured, and his lips touched mine again, harder, firmer, more possessive. The tip of his tongue touched my lips, lapped wetly over my seam asking for entrance, and I granted it to him and tasted him as he tasted me, anchoring my spinning world with my hands grasping his broad shoulders. He tasted warm, sweet, and nutty. Like mead. Like ambrosia. Flavored like the sun, tasting of the earth. He explored my mouth, tangled his tongue with mine, and I sucked upon him, lapped him up. I felt him twist and move against me as he freed himself of his clothing, and then his hands were finally upon me and I cried out at the joy, at the relief of feeling them. Of feeling him, naked and hard and ready against me. *Touch me, yes. Touch me.* And he did.

My world spun, tilted, and I was on the ground, my back crunching fallen leaves beneath as Dontaine covered me from above. His weight upon me was deliciously hard, deliciously dominating, as he parted my legs, and I felt him hard, thick, and poised at my body's entrance. I looked into his face above me, his nostrils flared wide as he breathed in my scent, my body's wet readiness, his eyes hard, intent, a glittering shining brown, almost blind in his driving urge to possess me, the slash of his cheekbones taut and flushed, reddened in rising desire like his lips, drawing my eyes to the chiseled perfection of his mouth, his strong chin, his every feature. Like a Greek god come to passionate life. I wondered how I could have turned from him before. And I stiffened as I remembered what he had offered me then. A child.

Desperately I struggled to push aside the lust-crazed need to mate. Tried to concentrate, focus, think on that very important fact. "Wait," I said urgently, and felt him hold himself coiled and still above me. And realized how terribly vulnerable I was to him in this position. One move and he would be in me and I would be unable to stop him. And I would no longer want to.

My eyes locked with his, and we held ourselves poised there for one terrible long moment, on the threshold of something wonderful. On the brink of something disastrous.

"I can't . . . No children, Dontaine. I can't get pregnant." Could not risk what I would pass on to a child in my possessed state. No other word for it. Possessed and driven by instincts not just Monère but demon dead.

I felt his entire body clench. Felt every powerful, strong muscle lock in silent protest as he fought himself. Fought against every screaming male and animal instinct he had to plunge himself into me and mate. His brown eyes glittered so sharply down at me that I was surprised they did not cut me. His face was tight, almost brutal, above me, and he growled. Actually growled. One poised terrible moment . . . then he rolled abruptly off me and lay on his side, breathing harshly.

I went limp with relief. With knowing how closely we had come to disaster. "Thank you. Thank you, Dontaine," I said, touching his shoulder. He flinched as if I had whipped him, his entire body coiled tight.

"We can have sex," I whispered tentatively, my hand frozen still on his shoulder. "Just . . . I can't risk getting pregnant. Not now. Not while I'm like this."

He took a deep, shuddering breath. "All right," he said, managing to sound oddly calm and reasonable, while every muscle in his body screamed with tension.

Hesitantly, I smoothed my hand down his shoulder, ran it lightly down his arm. And that stroking caress flared anew that drowning sensuality, that powerful draw of male to Queen. He shuddered as I drew myself against him, rubbed myself against his back. Stroked my hand against his chest, pausing to circle once each tight flat nipple. I lifted myself over him and rolled him onto his back, and he moved unresistingly where I wanted him to go.

I almost purred at the pleasure of seeing him spread out like a beautiful offering before me, and didn't even try to resist the bounty of his lovely body. I kissed his other shoulder, trailed my lips down a sinewy forearm. Whispered them over his puckered nipples, lapping my tongue roughly over the little soldiers that had come so attentively to attention, while my left hand roamed lower, following the lightly furred trail that arrowed down his middle, leading me to where he pointed straight up like a giant tree towering over thick brush. I touched him, ran my hand up and then down, measuring his length, grasping his generous width. Velvet hardness, pulsing life.

He made a deep rumbling sound, pushed himself against me, and his hands buried themselves in my hair as I suckled and laved his little nipples, then moved my lips lower, following the path my hand had blazed. A light kiss over a ridged abdomen, a gentle lick low over the belly that made him quiver, a nuzzle over where his musky scent lay most thickly, causing his thick shaft to brush against my cheek, allowing me to appreciate how butter-soft his outer skin really was—such softness to cover such hardness—and then my mouth was over him, on him, around him. He was of average length but so thick around that I had to open my mouth fully to take him in. I hummed with pleasure as he slid thick and smooth inside me. I ran my tongue around him, tasting him, more sharp, more bittersweet here.

Then I lost the sweet pleasure of it as my mouth suddenly

flared to burning life. As my teeth ached, my gums throbbed. As I realized that what filled that supple hardness in my mouth was not muscle but blood. Blood that called so strongly to me, so suddenly, that I ripped myself away from him, falling onto my back, my elbows. Because for one terrible moment I had almost plunged my teeth into him. Had almost felt his blood running hot and pulsing down my throat.

I cried out and my hand covered my mouth as if by that action I could stop the fangs from coming out. Dontaine knelt beside me, the powerful jut of his arousal too close, too tempting to my burning teeth. I fell back from him, hands raised up to ward him off.

"What's wrong?" he asked.

"Your blood. Too much blood down there. Too close to the surface."

"What do we do?"

"I don't know." I shook my head, finding it hard to think when I was so suddenly filled once again with bloodlust. Demon bloodlust.

"Let me." He moved down to my feet, touched my thighs gently, asking permission. Opening my legs to him, closing my eyes, I granted it. Yes, yes. Please, anything. Anything to take away that terrible urge, that terrible thirst.

It soothed, eased, with the first touch of his lips on my inner thigh. With the firm powerful grasp of his hands on my outer thighs, opening me up even more to him. To that questing, marauding, wicked, wicked mouth. A lick, a kiss, a gentle nip that stiffened me suddenly in fright, not lust.

"No blood. You cannot take my blood," I said, my heart pounding with the new threat. It was a strong Monère instinct to mark your lover. To break their skin and taste their blood. If he did, I did not know if the demon hunger that possessed me would pass on to him. "You must swear not to take my blood."

"My oath on it."

I went limp at averting that other near disaster. "God, I'm sorry. So many things you can't do . . . I just—"

"Hush. You are here before me, opened to my pleasure. All is well," he soothed, and played his lips upon my mound, nuzzling the curly hairs there, inhaling my scent, breathing upon me as the golden fall of his hair brushed the sensitive skin of my belly, my thighs, like a thousand whispering kisses. I was too grateful to him to be embarrassed at being exposed so blatantly like that. Too thankful at feeling the bloodlust ease and another lust rise and take its place as he lowered his mouth and licked me, a delicate teasing stroke.

Oh!

Nerves tingled to life within me. Pulsed deep in my core, wetting me, spreading my legs even wider for him. I whimpered, then jammed my hand to my mouth as if to stop the sound.

"No, let me hear your pleasure also as I taste it." And his words and the hot gust of his breath blowing over me there brought another low sound to my throat. Made me writhe, lift myself up to him. Begging, pleading without words to touch me again like that. With a low pleased rumble, he did. His head dipped down and his tongue lapped over me again with a surer, firmer stroke. Then another, and another. Driving me nuts. Giving me a taste of pleasure and making me want even more. "Tell me what you want."

"I don't know," I gasped. "Just more. Harder . . . Oh God," I breathed as he obeyed me, and sensation lashed me with sharp pleasure. He bent my knees, pushed them back so that I was completely opened to him. And I could only clutch his head, hold him to me as he spread me apart with gentle fingers and speared his tongue into me like a rapier thrusting sharp and deep. I cried out, arched up into him as he began a driving rhythm, pushing his tongue deep and repeatedly into me, his forefinger feathering lightly over my plump and swollen pearl that he had plucked free from the outer folds. And I didn't know which sensation was worse, or better, or more unbearable.

I surged against him like helpless waves lapping against the shore, begging him wordlessly, *Bring me home. Bring me home.* And he did, with a gentle squeeze, a pinching pluck of my swollen nub. A deep plunge of his thick tongue spearing into me, as if he were driving a blade home. I burst apart as light burst from within me. And a trembling rolling climax took and shook me, but didn't free me. I lay there in quivering aftermath, still hungry. Shit. Not for blood, though, thank the Mother. But for something else. *His* pleasure. And it wasn't just a woman's desire, but that something else. That something dark and Other that lay within me and held me, still.

I opened my eyes, saw those animal-brown eyes, the eyes of his beast, staring down at me. "You didn't come," I said.

"If you are well now, I can see you safe. Then shift, go hunt."

It was an astounding offer, unexpected, especially for someone who had challenged Amber once and risked his life for the privilege of my bed. I looked up at that handsome, patrician face and this time saw past the surface beauty to the generous heart beneath it, and the unbelievable control he wielded. And my heart melted at what I found there, unexpectedly. It wasn't the sex that opened my heart to him; it was this kind and selfless act. The gift he offered so easily—taking care of my needs and submersing his own. My heart cracked open without my willing it, filling me with something more tender than I had ever expected to feel for him—the softness and sweetness of love.

"No," I said softly, and drew him down to me, "I need you still." And kissed him gently with the new emotion I found welling up within me. Tasted myself upon his lips, his tongue. Sucked him deep into my mouth, fed upon him for a moment, then released him when the blood that filled him there also became too tempting.

"I need your pleasure, your release. I don't know why," I murmured, holding his head buried against my neck, safely away from my mouth. "But I need it. I'm sorry."

He laughed, his face pressed against me. Then lifting his head, he looked down on me. "I'm not. Tell me how."

"From behind." The only safe entry left to us. "Take me from behind." I ran my hands down the strong column of his back and over the tight swell of his bottom to feather over his anal pucker. "Here," I whispered. "I need more than just your tongue in me, sweet though it is. Take me here, please."

He looked at me for a heartbeat of time. Touched my face, as if what he saw there shining in my eyes was something he could not believe. Dared not believe. Looking at me as if I were truly seeing him for the very first time. And I was. I was. He trembled, and emotions too fast and fleeting for me to catch passed across his face.

"Mona Lisa," he murmured with shaking breath. Then as if the emotions, the awareness between us was too much, he lifted me up and turned me around so that my hands and knees were braced upon the ground. He wrapped himself around me, his head buried in the small of my back, and I felt something hot and wet fall against my skin. His tears.

"Dontaine—"

"Shhh. It's okay. I'm all right. Just give me a moment."

I wanted to turn around and hold him, but he would not allow it. His arms tightened around me, holding on to me as if I anchored his world. As if he would be cast adrift and drown if he let me go.

All I could say was his name, "Dontaine," softly and yearningly. He gave one big, almost convulsive shudder against my back then released me until only his hands were upon my hips. The softness of his lips pressed against me. Ran slowly, deliberately down my back, starting from my nape downward. The curtain of his hair fell like a silky halo lightly brushing over my skin. But the greatest sensation were those velvet-soft lips pressing feather-light against me. I couldn't believe how sensitive a back could be.

When he reached down past my hips and continued still . . . When the silky firmness of those lips and the warmth of his breath fell unerringly on my tailbone and pressed a little bit harder, a little bit firmer, just there . . . A lightning bolt of sensation shot from my tailbone straight to my groin, washing me with heat so suddenly that I bucked and swayed and cried out beneath him. Had his hands not held me at the waist, I would have fallen onto the ground.

"Oh God. Dontaine!" And his name was a demand, a plea.

"Trust me," he said.

"Yes." How could I not?

"I won't get you pregnant," he whispered. "Just let me play in your wetness for a moment."

I nodded but didn't really understand what he was saying until he lifted my upper torso up off the ground and eased me back against him to lie against his chest. "Just a little wider," he said huskily, and shifted my knees farther apart. My sensitive back was in bliss, cradled against the lean coiled muscles of his chest, my hips and bottom snuggled deep into his enveloping lap. He surrounded me from behind, bigger, harder. And the hardest part of him, that special wide thickness, slid between my legs in the space he had created for himself. He rubbed his shaft against my wet outer lips, so hard, so full, that I felt as if I rode atop a log. A hand, strong and sensitive, spread low over my belly in a stark claiming, holding me to him, holding me still, as his hips undulated gently against me. The softest of motion—a slow push forward, a slow wet slide back—to trigger such an avalanche of rich sensations.

The lush eroticism of what I saw—that claiming, controlling hand, the brief tantalizing peek of the red-purple head of him pushing out between my legs, then pulling back, disappearing from sight for a pounding heartbeat of time as if into me . . . it made my eyes flutter close, made me clutch his rock-hard thighs. Made me squirm back against him, groan his name in pleasure and suffering. Because I wanted him in me. So badly that my stomach clenched. And deeper, beneath his splayed hand, my empty womb tightened.

As if sensing my need, his hand pressed harder into me, assuaging my need for a moment, replacing it with an even greater need for his hardness to fill me. "How pretty you are," he murmured, his deep, husky voice a trilling vibration against my neck.

He covered me completely from behind, leaving me feeling oddly vulnerable, oddly naked, in front. It took me a moment to realize that as I could see us, so could he see me, and that he was watching a part of me that under his stirring gaze suddenly ached to be touched. My breasts, small and high, grew even tighter, more swollen beneath the caress of his eyes—the part of my body I was most sensitive about because I was no more than a handful, and barely that. But stroked so intimately below by his thickness, aroused so much by his voice, his careful touches, I was too far gone to be embarrassed. My nipples pointed outward, hard, peaked tips pouting to be touched. And he answered their call. His hands slid upward to cup my breasts, just holding their slight fullness, as if offering my nipples out to the darkness. And the sight of those long, tapered, sensitive fingers holding me so was as arousing as his actual touch.

"Please," I begged, trembled, arching against him, pushing my breasts outward and even more into those beautiful masculine hands.

"Yes," he said, and brushed his thumbs over my nipples. The pleasure of it jerked me back. Pulled a gasp from me. And started the play of moonlight once more upon my skin. A white trembling glow that started there, from where he touched me, spreading outward to the rest of my body. For one moment, I was a brilliant white thing against his skin made darker in contrast, and then light spilled onto him, and he began to radiate with light, also, spilling it out into the black velvet darkness. I watched as the light took us both, filled us, two children of the night aglow.

"Beautiful," Dontaine breathed, a whisper of sound in my ear. As the light played upon us, he played upon me, his artist hands molding my breasts, squeezing them, lifting them, plucking my berry-red tips, squeezing my nipples, pulling them, making me arch and cry out, writhe against him.

"Please, Dontaine. Please."

Heeding my plea, a hand left its nipple play and sought darker, more sultry depths. Two fingers sank into me, came back coated with my fluid. Reluctantly, he released me, urged me forward once more onto my hands. That wet hand touched me where I had touched him, circling my anal pucker, coating it with my own wetness. Eased in a finger gently past the tightness.

"So tight," he murmured, pushing in a second finger. I shuddered, groaned, as he stroked slowly in and out. Lovely, lovely, but I needed him. *His* pleasure, not mine, sweetly killing though it was. "I don't want to hurt you."

"You won't. God, you won't. Please, Dontaine, I need you in me."

"Then let me come into you." His fingers left me and I felt the hard wet head of him probe me for entrance. He pushed forward, but I was so tight and he was so wide, he did not enter. "I don't want to hurt you," he muttered, voice tight, strained.

"No, no. You won't. Please, please!"

"*Don't . . .*" He pushed in hard and the head of him popped in past the tight sphincter. "*. . . let . . .*" Another push. "*. . . me . . .*" A gentle slide. "*. . . hurt you.*" More of him filling me, cramming me.

"You won't . . . it doesn't! . . . Yes, yes, that feels so good . . . Oh, Dontaine," I cried when he was finally seated deep and full within me. And I both lied and told the truth. He was too big and I was too stretched for it not to hurt a little. But it hurt in a good way. Oh God, yes. So good, so good. I groaned as he shuddered against me, holding himself still, buried deep inside me.

"Mona Lisa . . ." I felt him trembling with restraint. But it wasn't restraint I needed. And pain did not matter. I needed his release.

I pulled forward then slammed myself back against him, and he gave a guttural cry at the tightness of me running over his length so unexpectedly like that. His hands clamped down on my hips, holding me still. "Stop," he muttered harshly. "You'll hurt yourself."

"You're hurting me by not moving," I cried plaintively.

"Behave," he said, his hands like iron manacles as I tried to rock against him. His tone became whiplash sharp. "If you don't, I'll pull out."

The threat stilled me as nothing else would have.

"I'll give you what you want," he said, breathing heavily, "but we do it my way. You'll take what I give you, as slow or fast as I want to give it to you. Do you understand?"

I nodded wildly.

His hands left me, and I stayed obediently still and trembling beneath him. A harsh breath, two, then he leaned over me, covered me, like a stallion blanketing a mare. His lips brushed across my nape. "Trust me," came his warm breath, stirring the soft hairs there.

"Yes," was my reply, and his teeth grazed lightly over my skin. So delicately, so dangerously. Setting off sunbursts of sensation where he touched.

"Don't . . . move," he said huskily, a stark command. Trembling, I obeyed him as his hand slid across my belly and then lower until his fingertips, calloused and rough from sword practice, lay just over the swollen nub of my pearl. Only his words, and his threat, held me back from surging forward into the waiting promise of his touch. One moment, two. Then he rewarded me for my restraint by pulling a tiny increment out of me and pushing back in. The slow push and slide of him like that pushed me forward with his downstroke, so that his fingertips grazed my swollen nub, spilling a hot wash of sensation in me in both front and back.

"Oh!" I moaned, cried, with that slight movement. But I held still.

"Yes," he crooned and licked my neck, a hot slide of tongue that was both soothing and arousing. "Yes." And did it again. Pulled out, an increment more. Pushed back in. And though he still crammed me, stretched me, it was not unbearably so anymore. The sharpness of pain faded beneath his careful rocking in and out, and more pleasure spilled out, zinging through me with each lengthening stroke. Each firmer, harder thrust back into me, pushing my pulsing, swollen clitoris more firmly against the rough-gentle play of his fingertips. It was exquisitely pleasurable torture, even more so because I had to hold still, had to endure it. I whimpered with my pleasure and with my restraint. He nipped me, grazing my neck again with his teeth.

"Ah, love," he murmured, groaning, burying his head in the fall of my hair. "You feel so good. Remember . . . hold still," he warned, and I braced myself for more wonderful, terrible things to come.

Like a pulse from deep within him, I felt his energy ease, loosen, rise. Grow sharper, more electric. Until my very skin tingled from head to toe where he covered me with his greater length. He touched me nowhere in front except for the tantalizing play of fingertips upon that most sensitive, swollen nexus of nerves within me, a touch that came and went as he did within my body. And because he touched me nowhere else in front but there, perhaps that was why I felt it most excruciatingly. Tingling, electrifying, shocking jolts that were both blissful and torturous. Both heaven and hell.

My need grew, swelled even stronger, as his thrusts grew harder, more wilder. Until that fine line of pleasure and pain became blurred and then became one, and it took me and threw me up into the heavens. Ripped me apart with agonizing pleasure while I floated there in the air. Convulsing me. But even in my explosive release, a part of me was still hungry, thirsty for something more. And that more was what surged within me like a wild tide battering against the shore. He pulled from me and then stretched me back anew, cramming himself into me with poling, thrusting force, with sharp gasping breath, with soft desperate cries. But still careful of me, not completely letting go. And therefore, still reaching for, still striving for his peak.

His balls, heavy, large, and tight, smacked into me, bounced against my bottom as he seated himself deep. I reached back and grabbed them carefully, and he stilled with his length and thickness buried deep within me as he felt my hold upon him. We both held our breaths as I squeezed his tight sac, his twin balls. Pulled lightly.

Like a rocket suddenly launched, he toppled free. And as he spurted within me, hot pulsing jets, I felt his energy—that electric, buzzing energy—explode out from him in a showering sparkle. His life-force. And that part of me that had been waiting, hungering for this moment, this release, opened up wide and sucked it—him—that part of him in. Swallowed it down as surely as demons swallowed down blood.

EPILOGUE

I'D joked before that I was like a vampire, sucking up my men's gifts. But I hadn't known before what I was talking about, and it hadn't really been true. Now it was.

My lover had given off energy during orgasmic release, spilt it out of him like firecrackers bursting, and I had drunk it down.

Okay.

I was lucky I was only hyperventilating and not grieving. I was lucky Dontaine wasn't dead.

He wasn't, thank God. He was peachy keen, in fact. With a cherry on top. But it was too close to what I had done with Mona Louisa. The fact that I'd sucked all her energy, all her light, her life-force, out of her—and I'd done that all by my little ole self, no demon-tainted ghost involved—and into me hadn't bothered me much. The bitch had deserved it. But this . . . doing this to someone I cared for . . . that just freaked me out.

Knowing that Halcyon, my Demon Prince, had sipped down a little of me when I had come apart, orgasming in his hands . . . that was fine with me. Actually nice, knowing how good it felt. But that was the trouble—it was *too* nice. *Too* wonderful. It could easily become addicting, like getting that necessary shot of caffeine every morning.

I glanced over at Dontaine, sitting next to me on the plane. His long, beautiful, tapered fingers wrapped around mine, and he gazed at me with an expression I'd never have imagined on that proud and arrogant face—the soft and tender look of love. A look that plucked an answering chord within me, God help me. He should have looked at me with fear instead. But that was okay. I had enough fear pounding in me for the both of us.

I looked at that handsome sculptured face sitting beside me and wondered if it were possible to love a man to death. The word *succubus* whispered through my mind. Creatures of myth, old legends, ancient tales. But the problem with myths and legends and ancient tales was that they were usually based upon a kernel of truth. A little kernel that could take root and grow into a frigging great big oak tree that could end up falling on top of you and crushing you.

I'd given my testimony before the High Council the next moonrise, and compared to what I'd just gone through, it had been a piece of cake. Calmly anchored by Dontaine's electrifying touch, I'd told them all I could truthfully tell them, and left out what I couldn't. I was as honest as I could be, but not stupid. I wasn't going to hand them my head on a platter. Halcyon's secret and mine were safe. For now. When some Council members tried probing into sticky demon matters, like how Halcyon had become weak enough to be captured by Mona Louisa, I'd told them I did not exactly know but that they could ask the High Prince himself at the next Council meeting. That, and a quick glance at Princess Lucinda sitting there with lazy observing menace, had shut them up.

Lucinda. She dressed the most modern, the most human, among us. But was actually the least so. The clothes might be contemporary, but that face, that striking face . . . And it really was striking when your gaze wasn't distracted by that lush, voluptuous body. With bold features, larger than life—or would that be death?—she had the face of a goddess of old. Something you worshipped, offered sacrifices to. Blood sacrifices. She'd sat there, far enough away from me not to trigger my new inhabitant, my inner demon, sated for now. With Dontaine's distracting touch—I'd clutched his hand like a safety blanket the entire time—we made it through with no screaming, no near possession, no crazy Mixed Blood Queen freak show. Cool. Neat-o. One fit per Council meeting was enough.

Why had I wigged out the previous night? Because the stress had triggered my beast. That was my story, and my men and I were sticking to it. It was the truth, so far as that went. Only they thought I meant my animal beast—I had two of them now, it seemed—when it was really the demon beastie in me causing all the ruckus. I made Dontaine and Tomas swear not to tell the others what had really happened. And they had given me their oaths because they were afraid for me, while I was afraid for them. Blaec, the High Lord of Hell, had killed all of Mona Louisa's men to keep his secret. I did not want the next men he slaughtered to be mine.

We were flying home. But we were not safe and not sound. Something dead, demon dead, resided within me, like an unpredictable bomb that could go off at any time. It wasn't safe to be around me. True in the past; even truer now. The men who loved me, who stayed around me, died. Only the threat now wasn't from others, it was from me.

I sent up a silent prayer to God for my human side. *Help me, please.* Then that other part of me that was not human but Monère looked out into the night sky, onto what had once been our home. I looked to the moon, so serene, pale, and distant, but hesitated. The last time I had asked for help, I'd ended up sucking Mona Louisa's demon-tainted essence into me. But old habits—and new habits, too, for that matter—died hard. I lived but did not learn. I sent a prayer winging out to that distant power, to our Mother Moon. *Please. Keep my men, my people safe,* I prayed. *Keep them safe from me.*

Dear Reader,

Luscious Lucinda is spinning off her own series beginning with Lucinda, Darkly, *the first book of The Demon Princess Chronicles, available now. Be very, very wary. Because danger may bite you when you are least prepared. But for every pain, my darlings, I promise there will be pleasure . . .*

For more on Mona Lisa and her beautiful men, indulge your senses with my novella in Over the Moon, *and my single titles* Mona Lisa Awakening *and* Mona Lisa Blossoming. *And coming in January 2008,* Mona Lisa Craving.

Sunny
www.sunnyauthor.com

NEW YORK TIMES **BESTSELLING AUTHOR OF** ***MOON CALLED*** **AND** ***BLOOD BOUND***

PATRICIA BRIGGS

IRON KISSED

COMING JANUARY 2, 2008

MECHANIC MERCY THOMPSON can shift her shape—but not her loyalty. When her former boss and mentor is arrested for murder and left to rot behind bars by his own kind, it's up to Mercy to clear his name, whether he wants her to or not.

Mercy's loyalty is under pressure from other directions, too. Werewolves are not known for their patience, and if Mercy can't decide between the two she cares for, Sam and Adam may make the choice for her…

www.penguin.com

EILEEN WILKS

USA Today **Bestselling Author of**
Mortal Danger **and** ***Blood Lines***

NIGHT SEASON

Coming January 2008

Pregnancy has turned FBI Agent Cynna Weaver's whole life upside down. Lupus sorcerer Cullen Seabourne is thrilled to be the father, but what does Cynna know about kids? Her mother was a drunk. Her father abandoned them. Or so she's always believed.

As Cynna is trying to wrap her head around this problem, a new one pops up, in the form of a delegation from another realm. They want to take Cynna and Cullen back with them—to meet her long-lost father and find a mysterious medallion. But when these two born cynics land in a world where magic is commonplace and night never ends, their only way home lies in tracking down the missing medallion—one also sought by powerful beings who will do anything to claim it...

www.penguin.com

Also from National Bestselling Author

KAREN CHANCE

AVAILABLE

wherever books are sold or at penguin.com

AD-01430C-Chance

LUCINDA, DARKLY

THE *demon* PRINCESS *chronicles*

AWARD-WINNING AUTHOR OF MONA LISA BLOSSOMING

SUNNY

"Fans of Laurell K. Hamilton will love Sunny."
—*New York Times* bestselling author Lori Foster

For every pain—there will be pleasure…

ON SALE NOW

AD-01430A-Sunny